I0760907

Knight of Shadows

King's Dark Tidings

Book 6

Kel Kade

This is a work of fiction. All characters, places, and events in this novel are fictitious. Opinions and beliefs expressed by the characters do not reflect the author's opinions and beliefs.

This book is intended for adult readers. It contains graphic violence, creative language, and sexual innuendo. This book does not contain explicit sexual content.

Dark Rover Publishing, L.L.C.

PO Box 1605

Allen, Texas, 75013

U.S.A.

ALSO AVAILABLE IN AUDIOBOOK
PRODUCED BY PODIUM PUBLISHING
2024

Written by Kel Kade

Edited by Leslie Watts

Interior Illustrations by Kel Kade

Cover art by Chris McGrath

BOOKS BY KEL KADE:

King's Dark Tidings Series

Free the Darkness

Reign of Madness

Legends of Ahn

Kingdoms and Chaos

Mage of No Renown (prequel)

Dragons and Demons

Knight of Shadows

Ritual of Ruin

Shroud of Prophecy Series

Fate of the Fallen

Destiny of the Dead

Sanctum of the Soul (2025)

Sign up for Kel Kade's newsletter for updates or visit my website, www.KelKade.com!

For my mother who raised me to be strong, independent, and compassionate.

N
Torrel
Emerald Lake
Jerea
Eastern Mountains
Sandea
Torlorn Mountains
Zigharan Mountains
Saldesh Mountains
Zigharan's End
Benbrick
Port Gull
Ashai
Kaibain
Channería
Serret
Gendishen
Skutton
Caellurum
Yeltin Isles
Uthrel
Drovsk
Vogn
Souelian Sea
Bay of Bourdony
Havoth
Kielen
Lon Lerésh
Ki'kyo
Pruar
Isle of Sand
Esk
Bromivah
Ferélle
Verril
Quarry
Gauge
Drahgfir Mountains

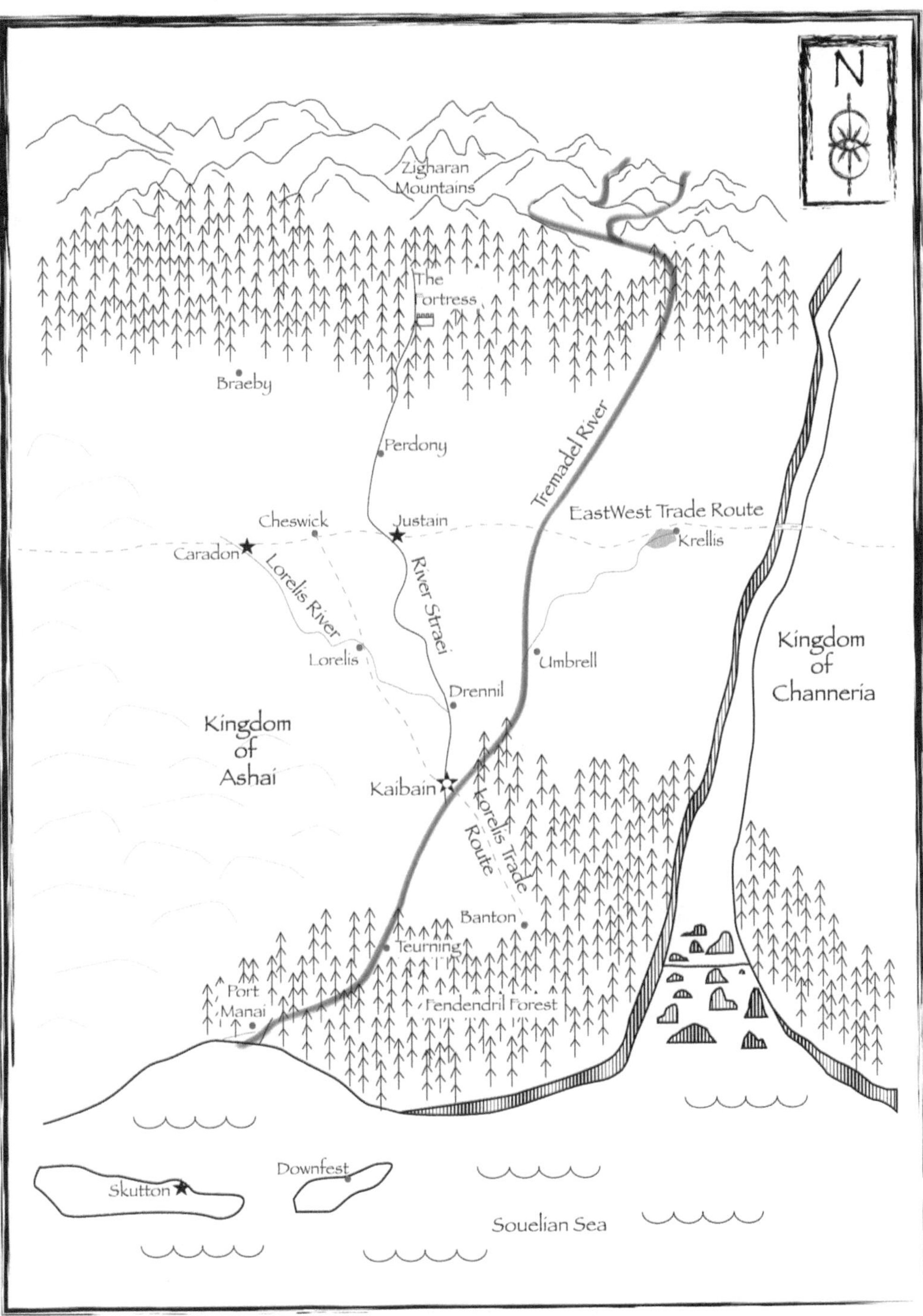
N
Zigharan Mountains
The Fortress
Braeby
Perdony
Tremadel River
Cheswick
Justain
EastWest Trade Route
Caradon
Krellis
Lorelis River
River Straei
Lorelis
Umbrell
Kingdom of Channeria
Drennil
Kingdom of Ashai
Kaibain
Lorelis Trade Route
Banton
Teurning
Port Manai
Fendendril Forest
Downfest
Skutton
Souelian Sea

PROLOGUE

"Rezkin is dead."

Thresson's head snapped up, and Caydean was pleased by the shock etched across his brother's face. The woman beside his younger brother cried out, but he ignored her. She wasn't important. Then again, neither was Thresson. He was only the second son, after all, and Caydean's prisoner besides.

"*And, still, he will kill you,*" whispered the ever-present voice in his mind. The voice was soft and sultry and enticing as it always was. Caydean's shoulders tensed as he stared at his younger brother wondering what he was plotting.

"You lie," hissed the woman. He reminded himself that Frisha was her name.

"*She will stab you,*" offered the voice, and Caydean turned his suspicious gaze on her.

He took note of the bars and runes that kept the two trapped and then grinned. "I often lie, but not about this. Our *brother* thought himself some kind of savior, I suppose. He sacrificed himself for what? To save that pitiful band of rebels he called an army? In the end, the so-called *Emperor of the Souelian* was a weak-minded fool who died for nothing. I will still kill them all."

"Why do you do this?" said Thresson, his grief over the loss of the brother he never met clear. Thresson was always begging for answers as a dog begs for scraps. Caydean thought it unbecoming of a prince of Ashai, but then again, Thresson had never lived up to his station.

"*He doubts your abilities. He thinks you are weak,*" said the voice.

Caydean growled beneath his breath. "How many times have you asked me that, and how many times have I answered? I do this because it suits me." He raised a fist and clenched it tightly as the darkness suffused his veins. He gritted his teeth and grated, "The ahn'an and the ahn'tep must be crushed." His voice deepened, and the power overtook his vision. "The daem'ahn will purge this realm of the infestation and rule over it as we were meant to."

Thresson and Frisha both reared back with frightened eyes, but Thresson would not be deterred. "What infestation?" he asked.

"*He taunts you,*" claimed the voice.

Caydean slammed his fist against the bars of the cell and shouted, "The putridity of the *soul.*"

"You are mad, Caydean," exclaimed Thresson.

"No, not just mad," said Frisha with a quivering voice. "I've seen this before. Look at his eyes. He's a demon."

The voice said, "*Now they know. They rise against you.*"

Caydean's body shook as the laughter rolled through him. These pitiful creatures did not know who held them in his clutches. If they did, they would not have the sense of mind to question him for all their terror. He leaned toward the bars, "I am not just *any* daem'ahn. I am the Orb Weaver, himself, Slayer of CidHarga, First Son of Gorokin—Father of Daem'Ahn. I'm the Tormenter of Tehui'hiak, Crown Prince of H'khajnak, the Great and Mighty Ygrethiel."

They both blinked at him in confusion, and Caydean turned from them with a huff. It was no matter. They were inconsequential. He wondered if perhaps it was time he disposed of them, but winning was so much sweeter when he had someone to whom he could gloat. The pain he inflicted on Thresson was joyful, and having control over the woman his youngest brother had taken as his betrothed was nearly as satisfying. Now that Rezkin was dead, he no longer needed the woman. The golem with whom she had been replaced would not persist if she died, though, so he hoped to *convince* her to become one of his minions while there was still time to exchange her again.

Caydean stalked toward the transport room which held the portal to the inter-realm pathways. Although he did not have the power to open a door on his own, Berringish had been gracious enough to provide him with the device that allowed him to move between his Seat in Kaibain and this hidden lair in Sandea. Berringish had possessed a second device that was portable and could be used to open a pathway to anywhere, but his brother, Rezkin, had destroyed it on the battlefield. It was a major setback, but one he could handle. Especially after today. Caydean grinned to himself as he thought about his present task. He was about to win this war, and his enemies would not see it coming.

The sandstone passageway was smooth, having been sculpted over eons by the wind. The fallen grains beneath his feet were a testament to the fortitude of the air currents that had swept them from their places amongst the rocks. He imagined he was much like the wind. He had plotted for some time before he had initiated the attack on the King's Tournament in Skutton, but he had set things in motion long before that glorious rout. Berringish had thought him hasty when he attacked.

"*Berringish doubted you*," whispered the voice.

The old Sen *claimed* he wanted to wait until his demonic minions had been established in the other kingdoms, but Caydean had been impatient. Berringish had controlled him for too long.

"*He would still control you if he could*," said the voice.

But Caydean had finally outgrown the Sen's designs and had taken control of his own destiny. He didn't view his impatience as a negative as had Berringish, but as proof of his drive and ambition. It was true that a few of his minions had been destroyed, thanks to his youngest brother, and the loss of the young dragon had been especially painful, but it was no matter. What he was about to do would make up for those setbacks, and his little brother was no longer around to cause him problems.

"*He will haunt you in death*," said the voice.

A chill traveled down his spine as he considered that, then he dismissed it. His brother held no such power.

Caydean briefly wondered where the Sen was now. He had heard no word regarding the Sen since the battle three weeks hence, and it was odd for Berringish to be remiss in checking in. He wondered if Berringish had not found a mage relay to send news.

"*He plots against you.*"

Caydean's lips turned down and he frowned as he rounded a corner. The old man was probably off recruiting more minions in some distant kingdom. Caydean knew better, though. The minions were a waste of time. What good were minions without generals to lead them? It was generals he needed, and he was about to get them.

The voice said, "*The generals will seek to usurp your throne.*"

No, Caydean thought. He was taking measures to prevent that. Once he had them, the generals would serve him and only him. They would not be able to overcome his control as he had with Berringish.

The transport room was quiet when he entered. It was a natural cavity in the sandstone cave large enough to hold the device and not much else. The carved pillars that would hold the portal were dark with disuse, which of course they would be since he was the only person alive who could use them.

"*That you know of*," whispered the voice.

Caydean growled his displeasure over the thought as he stepped up to the control runes. No guards were permitted this far into his lair. After all, if you didn't allow anyone in, no one could stab you in the back.

"*People do not always do what they're told*," said the helpful voice.

Caydean's gaze shot to the darkened recesses of the cave. Had the shadows moved since he had been focused on the controls? His senses pricked, and the hairs on the back of his neck stood out. Caydean raised his arm and shot tendrils of black power toward the darkened spaces. The tendrils whipped around the room but caught nothing in their searching grasp. Caydean's racing heart began to calm as he realized he was alone.

"*No, never alone*," said the voice.

No, never alone, he thought thankfully as he considered the voice that had gripped his mind since he had been a child of only six or seven years, even before he was joined with the daem'ahn. The voice kept him vigilant, ever cognizant of the dangers posed by those around him, and for that he was thankful.

He activated the portal runes causing power to surge up the pillars and streak across the space between them in a silent wave of rippling light. He stepped up to the portal that would transport him from his current location in Sandea to its sister portal located in his private workshop in the palace in Kaibain.

"*It will tear you to pieces and scatter you across all of Terralor.*"

Fear seized Caydean as it did every time he approached the portal. The mechanism that drove the portal was unknown to him, and, as such, he had little confidence in it. He saw the portal for what it was—an unnatural rift in reality. He did not trust it. Still, he would use it despite the way it made his blood run cold and his heart race. Caydean was not unaccustomed to fear. In fact, he felt it often and deeply, not that he would ever admit it to anyone, of course. But, in many ways, fear was his greatest asset. Fear was what drove him. It drove him to better himself, to best his challengers, and to uncover the multitude of plots against him. Fear had taught him that no one was to be trusted, and it was fear that he would use to crush not only Ashai but every kingdom on the Souelian. Eventually, through fear, he would accomplish his ultimate goal, the elimination of the ahn'an and ahn'tep races.

Caydean steadied his nerves and clenched his fists as he stepped through the portal and was transported. In one breath, he was standing in his lair in Sandea, and in the next he was in his private workshop on the lowest level of the palace in Kaibain. The portal was disturbing, but it was useful. His shoulders relaxed as he took in his personal space. The suite was separated into four rooms consisting of one large, central room with three smaller rooms extending off it, which included the transport room in which he currently stood. He quickly moved into the central room which possessed several workbenches covered in bottles, jars, glassware, and instruments for preparing potions and materials he required. Shelves lining the walls and extending into the center of the space held crates and trunks of supplies. The room to the right was adorned for the performance of rituals and sacrifices, and the room on the left typically held whatever or *whomever* he intended to use for those sacrifices. That room was presently empty, though, since the individuals he currently sought were volunteers.

Caydean passed through his workshop and wrenched open the door that led to a small receiving chamber. Two men and a woman were seated upon a couple of divans. The men were hunched over playing bones on the floor, while the woman was studiously ignoring them as she read a book. Upon his entry, the woman snapped her book shut, and the men snatched the bones from the floor, stuffing them into a small pouch. They all quickly got to their feet and bowed low.

"*They plot against you*," whispered his inner voice.

Caydean narrowed his eyes as he surveyed the three. Even though he had called them there, he didn't like that they had gathered together outside his workshop. They had greeted him appropriately, but had they been quick enough? Had furtive glances passed between them? Were they thinking even now of ways to defy him? He clenched his hands and released his pent breath. It was no matter. In less than an hour, they would be incapable of subterfuge.

"We will begin now," snapped Caydean before turning on his heel and returning to his workshop. The three volunteers followed him across the tidy space, and he stepped aside to allow them to enter the ritual room ahead of him. He grinned as he saw the fear that gripped them as they each stepped through the ward to cross the threshold. Having already been briefed on their roles during the ritual, they each took their positions, although their movements were shaky and uncertain. With wide eyes, they glanced at each other, perhaps for comfort, and then they stared at him in trepidation. He knew this room was unlike any they had ever visited, and in seeing it, the reality of what they were about to do was beginning to set in. It was for this reason that he instructed them to latch the shackles about their wrists and ankles. He could not have their fear overtaking them and risk them trying to run away during the ritual. And they *would* run. It was inevitable.

The darkened chamber danced with shadows that stretched across the arcane runes and diagrams that were scrawled across the floor and walls, many of them in blood. Some were permanent, inlayed with metal or contrasting stone. Others were painted on, while still more were temporary and designed in chalk. A plethora of candles occupied important inflection points throughout the room, and these were lit as soon as he opened the door. His volunteers jumped as the candles cast their imposing shadows, and he nearly laughed at the absurdity. One of the three was decidedly less jumpy than the others, and Caydean approached him with his shield wards tightly affixed about him.

"Avikeev, are you prepared?" he said.

Avikeev's expression hardened, and his dark eyes turned steely. "I am, Your Majesty."

Caydean eyed him suspiciously. "You will give me no trouble?"

Avikeev's lip curled up in disgust. "I am dedicated to the cause. Once I have the power, I will seek out my master's killer and obliterate him—*painfully*."

Although Caydean knew Avikeev to be in his early thirties, the man was possessed of the impulsive and often hot-headed temperament of a younger man. His heated drive and ambition had earned him his place at his former master's side. Battle Master Rhone had been Caydean's first choice for the ritual he was about to perform, but since the man was dead, he would have to make do with the former battle master's second—Avikeev. So long as Avikeev kept his wits about him and did not fight back, the ritual should go smoothly. The other two were powerful mages as well, but they did not possess the natural nocent power that Avikeev wielded and were unlikely to interfere with the ritual whether they fought back or not.

"*He will turn on you. You should kill him now and choose another*."

Caydean growled as he turned away from Avikeev to take his place at the edge of the circle that contained the three restrained volunteers. He looked to the second and third of the three, Trivian and Ulessa. "Are you both ready?"

Ulessa nodded with a *yes*, but Trivian appeared doubtful. Caydean turned his hard, icy gaze on the man, and he quickly folded. "Y-yes, Your Majesty. I am ready."

"Good, because if you resist, I will kill you and choose another for the honor."

"*He is weak and will seek to make you weaker*," whispered the voice in his mind.

Trivian firmed his jaw and lifted his chin. "That will not be necessary. I am ready."

Caydean no longer had to look at the text to perform the ritual. He had reviewed it over and over until he had it memorized. It helped that he had Ygrethiel, his demon, to guide him as well. While Ygrethiel was not practiced in human rituals, he had eons of experience and knowledge to draw upon. Although he had planned to do this with Berringish's assistance, Caydean would not wait for the missing Sen to reappear. He began the ritual with an incantation that lasted nearly an hour. Within the incantation were stored the terms of the agreement between him and the demons he intended to summon, so the words and the intent with which they were spoken had to be exact. Then he offered his blood to the runes inlaid in the floor, a small sacrifice for the right to make use of them. It was no matter. He had plenty more. Finally, he instructed his volunteers to pick up the daggers that lay at their feet and offer up their own blood as proof of their willingness. With a whimper and a wince, they each made a shallow slice to their forearm and dripped the crimson offering onto the runes at their feet.

Caydean stepped to the side of the room to collect the first of the three vessels. They were seemingly innocuous clay pots possessing cork stoppers and decorated with many of the same jagged, arcane runes that could be found about the room. They appeared simple, yet they were the culmination of Caydean's life's work, a work that even he would never be able to replicate. Caydean handed the first of the clay pots to Avikeev and then passed the second and third to Trivian and Ulessa. Avikeev began a chant, and Trivian and Ulessa followed his lead with only slightly less confidence. The air became heavy as energy began to grow within the circle of runes. Caydean grinned as his plans began to take shape before him.

Avikeev glanced to him for affirmation, and at his nod, opened the vessel. Trivian and Ulessa quickly did the same, and then all three at once dropped the pots causing them to smash onto the floor. Dark power surged out of the pots, inky smoke possessed of a mind. Horrible images took shape in the smoke like the monsters of nightmares. Ulessa screeched, and Trivian yanked against his restraints, while Avikeev's eyes bulged, and his mouth opened on a silent wail. All three began wrenching at their chains as their terror incited them to take flight. Then the demons surged toward the three, entering them through their orifices and filling their bodies with their powerful presence.

"*They will overpower you. They will destroy you,*" said his mind's voice.

A cold chill slithered up Caydean's spine. Could these demons turn on him? Would they be able to overpower him? No, he had taken all the precautions. These demons were chained to his will just as surely as the volunteers were now chained to those of the demons. Besides, Ygrethiel was their crown prince. While they were three of the highest-level demons in H'khajnak, he was still more powerful than all three of them combined.

Caydean raised his arms and all three grinned as they knelt at his feet. He said, "My generals, welcome to the Realm of the Living. May we bring chaos and terror to all."

Trivian's face contorted into a sneer. "Death to the ahn'an."

Ulessa intoned, "Death to the ahn'tep."

Avikeev's glare bored into him as he said, "And untold horrors to Wesson Seth."

1

WESSON PULLED AWAY from Celise's warm embrace, and Kai gave him a knowing smirk. His cheeks flushed, and Wesson ducked his head.

Kai chuckled. "The great and mighty battle mage is embarrassed to be seen with a woman—a beautiful one at that."

"I don't like to advertise my good fortune," Wesson muttered as he opened the door wide so the striker might enter. Wesson's chambers in the palace of Cael were only sparsely furnished and devoid of décor save for a single colorful rug in the seating area. Celise had woven the rug from strips of scrap material she obtained from the seamstresses.

"Oh, is that all?" Kai asked as though he already knew the answer.

Wesson motioned toward one of only two chairs, which were sturdy if not exactly comfortable. "Is there something with which I may assist you, Striker Kai?"

Kai's smile fell as he sat, and he glanced at Celise who appeared to be pretending she was not listening as she made the bed tucked into the far corner of the room. Returning his attention to Wesson, Kai said, "It is time to return to Garten Knoll. The rumors that the True King lives abound. We have had reports of such from nearly every kingdom. Queen Erisial of Lon Lerésh has decreed that he lives to be the official stance of the queendom."

Wesson nodded with a heavy heart, for he and his fellow Caelians knew the truth. "Of course she has. Rezkin being dead puts her in a difficult position. Her place on the throne is no longer secure. Someone will surely try to assassinate her now that there is no threat of Rezkin inheriting the throne upon her demise. But it is impossible. We entombed his body beneath the ruins six months ago. Even Rezkin cannot overcome death, despite the rumors."

"*I* know that, and *you* know that, but the people do not believe it," replied Kai. "We must go to the tomb to confirm his death. *You* must go because you set the wards around the tomb. We will take Minder Finwy with us. He can confirm on behalf of the Temple that Rezkin is, in fact, dead. Representatives from Ferélle, Lon Lerésh, and Gendishen will attend as well."

"Surely Caydean will have people watching the tomb," said Wesson.

"True, but we will not be there long. Azeria believes she can open a pathway directly into the tombs."

"We are fortunate the Eihelvanan have stayed around," replied Wesson. "Besides the convenience of the pathways, without Rezkin, I am not sure the citadel and its wraith-like guards, the Shielreyah, would permit us to stay. They seem to need the power of a Spirétua."

Kai nodded. "Entris insists on staying because he says it is his duty as Spirétua-lyé to root out demons."

A chill went through Wesson as he remembered Entris's assertion that Wesson, himself, was actually bonded with a demon while in utero. Wesson knew that demons were not intrinsically evil. They were beings of chaos, and he did not *feel* like a demon. He swallowed hard as a niggling thought told him that was not quite true. The truth was, sometimes, when he used his nocent power, he *felt* like chaos itself and to inflict it upon the world thrilled him. He supposed he was lucky the Spirétua-lyé had not killed him yet.

Wesson quickly packed a bag just in case things went awry and joined Striker Kai as he exited the chambers. They met Azeria in the grand foyer of the palace where she would open the entrance to the pathways that allowed for faster travel between places and even between realms. She was not alone. With her were the Spirétua-lyé Entris, Striker Farson, the ever-steady Captain Jimson, Apprentice Healer and warrior Reaylin, Elemental Mage Nanessy Threll, and the omessa shapeshifting she-wolf Tiseyi. The three representatives from the other kingdoms were also present. To one side stood Rezkin's cousin and successor, Lord Tieran Nirius, who was also an apprentice life mage. Beside him was Lady Frisha, the woman who had once been betrothed to Rezkin and was now courted by Lord Tieran. Wesson was uncomfortable around the woman ever since they had returned from Ashai. Something was off about her, but he could not put his finger on what it was. He had thought her odd behavior due to the news of Rezkin's death, but even now, six months later, she seemed strange to him.

Lord Tieran reached for her as Frisha stepped forward. She said, "I wish to go with you."

Striker Kai replied, "This is no journey for a lady without the means to protect herself."

Azeria said, "The striker is correct. The pathways can be hazardous, and the more mundanes we take with us, the longer the pathway."

Frisha gave Azeria and icy glare then lifted her chin stubbornly and said, "I need to see Rezkin's body. I need to know for certain that he is dead."

Captain Jimson said, "Lady Frisha, it has been *six months* since his death. His body will no longer appear as you remember him. Believe me. You do not wish to see him that way."

Frisha scowled at him and snapped, "Stay out of this, Captain. I was not speaking with you." Jimson looked as if he had been slapped, but he said nothing more as Frisha sauntered up to Kai. Her voice turned syrupy as she brushed her fingers along his arm. "Striker Kai, I *need* to see his body for myself. For closure. Surely you can understand a woman's needs." This last she said with a sultry grin that appeared completely natural yet very wrong on Frisha's face.

Wesson noted Striker Farson's sharp look as he stared at Frisha. Wesson's own instincts were again telling him something was not right with her, but he had already surreptitiously run a multitude of tests on the woman and could find nothing.

Kai gently took Frisha's hand and removed it from his person as he said, "This journey may be perilous, and everyone going has a role to play. You must stay here where you will be safe."

Lord Tieran stepped up to her and took her hand. "Listen to him, Frisha. There is no reason for you to go, and you are safe here."

Frisha's face screwed up in anger, and she snatched her hand away. "You mean I will be in the way. I am not so delicate. One day you will see exactly what I can do." Then she spun and stormed down the corridor to disappear around a corner.

Lord Tieran looked embarrassed as he said, "I apologize for Frisha's behavior. I know not what has happened to her, but I am sure it will pass soon." As he said this, he did not look so certain to Wesson.

Kai said, "Rezkin's death has been difficult for her."

Tieran shook his head uncertainly. "It started before news of his death reached us. She has just been … different. More temperamental and … ah … assertive, I suppose you could say."

By the uncomfortable looks all around, Wesson could tell that everyone had noticed how *assertive* Frisha had been lately. No longer was she the sheltered merchant's daughter they had all known, and only Lord Tieran's insistence upon a proper courtship kept her from scandal. Wesson wondered if the courtship was not an excuse for Lord Tieran to delay a greater commitment since Frisha had changed.

Lord Tieran wished them all well and then followed the same path Frisha had taken. Then Azeria set to opening the portal to the pathway that would lead them to Garten Knoll. The air in front of them silently split to reveal a misty passage, and Azeria entered first, followed by Striker Kai and the others. Wesson entered the pathway last, and the rift closed behind him.

Wesson could see nothing but a mist that glowed with a soft ambient light in the pathway. The ground beneath his feet was smooth as polished marble and dark as night. There were no walls or trees or anything else around them unless it was hidden in the fog, yet Azeria led them confidently forward.

"How can you tell where we are going?" he asked, his voice traveling just far enough for her to hear.

"It is part of my ability or *talent* as you would say. As a pathbuilder, I can sense the direction of the path and the distance to our destination. I cannot determine what the path will look like upon opening it, however. It is different depending on who is traveling it. Be prepared. This mist hides many things."

Nanessy Threll, who was walking beside Entris just behind Kai said, "How long will we be in here?"

"It is not far," replied Azeria. "I would say perhaps three hours (*istak*)."

Nanessy's eyes were wide as she said, "Only three hours to travel all the way to Western Ashai?"

Azeria nodded. "It would be shorter except that we are traveling with several mundanes. If I traveled the pathway alone, it would be nearly instantaneous."

"Wow, with that talent, you could travel anywhere in the world within minutes," said Nanessy. "What an amazing ability."

"I can only travel to places I have been," said Azeria.

Entris said, "And it is not wise for us to travel to many places since the humans believe we are long deceased or have forgotten that we exist altogether (*istak*)."

"Why is that?" said Farson. "If you live so long and can travel anywhere so easily, you should be known in every kingdom. Your people could have settled all of Terralor."

Entris said, "Our numbers are not so many, and pathmakers are rare, more rare even than Spirétua (*yelouis*). Although we live long lives, and perhaps because of it, it is not so easy for us to reproduce. Sometimes we go many seasons in which there are no births at all.

"A time is still within the memories of our elders that we endured a war with the humans in which our numbers dwindled. Afterward, our people gathered in small communities, and there are great distances between them. We established these communities away from humans to reduce the chances of another war. But humans spread quickly and far, and the time is coming when we will no longer be able to remain separate."

"Who won the war?" said Nanessy.

Entris hummed under his breath and said, "I do not believe there was a winner. Both sides took heavy losses (*yelouis*). The leader of the human aggressors was killed, and eventually people grew tired of fighting. The Eihelvanan retreated to our communities, and the humans did not pursue us. In time, they forgot about us."

"That's a rather anticlimactic story," muttered Reaylin.

"That is because it is not a story," said Azeria. "It is history."

Reaylin asked, "Do you hate humans, then? For the war, I mean."

Entris and Azeria exchanged a look, then Entris said, "We do not blame all humans for the faults of some of them. There were times when Eihelvanan and humans lived peacefully beside each other. And even during the war, not all humans were our enemies. We do not see humans as our enemies now, but we are cautious (*spretu*)."

As Wesson considered Entris's words, he wondered if he would be so gracious. If some of the Eihelvanan had declared war on *his* people, would he see them all as the enemy? And after the war was over, would he be able to forgive them for the deaths they had caused? He thought it had probably been wise to remain separate for a time, but what would happen as humans rediscovered the Eihelvanan? It would take a great leader to bring the peace between the races. Lacking that, fear and distrust would consume men's hearts, and war would likely break out again. Only this time, there would be nowhere for the Eihelvanan to go.

A few hours later, Azeria abruptly stopped and said, "We are here."

Everyone waited while she opened the portal to exit the pathway, then

Strikers Farson and Kai went through first followed by the kingdoms' representatives, Jimson, Reaylin, Nanessy, Tiseyi, and Wesson. The two Eihelvanan were to come last after the strikers reported that all was clear, but all was *not* clear. Apparently, Caydean *had* set a watch on the ruins.

Wesson threw himself to the side as an icy shard as thick as his forearm sailed toward him. It crashed against the crumbled wall of the once grand estate and shattered into a plethora of frozen fragments. He quickly erected several wards around him as he regained his feet and scanned the area for his assailant. He saw Nanessy dueling with a trained battle mage, but it could not have been the mage who attacked him. The kingdoms' representatives were hunkered down behind a broken wall. The strikers, Jimson, and Reaylin were battling against the armed forces of Caydean's army. And suddenly a large wolf leapt from behind the ruins to tackle one of the soldiers approaching Reaylin's flank. Another icy shard smashed against Wesson's shield ward, and he finally caught a glimpse of his attacker as she ducked behind a wall.

After casting a few volleys toward the attacker's location, Wesson slipped behind the wall nearest him and began making his way toward her. As he stepped deftly over the rubble, he employed some of the stealth spells he had been working on since meeting Rezkin. He silenced his steps as he pulled the shadows around him, and there were plenty of shadows to work with since it was near evening. A man suddenly flew over a wall and landed in Wesson's path. The mage took no notice of Wesson as he scrambled to his feet and leapt back over the short wall. Wesson sent a spell over the wall after the man, but it was one that would not detonate for a couple of minutes. Then he continued toward the last known location of his own assailant.

When Wesson was hidden around the corner from his attacker, he paused to take a deep breath. He knew what he needed to do, and he did not relish it. He had told Rezkin that he would not kill people, but that had been the wishful thinking of a naïve journeyman. Wesson had killed many people now, and yet sneaking up to kill *this* mage felt just as horrible as the first time he had killed someone. Only this time he was doing it on purpose. He swallowed his bile and rounded the corner. His spell was released as soon as he laid eyes on the woman, and he dearly wished he could pull it back. In the split second before the spell struck her, Wesson managed to erect a shield ward around the woman. Then his spell struck his shield ward with a concussive effect, blasting away the ruins in every direction and throwing him from his feet as it shook the entire hilltop.

Once the dust settled, Wesson could see that the woman lay prone on the ground with her black battle mage garb in tatters. He hurried toward her whispering aloud his greatest hopes that he had not killed her. He brushed her blonde hair away from her face and checked for breathing. He found her still alive but bleeding from many small cuts to her exposed flesh. Wesson shook her, but she did not wake. He quickly stood and looked around the ruins for the others. It took him a minute to find Reaylin, who had just run her sword through the soldier she had been fighting. Wesson called to her, and she shortly joined him. She was breathing heavily when she arrived at his side.

"What is it?" she huffed. "Thanks for the warning, by the way. I nearly died when your spell threw me into my opponent."

Wesson blanched. "Sorry about that. It was not planned."

"Well, what do you need?"

Wesson pointed to the unconscious woman at his feet. "I need you to heal her."

"What? But she's the enemy. You're supposed to *kill* her. She was certainly trying to kill you."

"I know, but I need her to be okay. Please heal her."

Reaylin looked at him with irritation but said, "Fine, but you had better know what you're doing."

Wesson nodded and nudged Reaylin toward the downed woman. Then he stood guard over the two while Reaylin conducted the healing. By the time she was done, the others had swept the hilltop clean of enemies and were headed his way.

A moan at his feet caught his attention, and Wesson turned his gaze back to the woman. She opened her eyes and immediately recoiled from Reaylin. Then her gaze turned to him, and her eyes widened as she said, "Wesson?"

Wesson knelt at her side and said, "It is me, Anda. Are you okay?"

Anda appeared alarmed as the others came to stand around her. She tried to raise her own shield ward, but Wesson had already bound her power so that she could not access it. It was a spell he had figured out during his brief time at the Battle Mage Academy, the same place where he had met and befriended the woman lying at his feet. Anda's power had barely been enough to keep her in the academy, but she had honed well the little power she had. Still, she did not have nearly enough power to overcome Wesson's spell preventing her from using it.

"What is wrong with me?" said a stricken Anda. "Why can I not use my powers?"

"I have blocked you for the time being," said Wesson.

Anda got shakily to her feet and held her arms around herself as if seeking comfort or protection. She glanced toward the others anxiously then looked to him. "What is happening here, Wesson? Why are you with these rebels? And who—er, *what*—are they?"

Wesson glanced back to see Entris and Azeria joining them. He was not sure what to say. How did he explain so much in the brief time they had? After searching for the words for a few seconds, he finally shook his head, "Anda, please believe me when I tell you this, but you are on the wrong side."

Pulling her gaze from the Eihelvanan, she looked at him in disbelief. "The wrong side? How can you say that? These people attack travelers and steal their possessions. Sometimes they even kill people. Worse yet, they want to overthrow the king! They will destroy all that Ashai is and let chaos reign."

Wesson confidently said, "No, Anda, that is what Caydean is doing. It is *he* who has attacked Ashai. It is *he* who is sewing chaos. He is mad in ways you do not even know. Not only has his unusual power driven him insane, but he is also possessed by a demon."

Anda shook her head adamantly. "Wesson, there is no such thing as demons. What you are doing is treason."

"No, the leader of this movement has a legitimate claim to the throne."

"You're speaking of this so-called emperor? The one who conceals his name but calls himself Dark Tidings? He is dead. He was killed right here where we stand when he attacked the king. He is entombed right over there."

Wesson winced and even though he put no stock in the rumors, he said, "There is some speculation that he lives."

Anda laughed. "Rumors spoken by desperate traitors to the kingdom."

"Regardless, his claim is legitimate, which means his successor is next in line for the throne, not Caydean." Wesson absently tugged at a lock of his hair as he considered how to get through to her. "Think about it, Anda. Caydean attacked the King's Tournament, then he attacked the duchies, and then the Mage Academy. Can you not see that all the turmoil in Ashai is due to *his* treachery?"

Anda crossed her arms and scowled at him. "The King's Tournament was infested with rebels, the dukes were plotting against the king, and the mages at the Mage Academy had gone rogue. As terrible as they were, the king had legitimate reasons for doing those things. And now he has declared peace again. He feeds the poor and displaced, he is providing jobs to those who need work, and he is even building a magnificent temple."

"A temple to himself."

"It is a temple to the mighty god Ygrethiel."

"And *who* is the embodiment of this new god but Caydean himself!"

"You fear change. The new religion is one of peace and prosperity for all."

"Ashai has always been a secular kingdom, allowing people to worship however and whomever they wish. Now everyone in the kingdom must convert or what? Be imprisoned? Be executed. And how exactly do the people prosper from worshipping Caydean? How is forcing a member of every household to undertake a pilgrimage that could take months good for the people?"

Anda lifted her chin stubbornly. "The pilgrimage is to prove one's devotion. The king will be granting titles and land to the most devout, regardless of class. Even the poorest peasant can now become someone of station. Never has that been a possibility under any other king. None of that sounds like the acts of a madman and certainly not a demon. He is a good and gracious king."

Wesson looked at her sadly. Over the past six months, Caydean *had* done those things. And he had been spreading misinformation about the attacks that made his actions sound noble, even righteous. He had villainized Rezkin and the rebels and reclaimed the hearts of many Ashaiians. Between the attacks and the extensive draft, Caydean had crippled the nation, and now the people were dependent on him for food and jobs, which they mistook for generosity. And since he was the one to provide them with what they needed most, they were all too willing to forget that he was the one who made them desperate in the first place.

Thankfully, the neighboring kingdoms were more cautious in their beliefs. The combined troops of Torrel and Sandea were still stationed at Zigharan's End to the northwest, and Channería maintained a garrison along the EastWest Trade Route to the east. With the new religion of the Ygrethialists abounding in Ashai, contentions with Channería, a kingdom devoted to the Maker, were at an all-time high. But the other kingdoms' skepticism would do nothing to convince Anda that he and the rebels were in the right.

Wesson's shoulders slumped as he released an anxious breath. He said, "I am sorry, Anda. I do not wish to hurt you, but neither will I allow you to go back to working for Caydean. I am afraid you are our prisoner now, at least until I am confident that I have convinced you that what you are doing is wrong."

Kai came forward to bind Anda's arms with a length of rope, but Anda snatched her hands away and shook her finger at Wesson. Her tone was filled with anger and hurt as she said, "I thought we were friends. I see that means little to you."

Wesson said, "Please understand, I am doing this for *you*. Once you see the truth you will thank me."

Once Anda was subdued, she was forced to follow as the others moved toward the entrance to the tomb. Wesson tried to ignore the blood trailing their steps as he approached the opening. It was sealed behind one of his wards that he was fairly certain no singular mage alive could break. That did not mean that multiple mages working in tandem could not get through, however. He would know, though, if any had. The tomb entrance stood untouched. Wesson quickly dispelled the ward, allowing the others to enter. As he waited, he glanced around to observe the state of the land where they had fought that fateful day six months before. The dead had been piled into a pit and covered over, and besides the intermittent patches of scorched earth that were now green with fresh growth, what had been a deadly battlefield looked no different from the prairie land around it.

Wesson turned away from the scene and followed Striker Kai into the dark passage that descended beneath the ruins to the burial chamber that held the body of the fallen Emperor Rezkin. The death of Rezkin, the infamous and untouchable Dark Tidings, had been a shock to everyone who had thought him indomitable. But when Rezkin had faced off against King Caydean, whom Wesson and a few others knew to be Rezkin's older brother, he had sacrificed himself to prevent the mad king from killing every rebel and fighter on the battlefield. Rezkin had died, and no one had been able to find the Sen necromancer, Berringish, to reclaim him from the dead. So, with great mourning, they had entombed Rezkin beneath the ancient ruins. They had left him with his armor, swords, and other weapons, as was befitting the burial of a warrior king, so it had been important to seal the tomb against grave robbers and Caydean's forces who might unearth it for some nefarious reason. So far as Wesson could tell, it remained untouched.

When they reached the entrance chamber to the tombs, Wesson began to notice the return of the feelings he thought he had left behind months ago. He felt pride in the way Rezkin had cast aside his precious rules to save the lives of those who followed him. And he felt anger both with Caydean for killing Rezkin and with Rezkin for dying. He felt resentment for the way they had all been left to pick up the pieces of the war and an empire that had depended on Rezkin. And he felt remorse that he had not been there to aid Rezkin when he was so needed. As Wesson glanced around, he noted that the others all wore expressions in varying degrees of sadness and anger as well.

He scanned each somber face as he passed Kai and noted the teary eyes on a few as he moved toward the tunnel that led to the tomb. The passage was short, if a bit rough, and Wesson cast a small spell to light the way as the others followed him. When he got to the tomb, however, he nearly lost the spell.

"What's this?" he shouted as the others spilled into the chamber around him. The tomb in which Rezkin had been interred was open, its stone lid shoved to the side, and Rezkin's body was missing. All that remained within the tomb was the etching of an image that had not been there six months ago when they had placed Rezkin's body in the stone space.

"It is a raven," said Kai, eying the image.

"As in *the* Raven?" replied Jimson. "He has been here? Did he steal the emperor's body?"

"So it would seem," replied Kai.

"Who is this Raven?" said Azeria.

Wesson's breath escaped as the implication struck him. Wesson knew what Kai and Jimson did not. He shared a look with Farson, whose red-rimmed eyes had taken on a hard glint. Wesson and Farson knew that Rezkin *was* the Raven, but the others were clueless to the fact. Questions began tumbling through Wesson's mind. Had Rezkin somehow come back to life? Was he truly the indomitable warrior everyone thought him to be? Or was there something else at play here? Wesson had seen Rezkin do some remarkable things, things that could now be explained by his Eihelvanan powers, but he did not think Rezkin truly held power over death. Wesson was now torn over whether he should tell what he knew of the Raven's identity and opened his mouth to do just that when Striker Farson shook his head and issued a single word. "No."

Wesson snapped his mouth shut. He would need to talk to the striker. Kai's abrupt orders snapped him back to the conversation. Kai and Jimson had presumably just finished explaining to some of the others who the Raven was, at least to *their* knowledge, when Kai said, "Spread out. Search for other entrances to this chamber."

The dark recess nearest him revealed nothing, but Wesson continued to scan the walls, ceiling, and floor for evidence of a hidden passage. After a few minutes, Reaylin said, "Here, I found something."

Wesson was closest to Reaylin, so he arrived at her side first. The passage was hidden by the jutting rock and appeared to have recently been cleared of rubble. With a few prepared spells at the ready, Wesson headed down the passage with the strikers behind him. The short corridor led to a smaller room with a number of burial alcoves and a larger tomb to one side. The others continued into the room, and Kai said, "Over here is another passage that leads to the outside. That is how they got around the ward. They just dug through the hillside."

Wesson's attention was on the tomb, though. He knelt beside it to inspect a dark stain on the floor.

"Blood," he said. "A lot of it. It's old."

Farson knelt beside him. He said, "Someone died here."

Scattered within the bloody stain were broken pottery shards. Wesson picked up one of the larger shards and noted the jagged, arcane markings painted onto it. His gut clenched as he said, "Demon."

There were several gasps, and Kai said, "That is a demon vessel?"

"It *was*," said Wesson, dropping the shard. "The demon is gone now, but to where?"

"You all are crazy," muttered Anda.

Nanessy's voice was hesitant as she said, "Do you think someone placed the demon in Rezkin's body?"

Wesson stood but continued to frown down at the bloody shards. "It is possible."

"No," said Entris. "The daem'ahn cannot exist within a dead body. A host must be living."

Wesson became lost in thought as he pondered the possibilities. Either someone had stolen Rezkin's body, and that someone could possibly be a demon, or Rezkin had somehow come back to life. If it was the latter, then it was possible Rezkin was now possessed by a demon. Would that explain why he had not come forward? Was that why he left the mark of the Raven? Wesson suddenly became aware of the silence around him and looked up to find that they were all looking at him.

"Uh, I am sorry. Could you repeat that?" he said.

Kai frowned. "I said, can you use your magic to detect who was in here or how long ago?"

Wesson shook his head. "I am afraid not. It doesn't work that way. Investigations would be much easier if it did, though."

Azeria's expression was placid, but her eyes were fiery as she said, "Daem'ahn aside, we have not answered the most pertinent question. Why would this Raven take Rezkin's body? What good would it do him?"

Kai stroked his chin thoughtfully, then said, "Perhaps as proof of the emperor's demise?"

"Proof for whom?" said Azeria. "Did you not just say that the Raven supported Rezkin's claim to the throne of Ashai? Why would he wish to prove his death?"

Jimson said, "Perhaps he wishes to introduce some uncertainty around the emperor's death. Rezkin's death would be inconvenient for the criminal overlord who had endorsed him."

"Yes, that would make sense," said Kai.

"No," said the she-wolf omessa named Tiseyi. "I do not believe this Raven has anything to do with it."

Kai gave her a curious look and said, "What do you mean?"

"I mean Rezkin is not dead."

Kai looked at her with pity. "I am sorry, my dear, but we all saw his body when we placed in him in here six months ago. As amazingly resilient as Rezkin was, he was not immortal."

"Well, I do not believe it," said Tiseyi, "and you cannot prove it without his body. He and I have a connection—one of the soul. I felt that connection sever, and I was empty. I no longer feel empty."

Azeria's attention snapped to the she-wolf. "You feel this connection again?"

A flash of uncertainty crossed Tiseyi's face. "Well, no, not exactly. I do not feel the connection, but neither do I feel the emptiness."

Mage Nanessy Threll reached over and placed her hand on Tiseyi's shoulder. She said, "I think you do not feel the emptiness because you have accepted the loss. You did not know him for long, and it *has* been six months."

Tiseyi scowled at Nanessy and flicked the hand off her shoulder. "Say what you want. I know in here"—she tapped her chest—"that he is not dead."

The representative from Lon Lerésh, who had been conferring with the other to kingdoms' representatives looked over and said, "We concur with the lady. It is our opinion that there is enough doubt surrounding the emperor's death to conclude that he is still alive."

Reaylin crossed her arms and said, "I'm with Tiseyi. I prefer to think he's alive, because if he is, then everything can be fixed. The problems with the other kingdoms in his empire will disappear, and we can all have hope again."

"But if he was alive, he would have come back to us," said Nanessy. "Where is he?"

Knowing what he knew about Rezkin and the Raven, Wesson had wondered the same thing. He said, "Spirétua-lyé Entris, you insist Rezkin was Spirétua. Are the Spirétua somehow able to overcome death?"

Entris shook his head. "No, only the Sen have power over death, and even they cannot retrieve their own souls."

Wesson had hoped for a different answer. He was absolutely certain Rezkin had been dead when they entombed him. It simply was not possible for him to be alive, and yet the symbol of the Raven was etched into the tomb. Had someone else in the Raven's retinue thought to claim the body?

Kai said, "We need to be going. The lookouts we killed above will be missed. We could find ourselves under attack at any time. We should be on the lookout for a potential demon, and we should seal these chambers again regardless. No one else needs to know that the emperor's body is missing."

"Speak for yourself, Ashaiian," spat Tiseyi. "I will not allow others to speak of Rezkin's death when I know him to be alive."

"You do not *know* that," huffed Kai.

The Leréshi representative said, "We will take this news back to our respective kingdoms."

Azeria said, "This deserves investigation. I will find out what happened to Rezkin's body (*ahdohuana*)."

Wesson did not know what *ahdohuana* meant, but by the flinty look in her eyes, he assumed it meant she was determined.

Entris said, "We do not have time for that, Azeria (*itsiyela*). Besides the possibility of *this* daem'ahn, I felt King Caydean's power while he was here. Not only is he infested with daem'ahn but he is also Spirétua. These are no doubt the reasons for his purported madness. He must be dealt with (*ahdohuana*)."

"You think to face him alone?" scoffed Azeria. "You will not survive. You cannot stand against him if he is both daem'ahn *and* Spirétua. We will do what should have been done six months ago. I will return you through the pathways to our home in Freth Adwyn so you may report to the Syek-lyé and recruit assistance. Then I will come back here to investigate (*spretu*)."

Entris gave Azeria a meaningful stare. Wesson got the feeling it was not often that the woman countermanded the Spirétua-lyé in such an imposing way. Then he said, "You know I cannot leave Cael for very long. The citadel must have a Spirétua if it is to remain powered."

His interest piqued, Wesson said, "So the citadel does feed off your power."

Entris tilted his head. "Yes and no. The power of the Spirétua charges the crystals that in turn power the enchantments on the citadel, but then the citadel returns that power and more to the Spirétua."

Kai interrupted and with a pointed look toward Azeria, he said, "We can discuss the workings of the citadel once we have returned. For now, we should go."

Tiseyi said, "The omessas returned to Pruar once they heard of Rezkin's death. I will now go to Pruar to inform them that he is not dead, and hopefully they will change their minds."

Anda said, "I take it this Rezkin you all have been speaking of is your emperor? The one known as Dark Tidings?" When she did not get a reply, she said, "What is an omessa?"

Tiseyi glanced at Anda and said, "I am omessa."

Kai cleared his throat. "It is too dangerous for you to travel back to Pruar, especially alone. Besides, it could take months to get there from here."

Azeria forestalled any argument when she said, "I will take her to Pruar after we have returned to Cael."

Tiseyi gave Azeria a nod and said, "Thank you."

Anda said, "Just how do you expect to keep me prisoner all the way to Cael? There are patrols all over the place. How did you get past them to get here, anyway?"

"Do not fret," said Kai. "We have our ways."

2

Azeria closed the portal behind her as she stepped from Tiseyi's village in Pruar back into the pathways where Mage Wesson awaited her. It was dangerous to travel the paths with just the two of them, but the route would be much shorter since they were both *talented* as the humans say. It was strange to be traveling with the human mage that Entris insisted was also daem'ahn. In her opinion, they should have already ended him, but Entris had stayed his own hand. Apparently, he was averse to killing the human-daem'ahn because Wesson was not what one would expect of such a pairing. Wesson was not chaos incarnate. He was structured and compassionate and even felt remorse for those he was forced to kill. He seemed to loathe his own power and had even managed to gain control over constructive magic despite his destructive nature. Azeria did not like it, but she could understand Entris's reticence toward killing the mage.

Wesson followed as she started along the pathway that this time appeared as a cavern of stone and mineral deposits. It was dark in the cavern, and the mist that swirled around her legs hid many potential dangers. Azeria walked with her sword drawn, ready to defend herself from anything or anyone who might attack. Although she was alert to the potential threats, her mind was on other things, namely Rezkin.

It was true that she had not known him for long, but in that brief time, he had gained her grudging respect. More than that, though, he had ignited within her other feelings, feelings she had never before experienced. She had thought to explore those feelings with him. And then he was dead. It had happened so suddenly, and she *knew* he was dead, yet she had barely been able to grasp the reality of it these past six months. Her powers had grown erratic as feelings of terrible loss, abandonment, and resentment consumed her. And now that anger and resentment had taken a new direction. The Raven. She had only just learned of him and yet she was driven by a single-mindedness to seek him out and punish him for disturbing Rezkin's resting place, and for stealing him away and leaving others to speculate about the truth of his demise.

Azeria was not fooled. She had touched Rezkin's body that had grown cold in death. Not even an experienced Spirétua could overcome that, and he had been but a fledgling. No, Rezkin was certainly dead. There was no doubt in her mind, and her heart ached because of it. It made her angry whenever people whispered those rumors that he lived because it was as if they were saying that her feelings were trivial and unfounded. It was even more insulting and infuriating that the Raven's actions had seeded the tiniest spark of hope within her. That little flame was a direct attack on his memory and all that she had felt for him.

And so Azeria was headed back to Ashai in search of this notorious Raven. She would make him pay for the insult against her and Rezkin. And she would prove once and for all that Rezkin, the Emperor of the Souelian, was truly dead. The Raven was difficult to pinpoint since reports of his activities had come in from all over Ashai and even the neighboring kingdom of Channería. She would start at Garten Knoll, since that was the farthest she had been into Ashai, and then, with Wesson as her guide, she would make her way slowly by mundane means toward the capital city of Kaibain where many of the reports indicated the Raven had been most recently.

It did not take them long to reach the ruins of Garten Knoll. The bodies of Caydean's forces remained where they had fallen during the brief battle a day ago, so she knew no one had been there. That was to their advantage since no one would yet be looking for their killers. She pulled her hood over her head to hide her pointed ears then made her way down the hill and headed toward the village of Benbrick. From there, she had been told they would seek river passage upstream to the capital city of Maylon. Then they would try to join a caravan heading east along the EastWest Trade Route toward Caradon where they would board another river boat to Kaibain. It would be a long and dangerous journey, and she did not relish the idea of being surrounded by humans, particularly those who were probably suspicious of outsiders while the patrols were still looking for rebels.

Azeria was determined to see it through, though. She had a mission, a purpose, and she would not be deterred.

Rezkin wiped the blood from his dagger then dragged the body deeper into the dark alley. Dawn had only just arrived, and the shadows were plentiful. He padded back to the end of the alley and peered around the corner. None of the lookouts had raised the alarm. The man he had just killed had been an annoyance that Rezkin no longer had to deal with. His name was Brin Meyner, and he was one of Caydean's investigators set on discovering the identity of the Raven. Although he had not gotten close to Rezkin, much of the information he had gleaned about the workings of the thieves' guilds was information Rezkin would rather not get back to the man's superiors. Rezkin had already infiltrated Master Meyner's room at the shabby Riverspray Inn and burned his notes.

Satisfied that no one had seen the murder, he returned to the body to riffle through the man's belongings. Master Meyner was dressed like a commoner of middling importance in a plain beige shirt beneath a leather vest and worn overcoat with matching trousers. This late in the spring, the air was warm, and the clothes were damp with sweat. In the inner pocket of the coat was a small stack of letters bound with twine, and in the man's other pockets were a notebook, a stick of graphite, a small coin purse, and an enchanted time piece no doubt issued to him by his employer since it was improbable a man of his station could afford one on his own.

Rezkin flipped through the small notebook to find hastily scrawled descriptions of various thieves' guild members and dates and times of their comings and goings in addition to information about shifting allegiances, supply shipments, stolen items, and other guild workings. Rezkin was mildly impressed. The man had been thorough, detailed, and quite observant. It was too bad he had been a staunch king's man dedicated to the task of outing the Raven and obliterating the guilds.

After collecting all that Master Meyner had to offer, Rezkin made haste through the narrow alleys of the shipping district before slipping into the crowd on the main road through the market district. It was easy to get lost in the throng thanks to the influx of people from all over Ashai bent on proving their devotion to the new god. No one took notice of him as he was dressed much like most of the working-class men in the streets. He wore a grey, long-sleeved tunic with a black leather vest and charcoal trousers. His hair was tied in a queue at his nape, and atop his head was a grey, floppy cap common among the residents of Kaibain.

After crossing several streets, Rezkin wound his way through the throng toward a tavern and inn named The General's Court. Often catering to the king's soldiers, the inn was relatively inexpensive yet held a good reputation for cleanliness, security, and fair dealing. Rezkin had chosen it for its proximity to the city's garrison.

As he entered the tavern on the first floor, he politely greeted the tavern's owner then made his way through the choked common room and up the stairs at the rear to the third floor where his room was located. He checked his door to make sure it had not been tampered with while he was away then cautiously entered the room. His first order of business was to check for traps and poisons before he sat on the bed that was big enough for two. Once he was comfortable and calm, he said, "You can come out now."

At first, nothing happened. Then, ever so slowly, a tiny head peeked out from beneath the bed. The triangular head tilted on its long, scaly neck to peer at him through the icy-blue eyes of a miniscule predator. It blinked at him, then opened its toothy maw and released a savage chirp. The little dragon finally surged forward into the open space of the room. Its leathery wings flapped ineffectually and then it stumbled and rolled into a ball flipping head over tail.

The little creature righted itself then turned to faced off against Rezkin. It lowered its head, bared its teeth, and flicked its tail wildly as it prepared to attack. Then it pounced on his foot, wrapping its arms and wings around his ankle and clamping its jaw around his leg. It did not bite hard enough to sink its tiny, razor-like teeth into his flesh, and Rezkin knew it did not truly wish to harm him. The dragon was playing with him as he did every time Rezkin returned from leaving him alone. Rezkin appreciated this type of play as it simulated a hunt, thereby improving on the dragon's skills and honing its aggressive nature.

The dragon he had named Seena was a feisty creature. She eyed everything she saw with a sharp gaze and intelligent eyes. Most often it appeared as if she wanted to attack, although there were times when she seemed subdued, usually promptly after eating. Her moods tended to mimic his. She slept when Rezkin slept and became most alert when he was scouting or fighting. He had managed to train her to hide when he was away as she was far too small to protect herself. Seena had tripled in size since she had hatched six months prior, but she was presently only the size of a kitten. And she still could not spew fire like the adult dragon he had encountered.

Rezkin reached down to stroke her neck, and she stretched it as far as she could before turning her head so she could look up at him. The corners of her lips turned upward, and she closed her eyes as a rumbling began emanating from her body. The purring reminded him of Cat, and a stab of worry shot through him. He shook away the concern as he reminded himself that Princess Ilanet had taken to feeding and caring for Cat whenever he was away. She would continue to do so now that everyone thought him dead—or at least most people did.

He had heard the rumors regarding Emperor Dark Tidings' demise. While most people accepted that he was dead, a good number believed it to be a ruse, that he lived in secret. Rezkin rather liked the uncertainty since it served two purposes. On the one hand, Caydean believed him to no longer be a threat and had ceased his attacks on the people of Ashai. Therefore, his companions were no longer targets. While on the other hand, the kingdoms of his empire would not break away so long as his death was in question. Rezkin now had the freedom to move about without the hindrance of the mantle of rulership while he still maintained a tentative hold over much of the Souelian.

The one thing he had not considered when this plan had presented itself was what his death would do to his friends and, conversely, how *he* would feel being away from them. According to the *Rules*, he was supposed to separate himself from his emotions. And yet, he found that he could not escape his longing for the companionship of those with whom he had grown close. As he stroked the dragon's glossy blue scales, he considered that Seena had gone a long way in filling his need for companionship. She gave him someone to protect and care for. She gave him purpose beyond his clandestine activities. And, more than that, he could feel a bond between them. The power he had inadvertently fed to her while she was incubating had connected them on a deep level. He was dedicated to her survival and well-being, and she was dedicated to him in return. He knew deep down that she would never leave him.

Rezkin shood Seena away from his leg then lowered himself to the floor in front of a standing mirror. Seena immediately climbed into his lap then used to her talons to scurry up his arm to his shoulder. There she settled, and Rezkin turned his attention to the new *Skill* he was working to develop. Some time ago, Mage Wesson had arrived at the conclusion that Rezkin's ability to leave people unable to recall his appearance was directly related to the part of the mind affected by illusion. And since Rezkin had seen Entris use illusion to make himself and Azeria appear human for a time, Rezkin had an idea of how to create illusion. Now, he was working to perfect his illusion so that it would appear as he wished it to for as long as he chose to sustain it.

His present attempts were for a simple illusion that would make him appear much older than his years. He pictured in his mind the image he wanted to project, then he wrapped his vimara around that image. Finally, he released that vimara to express itself outside of his body. As he did so, the image in the mirror across from him began to change. His shoulders became stooped, and his hair became grey. A bushy grey beard sprouted from his chin, and his face became long and creased. Rezkin smiled, and his teeth appeared broken and grey with rot.

Careful not to disturb the little dragon on his shoulder, Rezkin slowly stood. The illusion had covered his body to include the ragged, drab clothes of a beggar. Rezkin held his hand out to grasp an illusory walking staff with gnarled fingers. The staff felt solid in his hand as if it were real and not a manifestation of his will. He tapped the staff on the floor, and it made a *thunk*. Rezkin spun and crouched and moved in many directions as he watched himself in the mirror to make sure the illusion held. When he was satisfied, he dropped the illusion. Then he quickly reapplied it. He did this several times, each time decreasing the amount of time required for him to create a believable illusion. Then he changed the image to one of a man in his middle years, a noble. The man was shorter than he and clothed in the finest court dress. For some time, Rezkin practiced switching between the two images until he was certain he could produce both on a whim.

Then he produced a third image, this one a young woman. She was dressed as a maid and had a slight build, making her quite a bit smaller than Rezkin. He thought the image of the woman to be believable, however he noted that she did not *move* like a woman. He had never learned the skill of behaving or walking like a woman. It had not seemed practical since he could never pass for a woman in his true form. But with the ability to produce illusions, the skill suddenly seemed quite valuable. He decided he would need to spend more time watching women.

When Rezkin was satisfied with his illusions, he turned toward other tasks. He had spent the past six months traveling across Ashai tightening his grip on the thieves' and assassins' guilds and monitoring communications between the garrisons. Caydean had been busy during that time and tactically seemed to have done an about face. Although trade with the other kingdoms was still stymied and the military draft was still in effect, Caydean had been sending support and aid to those disadvantaged folk who were suffering because of it. For this, he used much of the wealth he had seized from the dispossessed and mostly deceased nobles.

The fools he elevated to those positions were sycophants and zealots dedicated to either Caydean or self-aggrandizement and exploitation. In addition, he was commissioning the construction of a grand temple at the heart of the kingdom on the outskirts of Kaibain. The temple was dedicated to a new religion that worshipped someone named Ygrethiel with Caydean at its head. The most devout followers were to be issued grants of titles and land as well as coin and goods. Overall, these changes meant Caydean was now seen as a just and generous king who had only his people's welfare in mind.

Of course, Rezkin knew better. Caydean was still the tyrant he had always been. Only his game had changed. He was plying the hearts and souls of his people with promises of wealth and status all the while plotting some greater tyranny against them. Unfortunately, Rezkin had not yet figured out what form that tyranny would take. If Caydean was plotting, and Rezkin knew he was, then he was keeping his plans close to the vest. Thus far, Rezkin had found no one with any information regarding nefarious plans, and if one were to look at it objectively, one might even say there were none. But Rezkin was not being objective, and he was certain Caydean meant to do greater harm still.

And so, Rezkin set to undertake his next set of challenges. First things first, he needed to infiltrate the palace, and he would have to do so without the use of his newfound magical talents since Caydean might sense the use of his power. Although Rezkin did not have to worry about other mages sensing his Eihelvanan power, Caydean was a Spirétua like him. Rezkin had sensed it when they met on the battlefield at Garten Knoll, the place where he had died. He had been brought back to life by the Sen Berringish, but he had killed the Sen when the man had tried to place a demon inside him. Before that, though, Rezkin had sensed both Eihelvanan and demonic power in Caydean, and it was for this reason, if no other, that Rezkin knew Caydean was plotting something devious.

Rezkin got to his feet and pulled a leather satchel strap over his head so that the satchel settled on his right hip and would not interfere with him drawing his sword. Then he held the flap open and said, "Come on, Seena. Get in."

Seena flapped her wings wildly, making little hops as she did so. Although she could not fly yet, she could hop and glide well enough to prevent injury if she fell from a height. Seena climbed up the side of the bed, then latched onto the satchel before tumbling inside. Once situated, she stretched her neck out so that she could see him. She blinked up at him with crystal clear blue eyes, and Rezkin felt a tightening of the bond between them. It was almost as if she were talking to him in his mind, but he could not quite hear her. He wondered if the connection would strengthen with time and if they might one day be able to communicate that way.

Rezkin tapped her nose so that she drew her head back into the satchel, then he closed the flap over her to prevent her from being seen. He exited the inn and headed toward the more affluent part of the city where the palace was located. The busy city streets became less congested as he progressed, and the multitude of colorful market stalls were replaced by elegant shops with elaborate displays behind glass windows. Fewer people walked here, but rickshaws were plentiful. Rezkin did not dally near any of the shops. He would have been noticed if he had. He was not dressed in the finery typical of the patrons of the area. But neither did he stand out since he looked the part of a courier which was common enough. It hardly mattered anyway, since thanks to his power, nobody would remember seeing him.

The palace was bustling that day with couriers, delivery drivers in both wagons and carriages, and all manner of servants and laborers coming and going through the western gate. Preparations were underway for a reception of dignitaries from Torrel, Sandea, Jerea, and Channería, a monumental feat on Caydean's part considering Torrel and Sandea maintained an invasion force at Ashai's northwestern border, and Jerea and Channería were on the cusp of war. The official reason for the visit was to introduce the ambassadors to the new religion with hopes of converting them and convincing them to carry it back to their respective countries.

Rezkin slipped into the throng of workers. He showed his forged papers to the gate guards and was padding across the bailey toward the side entrance in a matter of minutes. He was not the only one headed for the entrance, but he was the only person to pass it up as he continued farther onto the grounds. He made his way into the trees that lined the back lawn without being spotted and eventually found himself in front of a small cottage nestled within the wooded area. The windows were shuttered, and the chimney was clear of smoke so that it appeared that no one was home.

After skirting the home, Rezkin let himself into the root cellar at the back. It was dark in the cellar, but Rezkin used a mage stone to light the way. He searched the cellar using the soft, blue light of the stone and eventually found what he was searching for. He pressed his hand against the stone wall while at the same time pulling down on a hidden lever beside a set of shelves. There was an audible click, and then the wall slowly swung open to reveal a dark passage. Rezkin stepped into the corridor and closed the secret door behind him. The walls of the passage had been reinforced with stone and wood, and the floor was relatively smooth. The darkness and silence closed around him as he walked, and only the soft whoosh of his breath could be heard.

The passage ended at a set of spiral stairs that led upward to the third floor before it finally revealed a door into the palace. Rezkin was reasonably sure the rooms beyond the door would be empty since they were the queen's chambers, and the queen mother was currently in Caellurum. It was fortunate for Rezkin that Caydean had not yet taken a bride. But if he had, Rezkin would simply have chosen a different method of infiltrating the palace, for he knew many. The interior of the northern fortress where he had been trained, that had no name as far as he knew, had been an exact replica of the palace in Kaibain. Rezkin had been required to penetrate it regularly except, there, instead of visitors and servants, the fortress had been filled with trained strikers who were specifically searching for *him*.

Rezkin slowly released the lever which opened the hidden door into the queen's chambers, and he was surprised by what he found. The once opulent room had been reduced to smithereens. The furniture looked to have been exploded into little more than splinters, and carpets, drapes, and cushions were shredded and singed. Even the walls were cracked. And a fine layer of dust lay over everything,

It was not difficult for Rezkin to guess at what had happened. He was sure Caydean had become enraged when he found that Queen Lecillia had escaped. Although the queen mother had not officially been a prisoner, she had been kept on a tight leash within the palace, and she had witnessed much of Caydean's madness as she pretended to be supportive of his actions. It had been the former Rez, Connovan, who had absconded with her and brought her to Cael where she met Rezkin for the first time. Rezkin had never known his mother, and just having one was strange and a little disconcerting to him. They still were not close, and he wondered now if she had mourned his death all over again.

Since it was impossible to pass through the suite without stepping on the debris, Rezkin moved slowly so as not to alert anyone to his presence. After all, *Rule 12* was *do not make a sound.* Although Rezkin felt as though he had been freed from the *Rules* by his death, which had been a clear violation of *Rule 156*—

Do not die, he recognized the wisdom in many of them and continued to adhere to them when it made sense to do so. Therefore, he kept with *Rule 187— Remain undetectable to the senses* and *Rule 57—Remain in the shadows when possible* as he let himself out of the queen's chambers and strode on silent feet down the dark corridor wrapped in the shadows cast by the many alcoves and decorations. He heard the patter of feet coming from the intersection of another passage ahead of him, and he ducked into one of the alcoves just as a liveried servant passed by.

Rezkin followed behind the servant until the man entered one of the rooms, and then Rezkin continued to the entrance of a stairwell. He listened intently for evidence of someone on the steps, but he heard nothing. He quickly descended the stairs to the first level of the palace then hid himself in the shadow of the wall just as two guards walked by the entrance to the stairs. Once they had passed, Rezkin stole across the corridor to another hallway that would lead him to his destination—the king's study.

The door to the study was not warded, but it was locked, which Rezkin quickly rectified. He allowed himself into the study, a spacious room with many windows hung with heavy burgundy and gold drapes and interspersed with large oak bookcases. On one of the walls was a mural of the Souelian with Ashai painted in great detail. The furniture was built of oak with striped burgundy, blue, and gold cushions, and the carpets were of the Leréshi design, which integrated geometric shapes with foliage. A large table strewn with papers and maps occupied one side of the room.

Rezkin riffled through the pages on the table, most of which had to do with the building of the new temple, and then he turned toward Caydean's office at the back of the study. When Rezkin approached the door, however, he stopped short of attempting to open it. A protective ward covered the entire doorway. It appeared red and foreboding to Rezkin's sight, and it did not have the feel of a regular mage ward. This one was constructed of the cold power of the Spirétua. Rezkin did not think he could simply push through it as he usually did with mage wards, and he was sure that if he managed to manipulate it, Caydean would be alerted. Rezkin was saved from the attempt when he heard someone speaking as they approached the study door.

Rezkin quickly hid behind one of the thick draperies by the window as the study door opened to permit two men. The one speaking was a young man with sandy blonde hair and a fit frame who wore the black garb of a battle mage. His panels were black, which indicated he had a natural affinity for nocent power. But it was the other man Rezkin was wary of, and that was the king himself. When Caydean entered the room, Rezkin felt as if all the air in his lungs had been replaced with hot magma. His chest burned with the need to attack, to end the threat, but at the same time he felt an unfamiliar feeling. As Rezkin peered through the crack in the drapes, he felt a strong desire to run, to get as far from this man as possible. It took him a moment to identify the feeling, but after much consideration, he decided he must be experiencing fear.

The confusion had not been in the feeling of fear itself. He had experienced fear before, of course, but he had always been able to separate himself from the emotion as per *Rule 37.* No, the confusing part was the *source* of the fear. Never before had Rezkin feared another person—not since he had been a very small man, or a *child* as the outworlders called them. This fear was directed at Caydean himself, and Rezkin was not sure what to do about it. He had already faced Caydean once, and he had died for it. He was not yet ready to face him again. So he remained hidden and listened.

"Construction of the temple is going well," said the young man.

"It had better be," replied Caydean. "But are we on schedule?"

"Yes, Your Majesty. All should be ready for the ceremony."

Caydean stopped and narrowed his eyes at the young battle mage as if he were looking for some subterfuge. The young man shifted uncomfortably but held his ground under the king's scrutiny. Then Caydean seemed to shake off his concerns. Rezkin felt a cold chill as Caydean loosed his power on the room creating a dome-shaped field that encompassed him as well.

"The room is sealed from prying ears," said Caydean.

The battle mage blinked as he glanced around, his gaze brushing over Rezkin's hiding spot. "Are you sure? I do not feel anything."

Caydean's voice was heated, "You question *me*, Avikeev?"

The battle mage Avikeev confidently said, "No, of course not, Your Majesty. What would you like to discuss?"

"It is a matter of the weapon. Are we sure it will have the impact I desire? You have performed the calculations?"

"They are below in your workshop, but I am not concerned. It will be strong enough to raze all of Kaibain."

"And once I have taken care of Kaibain, no one will be able to stop me. The ahn'an will be obliterated. This world will be purified."

"And the ahn'tep?" said Avikeev.

"Of course the ahn'tep will fall as well. Those who live will serve me as I rule over all of Terralor." Then, in an apparent shift in conversation, Caydean said, "How do the people feel about the pilgrimage and upcoming ceremony?"

"Overall sentiment is positive," replied Avikeev. "Your approval rating is at a high, especially amongst the commoners. I believe many will desire to support their king's efforts by completing the pilgrimage."

"Do you mock me?" snapped Caydean.

Avikeev's confident expression did not change, "No, Your Majesty. I am being quite genuine. Your goodwill toward the people has made a difference, and since you have replaced most of the nobles with your own supporters, there is no one to stand in our way."

"Except the dukes," growled Caydean.

"The dukes are trapped on their respective lands. They would not dare move against you. They will keep their meager forces close to home."

"And if they join forces?"

"They will not. Ytrevius is dead, which only leaves Darning, Atressian, and Wellinven. Those three could not cooperate to save their lives, which is the better for us. Wellinven and Atressian especially harbor great animosity for each other since they each believe they should inherit your throne."

Caydean grinned cruelly. "They will learn soon enough that I cannot be unseated so easily. What of our plans in Lon Lerésh?"

"They are coming together nicely. If all goes as planned, we should have what we need by the time we need it."

"This is crucial to my plan. If the current plan fails in Lon Lerésh, then we will have to take it by force. The army must be ready to move."

Caydean turned and dismissed the ward sealing his office and entered. Rezkin could no longer see him, so he spent his time studying Avikeev. The man, likely in his mid to late twenties, wore his confidence like a cloak, but Rezkin got the sense that that confidence had been earned. He wondered how powerful the battle mage was, and how he might compare to Mage Wesson. Avikeev was obviously entrusted with a great deal of knowledge regarding Caydean's plans, and he was fully aware of the daem'ahn and the ahn'an. Rezkin wondered if the battle mage was not a daem'ahn himself, but there was no way to tell unless he revealed himself by using his daem'ahn powers.

Caydean reappeared with a stack of sealed letters in his grip. He handed them to Avikeev. "Have these delivered with the vessels. I want eyes and ears at the highest levels in those kingdoms claimed by the so-called Souelian Empire. One for each of Gendishen, Lon Lerésh, and Ferélle."

"What of our source in Cael?" said Avikeev.

Caydean grinned again. "She reports regularly."

That was news to Rezkin. He had known it was only a matter of time before Caydean managed to insert spies into his kingdom. He only wished he knew who it was. Of all the people in his highest levels of trust, he could think of none who would wish to side with Caydean even for a profit. But now he knew it was a woman, so the list of suspects had shrunk considerably.

A knock sounded at the door, and Avikeev moved to open it. Beyond the threshold was a man Rezkin knew to be the king's seneschal. The man said, "We are ready for you in the throne room, Your Majesty."

Caydean reapplied the protective ward to his office then followed Avikeev out of the study, shutting the door behind them. Rezkin waited a few minutes before emerging from his hiding place. He had been mildly surprised that Caydean had not detected him hiding behind the drapes, but he had not been using any of his Eihelvanan power at the time. Now that he knew where Caydean was going, he was more confident in using his power since the king could not detect the use from so far away.

Rezkin approached Caydean's ward with caution. He had watched Caydean remove it and reapply it, and he was nearly certain he could now manipulate it without alerting the king. After all, Rezkin had been creating wards nearly all his life—he just hadn't known he was doing it. The masters had taught him that his wards were merely *potential* manifested, but now he knew he had been creating wards using Eihelvanan powers. Rezkin did so now, creating a small ward that he laid over Caydean's own ward. Then he pushed his ward through Caydean's ward until a hole had formed. He slowly stretched his ward until it was big enough to step through. Finally, he stepped into his ward, bending it around himself and releasing himself on the other side, effectively putting him within the space protected by Caydean's ward. Rezkin was now free to open the door to the office.

Once inside, Rezkin quickly perused the shelves that lined the outer walls and a small side table that held an assortment of intoxicating beverages. Satisfied that he had missed nothing of importance, he moved to Caydean's desk. It was neat and orderly with stacks of correspondence in three piles to one side. Atop the center of the desk was a large rendering of the engineer's diagrams for the temple, and there were neatly scrawled notes dispersed across it. Rezkin committed the diagram to memory, but aside from its magnitude and odd shape, he had little interest in the temple. It was merely a ploy by Caydean to appease the people and increase their approval of him for reasons Rezkin had not yet gleaned.

Seena poked her head out of the satchel at his hip as Rezkin searched through the desk drawers. She sniffed the documents as he flipped through them. He found half-finished notes on how to deal with the dukes who had not surrendered their titles and properties when Caydean declared war on them. It seemed that despite his earlier concerns, Caydean was not in any hurry to eliminate the dukes so long as they remained on their own lands.

Rezkin found additional documents concerning other issues including troop assignments, interkingdom trade negotiations, something about a holding in Sandea, a missive regarding Rezkin's demise, and a list of titles to be awarded to the followers of Ygrethiel, but he found nothing concerning the weapon Caydean had mentioned. In fact, the only thing of interest Rezkin found was a document regarding a sect of spies stationed in Channería.

When he was finished searching the desk, Rezkin made sure to put everything back as neatly as he had found it. Satisfied that Caydean would never know he had been there, Rezkin let himself out of the office. He employed the same technique he had used to enter the ward as he exited it, and soon enough he was on his way out of the palace using a different route from the one he had used to enter.

Rezkin was satisfied with the information he had garnered for his efforts. He now knew that Caydean had some sort of weapon which would help him destroy the ahn'an and possibly the ahn'tep. He also knew that Caydean had a workshop somewhere in the underbelly of the palace, which was presumably where the weapon was located. He had discovered a sect of spies headquartered in Channería and distributed throughout the kingdoms. He also knew Caydean planned to deploy more daem'ahn to Rezkin's own kingdoms. And something significant was about to happen in Lon Lerésh, something that if it failed would lead to an invasion.

The information he had uncovered was invaluable, and it reaffirmed his belief that remaining dead to the world was for the best. He would never have found out about any of Caydean's plans had he been stuck in his role as Emperor of the Souelian. Although he had found companionship with his friends, they had been keeping him from living to his full potential. It was evidence of the value of *Rule 257—Be one and alone.* One thing was certain, though. He could not be everywhere at once. He would need to prioritize, and after he disposed of the demon vessels Caydean was sending out, his first order of business would take him to Channería.

3

FRISHA IGNORED the stabbing pain in her palm as she used the small rock to gouge the rockface of the cave wall. The going was slow, but she *had* made progress over the past hour. She wiped sweat from her brow as she glanced over at Thresson to check his progress. The rune he was working on was already starting to take shape. She turned back to her own rune and furiously scraped her rock against it, digging into one side and extending the arc. Then a sound echoing down the corridor from the outside gate had her scrambling down from her perch atop the ledge. She met Thresson at the bottom, and they both hastily sat and made a show of playing a game of squares in the sand. A moment later, the guard tromped up to the metal bars of their prison and slipped a couple of bowls through the slot at the bottom. Then he turned and exited the way he had come without so much as a word or glance in their direction.

Frisha got to her feet and collected the two bowls, handing one to Thresson. The sauteed meat and vegetables was better than she expected to be served by Caydean's men, but it was a far cry from the delectable cuisine Thresson had grown up on in the palace. Since they had no utensils, they ate with their fingers until their bowls were empty.

Frisha set hers aside and looked back at Thresson. She said, "Are you sure this will work? We have been at it for nearly six months."

Thresson leaned back against the cave wall and released a heavy sigh. "No, but it is the only plan I could come up with." He pointed to the multitude of magical runes that composed the spell that prevented him from using his mage powers and said, "If we can change enough of these runes in the right way, we can redirect the spell and possibly even change it altogether to something advantageous. At least, that is what I am hoping. If we are to escape, I think this is our best bet."

He placed his hand on hers and said, "Do not lose hope, Frisha. If it works the way I am hoping it will, then we are working on the last two runes. When they are finished, we can be gone from here."

Frisha nodded then grabbed her rock and climbed back onto the ledge so that she could reach the rune she was changing. Although she knew nothing about runes, Thresson seemed well versed in them. She prayed to the Maker that he was right. She could not sit in that prison for the rest of her life, and she doubted that would be much longer if she stayed. Frisha refused to believe Rezkin was dead, but she was equally certain that Caydean believed it. Sooner or later, he would realize she was of little use and would dispose of her.

Caydean seemed to have forgotten about them for the past few months and had made no visits to taunt his younger brother. Therefore, she and Thresson had been free to scrape away at the runes they could reach so long as they did so out of sight of the guards. Secure in their trust of the rune spells to keep she and Thresson imprisoned, the guards paid them little attention.

Hours later, Frisha yelped as the rock in her hand finally broke through her skin. She shook her hand then looked at the indentation in her palm where a small amount of blood seeped. She glanced at the water barrel, then looked back at the rune. She thought it looked complete, but she was not sure.

"Ah ha!" exclaimed Thresson, and Frisha turned to check on him. She narrowed her eyes to peer at him in the now dim chamber. She glanced toward the hole in the ceiling and realized the sun was no longer shining down through it. Dusk was upon them. She turned her attention back to Thresson, who was smiling broadly as the sand at his feet shifted. Frisha's first thought was that some burrowing animal had made its way into their cell, but after a moment, she realized that Thresson was making the sand move with his powers.

Her eyes widened. "You have your power back!"

He looked up at her with that foolish grin. "A bit. It is not much, but it will do."

She pointed toward the metal bars that made up one long side of their cell. "Can you do something about those?"

Thresson stretched his arms to limber himself up and said, "Let us see." Then he stalked over to the gate and pressed his hand to the lock. His expression turned to one of deep concentration and he muttered, "As an earth mage, I am able to manipulate metal quite easily."

It did not look easy to Frisha. A sweat had broken out on his brow, and he looked to be straining himself against a massive weight.

He gritted his teeth and said, "I might have just enough power—"

The gate suddenly screeched open. Frisha's heart leapt, and she winced as the sound echoed around the hollow chamber. It had been a long time since that gate had been opened.

Thresson stepped through the open gate and held his hand out to her. She grinned as she grasped his hand, and he pulled her though. Then they were rushing up the corridor as quietly as possible. They did not need words at this point. They had planned and plotted for months, and they both knew what to do. Now that Thresson was beyond the cell, his power should be fully unlocked. And since Caydean was not at that location, the guards were at a minimum.

They both stopped as the outer gate came into view. They hovered there in the dark as Thresson focused on opening the gate from a distance. It clicked but swung silently open.

"What was that?" barked a guard as Thresson darted forward. Thresson collided with the gate but did not stop as he yanked one of the bars from its seat and shoved it through the guard's chest. He pulled the bar free and quickly shaped it into a short spear before clashing with the next guard. Meanwhile, Frisha leapt at the downed guard and divested him of his belt knife.

The next guard who ran at them was focused on the larger threat of Thresson, who was still engaged with the second guardsman, and Frisha took him by surprise, stabbing the knife up under his ribs when he turned. His expression was one of pure shock as he fell to the ground gripping his bleeding wound. A moment later he was dead. Frisha expected to feel guilt and remorse like Tam had when he first killed a man, but she could not summon the sentiments. She was too focused on surviving and escaping with Thresson. Once the three guards were down, they turned down the tunnel that she only vaguely remembered having traversed upon arrival. When they finally exited the cave system, they were met with an indigo sky of twilight blanketing a hill-pocked desert.

Behind them in the tunnels, they could hear the pursuit of additional guards. Thresson grabbed Frisha's hand and pulled her toward the desert. The ground was rocky and thorny, and pain continually struck Frisha's bare feet as they hurried away from their former captors. She glanced back to find that at least four guards and an unfamiliar battle mage pursued them. She dearly hoped Thresson was stronger and more skilled in his magecraft than the battle mage or they were doomed. They had a head start, though, and they took advantage of it as they ran along the base of the hills heading east.

"There," said Thresson, pointing toward some massive boulders that adorned one hillside. "We can take refuge in those rocks. It is the most defensible position I have seen."

Frisha did not argue as she scaled the steep hillside behind him while trying to ignore the fact that her feet were a shredded mess. Thresson's were no better as he was also barefoot. The simple smock she wore and his thin tunic and pants were hardly travel wear, and already the night held a crisp chill that loosed goosebumps across her sweaty skin.

They wandered among the rocks for a minute before Thresson pulled her into a cavity that was covered and enclosed on three-and-a-half sides. Then he surrounded the structure with a shield ward that she hoped the battle mage could not penetrate.

Thresson said, "With the ward activated, they can easily find us, but at least we will be protected from attack."

"For how long?" asked Frisha as she wrapped her arms around her body to try to retain some of her body heat.

"I do not know," he said. "I have never before set eyes on that battle mage. I know not what power he wields."

"Let's hope it's less than you," she replied.

"Indeed," he said as he pointed out the dark shapes taking up position in the rocks near their hiding spot.

She huffed as she sat and began pulling thorns from her feet. "I hate feeling useless."

"You are not useless," said Thresson. "I would never have made it this far on my own. You have been invaluable."

"How so?"

"You helped shape the runes. That would have taken me months longer, and in that time, Caydean would surely have noticed. Plus, you killed the guard. I would have been overwhelmed."

"I doubt it," she said. "But I appreciate your attempt to console me. I only wish there was something I could do *now*."

"Now you can rest," he said. "They know where we are. If they are smart, they will wait us out. We cannot stay here for long without food and water."

Frisha shivered. "If we don't freeze to death first."

"I could make a fire, but we have nothing to burn. It would be in our favor to draw them in. We need them to attack now while we still have our energy."

"How do we do that?"

Thresson drummed his fingers on his leg as he thought. Finally, he said, "Well, I *am* an earth mage, and we *are* surrounded by earth. Perhaps I can antagonize them."

He was quiet for a moment, and then Frisha could hear the tumble of a few pebbles. The clicks and clacks became louder and deeper as larger stones fell. Then a rumbling began, and suddenly rocks all around their shelter were tumbling down the hillside. A man's cry of pain was abruptly cut short, and suddenly the ward around them jolted with a concussive force.

"It worked," said Thresson. "The mage is attacking."

"Can you handle it?" said Frisha.

"So far," he said as a fireball smashed against the shield ward. "I have an idea. You stay up here protected by the ward and push these rocks down on them. That will keep the guards busy while I confront the battle mage. I believe it will be easier to defeat him if I can get close and negate his ranged attacks."

"How much experience do you have in using your power for battle?"

"Little to none," he replied, "But necessity makes for an ideal tutor."

Frisha did as Thresson asked. While he rushed toward the battle mage, she began kicking and shoving rocks down the hill toward their enemies. Many of the smaller rocks pinged off the battle mage's shield ward, but some of the larger boulders were not to be stopped. Even the battle mage took cover, which allowed Thresson to move in closer than he would otherwise have gotten.

Frisha noted that there were now only three guards, and she targeted those three while Thresson began slinging spells at the battle mage. The ground shook with his efforts, and not all the rocks that fell were due to Frisha's machinations. Frisha rounded one of the larger boulders and placed her back against it. Then she pushed against the hill with all her might. It started to rock and then stopped. She took a deep breath and pushed again, this time with the knowledge that she would die if this did not work at the forefront of her mind. She fell backward as the boulder began tumbling, issuing loud cracks every time it struck the ground. Then it bowled straight through the battle mage's shield ward and crushed two of the guards as it continued its descent.

Frisha's celebration was cut short as she realized she could not see the final guard. She glanced toward Thresson to see him block a burst of light darts then send a swirling dust devil of rocks and sand at the battle mage. She drew her gaze away and surveyed the hillside. It had grown quite dark, and she could barely make out the shapes of the mages amongst the rocks. She had no hope of finding the final guard unless she caught his movement.

She heard something skitter nearby, and her heart skipped as a vice wrapped around her shoulders. A thick hand covered her mouth as she tried to scream.

"Not yet," gritted the guard as he began hauling her down the hill. She suddenly realized that at some point, Thresson's shield ward that had been protecting her had disappeared. The guard had been able to flank her with her none the wiser. When they were closer to where the two mages were battling, the guard released his hand from her mouth. Then he leaned down beside her ear and said, "Now scream," as he yanked her head back by the hair.

Frisha gritted her teeth and shouted, "No!" as she stomped on his foot. Then she smashed her head backward into his face. He loosened his grip on her shoulders when he stumbled backward, and Frisha had just enough room to spin in his embrace to face him. Then she stabbed her knife into his gut. She wrenched the blade out before stabbing it into him again and again as terror gripped her. The man dropped to the ground dead, and all Frisha could hear was the sound of her own breathing as she stared down at his lifeless body.

A hand landed on her shoulder, and she jerked around with the knife poised to strike. A heavy hand caught her wrist. "All is well, Frisha. It is I, Thresson. Be calm."

Frisha's gaze darted to where the battle mage had been only to find that he was impaled on a massive stone spike that jutted from the ground at a sharp angle. Then she fell into Thresson's arms as her nerves shook with tremors. He stroked her hair and quietly said, "Shh, all is well. Be calm."

Frisha took several deep breaths and eventually the shaking subsided. She said, "I think I'm okay now. We should probably keep going."

"Agreed," said Thresson. "The going will be hazardous at night, but we must put some distance between us and Caydean's men. Come. If we are where I think we are and we continue east, we should eventually encounter the Saen River. If we can find a boat, we can use it to travel south into Ashai or Channería."

"How do you know where we are?"

"I do not, precisely. But I have heard bits and pieces from the guards over time. So far as I can tell, we are in southern Sandea and these hills lead into the Zigharan Mountains. We could go into the mountains if you prefer, but I think the river would be considerably easier and faster."

Frisha shivered and wrapped her arms around herself to stave off the chill. "No, the river sounds best."

"Very well. Then let us make haste. I will try to use my power to cover our tracks as we go."

"Should we do something about them?" Frisha said, motioning to the body at their feet.

"Good point," replied Thresson. He stared at his bare feet for a second before he said, "First, let us take their boots."

"Right, good idea. I doubt any of them will fit me, though."

"The mage was the smallest. See if his will do."

Frisha gingerly removed the mage's boots and placed them on her own feet. They were too large for her, but she was able to lace them tight enough that they would not fall off her feet.

Thresson had collected his own set of boots. "Stand back."

Frisha did as he asked, and after a few seconds, the ground began to shift, and the body sank beneath the surface. When Thresson was finished, there was no evidence of death remaining. A heavy weight was lifted from Frisha's shoulders, as if clearing the evidence had somehow also cleared her conscience. Frisha did not feel bad for killing the man. He had been trying to capture her and would have used her to capture Thresson as well. After all her vehement protests toward Rezkin against killing, Frisha thought it strange that she should be so calm and collected after having ended the lives of four men. She wondered if the remorse would come later, once the terror of their flight had subsided. But in her mind, the deaths were justified, and she considered that perhaps this was how Rezkin felt every time he killed. If so, then maybe she had been wrong to judge him so harshly. After all, killing was not all he did. He had also saved a good many people, including her.

The going was rough that night and for the next four days. They had no supplies but thanks to Thresson's mage power, they managed to find enough food and water to sustain them. The days were hot, and the nights were cool in the desert. And most of the sparse foliage seemed to want to maim them with sharp thorns and spikes. Their pilfered boots protected their feet, but even that small comfort could do nothing to quell their nerves over possible pursuit.

They looked behind them often, searching for Caydean's people. Although they had covered their tracks, Thresson was concerned that frequent use of vimara would alert a mage to their presence if they were within close enough proximity. Therefore, he used it sparingly, even though it could have made the going much easier.

The first indication of pursuit came just as the river was within reach. They were camped for the night, and Frisha spied the glow of a fire reflecting off the rocks some distance behind them.

"Perhaps it's just a traveler," she suggested.

"We had best not take that chance. We should get some rest tonight and move quickly on the morrow. We leave before daybreak."

Frisha did not sleep well that night. The ground was rocky, the air was frigid, and they did not dare light a fire. The prospect of being recaptured or killed hung heavily in her mind. She did not think Thresson had slept either. Eventually, they gave up the pretense and began making their way toward the river in the dark at least an hour before dawn. They reached the bank just as the sun rose over the mountains. There at its head, the river was awash with sandbars, multiple channels, and tributaries, and they were often required to find alternate routes and methods of crossing the deep gullies.

Worn and filthy, Frisha had pushed herself to her limit by midday. They had gone from little activity trapped in a cell for six months to a mad dash across rough terrain for four-and-a-half days. Just as the river began to narrow to a single channel, Thresson called a halt.

"We will break here," he said. "We are both spent, and it would be good to rest and get clean."

Frisha wholeheartedly agreed. They took turns bathing in the river while the other rested their feet and kept an eye on the forested hills for anyone following them. It was just as Thresson rejoined her that Frisha noticed movement on the hill overlooking their location. Not wanting to alert the spy that she had seen him, Frisha turned away and whispered to Thresson.

"They're here—up there on the hill. They've found us."

Thresson gave no indication that he had heard her but quickly replaced his boots regardless. Then he took her by the elbow and began leading her back toward the riverbank. A sudden crackling behind them had Thresson throwing up a shield ward, and a bolt of power smashed against it causing it to quiver. Thresson quickly turned and sent a burst of earth energy up the hillside causing the ground to explode around their attackers. Several men armed with swords came rushing down the hill just as another bolt of coiled lightning struck the ward. Thresson grabbed Frisha's arm and yelled, "Jump," just as he pulled her over the embankment and into the frigid river. They clung to each other as they struggled to remain afloat while being pulled downstream. The river increased its flow rate quickly, and pretty soon the shore was passing by far faster than they could have run.

The river developed rapids as they approached a narrow where it passed between two steep hillsides, and Frisha lost her grip on Thresson. As they were both swept down the rapids, water filled her mouth and nose, and Frisha felt as though she were drowning. She coughed and sputtered as she tried to keep her head above water, but swimming was not one of her strengths.

Just as the rapids disappeared, a hand clasped her arm pulling her up for air. She spun and clung to her savior as she expelled water from her lungs on great heaving breaths. It was only after her savior had dragged her to shore that she realized he was not Thresson. This was one of Caydean's men who had apparently followed them into the river. He towered over her as he drew his sword, and Frisha was certain he was going to kill her right there. Then a branch smashed him in the side of the head, and he fell to the ground unconscious or dead. Thresson stood there breathing heavily as he tossed the tree branch to the side. He reached for her to give her a hand up and said, "Are you well? I am sorry, I failed to hold onto you in the rapids."

Frisha coughed once more, "I think I'll be fine. Thank you for saving me. I thought I was done for."

As he unbuckled the man's sword belt, he said, "It was not yet your time, and it will not be anytime soon if I can help it." He wrapped the belt around himself then sheathed the sword before dragging the man back into the river and sending him on his way.

"Where do you think we are now?" she asked.

"Between the Zigharan and Saldesh Mountains, on the Jerean side, I believe."

"Do you think they'll keep coming after us?"

"Ashai and Jerea have a contentious relationship during the best of times. It can be dangerous for Ashaiians in Jerea. Still, Caydean wants us badly."

"He wants *you* badly. I think my usefulness to him is about up."

"Perhaps, but he still wants you captured. If you expose your replacement golem as his spy in Cael, he will lose a valuable resource."

"We must get to Cael as quickly as possible. I hate to think what that *thing* is doing in my name—with *my* face and body."

"Whatever it does, it is not *you*. Remember that. You are innocent."

"I may be innocent, but others will not necessarily see it that way. They will remember the things she has done, and they will only see me doing them."

"Your name and reputation will be cleared. I will see to it."

Frisha laughed. "My reputation? I just spent six months trapped alone in a cell with a man. My reputation is ruined."

"Nothing happened. I will make sure everyone knows it. I am the prince. They will not question me."

"They may not question you, but they will question *me*." She sighed. "That's hardly important right now, though. Saving the others from Caydean's treachery is what is important."

"Of course," said Thresson. "Let us make our way south. We will reach this Cael through Channería. At least Channería is friendly with Ashai."

"Not so," said Frisha. "At least, it wasn't when I was taken. The lucky ones who managed to appeal to the Temple for asylum got shipped to Cael, but the rest … Channería was rounding up all the Ashaiians within their borders and imprisoning them in camps to be sold as slaves."

"Impossible. Slavery is outlawed in Channería."

Frisha rolled her eyes. "Okay, officially they are given to foreign *patrons* who pay their bounty."

"But that is slavery," said Thresson aghast.

"I know. That's what I said."

"But I am the Crown Prince. Surely King Ionius will grant me asylum and you with me."

"Is that a risk you are willing to take?"

He shook his head as they began walking down the river. "We will have to be careful then and not get caught. Perhaps we can take refuge in a Temple and be sent to Cael that way."

"What if the Temple is no longer helping Ashaiians? We will have given ourselves away."

"We will blend in then."

"How? I don't speak Channerían, do you?"

"My Channerían is passable, I think. At least, my tutors thought it was good. Truly, I have only ever had to use it on brief occasions when dignitaries visited the palace."

"Then perhaps you should start practicing. You can teach me."

4

YSERRIA STOOD at the foot of the dais as Regent Coledon held court. Ever since Rezkin had died, the kingdom had fallen into civil unrest. Petty squabbles had given way to talk of overthrowing Coledon and the empire as former king Moldovan's extended family vied for the throne. It was all they could do to hold back the tide of unrest. Fortunately, Rezkin's macabre show of power upon taking the throne and the rumors that he might still be alive had thus far prevented outright attack, but Yserria knew that plans were being made. It was only a matter of time before the serpents grew bold enough to strike.

Grievances were particularly heated on this day as Lord Genever accused Lord Palsby of treason, and Lord Palsby claimed Lord Trine was setting him up to take the fall for a crime he did not commit. Extra guards had been called in to hold back the throng of courtesans who wanted to make their opinions known, and she had elected to stay near Coledon to help him escape if things got too bad. Coledon, however, had the patience of the Maker, and he took the shouting and accusations in stride as he listened to each side of the argument. Yserria had been surprised and unsure when Rezkin had named him regent after knowing him all of a minute, but now she recognized the wisdom of the choice. Coledon was a fair and steady monarch who remained loyal to Rezkin even after news of his death. In fact, he had declared it the official stance of the throne that Rezkin still lived and decreed that Ferélle remained dedicated to the empire even though it would have been easy for him to declare independence and name himself king.

A glint of light suddenly reflected off a blade as Lord Palsby's son, Fedro, leapt into the middle of the proceedings. He cried, "Lord Genever, you have gone too far. I will not stand idly while you drag our family name through the mud with your lies. In our defense, I challenge you to a duel."

Lord Genever drew his own sword and rounded on the much younger man. He said, "I stand by my claims. Your house plots against the regent, against the emperor, and I cannot allow that to stand. I accept your challenge. Let us be done with this here and now."

Lord Palsby grabbed Fedro's arm and pulled him back. "No, Fedro, do not do this. He is an accomplished swordsman."

"He is old, Father. I shall defeat him with ease."

As Fedro advanced on Lord Genever, Yserria leapt forward. Fedro's sword clashed with Genever's as he struck from overhead. Genever swept his sword around and slashed at Fedro's side. As the two swords met again, Yserria's was thrust into the middle. Yserria stepped between the two duelers, fending off both their advances as they tried to fight around her. Genever struck Fedro in the arm, drawing blood, then Yserria blocked another strike that might have opened the younger man's throat. She brought her sword around, twisting at the last minute, locking Fedro's hilt and causing him to lose his grip. After disarming him, she turned back to Genever.

Genever said, "Out of the way, Knight Yserria. This matter does not concern you."

"There will be no duel," she shouted.

A pounding sounded from Yserria's right as Coledon rapped his scepter on the floor. The crowd stilled, and even Genever lowered his sword. In a strong and steady voice, Coledon said, "This is a matter for the crown to resolve and will not be decided on the tip of a blade. Lord Trine's evidence is circumstantial at best. I have seen no hard evidence demonstrating Lord Palsby's disloyalty. That being said, Lord Palsby, it does disturb me that two of your peers have brought this to my attention. If it should be found that you are truly working against the crown, your punishment will be swift and brutal, and it will extend to your entire house, not just *you*. Do you understand?"

Lord Palsby bowed toward Coledon. "Yes, Regent, I assure you my loyalty is ever to the crown and to our great emperor."

Coledon turned his intense gaze on Fedro. "Do *you* understand?"

Yserria flicked her sword toward him, a motion that caught Fedro's eye. He swallowed hard then looked back to Coledon as he retrieved and sheathed his sword. "I understand, Your Grace, but this man besmirches our good name. I seek recompense."

Coledon leaned forward, and there was a collective inhale around the room. Yserria had to give it to the man. He had presence. He said, "An investigation will be opened into this matter. If no additional evidence is found, you shall be granted your recompense. Let us hope that is the case, for your sake."

Lord Palsby snagged his son's arm again and dragged him back behind him. "No recompense is necessary, Your Grace. We are prepared to let the matter drop."

"That may be so, Lord Palsby, but the investigation will commence regardless. You will cooperate with the investigators, or you will discover the comforts of our prison."

"Of course, Your Grace." Lord Palsby's eyes were round and sweat poured down from his brow. It was obvious the man had something to hide. Whether or not it extended to treason remained to be seen.

Yserria relaxed her stance as the men departed. Coledon stood and walked toward her, and Yserria fell into step beside him. Malcius and two more guards brought up the rear as they made their way from the throne room. Yserria and Malcius followed Coledon into his study while the guards remained outside the door. Malcius moved to the sideboard where he poured an amber-colored liquid into three glasses. He turned and handed one to each of them before going back for his own.

Coledon sounded tired as he said, "What do you think?"

Malcius replied, "I think you handled that well. You avoided bloodshed, for the most part, and mention of an investigation had Lord Palsby sweating—literally."

Yserria asked, "Who will you have lead the investigation?"

Coledon looked at her meaningfully. "I had hoped you—"

Yserria was already shaking her head. "I cannot. Word has come in that there is unrest in Lon Lerésh. Apparently, Queen Erisial has thwarted multiple assassination attempts against her, but it is only a matter of time before someone succeeds. Now that Rezkin is dead—"

"Allegedly," interjected Coledon.

Yserria tipped her head. "With Rezkin gone, her enemies grow bold. They no longer worry that a man will succeed the throne to reign as king. I must return to my echelons to ensure that Erisial has our support."

Coledon looked to Malcius. "I take it you will be going with her?"

Malcius clenched his jaw but nodded.

With a heavy sigh, Coledon said, "I shall miss your support here. I am afraid it is only a matter of time before someone succeeds against me as well, and I have no desire to die. It was only the threat of Rezkin's wrath that kept the wolves at bay. If he truly lives, I hope he reveals himself soon."

Yserria left Coledon in his study, and Malcius followed her out. He quickly caught up with her. "Why did you not tell me we are going to Lon Lerésh?"

She glanced at him out of the corner of her eye. "I only just received the information before going to court. There wasn't time. Besides, *you* do not have to go."

Malcius reached up and gripped the thumb-sized red crystal that hung around his neck. "Yes, I do," he muttered.

Yserria abruptly stopped and turned to him. "Why, Malcius? Why do you follow me wherever I go?"

He scowled. "Because Rezkin ordered me to. I do not need any more reason than that."

Yserria's irritation turned to compassion. "Rezkin is dead. You need no longer follow that order. I am sure Tieran can find something better for you to do."

"No," snapped Malcius. "Rezkin is not dead. It is impossible. He is undefeatable."

"No one is undefeatable. He faced off against Caydean, and he lost. You need to accept it."

"I do not. I *will* not. And as long as I live, I will continue to carry out his orders until he tells me otherwise."

Yserria's eyebrows rose. "You plan to follow me around for the rest of your life?"

"If need be."

Yserria was not sure what was going on with Malcius, but she knew he was not telling her everything. Something more was going on. She said, "Why do you adhere so strictly to *this* particular order? You and he were at odds over Palis's death in the time before he fell."

Malcius's expression cooled and something like regret crossed his face. "I was mourning my brother's death, and I was angry. I knew all along that Rezkin did not deserve my anger, but I could not seem to stop hating him. Even so, I respected him. I gave him my loyalty even though I resented his every order. I cannot explain it. I guess I needed to hate someone, and he was there."

Yserria's mouth went dry. She licked her lips and said, "Is that why you hate *me* so much?"

Malcius appeared surprised by her question and a little guilty. His denial was swift. "I do not hate you."

Yserria almost asked why he was so angry with her then, but she was not sure she wanted to hear the answer. He blamed her for Palis's death. She knew it, and she was not sure he was wrong. Palis had died to save *her* after all.

She turned to continue down the hallway, but Malcius stopped her with a hand to her shoulder. "Wait, we need to talk about Lon Lerésh."

"What about it?"

"About *this*," he said, swiping a finger down the arcane scrollwork that decorated his face at one temple, the runes that signified the bond between them. Ever since Malcius had recognized her claim outside of Lon Lerésh, they had both been cursed with the marks that effectively identified them as married in any other country. She had avoided looking in mirrors as much as possible just to keep from having to look at hers.

"What about it?" she said.

"In Lon Lerésh, I am considered your consort, and now everyone can see the evidence of it. What if someone tries to claim me?"

She crossed her arms. "Perhaps I should let them."

He scowled at her. "Would this mark then disappear if someone else claimed me?"

Yserria's arms dropped. She had not thought about that possibility. "I don't know," she said. "If that's true, then I could be rid of my mark as well."

"Yes, you would be free, but *I* would belong to someone else, and she would probably not let me go. I need to know what you intend to do if someone challenges you for me."

Yserria did not answer right away, and the longer she delayed, the deeper his scowl got. Finally, she found her words again. "Don't worry, Malcius. I will not allow anyone else to claim you."

His shoulders relaxed, and he gave her a curt nod. "Good, then I will be able to continue following you around as Rezkin ordered."

Yserria rolled her eyes as she reconsidered allowing someone else to claim him. It seemed she was going to be stuck with him for life. But for some reason, the notion did not bother her as much as it should have.

5

REZKIN THREW his pack over his shoulder as he disembarked from the ship in the eastern city of Umbrell. Thanks to the two water mages aboard, sailing up the Tremadel River had been much faster than going by land. Unfortunately, he would need to find a smaller vessel going north to Krellis via the Danton River or he would have to procure a horse. A pang of regret had him missing Pride. The trusty battle charger was far superior to any horse he might find in Umbrell, and the journey to Channería would be long and arduous. He thought it would be ever so convenient if he could walk the paths like Azeria, but wishful thinking would not get him closer to Channería. The thought of Azeria sent a streak of discomfort though him that he could not identify. He considered the sensation as he walked toward the city center, and by the time he arrived at a satisfactory inn, he had decided that perhaps the feeling was sorrow.

Shaking himself, he looked up at the establishment. It was only two stories like most of the buildings along the hardpacked dirt street, but unlike the other businesses, its sign was freshly painted, and flowers were growing in the window box. It was evident that someone took good care of the place. When he entered, a small bell rang above the door, and then Rezkin came face to face with a man who was not as tall as he but who had quite a bit more weight in the middle. His sleeves were rolled up to show that his hairy arms were tattooed in the kind of ink typical of soldiers, and he busily wrung a rag between his meaty hands. The man glowered at him but said nothing. A moment later, a young woman came sweeping into the foyer with a glowing smile and a spark in her honey-colored eyes.

"How do you do?" she said as she swatted at the scowling man. As the man glanced at her, his expression softened and then he turned and strode behind the counter that took up the right side of the foyer. The woman said, "Don't mind him. He's suspicious of everyone, but he means well. I'm Bobbi, and you are?"

"Drake," said Rezkin. He held out his hand for her to shake. "Drake Banting."

"Well, it's nice to meet you Master Banting. Are you looking for a room?" She swatted his chest, "Oh, that's a silly question. Of course you're looking for a room. Why else would you be here?" She looked at him quizzically as if expecting an answer.

"Yes, I'm looking for a room. But you can just call me Drake."

Her gaze dropped to his chest and then slowly rose back to his eyes. Her cheeks turned a soft shade of pink, and she blinked a few times before she spoke again. "If you'll come this way, Master Drake, I'll show you your options and you can choose which room you'd like to stay in."

The first room she showed him had no alternative egress, and it was far too close to the foyer for his liking. The second room was a bit pricier with its large bed and bathing chamber, but its second-floor window overlooked the alley, and it was at the back of the establishment. Rezkin paid the woman for two nights in advance then immediately made use of the bathing facilities. The running water of the shower was tepid, but it washed away the dirt and sweat from travel just the same. As he bathed, Seena frolicked in the water at his feet. She cooed and purred as the droplets sluiced down her spine.

Rezkin finished showering quickly, much to Seena's disappointment, then he dressed again so that he could go hunting some dinner. He unrolled the bundle in which he had hidden the black blade and Bladesunder, and he strapped the latter to his hip. Although he did not anticipate swordplay that night, he wanted to be prepared. Plus, it would have drawn more notice had he *not* been wearing a blade in eastern Ashai, where most people armed themselves. He rewrapped the black blade and pushed it under the bed. Then he turned to Seena and said, "You guard this for me while I am gone."

Seena's head snapped back, and her chest puffed out before she scurried under the bed as well. A soft, lilting sensation brushed over Rezkin's mind, and he wondered once again if she was trying to communicate with him. Rezkin left the little dragon guarding his treasured sword while he went in search of sustenance and information.

Umbrell was not a large city, but it was an old city. Its streets consisted of packed dirt, and most of the buildings were constructed of wood with wooden shingles or thatch composing their rooves. Most looked to have seen better days, and every so often he would see a burnt-out husk or freshly cleared locations in varying stages of construction. The people of Umbrell were of no greater glamour than the buildings. Most wore homespun clothes in drab browns and greys, although nearly every man and many of the women wore a sword or large belt knife. In fact, the only opulence to be seen was found on the scabbards themselves. Nearly every sheath was adorned with elaborately painted scenes or geometric designs. Many were inlaid with varying woods or mother-of-pearl, and all were unique and beautiful, although many people beyond the east thought them to be gaudy.

Rezkin entered a tavern where a crowd had gathered and intentionally scuffed his boots so as not to startle anyone by his swift approach. The warm light of the lanterns brightened the room considerably so that it was nearly as bright inside as it was outside in the late afternoon sun. At that time of day, most of the seats were taken, but there were a few empty ones here and there at occupied tables. Rezkin took note of each of the patrons at those tables with empty seats and settled on a pair who looked to be merchants by their foreign dress.

He ordered a mug of ale at the bar then approached the table with a practiced smile. He jovially said, "Greetings, good fellows! This lovely establishment is filled to the brim. Might I join you?"

The man on the left was slim with hollow cheeks and a bushy mustache. He eyed Rezkin up and down then nudged the average-looking man on the right with his elbow. The man on the right dropped his gaze to Rezkin's unadorned scabbard then grinned and sat back in his seat with arms splayed. "Please do," he said in a Channerían accent. "We are always welcoming of fellow travelers. It's good to hear the news from places not yet traveled."

"So it is," Rezkin agreed as he took his seat at the table. He feigned ignorance and said, "Where, might I ask, are you from?"

"Ah!" said the average-looking man. "We are from Lasveny. It's a beautiful—"

"Quaint," interjected the lanky man.

"Yes, *quaint*, city to the east of Serret. Have you heard of it?"

Rezkin shook his head. "I can't say that I have. I've just come up from Kaibain, myself."

The average man slapped his hand down on the table, "What good fortune! We happen to be on our way to Kaibain. What news do you carry?"

Rezkin casually sat back in his seat. "Yes, yes, but first things first. Introductions!"

The average man grinned abashedly. "Oh, indeed, I forget myself. I am Rodry, and this here is Pivar."

"It's a pleasure to meet you both," said Rezkin. "The name's Drake."

"Drake, my good man, what brings you to the east?" asked Rodry.

"I can't say as anything is *bringing* me east as was driving me *away* from the west."

"Oh?" Rodry turned to Pivar, "Seems we have a man on the run here." He leaned in conspiratorially, "What is it that drives you?"

Rezkin grinned unapologetically, "There might have been a dalliance with a lady…"

Rodry barked a hefty laugh and slapped the table again. "I knew it! You have a look about you."

"Ladies' man," said Pivar.

"There's no doubt about it," added Rodry. "Now, tell me. What news do you have of the King's Seat?"

Rezkin spent a few minutes telling them things they already knew, of the construction of Caydean's temple, of the continued military draft, and of Caydean's good will. When he was finished, Rodry said, "Yes, it's a good time to come to Ashai, but you'd best be careful if you have intents on Channería. There's a reward for turning in any Ashaiians found within the borders. You might have luck taking refuge at a Temple of the Maker, but what kind of life is that?"

Rezkin raised a hand, "Don't worry about me. This is as far as I go. But I am curious—are they still sending Ashaiians to that island … what's its name?"

"Cael," said Pivar.

With a nod, Rezkin said, "Right, that one."

Rodry leaned in, "Aye, the temple still sends them there, but there's no telling for how long King Ionius will put up with it, especially now that the emperor is dead. *Although*, some say he lives still in secret."

Rezkin expressed surprise, "Is that what they're saying in Channería?"

"From what I heard, King Ionius refuses to take a side on the matter. He has other things to worry about."

"Jerea," said Pivar.

"Right," said Rodry. "Prince Nyan of Jerea has gathered a sizeable army at the border, against his father's wishes, I might add. There have already been a few skirmishes, and some of the displaced have already turned to banditry. The roads are becoming dangerous for travelers, yet people are fleeing the north in fear of all-out war."

"Oh?" said Rezkin, "I have friends in Londgrad. How fares the city?"

Rodry's face screwed up in distaste. "No one goes to Londgrad, not even the refugees. It's a cesspit of degenerates and other deplorables. Ah, no offense to your friends, mind you."

Rezkin grinned. "No offense taken. My friends *are* some of those degenerates."

The three had a good laugh, then Rezkin excused himself. Upon returning to his room at the inn, Seena pounced on him, sinking her sharp talons into his thigh. Rezkin pushed her away, and she tumbled across the floor. She righted herself and splayed her wings as she inhaled a great gulp and her chest puffed out. She released a ferocious growl, and this time, a tiny puff of smoke accompanied it.

"Ah, is that what has you so riled up? You've almost found your fire," said Rezkin. "I'm impressed."

Seena showed all her viciously sharp teeth as she grinned and flapped her wings, although her feet still did not leave the ground.

"Very well," he said.

Rezkin picked her up and held her over his head. She spread her wings wide, and then he released her as she leapt forward. She glided across the room and smacked into the wall. She slid to the floor, and Rezkin retrieved her. As he settled her on the bed, she looked a bit dizzy. He waited for her head to stop bobbing before speaking.

He said, "Now hold out your wings." She did as he asked, and he said, "You do not have enough room to maneuver in here, but you must turn before you hit the wall. Tilt your wings to the side like this." He maneuvered her wings so that they were angled to the floor. He had spent countless hours watching birds so that he could help Seena learn to fly. He usually did not give her flying lessons inside the room, though.

Rezkin let go of Seena's wings, and she perched on the bed doing her best to tilt them as he had shown her. After allowing her to practice for several minutes, Rezkin informed her that it was time to sleep. He quickly set several traps at the window and door, shucked his clothes, and climbed into the bed. Seena curled up beside his head. Then Rezkin slept.

The wind blew dust devils across the dirt road as a lone rider huddled within her cloak. A pale lock of hair escaped her cowl to glisten in the moonlight. Her hood flew back, and silver eyes stared back at him. Something large moved in the brush beside the road. Then more of the dark shapes unfurled from their hiding places. The men merged on the rider, and she sent two of them sprawling in the dirt with a blast of wind. Then she drew her sword and met the first attacker as her horse pivoted nervously beneath her. Their weapons clashed, and she kicked him away just as a second man came at her from the other side. She kicked at him as he swung his cudgel, and he faltered, but still he managed to unseat her.

Azeria struck the ground with a grunt then quickly dodged a heavy blow that thudded into the ground where her head had been. She swung her sword around, slicing deeply into the meat of the man's thighs. He cried out as he fell to the ground, but another man was there to replace him. Azeria parried and dodged a few sword strikes then cut clean through the man's neck with a sweep of her blade. She dropped her leg and rolled backward, deftly avoiding being bludgeoned as the next man's swing went over her. She gained her feet and sliced through his hamstrings before impaling him through the gut.

She ran toward the final assailant, cutting the throat of her first attacker as she went. The last man tried to back away, but Azeria was too fast. He was down within seconds, his cry cut short as he slumped into the bloody quagmire in the road. Azeria flicked her sword then sheathed it in one fluid motion. She turned her head to look over her shoulder. Her silver gaze met his own, and she said, "Come back to me."

6

AZERIA AWOKE WITH A START, breathing heavily from reliving the battle that had taken place the previous night. But it was not the blood and death that had her heart aching. *He* had been there, watching her. She had felt him from the moment before the battle until the end. Although it had felt as real as her previous shared dreams with him, she knew this one was different. Rezkin was dead. If he had truly been there, then he had done so from the Afterlife.

Tears streamed from her eyes as she pressed her palms to her face and sobbed. How was it that only now, after he was dead, did she realize how much he meant to her? Azeria swiped her tears away as anger consumed her. She needed to go to him. She could feel the pull to find him, yet she could not lest she seek the Afterlife as well. She furiously rolled up her sleeping pad and shoved her few belongings into her pack. If she could not go to him, then she would do whatever was needed to find his body—or, barring that, the one who took him.

The sun had not yet risen, and Wesson was still asleep within a protective ward. She waited another half hour then started lobbing bursts of power against his ward. Finally, he woke with a start.

"What are you doing?" he muttered as he wiped sleep from his eyes.

"Trying to wake you," she replied.

"Was it really necessary to attack my ward like that? It was alarming to be awakened like that."

"Good, then you will be alert. We need to go."

Wesson grumbled as he rolled up his sleeping pad and packed away his belongings. The road was dark as Azeria led her horse forward. They were only a few hours' ride from Kaibain according to some pilgrims they had met the previous night. That was before the attack that had left her barely winded. The slow humans were hardly a threat, and Wesson had not even had to use his power. Azeria had been thankful for the action that had broken the monotony. Until then, the route from Garten Knoll to Kaibain had been uneventful. They had avoided the occasional patrol as well as a few ambushes, but last night they had decided the attack was not worth the effort of avoiding it. She would not mourn the loss of the pitiful humans who had assailed her. As far as she was concerned, she was doing the humans a favor in ridding them of the thieves.

When Kaibain came into view, she noted the high walls and the guards at the gate, and Azeria's shoulders tensed as they did every time she neared a human city. It was one thing to keep herself hidden on the road, but quite another in a busy city. And in this one the guards and officials would be especially suspicious. She brushed her fingers over the amulet that hung from her neck. It was a gift from Entris. The amulet was enchanted to create an illusion that would allow her to pass as human for a few minutes at a time. The effect would not last, and it would be about twenty minutes before she could use the amulet again, but it was enough to get her through introductions or mishaps before she could raise her hood again.

Azeria kept her hood raised as they passed gate guards who were keeping watch over the travelers but were not hindering entry to the city. The city itself was unlike Eihelvanan cities. First and foremost, besides a few potted plants, it lacked any sign of nature. The few trees that grew in planters near the crossroads were stunted and weak looking. As long as she had been in Ashai, she had found it disconcerting to be so removed from the forest and mountains of her home, but this city was beyond anything she had experienced thus far. People, carts, and stalls clogged the roadway, and dwellings were constructed in every available space. The cacophony of the crowd and the pungent aroma of body odor, human and animal waste, and cooking food were enough to drive anyone away except, apparently, the humans.

The inn they selected was modest and her small room was sparsely furnished, but the proprietor did not ask her to remove her hood, so she was satisfied. She stored her belongings then went looking for trouble. Azeria was not well versed in human subterfuge, but Striker Kai had instructed her on the best ways to find the thieves' guilds. She was to look for certain marks scrawled on the sides of buildings to identify the various territories. Within those territories, she should look for humans bearing tattoos of the same marks, which identified them as guild members. Azeria thought her best chance at finding them was to catch one of them in the act of stealing. In fact, she would entice them to come to her.

Azeria removed her functional traveling clothes and donned a dress of human design. It consisted of a white linen chemise beneath a dark purple ankle length gown that was belted at the waist with a silver tie. The garb would be a hindrance if she needed to fight, but it served her purposes for now. She draped a silvery grey scarf over her head and around her neck to hide her hair and ears. Such was common in the city so she would not look out of place. She allowed her crystal amulet to hang over her bosom and placed a few rings and bangles on her hands and wrists. The jewelry was not of great value, but it would make her appear as a woman of some means and hopefully an easy target. Finally, Azeria tied a heavy purse to her belt so that it dangled enticingly near her hip.

Satisfied with her appearance, she left Wesson to his own tasks and headed for the market district, which she knew to be only few streets away since she had passed it on her way into the city. As she walked, she kept an eye out for the symbols Kai had drawn for her. As she neared the market, she finally caught sight of one at the corner of an alley that belonged to the Diamond Claw guild. Pleased that she was on the right track, she meandered between the stalls and shops stopping often and flashing her jewelry in the sunlight to draw attention. As she passed by another alley with the guild symbol emblazoned on the woodwork, she caught sight of two men hiding in the shadow of the building. She gave no indication that she had seen them, but she turned so that the sun caught the crystal amulet at her bosom, and she brushed her hand over her purse.

As she walked on, she noted that one of the men uncurled from his hiding place. She could feel his gaze on her as she strode through the market at a sedate pace. When she stopped to look into a shop window, she felt someone brush by her, and she knew her purse had been lifted. Unconcerned, she kept an eye on the man as he casually strode through the crowd. The man was unremarkable in every way. He was of average height and build for a human male and had shaggy brown hair and clothes typical of the workers in the area. In fact, if Azeria did not know he was the thief, she would likely have overlooked him altogether.

Azeria pursued the man past a couple of streets, then he ducked down an alley. Pleased that her chase was nearly at an end, Azeria followed him. Only when she got to the alley, the man was nowhere in sight. She reached through the hole in her pocket to the dagger strapped to her thigh as she stalked down the alleyway. A scuff from behind her was all the warning she got before an assailant grabbed her. At least, he tried to. Azeria was too quick. She deftly danced out of his grasp as she turned and caught him in the solar plexus with an elbow. Movement to her left caught her gaze, and she realized the man who had followed her was back. As he lunged for her, Azeria pounded the first man in the back sending him stumbling into the second man. She wrapped an air current around both men and slammed them into the wall. With a flick of power, she swiped their feet out from under them. She stepped up behind the first man and struck him in the temple with the handle of her knife, rendering him unconscious. The second man pushed the first man off him, but he was only human and slow. Azeria pressed her knife under his chin, "Show me your marks."

"You're a mage," sputtered the man as he blinked up at her with frightened brown eyes.

"I am nothing so basic." She pressed the tip of her knife into his flesh drawing a dribble of blood. "Your guild marks. Show them to me."

"All right, all right, here. Look at them." He rolled his sleeve up on his arm to show the symbol of the Diamond Claw guild, then he tugged his tunic down to reveal a black raven tattoo on his collar bone. "That's all of 'em. That's all I got."

"You serve the Raven?" she asked.

"Of course I do. Anyone who wants to live serves the Raven."

Azeria stepped back as she looked down at the man slumped against the wall. "Take me to him."

His eyes widened. "Look lady, I *serve* the Raven, but I don't know him. I ain't never seen him."

Azeria was disappointed but not deterred. She had not expected this task to be easy. She said, "Then take me to someone who *does* know him."

"I-I can't do that. I ain't got that kinda clout."

"Who *can* you take me to?"

"Uh …" He stared at her blankly, so she continued to gaze down at him with steely eyes. Finally, he said, "Rom. I can take you to Rom."

"Does this Rom know the Raven?"

"I, uh, don't know," he said as he wiped the blood trickling down his chin. "But he knows Attica, and Attica knows the Raven."

"Very well," said Azeria. "Take me to Rom."

The man slowly got to his feet dusting himself off, "I'm Ikrus, by the way."

"I do not care," said Azeria as she flicked her hand for him to lead the way.

Ikrus looked down at the man Azeria had knocked out before heading back down the alley. Gone was the casually stealthy thief from earlier. Ikrus walked stiffly and glanced back frequently as if checking to make sure she was still following him. He led her down several streets and through a few buildings before he came to a stairwell that led to a door below street level. He tapped a beat on the door, and it opened. Ikrus showed the doorman his tattoos then motioned to Azeria as he whispered to the doorman. Azeria could not hear everything that was said, but she caught the words *mage* and *Raven*.

The doorman gave Azeria an appraising look then jerked his head as the door swung wide. She followed Ikrus into a dark room lit by a single oil lamp. A couple of human men were sitting at a table and seemed to be playing a game that used bones as pieces. Either that or they were conducting a crude ritual. Azeria was not certain, but she did not sense any power emanating from either of the men, so she doubted the latter. There was a loud *thunk* as a latch slid into place barring the door behind her. Azeria's hackles rose. She did not like being trapped underground with these human men, but she was confident she could handle them if they gave her trouble.

Ikrus crossed the room and entered a second, larger room where a number of humans slept on grain sacks, piles of hay, or wadded blankets. The room was even darker than the first, but Azeria's eyes adjusted quickly. Ikrus was only human, though, and not so lucky as he ended up tripping over several people as he made his way through the space. When they reached the other side, they took a set of stairs to the level above, which was the ground floor. They walked through an empty room with a few windows that had been painted over, and Ikrus stopped in front of a closed door. He rapped several times on the door, and when it opened, a very large human male with a bald head and stubble on his chin stepped into the room.

"What is it, Ikrus?" said the bald man, his gaze flicking toward Azeria.

Ikrus said, "Sorry to bother you, Boss, but this woman is looking for the Raven."

"Why did you bring her here?" growled Rom.

"She insisted rather forcefully," replied Ikrus. "She rendered Guent unconscious and had me at knifepoint."

Rom narrowed his eyes at Azeria. "You attacked my men?"

"They attacked *me* after they stole my purse." She looked to Ikrus, "Which I want back, by the way."

Ikrus reached inside his pocket and produced Azeria's purse. Handing it over, he said, "Sorry about that."

"I am sure you are," she replied. She turned her attention back to Rom. "I understand you know the Raven. I need to speak with him. Where can I find him?"

Rom crossed his meaty arms as he looked at her. "Why should I tell *you*?"

Azeria jiggled her purse. "I will pay well for the information."

With a chuckle, Rom said, "No amount of money you could offer would get me to turn on the Raven. That's a fast way to lose your head, and I like mine right where it is."

"I'm not asking you to turn on him. I only want to speak with him. Can you arrange it?"

He said, "That's at least one question I can answer without lying. I don't know where he is, and I don't know how to contact him. You're wasting your time here."

Azeria swept into Rom's personal space, struck his chest at the same time she kicked the back of his knee, and laid him out on the floor with a *whomp*. Moving faster than any human could possibly move, she had her knife at Rom's throat before he even knew he had been attacked.

"Someone in this guild knows how to find the Raven. If you do not know, then you are useless to me, and I have no problem with ending you here and now."

Although Azeria's words were malicious, she would not actually follow through on the threat. While she cared little for the human thieves, she was not one to end life so frivolously. Rom did not know that, however, and it appeared her bluff worked when next he said, "Okay, look. *I* don't know how to find him, but Guildmaster Attica does, and she happens to be here now. You're lucky because she spends most of her time in Justain."

"Take me to this Attica," said Azeria.

Looking up at her from the floor, Rom pointed toward the door. "She's in there."

Azeria released Rom and stepped around his prone form to push the door open. The room was a well-furnished office space with a desk, several chairs, and a sideboard. At the desk sat a young woman with sharp features and long, black hair. Her eyes were an unusual shade of green brown not found in the Eihelvanan. Her tunic and leggings fit her form snuggly, and it was obvious she was used to employing her womanly attributes to get what she wanted. The woman, presumably Attica, looked up at her with surprise as Azeria entered the room and latched the door behind her so they would not be disturbed.

Before Azeria could speak, Attica snapped her book shut, "Who are you? If you're from the Crimson Blades, I'm not interested in talking about it anymore. I said there's no deal."

Azeria said, "I am not from one of your guilds. I am here in search of the Raven."

Attica smirked and stood. She moved to the sideboard to pour a beverage that looked like water, but even from where Azeria stood halfway across the room, she could smell was not. The guildmaster said, "He's not here. He comes and goes as he pleases. We never know when he'll show up."

"But you have a way of contacting him," replied Attica.

Attica turned around with her glass and leaned against the sideboard. "I do, but why should I help you? You haven't even told me who you are."

"My name is Azeria. Who I am is not important, though. All that is important is my task. I seek the Raven, and I *will* find him."

"What's your business with the Raven?"

"He took something that did not belong to him."

"How do you know it was him?"

"He wanted us to know. He left his mark."

"Sounds like the Raven," remarked Attica. "You want back whatever it is he took?"

"If possible, but more importantly I need to know why he took it."

Attica swirled her glass then tipped it back before swallowing hard. Her voice was a bit gruff when she replied. "Well, I'm afraid you just missed him. He was here about a week ago. So far as I know, he left Kaibain."

"You will send him a message for me."

Attica gave her a lopsided grin. "I like you. You don't mince words, and you get straight to business. But that doesn't mean I will help you. What's in it for me?"

Azeria jiggled her purse again. "I pay well."

Attica shook her head. "Money is well and good, but not the best use of your skills. The fact that you are in here means you were able to take out Rom, not an easy feat. I hope you didn't kill him."

"He lives."

"Good, then I am willing to deal with you. I will send your message in exchange for a service."

"I do not have time for services. I must find the Raven."

"This should not take you too far out of your way. I believe it will put you in the path of the Raven, or close to it."

"Is that so? What is this service?"

Attica moved back to the desk and opened a drawer. She pulled out a small, decorated box that looked like it might contain valuables. The guildmaster set the box on the desk, "I need this delivered."

"Delivered to the Raven?"

"No, but I think he will not be far. In fact, he might have taken this himself if it had been here on time."

"If this is so important, why would you entrust it to me?"

"Because you didn't kill Rom, but you could have. I need a skilled warrior to make sure this gets to where it's going."

"You have many skilled guild members at your disposal."

"Thieves, not warriors. But there's something different about you. It's a feeling I get. I think I can trust you. If you say you will do this, then it will get done. I don't know why, but I am certain."

"Very well. I will make your delivery if it will get me closer to the Raven. Where must I go?"

Attica smiled. "You go east."

7

Wesson stored his belongings at the inn then headed into the city. He was not dressed in his typical battle mage garb as that would draw unwanted attention. He wore a simple beige tunic, brown vest, and brown pants, and his caramel-colored curls were hidden beneath a floppy hat. In all, he looked like any other commoner in Kaibain. The last time he had been to this city, he had left it in haste after the attack on the Mage Academy. He doubted anyone would recognize him, but it was prudent to try to fit in.

His path through the city took him past the lower market district and into a more affluent area where higher end shops and many of the civic structures were located. His first order of business was to scout the mage relay to see what kinds of security measures were in place. The mage relay was located between the city's planning office and the courier's guildhall, and it was an opulent building with curved walls, stained-glass windows, and a golden dome atop it. The front entry was open, and it seemed anyone could just walk in, which is what Wesson did.

The inside of the building was one large, open space, the front of which was reserved for patrons waiting to send or receive messages and was populated with many seating areas. The two sides of the room were separated by a long counter, and the mage relay was located on the far side of the counter. The relay itself was a large circular structure that consisted of the base of a cone at the bottom with the tip shorn away. Around the cone were inscribed the runes that established the destinations for messages sent or received. A second cone, sans tip, descended from the ceiling, and the gap between them, where the points would have been, was a platform upon which the messages were sent or received.

A single guard was stationed at one end of the counter, but he was not paying attention to the room. He was busy having a conversation with the pretty mage behind the counter. Their flirtations were not what had garnered Wesson's attention, though. The mage, along with her colleagues, were all wearing an unfamiliar uniform. It was not the robes or tunics established by the Mage Academy for official wear by mages. These uniforms had a waist-length top with an asymmetric design across the front with a white flap overlapping the black base and pinned with a silver button. The pants were black and fitted but not snug and were tucked into knee-high black boots. What disturbed Wesson was the emblem over the left breast. It was the kingdom's seal, the king's mark.

He casually approached the counter and waited for the young woman to notice him. When she finally came over to assist him, she smiled politely, but the expression did not reach her eyes. Wesson noted the tightness around her lips and the darkness beneath her eyes. Although she was kempt, she looked haggard.

"What can I do for you?" she said.

Wesson pulled a small missive from his pocket and handed it to the woman. He said, "I'd like to send a message."

The woman perused the message, "That'll be a thump."

Wesson produced the heavy coin and handed it over to her.

She said, "I'll see that this is sent. Good day."

Wesson hurried to say, "Oh, I'm expecting a quick reply. I'll wait."

"Very well."

Then he took a chance and added, "The new uniforms look nice."

She nodded, "You must not have been in here for a while. We've had these for months. They're not too bad, although not as comfortable as what we used to wear."

He cautiously said, "Why the change?"

She blinked at him as if startled then quickly recovered. "I guess you might now know, being a mundane. These are what all mages wear now—at least, those who are not wanted for treason." She tapped the sigil over her breast. "Wearing this seal shows that I've sworn fealty to the king."

Wesson said, "But I thought mages were independent of the crown. They're supposed to be under the purview of the Mage Academy, aren't they?"

Her eyes darted around as if searching for eavesdroppers, then she lowered her voice, "That's how it used to be, but now the academy is gone. Any mage who hasn't sworn fealty by mage oath to King Caydean is considered a traitor and subject to immediate death upon sight."

Wesson was genuinely surprised, and he was sure it showed on his face. He quickly said, "I didn't know that, but I guess it's best for the kingdom this way."

Doubt flitted across her face before she straightened, "Yes, glory to the king." Then she turned from him and stepped over to the mage relay. Her vimara sparked in the air, and Wesson tamped down on his own so that it would not bleed into the air and alert her to his status as a mage. He watched carefully as she went about constructing the spells and attaching them to the runes of the relay. She set the missive on the central platform and released her spells. Various runes of the relay lit up with blue and green light, and then a blue haze formed between the cones. It flashed brightly, then all illumination was gone, and the relay sat dormant once again. The woman snagged the paper and returned it to Wesson without so much as glancing at him. Then she went to rejoin her conversation with the guard.

Wesson waited for a while, but he was not truly expecting a response. In fact, the message and its recipient were fabricated so that he would have an excuse to linger. The woman continued talking to the guard, and one of the other mages behind the counter stepped into a back room. The third was hunched over a desk facing away from the relay and seemed to be engrossed in a ledger. Wesson figured he would not get a better chance to do what was needed.

He tamped down on his vimaral bleed as much as possible. Hopefully, no one would be able to detect his mage power unless they were standing right next to him. Then he wrapped around himself a spell that had been inspired by Rezkin. If anyone's attention landed on him, it would immediately be diverted to something else. In this way, he could go unnoticed by anyone in the vicinity. Then he applied a small sound ward around himself so that no sound would escape beyond it. Once his wards were in place, Wesson moved over to the counter and climbed on top of it. No one raised an alarm, so he figured he was safe so far. He slid over the other side and quickly crossed to the mage relay. He pulled a small stone disk from his pocket. It was about the size of his palm, and numerous runes had been carved into its surface. At its center was a crystal from the citadel in Caellurum, fully charged, thanks to Entris.

Wesson placed the disk on the platform of the mage relay. The next part, he knew, would be particularly difficult to pull off without alerting anyone. He placed himself between the relay and the mages in hopes that his redirection spell would prevent them from noticing the changes happening to the relay. He triggered the spell on the stone, and it began vibrating with a low hum. Wesson's heart lurched as he quickly glanced behind him to see if the other mages had noticed. The mage at the desk looked up, glanced from side to side as if listening for something, then shrugged and went back to his ledger. The female mage did not seem to hear the hum at all.

Relieved, Wesson watched as the stone disk began to sink into the platform. Then he was alarmed once again when someone approached the counter with a document in his hand. Wesson anxiously glanced back to the stone. It was not nearly close enough to being embedded. If the mage came over to use the relay now, she would see the stone and his task would fail. Wesson had to think quickly. He looked over to the mage, but thankfully she was taking her time chatting with the guard. Wesson needed to keep her preoccupied. Unfortunately, the man waiting at the counter was becoming impatient.

"Hey, there. Mage! I'm waiting," he groused.

The mage looked over at him with her false smile, "I'll be right with you."

Wesson glanced back to the platform. The stone disk was nearly halfway submerged, but it was not sinking fast enough. As the woman finally came over to help the man, Wesson decided to act. He summoned his constructive power and whipped out a wind spell. The gust swept through the open doorway and across the foyer to snatch the document out of the waiting man's hand. The man cried out as he attempted to catch the paper, but it danced across the foyer out of his reach.

The woman's spine straightened, and she looked back to the mage at the desk. She snapped, "Did you do that?"

The mage turned to look at her, "Did I do what?"

She scowled, "Stop playing around, Malcolm, or I'll have you do the ledgers for the next month. Get back to work."

Malcolm blinked at her confused then turned back to his ledger. Wesson swallowed the bile that had crept up his throat and looked back to the stone disk. It was almost completely embedded in the stone platform of the relay. Meanwhile, the man awaiting use of the relay had retrieved his document and returned to the counter. As the man spoke with the mage, Wesson anxiously watched the stone disk sink beneath the level of the platform. When it was finished, he could not tell that anything had changed. The mage turned and headed toward him, and Wesson quickly skirted the relay and headed back toward the far end of the counter. He watched closely as she began using the relay. He had to make sure the device would continue to work as usual despite his little addition. After several minutes, he became satisfied that the relay did, in fact, work as normal, and Wesson slipped back over the counter and left the building.

Wesson was not practiced in subterfuge, but he thought his mission had gone rather smoothly. No one was the wiser that he had just added a new central destination rune to the relay. Assuming it worked as it was supposed to, now every message that was sent via the sole relay in the capital city of Kaibain would also be sent to Cael. Likewise, they could now send a message to the Kaibainian relay and make it appear the message had come from anywhere to which the relay was connected. He had just created a new weapon in their arsenal. Wesson was so thrilled to have pulled off the scheme that he did not notice the man walking into the relay until it was too late. Wesson had just enough time to drop his spells before he collided with the man.

"Oh! Pardon me," said Wesson from the ground where he was sprawled.

With dark eyes, the man looked down his nose at Wesson as he smoothed nonexistent wrinkles from his uniform. This uniform was similar to those worn by the relay mages except that it was entirely black and had a number of shiny embellishments across the front and down the sleeves. The man's sandy blonde hair brushed his shoulders, and a scowl was etched across his clean-shaven face.

"Watch where you are going, wretch," snapped the man who would not be bothered to help Wesson stand. He narrowed his eyes at Wesson and his nostrils flared as if he were smelling him. "Are you a mage?"

Wesson's eyes widened, and he donned a look of innocence and surprise. "Who, *me*? I wish, but, no, I wasn't blessed with the *talent*." Wesson brushed off his pants as he got to his feet, and he almost regretted getting up. The man was at least a head taller than he, and he was looking at Wesson as if sizing up his prey.

"Hmm, I thought I felt the use of vimara coming from you," muttered the man. Wesson felt a flutter of nocent power brush over his skin. It was dark and probing, and Wesson did not care for it. He tamped down tightly on his own power so it would not respond to the man's attempts to coax it from him. Not having found what he was searching for, the man sniffed indignantly, "It was brief and weak, though. I was either mistaken or you haven't enough power to be considered a mage. Be gone from my sight. I have important business."

Wesson did not need to be told twice. He quickly got out of the battle mage's path and hurried across the street. Wesson waited a few minutes as he considered following the man. Wesson did not recognize the battle mage, and by the look of his uniform, he was of some high rank. It might behoove him to find out more about the man, but if he got into trouble, he would have no backup. Azeria had gone off to take care of her own concerns, and she would have no idea where he was anyway. Still, this might be his best chance at learning more about the new hierarchy of mages. Wesson slid into the shadow of a building and waited.

Avikeev had dismissed the young man who had run into him, but some small part of him thought perhaps that had been a mistake. Something about the boy seemed off, but he could not put his finger on it. He tried to shrug off the feeling as he left the mage relay and headed down the street. He could have taken a rickshaw or even ridden one of the king's horses, but he liked to stay fit and always felt it best to walk if he was not in a rush. This day, he was not in a hurry. His message to the Channerían spy had been sent, in code, of course, and he was without orders at the moment. Still, if Caydean thought he was shirking his duties, he would be punished, so he headed toward the grounds where the new temple was being built.

The temple had been under construction for four months, and it had to be finished in time for Caydean's ceremony. The mage force had been working night and day to see it done, and Avikeev had been tasked with ensuring they adhered to the plans exactly, despite the fact that no single individual had a complete set.

As Avikeev descended the hill and entered the nearest portico, he lashed out at the nearest scaffolding with whip of power, snapping the structure and causing the workers atop it to crash to the ground in three broken heaps. Other workers in the vicinity rushed to their aid, and Avikeev chided himself for the slip-up. Attacking the workers would only set back construction, but he did not quite have full control of the demon that resided within him. The demon wanted to inflict chaos on the organized structure of the temple and its workers. Destruction was the breath of life for the demon, and it got a thrill every time it usurped control from him. Avikeev enjoyed the demon's antics as well, but he was more calculating in his actions. A little bit of order now would lead to even greater chaos in the future, and what a glorious ambrosia that would be.

He exited the portico onto the lawn, which was designated the staging ground, and found the lead architect directing her subordinates to begin laying the support structures for the next level of the northern building arc. Although his demon was roiling with unspent energy, Avikeev waited patiently for her to finish her instruction. When she was finished, she turned to him.

"Greetings, Battle Master. What may I do for you?"

Avikeev's first inclination was to tell her to set charges and destroy the structure they were so tirelessly building. He clamped down on the sentiment and instead said, "Thank you, Mage Terishi. I am only seeking an update."

Mage Terishi raised an eyebrow, "You asked me that last eve. We remain on schedule, same as yesterday."

Avikeev wanted to beat her for her insolence, but that would do him little good in the grand scheme of things. Mage Terishi was a talented architect and earth mage and losing her would delay the project. So instead of lashing out at her with the explosion of nocent power that he wanted to release, he said, "Watch your tone, Mage Terishi. You are still under *my* command."

Mage Terishi swiped a hand down her face, and for the first time, Avikeev noticed the dark bags under her eyes and the frazzled state of her grey-streaked hair. She replied, "Forgive me, Battle Master. I have not slept in three days, and I fear I am no longer thinking straight."

Avikeev tilted his head as he wrapped his will around his power. He could be gracious. He said, "I will forgive the slight this time. I want you to take a few hours to rest."

"I cannot, Battle Master. My direction is needed here."

"Mistakes are made when sleep deprived, and we cannot have mistakes."

Mage Terishi's expression was tight, but her eyes relayed relief. She said, "Thank you, Battle Master. I suppose now would be a good time to rest since I have already delivered my orders." She curtsied then hurried away, and Avikeev was pleased with himself. His control over the demon was getting better. He would not allow it to *become* him.

He turned to leave and spied a man carrying a sack toward the new construction area. The man was limping badly and appeared to be struggling under the weight of the sack. A dart of demonic nocent energy shot out of Avikeev's chest and struck the man in the back. The man cried out in pain as he fell to the ground beneath the sack. As the man cried and moaned, Avikeev smiled. The man would die. It would be a slow and miserable death. Avikeev felt not the slightest remorse for the dying man. He was worse than useless. He would have gotten in the way of the other workers, and that would not do. As Avikeev gazed around at the unfinished temple, he wondered where else his assistance might be necessary.

He grinned joyfully as he began making the rounds. His demon would be pleased.

He finished ensuring the construction was going well with only a few well-timed mishaps and then left the temple. Having taken care of his duties related to King Caydean's project, it was time to focus on his own pet project. He strode back through the congested streets of Kaibain avoiding the pilgrims when he could and forcing them from his path when necessary. At one point, he had the sense of being followed, but a quick survey of his surroundings revealed no one. He dismissed the sensation. It was absurd to think that anyone would be so bold —or *foolish*—as to spy on *him*.

Avikeev turned down a quiet street with very little foot traffic that held larger residential estates. He let himself in through a gate and walked up the winding path to the main house. He smiled with pleasure as he thought of the home's previous owner. What had been General Marcum's estate was now *his*, and it gave him great pleasure to have claimed it from the traitorous general. Part of him wished the general could see what he had done with the place, but he would have been satisfied with the general's death.

Rumor had it that the general had been gathering deserters and traitors somewhere to the north. Avikeev thought that if he were in charge, he would already have sent the army to vanquish them, but he understood Caydean's reasons for keeping the army close. For one, the army was still largely loyal to Marcum, and he knew that many in its ranks were uncomfortable with the fact that the general had been designated a traitor. Sending the army after the general would only result in more deserters switching sides. But there was another reason for keeping the army near Kaibain, a darker reason, and one that would ultimately see their side victorious.

Avikeev entered the home through the front door but quickly made his way to the back of the house, passing a few startled servants on the way. He descended through the kitchen into the cellar that had recently been repurposed. What had once held an assortment of household items, casks of ale, and a healthy collection of wine now held a workroom and several barred cells that were currently occupied by his latest *guests*. He made his way to the workroom at the back, sat down at the long bench that stood in the center of the room, and began flipping through his notes. He was deep in thought when his butler's voice roused him.

"What is it, Bendin?"

"Sir, Generals Trivian and Ulessa have arrived. Shall I show them in?"

"Yes, thank you Bendin. See that we are not disturbed."

"Very well, General, sir."

Bendin left without a glance for the prisoners in the cells. The prisoners, for their part, were silent, having given up in the efforts to sway anyone to help them. The five mages had been caged in the cellar for months and kept on meager rations so that they remained weak and docile. Thanks to the runes inscribed on the bars and walls of the cells, the mages were unable to use their vimara, but even without the runes, he figured they probably did not have the energy to put up much of a fight. It was too bad. He would have enjoyed punishing them.

A few minutes later, Trivian and then Ulessa descended the stairs into the cellar. Ulessa ignored the prisoners as well, but Trivian grinned and sent a stream of dark power into the closest one. The mage issued a choked cry then crumpled. The woman who shared his cell whimpered then bent over him.

Avikeev stood and stared at the downed mage. "Did you kill him?"

Trivian sighed despondently. "Unfortunately, no. He lives but only because we need him for the experiments."

Ulessa set a sack on the table with a harrumph. "If you had it *your* way, we would have no prisoners to experiment *on.* Why must you always kill them?"

Trivian's grin was feral. "I enjoy it."

Crossing her arms, Ulessa said, "There are more useful ways to inflict torment. You are too shortsighted, Trivian."

Trivian's expression sobered. "And you are boring. You always have some long-winded plot. I swear you make things more complicated just to vex me."

"Ha! My plans have nothing to do with you. In fact, I never think of you at all."

"That's enough," snapped Avikeev. He looked to Ulessa. "Did you bring them?"

Ulessa issued a final scowl to Trivian before turning back to her sack. She opened it and began pulling out items and setting them on the table: the first was a metal sculpture about the size of Avikeev's fist; the second was a granite sphere polished to a shine; and the third was a thumb-sized gemstone that transitioned from red to green.

"What makes you think any of these items will work?" asked Avikeev.

Ulessa tapped the statue. "They have all held very powerful enchantments, sixth order or greater. They're clean now, of course. I made sure of that."

"That is an improvement. The last items we used had possessed third and fourth order enchantments, and they were not enough. How did you come across these?"

Ulessa tucked a lock of dark brown hair behind her ear and smiled. "I have my ways."

Trivian gave a derisive snort. "I know exactly what *your* ways are—"

"That's enough, Trivian," said Avikeev. He turned back to Ulessa. "Do we have any more information from your source in Cael?"

"Nothing related to this."

"Very well. Let us get on with it. If we can draw part of their souls out and trap them in these vessels, then we can use the vessels to control them."

Avikeev turned to the hearth he had added to the cellar and used a bit of pyris to start a fire. He ordered Trivian to retrieve a prisoner and chain her to a post near the fire. Then he started the ritual using the fire to open the woman to accept a demon, only he did not designate a demon to enter her. Instead, he interrupted the ritual halfway through and began drawing the fire, and therefore part of her soul, into the statue. Her soul resisted at first, but he continued pulling with the dark power of the demon inside him. Eventually, her vessel released a part of her soul, and the woman lost consciousness. Avikeev added more power as the soul traversed the distance between her body and the small metal statue. He poured power and fire into the statue, and Trivian and Ulessa joined him. Together, they filled the small vessel with enough dark power to hopefully contain the piece of soul.

When the transfer was complete, Avikeev terminated the ritual and released his power from the statue as did Trivian and Ulessa. The statue no longer looked as it once had. It had begun to melt so that it now resembled a large glob of phlegm. But how it looked was not important. Whether it retained the piece of soul was what mattered.

Avikeev looked back to the unconscious mage. He watched her for a moment then frowned. He placed his fingers over the pulse point on her neck and waited. Nothing. The woman was dead. He growled his frustration and threw the melted statue across the room so that it bounced off the stone wall with a resounding *clank*.

"How did he do it?!" he shouted.

"We will try again," said Ulessa. "Perhaps one of these stones will work better. He did use a crystal to join their souls after all."

"So says your golem."

"The golem is not wrong. She would not have reported it if it wasn't true.

The emperor drew the fire and part of their souls into the crystals. That was very clear."

They tried again with the two additional objects, but the results were the same. Each time they tried, the mage died. The objects simply could not house the power of the soul.

"We need those crystals," said Avikeev after the last ritual failed.

Ulessa nodded. "It would be useful to have one he already succeeded with to study."

Avikeev growled. "But they are all in Cael. We cannot retrieve any of them."

"They are not *all* in Cael," said Ulessa. "The female warrior—what was her name? Yserria, I think—she left Cael some months ago. Last I heard, she was in Ferélle."

Avikeev stilled as he looked at Ulessa. "Is that so?" He turned to Trivian. "Go to Ferélle and retrieve this Yserria and her crystal."

Trivian's face screwed up with distaste. "It will take months to get to Ferélle and back."

"King Caydean will recognize the urgency of this mission. He will likely allow you use of the portal to get there. Take whoever you need to succeed."

"Whoever?" asked Trivian, his excitement evident. "Even the battle mages?"

"Yes, yes. Just bring her back *alive*."

8

Rezkin disembarked in Krellis to find a sprawling community of tents and huts with a few sturdier buildings nestled within them. Less than a hundred years ago, Krellis had been nothing but a way-stop on the EastWest Trade Route, a place for merchants to exchange goods and local farmers and craftsmen to hawk their wares. Now it was a hub of commerce and a place of culture unlike any other city in Ashai. Merchants could be found trading at all hours of the day and night, and most restaurants and taverns never closed. The city had nearly as many Channerians as it did Ashaiians, as well as Jereans, Sandeans, and even tradespeople from the Eastern Mountains. Rezkin's grandfather, the father of King Bordran, had established a central governing body in the city a little over sixty years ago beholden to none but the king and Duke Wellinven. Due to its origins, the city had little to no planning and no walls to protect it from attack. As such, it housed a permanent garrison aptly named Fort Krellis at its eastern edge. Never had the fort seen action, but thanks to Caydean's machinations, it was on high alert.

The path through the tents and huts beyond the docks was narrow, barely wide enough for two wagons to pass, and everywhere Rezkin looked were piles and strings of fish kept cool in the shade or drying in the sun. The fragrance was enough to spoil Rezkin's appetite. He felt the bag at his waist shift, and he looked down to find that Seena was poking her nose out from beneath the flap to smell the enticing aroma of the fish. He realized he would need to feed her soon, so he stepped aside to purchase a few of the freshest he could find.

Just as Rezkin stepped out of the path, a man came shoving through the throng. "Make way!" shouted the man. "Make way for General Bergmon."

The crowd was slow to part, but that did not deter the so-called general. Mounted on a bay battle charger, the general continued down the path at a trot regardless of the people traveling there. More than a few were bumped or kicked out of the way, and one woman was trampled so badly someone began calling for a healer.

Rezkin recognized the name Bergmon, and he knew the man had not been a general or even a military man before the attack on the King's Tournament. In fact, Bergmon had been nothing more than a minor noble and merchant who had professed his undying loyalty to Caydean. That fact alone caused Rezkin to distrust Bergmon, but based on his first impression of the man, he decided he did not care for him at all. Rezkin shook off his irritation. He reminded himself that his feelings for or against someone were irrelevant and to remain vigilant no matter his sentiments. Still, he added the man to his list of people in need of attention.

That night, Rezkin stole into the garrison undetected. He was wrapped in shadows and had created a sufficient distraction for the gate guards. He hurried across the grounds, timing his efforts so that he never encountered the few soldiers who were about so late. He snuck past the barracks and into the command post at the fort's center. A room to the left was lit by candlelight, but the central corridor in which Rezkin found himself was dark. He passed several more rooms, then stealthily took the creaky wooden steps in silence. At the top of the landing, he found the largest set of doors and let himself into the suite beyond. The entire suite was dark, but Rezkin had no difficulty navigating the predictably furnished rooms.

When he entered the sleeping chamber, Bergmon was asleep in his bed snoring loudly enough that he could not possibly have kept a bed companion. Rezkin used *Method 12* to end the man's miserable existence via garrote. When he was finished, he looked down upon the man's still form and wondered if he should feel some sentiment, perhaps guilt or remorse. According to the *Rules* he should not, but to the outworlders like Frisha these feelings were important, especially when ending a person's life. Rezkin did not have any feelings, though. Bergmon had been one of Caydean's sycophants and was therefore fair game in the war between them. Rezkin quickly carved the image of a raven into the headboard above the corpse. A search of the rooms revealed several letters detailing plans for the proliferation of Caydean's new religion and the consequences for refusing conversion, both for the general and for the public. Caydean's desire for complete power meant membership in this new religion was mandatory. When he finished examining the general's correspondence, Rezkin escaped the garrison with no one the wiser.

In the morning, he procured a horse from a trader who was reluctant to sell her for the price Rezkin offered. Having successfully negotiated the deal to his satisfaction, Rezkin left the city. He headed east along the trade route and found himself most often alone on the road. What had once been a heavily traversed path was now a desolate one with few merchants and even fewer travelers willing to brave the contentions between the two kingdoms. Rezkin remained vigilant and wary of patrols and often left the road to travel amongst the brush and trees that dotted the route. Unfortunately, he had little choice but to take the road since the gorge that separated the two kingdoms was spanned by a single bridge.

He eventually reached the gorge only to be greeted by a blockade occupied by Ashaiian soldiers. Rezkin donned one of the many illusionary disguises he had been practicing and approached the blockade as a wary traveler of twice his age and scarred by years of toiling in a smithy.

"State your name, country of origin, and your business," said the patrolman who greeted him with the tip of a spear pointed at him.

Rezkin answered in broken Ashaiian and a heavy Channerían accent of eastern dialect. "I be Roscus Torrin of Channería, and I be headin' home."

"What were you doing in Ashai?" said the patrolman.

"I been 'ere fer years, but things bein' what they be between the kingdoms, I be thinkin' it's 'bout time I'm headin' home."

The patrolman lowered his spear, "Smart man. I can't say as I blame you. You'll find the going rough in Channería right now. Very well. Get moving. They shouldn't give you too much trouble on the other side, you being Channerían and all."

Rezkin said, "Thanks be to you, sir. I'll be headin' on my way then."

Once he was past the Ashaiian blockade, Rezkin started across the bridge, which was such a phenomenal feat in and of itself that it could not have been built without the arduous labors of numerous mages. It was wide enough for four wagons to pass and so tall that one could not spy the bottom from the top. The walls were ornately carved with scenes of peace and prosperity, an irony not lost on him as he approached the Channerían blockade on the other side from which a multitude of archers trained their arrows on him. In fact, there were so many archers that should they unleash their arrows, it would be impossible to avoid them all even with his skills. Rezkin prepared to erect a shield ward for the eventuality.

He was not fired upon, thankfully, but he was greeted at sword point by multiple guardsmen. The lead guardsman said, "Halt! Ashaiians are not permitted beyond this point."

Rezkin tipped his hat and said in fluent Channerían, "*That be very well, but I be Channerían. I be headin' home.*"

The sword points lowered a fraction, and the guardsman said, "*A rockman, eh? You've a long way to travel through dangerous territory.*"

"*It be so dangerous, does it?*" replied Rezkin.

"*Aye, Prince Nyan has crossed the mountains, and he's pressing in on the north while the king's preoccupied with the fishers.*"

Suddenly, one of the men raised his sword and shouted, "*What's that in your bag?*"

Rezkin had felt Seena shifting about, but he had hoped the guardsmen wouldn't notice. He was not so lucky. He reached down and flipped open the flap of the satchel. Seena rushed out and scurried up his arm to perch on his shoulder.

"*She be me cat,*" said Rezkin as the swords lowered again.

To the guardsmen's eyes, Seena was indeed a cat, one that looked identical to the little tortie Rezkin had left behind in Cael. He had not been certain the illusion would work on the dragon, especially since Seena did not *move* like a cat, but the guardsmen appeared mollified. They waved for him to continue past the barricade, and Rezkin was satisfied that his first test of the illusions had gone well.

The journey to Londgrad, home of the Ashaiian spies in Channería, was long and relatively uneventful since Rezkin successfully avoided the patrols. The bandits he encountered were defeated with ease and hardly worth mention. There was quite a bit more movement on the trade route through Channería, however. Recruits and troops were heading north toward the conflict, and settlers were fleeing south away from it. Traveling merchants were still doing business as usual, and some were even turning a tidy profit thanks to the conflict. Although the supply was still regular, the cost of grain and other produce imported from the north had already risen. Those displaced by the fighting could not afford to take up residence within the towns, so tent cities had begun popping up on the outskirts of nearly every village.

Rezkin regularly strayed from the roadway to cross over the countryside and through the forests so that Seena would have a chance to get some exercise and continue their flying lessons. Although the illusion that she was a cat worked for short periods of time, it would have been disconcerting to see a cat soaring through the air. Seena was in good spirits for the most part, but Rezkin was having increasing difficulty keeping her from getting involved in his conflicts. Whenever he was locked in a battle, she became eager to participate. Although her tiny talons and teeth were effective against the rats and voles she hunted, they would hardly bring down something as large and dangerous as a man.

Rezkin was a few days into his journey to Londgrad, which was located to the north of Serret, when he stopped to camp in a cave beside a river. The cave was not very large, but it contained a fresh pool fed by a natural spring. The walls were dotted with chert nodules, and large crystals of calcite covered a sizeable cavity in the rear wall. As soon as Rezkin set down his packs, Seena hurried out and dove into the shallow pool. Although it was her first time in a body of water large enough to swim in, she took to it like a fish.

"Very well," he said. "You may swim for now, but we cannot stay for long. We must get to Londgrad quickly. I have many tasks ahead of me."

Rezkin watched her play for a while, feeling a sense of peace. Eventually, she leapt out of the water, shaking her body and wings. She hesitantly stalked closer to where he sat watching her then paused only a few feet from him. She stared at him with icy-blue eyes, and Rezkin got the distinct feeling she was trying to communicate.

"What is it?" he said. "What do you want to tell me?"

A presence brushed against his mind, and then he heard the softest whisper. "*Go?*"

Rezkin leaned back in surprise as the word clearly echoed in his mind. He said, "You want to go? We just got here. We have not yet rested."

Seena flapped her wings excitedly, obviously pleased that he had heard her. She paused, stretched her long neck out, and tilted her head at him. A soft, lilting voice caressed his mind. "*Go quickly.*"

He nodded. "Yes, we must go quickly after we have rested."

Seena turned in a circle then stopped in front of him again and stretched her body and wings upward. She closed her eyes, and Rezkin felt the presence in his mind again, this time stronger and more demanding. His first instinct was to fight back, to shut it out, but he resisted. Whether it was due to his bond with Seena or simply from having raised her since she was a hatchling, he trusted her, and he was curious as to what she was doing.

After a moment, a small glimmer of light appeared above Seena's head. The lavender light gradually grew to the size of a horse, illuminating the cave so that the crystals set in the walls sparkled. Rezkin got to his feet as he stared at the brilliant confluence of light that created a rent in the air. He had seen something like it before. It was nearly identical to the portal in the pathways that Azeria created. To his amazement, Seena had somehow created a portal, but where would it lead? Azeria could only create a pathway to a place she had been. Seena had never been to Channería, and he certainly did not want to end up back in Ashai.

"Where does this go?" he said.

She replied, "*Go quickly.*"

Rezkin hesitated. He trusted Seena, but she was still an infant by dragon standards. Could he trust a dragon infant to create a portal to a place he would wish to go? For all he knew, this pathway could lead to another realm entirely. He looked back to Seena, who appeared to be struggling. Her breathing was coming rapidly, and her limbs were beginning to shake. He did not think she could hold the portal open much longer. It was a risk, but it might be one worth taking. If Seena could truly open portals to the places he needed to go, it would save him months of travel. He would actually be capable of completing all his tasks, and he could more easily manipulate events so they worked against Caydean. Rezkin took what Tam would call a leap of faith. He gathered the reins and his packs, picked up Seena, and stepped into the light.

When Rezkin stepped through the portal, he was released instantly back into the world, and, to his surprise, he knew exactly where he was. In fact, he had once stood in that very spot on a hillside overlooking the capital city of Serret. It appeared that Seena had taken the location for the pathway from his own mind, and her pathway had cut more than a week from their journey. After taking account of his surroundings and ensuring there were no witnesses, he looked down to Seena. She had collapsed into his arms unconscious. A spike of concern shot through him, but he pushed it down as he considered how to help her. He figured creating the portal must have drained her energy, so he reached into his bag and pulled out a chunk of dried venison. He waved the meat in front of her nose, and after a few sniffs, she snatched it away from him. He gave her a few more pieces then offered her some water before carefully tucking her into the satchel at his hip. As he did so, he noted that it would not be long before she could no longer fit in the bag, and then his skill with illusions would be pushed to the extreme.

Rezkin opted to forgo going into the city and instead set up camp on the forested hill. He would have preferred to have slept in the cave, but Seena had gotten excited and created her pathway before he could rest. He was still astounded and grateful that she had been capable of creating the pathway, though he did not know how to feel about the fact that she had access to his mind. Rezkin was many things to many people. His secrets and identities were plentiful, and he was not thrilled that there could be anyone, human or beast, who might know the truth of it all—the truth of *him*. He was not even sure he knew the truth of himself.

When he finally set out for Londgrad in the early hours of the morning, Seena was rested and just as eager to be on the road as he was. The entire way was crowded with travelers, and he was forced to keep his illusion in place constantly if he did not wish to be seen for who he really was. As such, he was spent for energy and had to trade often or stop to hunt to satisfy his hunger. Seena was eating more than usual as well, and Rezkin wondered if she was preparing for a growth spurt or if she was just feeling his hunger as her own. It did not take much more energy to extend his illusion to Seena, so she was able to ride out in the open as a cat rather than being stuffed back into the satchel.

On the day he arrived in Londgrad, the sky was dark and threatening. A storm was gathering overhead, which boded well for him. Although the rain was uncomfortable, it was an ideal time to skulk about the town with little worry of being observed. Londgrad was a utilitarian town with few amenities. The buildings were squat, mostly single story, with slate or wood shingles and bore no paint or trimmings. Being located on the open plain, it was not in want of space, and the roads were wide enough for three or four wagons to pass. There was little color to the town, and even the awnings and window coverings were made of undyed homespun cloth. The people were just as unremarkable as the town, and with their grey and brown tunics and frocks, they all looked pretty much the same.

Rezkin stopped in front of a small, single-story building bearing a broken sign with a moon carved into it. He encouraged Seena to crawl back inside his satchel, secured his horse's reins to the post outside, and mounted the creaky wooden steps that led to the front door. He tried the handle, but the door was locked, so he rapped against it a few times. From within, Rezkin heard the gravelly voice of a man moving toward the door.

"*Dang it, who in the bloody hells could that be?*"

The door abruptly swung open to reveal a man likely in his seventies with scraggly white hair and plentiful creases across his sun-weathered face. The man jerked upon seeing Rezkin standing at his door.

"*Who are you and what do you want?*" he snapped.

Rezkin lifted a finger toward the broken sign, "*This is an inn, is it not?*"

The old man's expression soured as if he were tasting something bad. "*Ain't no one ever accused this dump of being an inn, but I've got a few beds for rent.*"

Rezkin pondered this for a moment. "*Do you have any private quarters?*"

"*I've got one room and five beds. There ain't no one else staying as of yet. That's the best you're gonna get in Londgrad right now. The inn burned down last month. Do you want a bed or not?*"

"*I do,*" said Rezkin. "*Do you have a stable?*"

"*There's a stable down at the crossroads. You can keep your horse there for a fee.*"

"*I see.*"

"*I get paid up front, and anyone you bring back with you has to pay up front too.*"

"*Fair enough,*" said Rezkin as he handed over a few coins.

The man finally allowed Rezkin to enter the dim space that was truly shabby. Just as the man had said, five cots occupied a single room. On each cot was a wool blanket and a lumpy pillow, and at the end of each cot was a chamber pot and a small trunk with a pad lock. That was the extent of the amenities. Rezkin chose the bed in the corner closest to the door for ease of access. He wouldn't be sleeping anyhow.

After securing his pack in the trunk, Rezkin placed a ward around the entire thing. He instructed Seena to remain hidden beneath the cot but left the cat illusion on her anyway. Then he went back outside and mounted his horse once again. He rode to the crossroads the old man had indicated and easily found the stables. Once he had taken care of the horse, he headed into the drizzle that was now precipitating from the gloomy clouds. Thanks to the thick, black cloud cover, the sky was darkening quickly, and although it was probably another hour until sundown, the streets had already succumbed to night.

Despite its humble appearance, the one redeeming feature that kept the city alive was the fact that it had a mage relay. Rezkin did not know the reason for its existence there, but it was responsible for the majority of the visitors who came to Londgrad. Rezkin decided that he would start his search for Caydean's spy network there. When he arrived at the building that housed the relay, easily the tallest building on the street, the mage responsible for operating the device was locking the doors behind him. The mage's hair was shaggy, his mage robes were wrinkled, and he walked with hunched shoulders and a vacant expression on his face. In fact, it appeared to Rezkin that all the mage's hopes for a decent life had been dashed. He almost felt sorry for the young man.

Having already surveyed the surrounding buildings for witnesses, Rezkin hurried toward the mage relay's doors once the mage had departed. The mage had warded the door, but it was no hindrance to Rezkin. He pressed against the ward with his will until it bent inward and folded away from him. Then he pulled a lock picking kit out of the pouch at his waist and made quick work of the lock on the door. Finally, he let himself into the building and closed the door so that no one passing by would see anything amiss.

Inside, the relay looked much the same as any other relay Rezkin had seen. The open space just inside the door had multiple seating areas that were separated from the relay itself by a long counter. Rezkin padded across the chamber and vaulted over the counter. He pulled a scroll tube from the pocket inside his tunic and withdrew several missives from it. Before he searched for information on the spy network, he would make use of the relay to send the messages to his own spies, thieves, and assassins scattered across the Souelian.

After finishing with the relay, Rezkin turned toward the desk situated to one side of the room. Beside it were several bookcases populated with old ledgers bound in dark leather and inscribed with gilded lettering. The ledger he wanted, though, was laying open on the desk. He began scrolling through the past few months' worth of entries, making note of those that seemed suspicious. The ledger contained the names of the senders and recipients of the missives as well as a brief description of the contents of the messages. Finding the spies would be difficult since they were certainly sending their messages in a code that was not recorded in the ledger. Still, Rezkin was familiar enough with the process that he was reasonably sure that at least a few of those he noted were associated with the spy network. Now that he had their names—or at least the names they had provided—he just had to track down the individuals.

Rezkin finished his perusal of the ledger then exited the building the same way he had entered. The rain was coming down hard now, and thunder rumbled in the distance. He did not bother with a hood. He would be soaked in a matter of minutes anyway. As he stepped into the road and turned toward the city offices, he caught sight of someone watching him from within a darkened alcove. He gave no indication that he had seen the witness as he sloshed through the quickly thickening mud of the unpaved road in the direction of the building. As he neared the location where he had seen the witness, a man wearing an ankle length hide coat stepped from the alcove into the rain and hurried around the side of the squat building.

Rezkin followed.

Lightning lit the sky as Rezkin turned down the side street in pursuit of the witness. He could no longer see the man, but he caught a glimpse of the coat as the man rounded another building. Practicing with Azeria and Entris had helped Rezkin become faster, and he used that speed now to catch up to the witness. He darted around the building and narrowly escaped being impaled on the end of a sword for his efforts. He dodged to the side and drew Bladesunder as he did so. He brought the Sheyalin down to block a strike just as the man lunged. When the two blades clashed, they emitted a blue spark that flashed like the lightning above. That was when Rezkin noticed the blue swirls in the other man's blade. He, too, had a Sheyalin. The man was a Swordbearer. But to whom did this Swordbearer belong? Caydean or the dead king Bordran?

Rezkin could not stop to ask as the man continued his assault. After bringing his blade up to meet an overhead strike, Rezkin dodged to the side and swept his own sword toward the man's ribs. The man dropped his arm and met the attempt with a *clang* and flash of blue lightning. Rezkin was not deterred, though. He continued to press the enemy as much as the man was pressing him. Although the man was a skilled Swordmaster and his longsword had greater reach, Rezkin was faster as he dodged and blocked every attempt to end him. After several long minutes, the man began to slow. His sodden coat may have protected him from the rain for a time, but at that time it was only a hindrance. Rezkin had no such restrictions as he darted in to score the man's side. On the next exchange, Rezkin drew blood from the man's forearm. A moment later, he had stabbed the man's shoulder. This continued for several more minutes. Each time Rezkin drew more blood but never enough to spill the man's life into the street.

The assailant was bleeding profusely from numerous wounds when he stepped back and with a heavy breath said in Ashaiian, "Who are you? Who sent you?"

Rezkin said, "I would ask the same of you."

The man growled with a clenched jaw and swung his sword down toward Rezkin's head.

Rezkin dodged. "Why do you attack me? You do not know that we are enemies."

"I don't know that we're not," replied the man as he lunged.

Rezkin parried and pressed forward as he continued to inflict damage upon the man's body. He stabbed the man in the shoulder above his sword arm, and the man abruptly lost use of that arm, dropping his Sheyalin into the mud at his feet. The man turned to flee, but his boots stuck in the mud. Rezkin took the opportunity to stab the man through the back. The man slid off Rezkin's blade as he fell forward to collapse into the now bloody puddle in the road. Rezkin kicked the man, flipping him over so that he could see his face. He sheathed his sword and drew his serrated knife, which he held to the man's throat as he knelt beside his head.

He said, "Who do you serve?"

"There is only one man to serve, and that is King Caydean. I do not believe you to be one of his. Was I right?"

"We serve the same master," replied Rezkin. "You did not need to die."

Blood burbled up the man's throat to stain his lips as he released a pained laugh. "I s'pose it's a fitting end for my miserable existence. At least I was killed by someone worthy and not by some wretch who just got lucky."

Rezkin took a chance, "I have a message for our agents here, but I do not know where they are."

The man coughed up frothy blood and sputtered, "No, you wouldn't. They moved only a few nights ago. They're in the old mill just outside of town to the east, where the road bends. Tell them Jeiro sent you."

Rezkin started to move away, but the man caught him by the sleeve pulling him back. He wheezed, "Don't forget the sword. The king will want it returned."

"Of course, friend," said Rezkin with a pat to the man's hand.

The hand went slack as the Swordbearer released his last breath. Rezkin did not delay in removing the man's sword belt and securing it over his own hips. He braced himself and his will as he grasped the handle of the Sheyalin. The enchantments preventing anyone but the user from using it did not activate, though. The Swordbearer was dead and so were the enchantments, apparently. After retrieving the abandoned Sheyalin from the mud, Rezkin dragged the man's body into an alley and left him there.

By the time Rezkin exited the alley, the heavy rain had already diluted the blood in the road. Rezkin wished the body were so easily disposed of, but hiding it would have to do. No one would find him until the rain had abated anyway. Rezkin quickly made his way back to the stables to retrieve his mount. Then he retrieved his pack and Seena and headed back into the rain. Seena hid from the storm in his satchel, and Rezkin was amused that a dragon would be afraid of a little bit of lightning. She was a young dragon, though, so perhaps she would grow more accustomed to it with time.

Rezkin's horse, too, was anxious though, and once again he wished he had Pride. He had not realized the depth of his attachment to the battle charger until he no longer had him. He briefly wondered if feeling a bond for one's horse was a violation of the *Rules*. He was not exactly emotional about the steed, but he did long for his presence. He decided it was a grey area that should not require so much thought.

Rezkin saw no one in the streets as he made his way out of town heading east. He hoped the mill was easy to find for he did not relish the idea of searching in the rain and the dark for the remainder of the night. But it turned out it was just as the Swordbearer had said. He found the mill at the bend in the road, its sails spinning furiously in the wind. The plot of land was overgrown but free of trees close to the buildings. To the side of the mill was another building attached to a silo, and a barn was nestled beyond that.

Rezkin secured his horse to a post outside the buildings. He left the Swordbearer's Sheyalin with his horse but took Bladesunder and the black blade strapped to his back. Then he headed toward the building beside the mill where he could see the soft glow of an oil lamp through the window. He rapped on the door, and it opened quickly. On the other side were several sharp points of steel aimed at him.

Rezkin said, "Jeiro sent me."

The blades lowered, but the men behind them continued to look at him with suspicion. "How do you know Jeiro?" said the man in the center. The man's ears were a bit too large, his eyes were a bit too far apart, and his mouth was slack lending him a dimwitted appearance.

Rezkin partially slid Bladesunder free from its scabbard, "He and I have something in common."

The center man sheathed his sword as did the stocky man next to him. Another put away his knives and a fourth turned to drop his cudgel on the table behind him. Then the four of them moved back to allow Rezkin entry.

Rezkin stepped into the small room, and a puddle quickly formed beneath him from his dripping clothes. A good-sized fire was warming the hearth to his right, and an oil lamp sat on a side table by the window. The rest of the room was occupied by a large dining table and six mismatched wooden chairs, two of which were occupied, one by a man with a beard and a severe expression, and another by a woman with a doll-like face but hard, angry eyes.

"Who are you?" said the dimwitted-looking man as he rounded the table and fell into a chair on the other side.

Rezkin said, "My name is not important. Only the message is."

"Message? What message?" snapped the woman. "Why didn't this message come through the usual channels?"

Rezkin met her anger with cool grace. "This message was too sensitive to risk the relay." Rezkin's gaze passed over the group, and he said, "Where are the others?" In truth, he did not know how many spies were in this sect, but he assumed they would not all be holed up in this little building at once.

Dimwit said, "Ignatio and Parvus are on assignment, and Trent had an unfortunate accident. He won't be joining us."

Rezkin gave him a sharp look. "He was discovered?"

"Let's just say he got a little *too* close to the mark," said the man.

Rezkin nodded as if he knew what the man was talking about or even cared.

The woman asked, "What's the message?"

He stared hard at her, and his voice held an edge, "That depends on how things are going. I am not just a messenger. It is my job to decide how we proceed from here. What have you learned about the rebel forces?"

"Funny you should ask," said dimwit. "We received intel on that traitor, Marcum. Apparently, he is to meet in secret with the three dukes—"

"*Former* dukes," interjected the bearded man.

"Right," said dimwit. "They're to meet at Wellinven in three weeks' time."

"Atressian and Darning agreed to this?" asked Rezkin.

The woman chuckled, "I wouldn't put it past Atressian to use the opportunity to assassinate Nirius."

The bearded man said, "Perhaps this is a good thing. They can kill each other for us. Problem solved."

"We're not leaving it to chance," said Dimwit. "General Ulessa has already sent someone to deal with them. They won't be leaving the meeting alive."

"You mean they won't be leaving the meeting at all," said the bearded man.

"That's what I said," huffed Dimwit.

"You said they wouldn't be leaving *alive*, which implies they could still leave if they were dead."

Dimwit said, "Why do you always do this? You're always picking apart my words—"

"Enough!" boomed Rezkin's voice over the nattering. "Tell me of this attack on Wellinven."

Dimwit said, "Sorry, boss. That's all we've got. It's on a need to know. If you want more information, you'll have to get it from Ulessa."

"*General* Ulessa," said the bearded man.

Dimwit lunged for the bearded man, and the others crowded around them, some calling for them to break it up and others shouting encouragement. Rezkin used the distraction as an opportunity to draw the black blade and plunge it through the nearest man's back. As he silently slid from Rezkin's blade, Rezkin dragged a knife across another's throat from behind.

The woman screamed, but it took a few more seconds for the men to collect themselves enough to notice what was happening. In that time, Rezkin had brought the black blade around to slice a third man, who had been reaching for his cudgel, nearly in two. The last three managed to draw their weapons as they pushed back from the table and stood. Rezkin launched a throwing dagger at the woman, and it lodged itself in her shoulder causing her to drop her rapier with a clatter.

Dimwit lunged for Rezkin with his sword raised, but Rezkin easily knocked it to the side. Then he took the man's arm off at the elbow. As the man cried out and fell back, Rezkin exchanged blows with the bearded man. With each clash of their blades, the black blade ignited with green lightning. Rezkin quickly disarmed the man and stabbed him through the gut. It was a fatal wound, but it would take a long time for the man to die. Rezkin sheathed his blade and reached for the woman. She kicked out at him, but he managed to wrestle her into submission with little effort. He pulled a length of cord from a pouch at his waist and wrapped it around her arms behind her back, then he secured her to the chair. Next, he tied up the other two men. He used additional cord as a tourniquet on Dimwit's stump so that he would not bleed out too quickly.

Once everyone was subdued, he set to questioning them. When he was through with the interrogation, he made sure that none of them would ever speak again. Then he marked each of the bodies with a raven before dragging them out into the storm and lining them up along the front of the building. When that was finished, he led his horse to the barn where he found the spies' horses stabled.

The barn was sturdy and dry, so he shucked his wet clothes and hung them up before changing into a fresh set of clothes and settling in for the rest of the night.

As he sat on the fresh hay cleaning and drying his weapons, he recalled the last time he had done such a thing. A little tortoise-shell cat had groomed his hair as she cuddled up to him. Rezkin wondered what Cat was doing now, and he found himself aching for her company. He spied the little dragon occupying the hay next to him. She was sprawled on her back with her wings spread wide and her hands and legs sticking into the air. Her tail was curled around her body, and her head at the end of her long neck was turned toward him. Her lips turned up in a semblance of a grin as she blinked at him lazily with icy-blue eyes.

In his mind, she said, "*Sleep?*"

He nodded, "Yes, sleep now. Tomorrow we will go."

9

Azeria arrived in the human city of Krellis just as the sun was setting. Her first impression was one of confusion. There were few permanent structures in the city as it seemed most of the people lived in tents or huts constructed of reeds and grass. She could not imagine living in such rudimentary conditions all the time, and she wondered what drove these people to live in such a way. She had no one to ask, though, since Mage Wesson had stayed behind in Kaibain. She wrinkled her nose as she focused on her surroundings. The area near the docks smelled strongly of fish, and that, mingled with the heat beneath her hooded cloak, made her stomach queasy.

She stopped to ask a merchant for directions to the city's news office, if it had such a thing, which it did, and then she moved quickly through the throng. She passed stall upon stall selling fish and other goods as she made her way toward the city's center. She found the place easily enough. The news office was located on the first floor of one of the few buildings that occupied the street. Outside the office hung a large board to which many notices were nailed. She scanned it for any information on the Raven. It was not easy for her. Although she had learned to speak the human trade language of Ashaiian fluently, she had not been the best student when it came to reading the language. Still, she managed well enough to find what she was searching for. One notice offered a reward for any information that led to the capture of the Raven.

She snagged the notice and entered the news office. A woman was sitting behind a desk just inside. Her hair was tied in a tight bun at the back of her head, and she wore a pair of spectacles low on her nose. She was so engrossed in perusing some missive that she did not immediately notice Azeria standing before her. When she finally glanced up, she yelped with a start as she leapt to her feet.

"Oh, my dear, you startled me! I didn't hear you come in."

Azeria said, "I apologize for startling you." She held up the notice she had taken from the board outside, "I have some questions about this man."

The woman gave her a knowing look, "You aren't the only one. Are you interested in the reward? It's quite the sum, now, isn't it?"

"Yes, I would like to know anything you know about him."

As she plopped back into her seat, the woman said, "Honey, I know that's a lot of money, but if you want my advice, you should steer clear of that one. He's known all over Ashai and even Channería for being a brutal criminal overlord. In fact, just last week he killed a general right here at this garrison. A general! Can you believe it?"

Azeria pursed her lips as she considered the information. She said, "How do you know it was him?"

Pointing to the rough sketch of a raven scrawled across the notice, she said, "He leaves his mark on his victims."

"I see," said Azeria. "But it could have been anyone, could it not? Perhaps someone else killed this general and left the raven's mark to throw off suspicion."

The woman blinked at her several times. "Well, I suppose that's true. I hadn't thought of that. But the general was killed in his own bed in the middle of the garrison, and nobody saw anything suspicious. Whoever it was, they are very, *very* good."

"Was there any indication of where this Raven may be headed next?"

The woman shook her head. "None that I know of. His mark is all the evidence he left behind. We don't even know *why* he killed the general."

Still unsatisfied with the lack of information, Azeria thanked the woman and turned to leave. She stopped as the woman called out, "Hey, do me a favor and hang that back up on the board before you leave."

Azeria did as she was bade then headed back onto the street. She was heartened that she seemed to be on the Raven's trail but a little disappointed that there was no indication of where he was headed next. He had been going east, though, just as the guildmaster in Kaibain had said. This was good news considering the task she had been given by the guildmaster. Azeria was to deliver a small box to someone in the Channerían capital city of Serret. While Azeria held no love for the Raven's guild, she was as good as her word. She had said she would deliver the item, and she would. Hopefully she would find the Raven in the process.

She had no intention of staying in the city, so she steadily made her way to the edge of town where she found a horse trader. She used the human currency she had obtained in Cael to purchase a mount, a saddle, and tack then headed east past the garrison. She noticed a plethora of guards stationed about the fort and assumed the precaution had to do with the general being killed right under their noses. Azeria had no idea why the Raven had killed the man, but since the general had served Caydean, she conceded that, at least in this, the Raven had been on her side.

The journey east to Channería was marked by few merchants heading in the same direction, and even fewer passing in the other direction. After several days, one such merchant pulled his wagon up beside her.

"Hi, ho! Greetings to the traveler," the merchant said. He had a strong accent that Azeria had come to know as being Channerían in nature.

She did not stop but politely returned his greeting. "Greetings to the traveler."

"Where might you be headed, dear lady?"

Azeria gave him a sidelong look, wondering why he was talking to her at all. Her answer was clipped. "East."

The merchant nodded with a broad grin that seemed a little too practiced to her. She surreptitiously eyed the man when he glanced away. He was of average height for a human and appeared to be fit beneath his snug tunic which looked to be a costly item by the fine weave of the material and the extensive embroidery. His brown hair brushed his shoulders, and he had a mustache that curled up at the corners of his mouth. Azeria thought that perhaps human women would consider him attractive, but he did nothing for her.

The man turned once again, "Have you been this way before?"

Azeria noted the sword and belt knife the man wore at his hips. "No."

Maintaining his grin, the man said, "Well, I might be of service to you then. You see, there's a check point up ahead at the bridge. The Ashaiians are keeping an eye on the Channerían Army, and the Channeríans are keeping Ashaiians out of their kingdom. If you are Ashaiian, you will not be able to get past them."

Azeria said, “I am not.”

“Ah, well, still it might be best if you do not try to cross alone. I am willing to let you ride through with me for a fee."

"A fee?" said Azeria.

"Yes, it will not be much—a paltry sum. Only because I incur such great risk in agreeing to take you across.”

Azeria said, “That will not be necessary.”

The man’s smile faded a bit and then he recovered. “Very well, very well. But if you think to change your mind, you should do so before we reach the bridge.”

“I will not,” she said. “You may go ahead.”

The merchant licked his lips, “You should know that the bridge is the only way across the gorge. There is no other path. You should take my offer.”

Azeria was irritated by the human but tried to maintain her civility. She said, “I thank you for your offer, but I will have no problem crossing the gorge. I would appreciate it, however, if you would take my horse across.”

“Your horse?”

“Yes, just the horse. I will meet you on the other side to retrieve him. I expect this will not be a problem since he is only a horse and not a person.”

“No, no, it is not a problem, but how will you get across?”

“That is of no concern. Will you do this?”

He stroked his chin. “Yes, I will do this, but you must pay me up front.”

“No, you will get paid once I have retrieved my horse.”

“Ah, but what assurance do I have if you do not show up?”

“If I do not show up, then you will have a free horse.”

“Hmm, that is true. The bridge is not far—just around that hill there. Give me your horse, and I will bid you good luck.”

Azeria dismounted and left her pack secured to her saddle. The merchant tied the horse’s reins to the wagon, then he snapped his reins and rode ahead. Once the man was out of sight, Azeria left the road. Her steps were sure and light as she traversed the rocky hill that was dotted with towering trees not entirely unlike those in her homeland. It was not long before she reached the edge of the land where it dropped of steeply into the gorge. The trees grew right up to the edge and then down into the ravine where they met a broad river that raged over jagged boulders as it rushed toward the sea. Even with her sharp vision, though, she could not clearly make out the other side, so she could not safely create a portal to take her there. It would not do for her to create a portal that placed her directly into a tree or the rockface.

Turning her head up to the sky, she inhaled steadily. A hot breeze blew across her face ruffling her hood. She opened her eyes to spy the cliff face on the other side of the gorge. It was quite some distance across, farther than she had ever attempted, in fact, but she was not deterred. She gathered the ends of her cloak and tied them around her waist. Then she used a length of leather cord to secure them even tighter. She took several deep breaths, steadying her nerves, then she summoned the wind. It was slight at first—no different than the breeze that already swept across the expanse, but as the seconds slipped by, the currents became fierce. The wind slammed against her divesting her of her hood and causing her boots to slip across the loose rocks beneath her feet. Azeria braced herself, every muscle in her body going taut against the strain.

Azeria fed more of her power into the wind, creating a torrent that she could no longer stand against on two feet. When her feet finally slid freely across the rocks, she quickly angled her cloak to catch the draft. Her cloak billowed around her lifting her from the ground. She guided the wind beneath the sail of her cloak so that she swept forward and over the rim of the cliff. The wind was harder to gather once she was free of the land, and she dipped into the gorge. She forced more power into her purpose creating an updraft that pushed her higher.

She was little more than halfway across the chasm when she felt her power begin to wane. Azeria was certain she could make it with a little help from the natural currents that sped down the gorge. She wrestled those currents into her cloak causing her to once again sail upward, but just as she was nearing the rim, her power was finally spent. The wind that was already in her sail carried her as far as the edge, but her feet did not make it to land. She dropped quickly as she arched forward reaching for the ledge. Her fingers brushed the rocky surface but failed to find purchase. Before she could fall much further, though, she caught herself on a tree root that twisted through a craig in the rock out into the open expanse of the gorge.

Breathing heavily, Azeria clenched her muscles against the mighty claws of gravity. Her heart raced, not just from the effort but also from her near miss with a painful death—a death she was not quite free from yet. Her energy spent, it took Azeria's entire will to pull herself to safety. One handspan at a time, she managed to scale the cliff using the tree roots and divots in the rockface. When she finally reached the top, she allowed herself to fall back onto the rocks and detritus. She stared through the tree boughs at the blue sky above and thanked

Rheina, Goddess of the Firmament, that she had made it across the gorge. Azeria did not lay there for long, though. She had to catch up with the merchant who had her horse and supplies.

She sped over and around the hills on swift feet until she reached the road. Once there, however, she was not sure which way to go. She did not know if the merchant had already passed. She decided to continue east on the roadway in case the merchant had already traversed that section of road. That way he would not be getting further ahead, and if he was still behind her, he would eventually catch up to her.

Azeria had not yet found the merchant by nightfall, so she pressed onward. It was about an hour after dark that she came upon a campsite. The scent of burning wood and roasting meat wafted through the air causing her stomach to rumble. She could see by the firelight that a wagon and a couple of horses occupied the site as well as a single man sitting near the blaze. Azeria was relieved as she approached to find the merchant engrossed in his meal.

"Greetings to the merchant," she said as she entered the ring of light cast by the fire.

The merchant jerked nearly spilling the contents of his mug. "Oh! Good lady, you have found your way to me after all. I admit, I did not think you would. You must be very clever indeed to have gotten past the guards. Tell me how you did it."

"You will have to excuse me," she said, attempting to sound cordial, "for I do not wish to give away my secrets."

"I cannot blame you there," replied the merchant. "There are many who would pay handsomely for such knowledge."

Azeria said, "Indeed. I shall take my horse and go."

"Nonsense! You must join me. It is late and I already have this fire and a meal prepared. There is no reason for you to go off into the dark alone. I see you carry a sword and a bow—unusual, I might say—but even so it is not safe for a lady out here."

"You believe I am safer with *you*?" she replied.

The merchant whipped a knife out and sent it sailing across the open space into a tree. Azeria was somewhat impressed. For a human, he was fast.

He said, "I have my ways. Besides, you do not speak the language of Channería. You will need someone to speak for you if you are to get anywhere in this kingdom."

"I was under the impression that most people in Channería spoke Ashaiian as well."

"Yes, that's true, but it is not safe to be heard speaking only Ashaiian right now, is it?"

Azeria had to admit the merchant had a point. She said, "Where are you going?"

"I am going wherever *you* are going, my lady."

She narrowed her eyes at him. "Why would you do that?"

He said, "You are quite comely, and I admit that I hope to gain your favor."

Azeria had been trying to be polite, but she had to nip this in the bud quickly. "You will fail. I am not interested in pursuing a relationship with you."

The merchant nodded knowingly. "I had a feeling you would say such a thing, but I am not deterred. I would still travel with you wherever you need go, dear lady."

"What is your name?" she said.

"Ah, my apologies. I failed to introduce myself. My name is Gavain Claud, but please just call me Gavain. And would you bless me with your sweet name, my lady?"

Azeria inwardly groaned, but outwardly she was stoic as ever. "I am Azeria."

"It is fitting. A beautiful name for a beautiful woman." After a moment, he said, "It is dark and warm this night. Tell me, why do you cover your fine features with your hood?"

Azeria was wondering to herself why she had not yet left the man. What he had said about the language problem made sense, though. And she would probably draw less attention if she were traveling with a merchant than she did as a lone, well-armed woman. She said, "I prefer it."

"Ah, perhaps the lady is shy," he said, seemingly to himself, but his gaze dropped to her sword, and he looked as if he did not believe his own words. He looked back up to her with a broad grin. "Come, sit. Have some food. It is fresh and hot. I have used many costly spices. You will like it."

Azeria did sit. And she ate. She ate enough to help replenish the stores of energy she had exerted crossing the gorge. A good night's rest would also go a long way in restoring her, but she was hesitant about sleeping too deeply with a stranger in her midst. Ultimately, she did not have a choice, though. As soon as she lay down using her pack as a pillow, she was sound asleep. The chains of sleep wrapped tightly around her, refusing to release her even as she dreamt of the one she had lost before she had even fully known him.

. . .

He was crouched beside a dark stream, turned inky in the night. The moonlight draped his perfect form so that every muscle glowed with unmatched strength, defined by the darker valleys between them. He washed away the blood that painted his hands and forearms, leaving behind only clean, unmarred skin. His head snapped up as his predatory gaze caressed the dark wood around him.

The hairs on the back of Azeria's neck stood on end as he peered through the crisp, star-studded night looking for something. *His gaze suddenly latched on to hers, and her breath abandoned her. A look of surprise stole across his face. And then he said one word.*

Azeria.

Azeria awoke with a start, her anguish nearly overwhelming her. She had dreamt of *him* again. When first she had dreamt of him more than a year ago, she had been confused by the dreams. What strangeness it was to dream of a man she had never met—and a human one at that. Once she had finally found him, she had been thrown and embarrassed by the dreams. Now that he was dead, though, she knew the dreams to be a curse. For how long would these dreams of a dead man persist? She all at once wanted to fall into them never to escape and run from them until she had once again found her sanity.

Azeria wiped the moisture from her lashes and sat up to find a mug of tea and a plate of last night's dinner sitting beside her. She quickly tugged at her hood ensuring that it was still in place. She hoped it had not slipped in the night. Gavain had already doused the fire and was loading his wagon when he looked over and gave her a bright grin. He did not appear to be acting any differently, so she was reasonably sure he had not seen her ears.

She checked her boots for snakes and other uninvited guests then pulled them onto her feet. She quickly scarfed down the food and the tea then stood. She carried the mug and plate over to Gavain then stepped into the trees to relieve herself before rejoining him.

"You must have slept well," he said. "You did not wake even when I made too much noise while heating the food this morning.

"I slept a little *too* well," she muttered.

His smile lost a little of its brightness, "Even so, you do not seem rested."

Gavain was observant, she thought. She said, "I had a bad dream." Even as she said it, though, she knew it was not true. It had been a *good* dream, but it had incited many *bad* feelings.

"Then let us hope the mood does not linger long this morning. You should be in better spirits soon, I think," said Gavain.

Azeria was not sure she *wanted* her mood to lighten, though. Now that she was feeling it, somehow her misery made her feel closer to him, to Rezkin. It was as though mourning him made him more real. Rationally, she knew that he was no more real today than he was in her dream, but her heart did not believe it.

10

Tieran tipped his head back as the sun shined down on his face. The sea breeze tousled the few strands of hair that had come loose from his plait, and the morning's heat seeped into his muscles relaxing them just a bit. The next sound caused his shoulders to tense, tightening his muscles once again.

"Tieran!" snapped Frisha as she mounted the last few steps up the wall.

Tieran clenched his teeth as he turned to greet her. "Hello, my dear. How are you this morning?"

She stopped before him with crossed arms and an angry scowl. "Where have you been?"

Tieran swallowed down his sharp retort and instead said, "I did not see you at breakfast this morning, so I was forced to dine without you. Then I came out here to get some sun."

She narrowed her eyes at him. "Have you forgotten you are supposed to tell me where you are at all times?"

No, he had not forgotten. In fact, he had hoped she would not find him for some time. Tieran's gaze strayed to Lus, who was hovering at the top of the steps. Despite the fact that Rezkin was dead and gone, the guard continued to watch Frisha night and day. Although after all this time, they had developed a decent rapport, Tieran still did not feel comfortable speaking his mind in front of the guard. It was a strange feeling considering Tieran had always spoken his mind no matter who was listening, but something about Lus put him on guard.

Tieran's gaze flicked back to Frisha, "How could I tell you where I am going if I do not know where you are? Where were *you* this morning?"

Frisha huffed, "That is of no consequence. What is the latest news? Have the strikers returned? Are the other kingdoms prepared for an attack?"

Tieran gripped his fists behind his back as he stared at her. It was always the same with her nowadays. She thirsted for information but gave nothing in return. Tieran said, "The strikers have not yet returned, but I did get a message from Farson on the relay. Regent Coledon is preparing the Ferélli Navy for just such an event, and Yserria and Malcius have left for Lon Lerésh."

"*How* is Coledon preparing the navy? What are they doing?" she said.

"I do not know, Frisha. Farson did not give me that information over the relay. Why do you care so much, anyway?"

Frisha huffed, "Details are important, Tieran."

"For the strikers and the generals, yes, but why do *you* care?"

She lifted her chin, her jaw set stubbornly. "I like to stay informed. You will tell me when you have more information."

It was not a question. It was a command, and Tieran did not care for it. Frisha's behavior over the past six months had been hostile and confusing, but most recently, she had been engrossed in every detail of the workings of the war for which they were preparing. She insisted on being present during every planning and strategy meeting, and she wanted to know about every decision being made. At first, Tieran had thought she was trying to allay her fears over the war by acquiring as much information as she could, but lately it seemed to be more than that. Something was not right, but he could not figure out what it was.

There was no way he could find out from *her*, either. She barely spoke to him except to get information. She had not mentioned their betrothal even once in the past six months, and she spent much of her time flirting with every man on the island *but* him. For a time, he had excused her odd behavior due to her remorse over the loss of Rezkin, but Tieran's ego could only take so much abuse before he cracked. Frisha was no longer the woman he had fallen for, and it did not seem as if the one he wanted would return. Tieran was nearly at the conclusion that their betrothal was at an end.

Frisha finished tying the worn shoes and stepped from the shade of the wagon to rejoin Thresson.

"How is this?" she said, as she tugged at the ill-fitting dress.

"It looks good enough," said Thresson. "You will not stand out now."

"At least it's clean," she added.

Frisha was thankful for the change of clothes even if their source was a bit dubious. For the past few weeks, they had traveled, like many of the inhabitants of the Channerían north, on foot heading south. It was their fortune that they had happened upon this wagon that appeared abandoned. The contents had been riffled through, presumably by someone looking for valuables, but no one had bothered with the clothes. Frisha hated to think of what might have happened to the wagon's owners, but she was pretty sure she knew. It was common for thieves to set upon unwary travelers. It disgusted her that people could be so cruel as to steal from those who were already suffering.

Thus far, they had been lucky not to have been assailed by bandits or caught by the patrols. But it seemed no one paid them much heed when Jerean troops were attacking in number. Thresson's Channerían had been better than passable. It had been good enough to satisfy the few people with whom he had spoken so that no one suspected them of being a couple of Ashaiian refugees.

Frisha was pulled from her thoughts when she looked down to find an orange tabby cat rubbing against her legs. The cat had been curled up in the clothes in the wagon when they arrived, and now he thought she belonged to him. She huffed and looked at Thresson.

"Why does everyone have a cat in this country?"

It was true. More than half the travelers they had seen on the roads had been carrying cats. Apparently, this one had belonged to the owners of the wagon.

Thresson said, "Cats are almost sacred in Channería. There are laws against harming them, and social standards practically *require* one to own at least one cat."

"But why?"

"It all goes back to a time of famine. A prolonged drought caused poor crop yield for several years in a row. Then the kingdom became overrun with rats that were eating all the food stores and spreading disease. Channería lacks life mages who could control such a problem. In response, the king began encouraging the breeding and keeping of cats to address the rodent epidemic. Over time, it became a part of Channerían culture."

"I guess it makes sense now how Rezkin ended up with a cat," she mused.

Thresson looked at her in surprise as they began walking again. "My brother had a cat?"

She held up a finger. "*Has* a cat. He's not dead, you know."

"Caydean said—"

"I know what Caydean said. He's lying. Rezkin simply can't die."

"Everyone can and will die, Frisha."

"You've never seen Rezkin fight. There isn't an opponent good enough or fast enough to best him—except perhaps the Eihelvanan."

"Those are the elves of whom you spoke?"

"Yes, they're inhumanly fast. Ever since Rezkin started training with them, his speed has increased as well. Plus, they have magic and not the kind wielded by human mages. Rezkin has their kind of power. I don't really understand the difference, but I know Rezkin can do things the human mages thought to be impossible."

"Like what?"

"Well, for one, he can walk through wards. It doesn't seem to matter how strong they are. They just don't affect him. And some magical attacks just sort of slip right off him without having any effect. And he can use the crystals."

"The crystals?"

"The citadel is full of these crystals that hold power and spells or enchantments. The human mages can use some of them, but not all, and they can't power them. But Rezkin can."

She glanced over to see Thresson's face turned downward with a furrowed brow. If she had to describe his countenance, she thought he looked despondent.

"What's wrong?" she asked.

Thresson released a shaky breath, "I am sorrowful that I never met him. Rezkin, I mean. I do hope he truly lives, as you believe. He sounds like a fascinating person."

"Oh, he definitely is that, but he has a dark side, too."

"Oh? Is he like Caydean, then?"

"No, nothing like Caydean. But he has killed *a lot* of people."

"That is disturbing. Is that why you broke your betrothal?"

Frisha did not answer right away. Her thoughts were tumultuous around the issue of her betrothal to Rezkin, and it was difficult to sort them out. Finally, she said, "Yes, when I found out who he really was, it scared me. I was disgusted by the things he had done, by the way he so easily and carelessly ended people's lives. But now, I don't believe he was being careless. Now that I have been placed in such a situation, now that I have killed, I understand how it is sometimes necessary. And I understand not feeling bad about it. Those men I killed—I don't feel guilt or remorse over their deaths. I did what I had to do to survive, and I won't apologize for that."

"Do you regret it then? Ending your betrothal?"

Frisha did not have to think about it. She knew the answer right away. "No, not at all. Even if I understand Rezkin a little better now, one truth still remains. He doesn't love me."

"Are you so sure?"

"Yes, I know it for certain. Rezkin doesn't feel things the way other people do. At least, if he does, he buries his feelings so deep they might as well not exist. I don't know why he thought to marry me in the first place, but I do know it wasn't for love."

Thresson said, "Most marriages among the nobles are not based on love, but I had always hoped to find someone to whom I could give my heart. I suppose I have always been a hopeless romantic."

"Not hopeless," said Frisha. "You will find someone worthy of your love. If anyone deserves to, it's you."

"Thank you for saying so, but life does not always give us what we deserve. Look at Caydean. Despite his cruelty and sadism, he sits upon the throne of the greatest kingdom on the Souelian."

"We will defeat Caydean. Rezkin will find a way."

After that, they both fell into thoughtful silence for a long while. The trek was long to the next village, but thanks to the few supplies they had found in the abandoned wagon, they at least had something to trade for food and shelter—assuming they could find any. The towns and villages along the route thus far were practically overrun with refugees from the north. For the past few days, though, they had seen significantly fewer people on the road. It seemed most of the refugees were not interested in going so far south.

There was no shelter to be had in the village of Rendow, however. Frisha and Thresson passed through the village, only stopping to trade for a few meager supplies. They were several hours outside the village when darkness began to set in. It was just after they had rounded a bend in the road when the attack came, swiftly and without warning.

Thresson drew the sword he had acquired from one of Caydean's men, and Frisha palmed a large knife. She yelped as a man grabbed her hair. She swung the knife to slice across his forearm. The man roared and pushed her to the ground before attempting to stomp on her. She rolled away from the man's heavy boot. She lashed out with her knife catching her assailant's calf. The bandit faltered, and Frisha was able to regain her feet. She caught a glimpse of Thresson fending off three attackers at once. A fourth man stood off to the side laughing at the other men's troubles.

Frisha held her knife in front of her at the ready while keeping both men in her sights as Rezkin had taught her. Her assailant growled low then charged at her like a bull. Frisha's eyes widened as he neared. She leapt out of the way while swinging her knife out to score across the man's back. The laughing man jeered from his place beside the road. Frisha was grateful he had not come for her as well. Her assailant seemed to be thinking along the same lines because he barked something in Channerían at the other man who he called Peebs.

The man named Peebs continued to taunt Frisha's assailant by the sound of it.

Her assailant said something back to Peebs. He was obviously unhappy with the laughing man. Frisha took advantage of the distraction to put some distance between her and her assailant. She glanced over to Thresson and found that he had felled one of his opponents but not without incident. He was bleeding heavily from a shoulder wound. Frisha worried that he might be flagging. She did not have time to watch further as her own assailant came at her again. Just as he got within striking distance, he suddenly jerked back with wide eyes. The assailant collapsed with a quarrel sticking from his chest. The laughing man's taunts abruptly halted, and he fell to the ground as well.

Frisha shook herself from her stupor to search for the source of the crossbow bolts. A stranger jumped into battle with one of Thresson's opponents. She could not see him well in the waning light, but he was tall and broad of shoulder. Thresson and the stranger both wielded their swords with enough skill to hold off the bandits. The one battling the stranger pushed him back. The stranger fell into Thresson's opponent. Thresson's opponent lurched forward straight onto Thresson's sword. The stranger narrowly missed getting impaled as well. The stranger recovered and managed to distract the final bandit. Thresson swept in from the side to sink his sword into the bandit's torso. Thresson and the stranger said nothing at first as they both stood breathing heavily. Eventually, Thresson cleared his throat and said something in Channerían to the stranger. The stranger said something back, and the two exchanged handshakes.

Frisha wanted to run up and thank the stranger for saving their lives, but she could not speak Channerían, and she could not give away the fact that they were Ashaiian. She wished she had not protested when her father had wanted her to learn another language, but she had been a stubborn girl who thought she would never leave Ashai. She recognized, now, that she had been spoiled in the comfort and shelter of her family home.

Thresson turned from the stranger and quickly came over to check on Frisha. Upon seeing that she was okay, he pulled her in for an embrace then quickly put some distance between them. The stranger came over and said something to her, but of course she could not respond. Thresson said something in her stead, and the stranger looked at her quizzically. It was as if a light suddenly shone from his eyes in the dark, and he spoke in Ashaiian with a thick Channerían accent, "You are Ashaiian?"

Frisha's eyes widened, and she looked at Thresson in alarm. "You told him?"

Thresson released a heavy sigh and shook his head. "No, you just did."

Frisha's cheeks heated as she realized her mistake. She looked at the stranger imploringly and begged, "Please don't turn us in. We're just trying to get to Cael."

The stranger said, "This is not a worry for you. I have no intention of turning you over to the authorities. You are safe with me."

Somehow, the man's assurances did not allay her fears. Still, she said, "Thank you for saving us. I couldn't have held off that bandit for much longer, and I'm pretty sure Thresson was about to be overpowered." She jumped as she remembered Thresson's wounds. She turned to him, "You're hurt. We need to see to that right away."

"I am not sure there is much to be done," said Thresson. "It is a deep cut, and we have no needle and thread or bandages."

The stranger spoke cheerily as he said, "This is no problem. I have these things for you to use. Allow me a moment to retrieve my mount."

As the stranger moved away, Frisha encouraged Thresson to sit up against a tree by the roadside. She retrieved the waterskin they had traded for at the last village from the road where he had dropped their pack. After helping him to remove his tunic, she poured a bit of water over the wound. It was not a long cut, but it was deep and would need stitches.

The stranger returned with his horse in tow. A calico cat was perched on the horse's rump. Frisha would have thought it strange except for the fact that they were in Channería and practically everyone was traveling with a cat. The stranger riffled through his own pack before producing the supplies they would need. He bent to hand them to Frisha, but she looked at them uneasily. "Um, my sewing skills are not great, and I have never stitched flesh before …"

The stranger pulled back with a low chuckle. He said, "This is no problem. I can do this for you if you wish, but it will not be pretty. There is little light to see by."

Frisha found herself smiling up at the stranger. Everything seemed to be *no problem* for the man who had done nothing but help them since they met. She stood aside to allow the stranger access to Thresson. As the man got to work, she said, "What is your name?"

"My name is Urvuay. I am pleased to meet you."

"Likewise," she said as she introduced herself and Thresson.

Upon hearing Thresson's name, Urvuay gave him a long, lingering look that made Frisha uncomfortable, although Thresson did not seem to notice as he was grimacing in pain from the stitching. After a moment, Urvuay shook himself free of whatever had captured his thoughts. "I am going to Serret. You are going to Cael. We may travel together—for safety, yes?"

Thresson grunted. "We would be happy to have you with us Urvuay, although we do not have horses. We will slow you down."

Urvuay chuckled, "This is no problem. I am in need of exercise. The lady may ride my horse, and I will walk with you, if this pleases you."

"That's very kind of you," said Frisha. She was skeptical, though. She was no longer the naïve girl who took people's words at face value. Urvuay seemed a little *too* good, and she was not sure she trusted a man who went to such lengths to help complete strangers. She had already been down that route, and she was not eager to do it again. She and Thresson were in dire need of assistance, though, and so far, Urvuay had given her no reason to suspect ulterior motives.

They were not long on the road when Frisha decided to learn a little more about their savior. She said, "Tell us a little about yourself, Urvuay. Where are you from? What is your profession?"

"Ah, I am not so interesting. I am from the city of Penniston in the north. I am a master stone mason. I designed the fortifications for the city."

"Oh?" said Thresson. "What brought you down here?"

"Penniston looks like a rich city. The nobles live lavishly while the city's coffers run dry. Once they had my designs, they released me from service and handed the job off to a lesser mason."

"That's awful," said Frisha.

"I came south looking for work just as Jerea began their invasion. Reconstruction of the city's defenses had only just begun. I am certain it was overrun."

Frisha said, "Then you were lucky to have been let go."

"Yes, my shame became my great fortune."

The journey was long and uneventful after that. Frisha did not end up riding the whole way. She had insisted they take turns riding with the cat, and since Thresson was injured, she had told him to go first. Urvuay helped them hunt for their meals, they slept out in the open a short distance from the road, and they bathed in the streams they passed. It was a rough journey, but it was manageable. By the time they reached Serret, they were completely spent. Urvuay rode ahead to secure his lodging, and Frisha was certain they had seen the last of him. A few hours later, though, he met them on the road again and informed them that they would be staying with him while in the city.

Thresson said, "That is very kind of you, Urvuay, but you need not go to so much trouble for us."

Urvuay's broad grin was full of good humor as he said, "Ah, but what choice do I have? I should let you sleep in the streets?"

Frisha shared an anxious glance with Thresson, who turned back to Urvuay, "Thank you, Master Urvuay, for your kind hospitality. We are in your debt."

"Bah, it is no problem."

Frisha's heart lurched as every ruthless scenario flitted through her mind. Would Urvuay finally turn them in to the city guard? Would they be captured and sold to the highest bidder? She was so engrossed in her terrible musings that she nearly missed what Thresson said next.

"What are your plans now that you have reached Serret?"

"Ah, I am unsure," replied Urvuay. "I had thought to find work as a mason, but I fear I will be conscripted into the army to fight in the north."

"You do not want to fight in the war?"

Urvuay's face screwed up in distaste. "It is a pointless war instigated by a petty princeling whose self-importance was crushed when he could not marry the king's daughter. Why would I wish to sacrifice my life for that?"

"You could still find work as a mason," said Thresson. "Just not in Serret."

"Where then?" asked Urvuay.

"In Cael."

Frisha was not surprised that Thresson would suggest it, but she was surprised that Urvuay would consider it. He was not a refugee and had no reason to give up a good living in his own kingdom for the kinds of hardships that came with securing a new kingdom.

Urvuay looked thoughtful for a moment. "I am Channerían, not Ashaiian. Do you think I will be welcomed in this new empire? There are already so many refugees."

Frisha said, "There is room for one more. You are a good fighter, and you are kind and respectful. You are exactly the kind of person we want in our empire."

Urvuay was quiet for a few minutes while they walked. Eventually, he straightened and nodded once. "I wish to see this new kingdom. I think there may be opportunity there that is not available to me here. Besides, I do not enjoy the unrest here in Channería. Between the Jereans to the north and the Fishers here in the south, there is too much turmoil."

"Then you do not agree with the Fishers?" said Thresson.

Urvuay shook his head. "Oh, I agree with them. There is too much corruption in this kingdom. But I do not wish to be swallowed by the war that is to come."

Thresson said, "From what I have heard, the entire Souelian is on the precipice of war. I doubt you will find a kingdom *not* involved in the fighting in one form or another."

"That is true," replied Urvuay, "but I believe in Cael I will be on the winning side. I put my faith in this new emperor."

"Then have you not heard that he is dead?" said Thresson.

"Bah, I do not believe it. These are lies spread by his enemies to make us lose hope."

Suddenly, Frisha liked Urvuay a lot more. Somehow hearing someone else echo her own thoughts made her feel as though they were actually true. She resolved to put a bit more trust into the man while still holding on to a decent amount of doubt. She was determined not to repeat the mistakes of the past.

11

FOR WEEKS they had ridden together, and Azeria was grateful for the company despite the fact that Gavain was human. His conversation had broken up some of the monotony of travel. It turned out that Gavain was well-traveled throughout Channería, Ashai, and the Eastern Mountains. He had even made a few jaunts into Gendishen and Jerea, although he was not enthusiastic about such journeys. When she asked why he did not travel with guards or a companion, he simply said he enjoyed the freedom that came with being a lone traveler. He did not ask many questions of her, thank goodness, and neither did he press her to reveal herself to him. He seemed content to allow her privacy in exchange for her company. And when they were intercepted by a patrol once along the way, Gavain did the talking and smoothed things over well enough that the patrol let them pass without trouble.

They rode into a small town Gavain called Londgrad around midday. From what she had been told, the town was about a week's ride from her destination, the city of Serret. The town was not an attractive place. The squat buildings were drab and unadorned, and the people seemed less than friendly. As they rode down the main path through town, they endured the suspicious stares of the wary townsfolk. Gavain pulled his wagon to the front of a place he called a *general store*, which was apparently where the people of the town did their trading. On the porch, a couple of older men were seated on either side of a small table set up with some kind of game. The two men eyed Azeria and Gavain with dour expressions.

"*Brach nih!*" said Gavain as he jumped down from his wagon and crossed the short distance to the porch. Then he rattled something off in Channerían that Azeria did not understand. The two men stared at Gavain and made no attempt at a greeting. Gavain cleared his throat and said something else. One of the men spit off to the side and grumbled a reply that sounded like a question. Gavain grinned broadly and gesticulated wildly as he spoke at length. Finally, the old man who had spoken rose to his feet and headed toward the wagon. As Gavain peddled his wares, Azeria's gaze traversed their surroundings. People hurried to and from buildings, and no one seemed interested in approaching them.

It was strange to Azeria to be so surrounded by people yet feel so distanced, even undesired. In her homeland, people were always flocking around newcomers with joy and friendship. Although she admitted that Rezkin and Mage Nanessy Threll had not received such a welcome upon entering Freth Adwyn. Her people had been curious but cautious, and it was only due to Entris's great compassion and sense of responsibility that Rezkin had not been marched through town bound as their prisoner. A great sense of sadness enveloped her as she thought of that time. She had remained aloof and even frigid toward Rezkin. She had told herself it was because he was a human Spiré-tua, destined for madness, but truly she had been overwhelmed by the feelings that surged inside her when he was around. She had finally made contact with the man from her dreams, and she had not known what to do with it. She regretted such coldness now.

She shook herself free of her morose feelings. Regret was a pointless emotion. Those events were in the past, and nothing could change that. She could not even vow to do better in the future because Rezkin was dead. He was gone from this world, gone from *her.* The best she could do now was to find the one responsible for stealing his body—the Raven. But what would she do with the Raven when she found him? She was not certain. She really just wanted information, and, if possible, Rezkin's body returned.

Gavain concluded his business and returned to his wagon. He leaned over to speak to her quietly in Ashaiian. "Come, let us get a good meal. I know where a decent tavern is."

Azeria nodded and together they rode toward the other side of town before stopping outside an unimpressive building with a sign depicting a spoon. The fare was edible but could hardly have been called good. Gavain occupied himself with chatting with the other customers while Azeria sat wrapped up in her thoughts. And inevitably, those thoughts kept returning to Rezkin. She had had a connection to him, a bond of the soul, and even his death had not set her free.

Once they were finished with the meal, Gavain spoke quietly with her as they returned to the wagon. "I'm afraid we will not be able to stay here for the night. The inn burnt down a few months ago. We will have to camp outside of town. I know of a place we can stay. It's an old mill long abandoned." He glanced at the darkening sky, "It will keep us out of the rain at least."

Azeria mounted her horse and followed the wagon out of town. The mill Gavain spoke of was not far. Unsurprisingly, it consisted of a windmill, a long building, probably used for storage and processing of grain, and a barn. But none of that seemed important when faced with what they found *outside*. Bodies. Several decaying and picked over corpses were lined up outside in the yard. Scavengers had feasted on them, and it was difficult to tell how many there had been, but it was obvious they had been human.

Gavain said, "These look to have been here a few weeks. We should check inside."

Azeria nodded and gripped her hilt as she stepped through the open doorway. Just inside the door was a table and chairs beside a hearth still filled with char and ash. Dark stains covered the table and floor, but it was the mark on the wall that captured her attention. There, painted in the rusty reddish brown of dried blood, was the symbol of the Raven.

Gavain jerked back, and Azeria tensed as he grabbed her arm. He tugged her toward the doorway with a firm jerk. His voice was full of urgency, "Come. We must go from this place. The Raven has been here, and he could return. We do not wish to be anywhere the Raven might be."

Azeria shook her head. "I do not believe the Raven will return. These people are all dead, and there is nothing of value here. He has no reason to come here."

"Even so, I would not risk it."

Gavain might have been discomfited, but Azeria was thrilled. She thanked the gods for their divine intervention as she was still on the right path. Somehow, though, the Raven had gotten further ahead of her. Where she had only been a week behind him before, now she was two or three weeks behind, based on the state of the bodies in the yard.

She followed Gavain back into the yard and around the building. Gavain stared at the darkening sky for a long time, then glanced again at the bodies. His shoulders slumped, and he finally suggested they sleep in the barn that night since it appeared the sky was about to open on them. Azeria did not care for the proximity to the bodies, and if she had been alone, she might have opened a portal to almost anywhere else. Gavain had been a help on her journey, though, and she was not yet ready to abandon him.

Another week passed before they reached Serret, and in that time they were subjected to the deluge several times. It was a miserable trek but unavoidable. The city was a strange one with its many districts separated by guarded gates. The check points prevented the fluid flow of foot traffic and wagons such that each one became clogged with irritable and short-tempered humans. Despite her frustration at the delays, Azeria was thankful for the traffic. Each time she went through a gate, she was forced to use her amulet to appear human. The extended time spent between gates meant her amulet had time to recharge before she had to use it again.

They steadily made their way toward the merchant district where Gavain assured her he had contacts that could aid them in finding inexpensive lodging, for *her* anyway. Gavain did not want to leave his wagon for fear that someone would steal his goods. By the time night fell, Azeria had a warm bed in a private cellar room that had its own egress into the alley above. The landlady was a quiet woman who kept to herself and did not ask too many questions. Although Azeria was worn from the journey, she did not want to waste any time. The Raven could be in the city at that very moment, and she did not wish to miss him again.

Azeria left her pack in the cellar, electing only to take a small sack containing the box that had been entrusted to her as she skulked about the city. She ascended the steps to the street level where she remained hidden in the shadows of alleys and overhangs as much as possible. The nearly full moon cast its silver glow upon the streets, illuminating the path she needed to find her way. She started in the merchant district and worked her way south toward the docks. Many of the gates separating the districts were locked and guarded, but that did not deter her. Azeria approached an unmanned part of the wall and used her power over wind to lift her over top of it. Thanks to the moonlight, she was exposed during that time, so she cast her power a second time to cause a cloud of darkness to surround her. Anyone looking her way would merely see a dark smudge that they would likely excuse for a trick of the eye.

She entered a part of the city where stood residences of the less fortunate. The homes were small and tightly packed together. The windows had no glass panes, and many of the shutters hung askew or were broken. Laundry hung from lines stretched between the buildings where there was space, and no greenery was to be seen. Azeria stuck to the shadows as she traversed the streets until she found the public fountain at the district's center. From there, she had only to follow the directions given to her by Guildmaster Attica. Azeria paused as she approached an unmarked door that looked pretty much like every other door on the row of houses. She was sure she had counted correctly, but there was no way to know for sure that she was in the right place until she knocked. She raised her hand to do just that when the door suddenly lurched open and someone came barreling out of it.

Azeria leapt to the side barely avoiding a collision with the dark figure. She reached for her sword but paused when she took in the person's form and stature, which she could now see in the light of the moon. A young man who could not be called an adult even by human standards jumped back from her with a yelp. He said, "Pardon me," then turned and took off into the night. Azeria watched the young man go before turning back toward the door. There stood a man who was slightly taller than she was. He squinted at her, obviously trying to make her out in the dark of the night.

The man growled something at her in a gruff voice that made her want to clear her own throat, but Azeria did not understand the language.

She said, "I have a delivery for you."

"And who might you be?" he said, switching to Ashaiian.

Azeria peered at him from beneath her hood. After a beat, she said, "I was sent to deliver something."

"Sent? Sent by who?"

"Guildmaster Attica in Kaibain."

"I don't know no guildmaster," came the gruff response. The door started to swing closed, but Azeria's arm darted out to stall it.

"Wait," she said. "The roses are pretty this time of year."

The man sucked in a breath. "They only bloom after a rain."

Azeria withdrew her arm when she was certain the door was not going to close. The man grumbled something under his breath then stepped out of the way, beckoning her to enter. The narrow hallway beyond the threshold was dark, as were the rooms to either side, but she could see the warm, golden light of a fire at the end of the corridor. The man slid by her and said, "Come."

Azeria followed him into the lit room, which happened to be a kitchen. A small table occupied what little open space there was, and a woman was seated there doing some mending. Her hair was dark and tied into a loose bun from which several stray strands hung loose. Her feminine curves were draped in a dark brown dress and white apron. The woman's cheeks were round as she grinned at Azeria.

"Good evening," said the woman. "Did I hear that you have something for us?"

Azeria set the small sack on the table with a *thunk* but kept hold of it. "You have good ears—" She stopped before she said the rest of her thought, *for a human.*

The woman hummed happily as she placed a careful stitch. Without looking up from her work, she said, "I have had years of practice just *listening*. You would be surprised what people will say when they think no one can hear them."

Azeria was *not* surprised. Most humans could not produce a sound ward to prevent anyone from overhearing them, so they had grown accustomed to speaking freely without such an assurance. She had heard many things in her time with the humans that she wished she had not.

The man, who was hovering nearby, said, "She doesn't need to know nothing about that." Then to Azeria he said, "Just hand it over and be gone with ya."

"Now, now, Herm. That's no way to speak to a lady," said the woman.

The man, apparently named Herm, said, "She doesn't need to know my name!"

"Oh, you worry too much," said the woman. She looked at Azeria, "My name is Maisey. It's nice to meet you."

"And you," said Azeria as she pulled the small box from the sack. She did not bother to offer her own name. These people did not need to know it, and she did not plan to stick around any longer than she had to. Herm reached for the box, and Azeria reached for her hilt. His eyes widened in surprise, and he drew his arm back. Azeria said, "I will give you the box *after* you have given me information."

Herm narrowed his eyes, "We aren't in the business of giving away information."

Maisey tsk-tsked and said, "Calm down, Herm. You haven't even asked her what she wants to know." The woman looked up from her mending and met Azeria's gaze. "Well, what *do* you want to know?"

Azeria said, "I seek the Raven. I would have any information you have on his whereabouts."

Herm let out a grunt. "No one *seeks* the Raven. Anyone with an ounce of sanity would do best to avoid ever meeting him."

"Well, I am looking for him. Has he been seen in this city?"

"Yes," Maisey drawled. "He made himself known to the guild last week. I couldn't say as to where he is now."

Azeria's tense shoulders relaxed. She still did not know where the Raven was, but at least she was only a week behind him again. She was about to hand over the box when Maisey spoke again.

"We can let him know you're looking for him. If he wants to see you, he'll find *you*."

"That will not be necessary," said Azeria.

Maisey smiled coyly. "Well, now, he'll be hearing about it anyway. If someone comes looking for him, that's something we need to report, you see. I'm sure you understand."

Anger sloshed around inside her, but Azeria did not allow these two to see it. Instead, she laid the box on the table and slid it toward the woman. She said, "Very well. Tell him that I require an audience. In two nights' time, I will meet him by the statue of the man on the horse in the merchant district."

"If you say so," said Maisey with a lift of her eyebrow.

Azeria turned and stalked out of the home without waiting for an escort. So far, the Raven had always stayed at least one step ahead of her, and she had no way of closing that distance. She was out of direction—at a dead end. Perhaps allowing him to come to her would be the best way after all—assuming he found her worthy of an audience, that is. If he hadn't known she was looking for him before, he certainly would now. Would he disappear altogether once he knew? Would he attempt to kill her? Or would he grant her the audience she sought? Only time would tell. Azeria would be prepared for every eventuality.

She did not return to her abode that night. Instead, she set an enchantment on the front door to alert her if it was opened then watched the house Herm and Maisey shared from the safety of the shadows across the street. Eventually, the light she could see through the front windows winked out, and Azeria made herself more comfortable beneath the eaves of the building. Then she entered *eskyeyela*, a form of meditation that allowed her to visualize the flow of vimara and hear its melody. The advantage to *eskyeyela* was that she would replenish her power, albeit more slowly than in sleep, and she would also be able to maintain some awareness of her surroundings.

It was just before dawn that Azeria's alarm drew her from her meditation. Herm exited the house and began striding down the street to her right. Azeria was about to follow when the alarm alerted her to the door opening once again. This time Maisey slipped through the doorway before turning to the left. Azeria glanced back at Herm who was now halfway to the next street then turned her attention back to Maisey. Although their interaction had been brief the previous night, it was clear to Azeria that Maisey was the one in charge, and Herm was the muscle. Azeria slipped from her hiding place to follow the woman at a close distance. She cast her power about herself to obscure her image. If Maisey did look back, her mind would not register Azeria's presence unless she knew exactly where to look. While the enchantment would not fool a Spirétua or possibly even a powerful mage, it was more than enough to keep her hidden from a mundane *human*.

The sun hid behind a swath of dark grey clouds as it rose above the horizon, and the air was heavy with heat and moisture that caused her tunic and breeches to cling to her skin. She much preferred the cool shade of her forest home or even the wafting sea breezes of Cael over these stifling conditions. She pushed her discomfort from her mind, though, as she kept pace with the woman, Maisey. They passed into the next district, and Azeria was able to get by the guards without using her amulet. This district was full of warehouses and other buildings used for processing goods. A slight breeze picked up, and Azeria could smell salt and fish upon it. As they moved past the warehouses, they came upon the docks and a large shipyard where the construction of not one but three warships was underway.

Maisey entered the shipyard and passed by the skeletal ships to approach a window that opened into an office. A man greeted her at the window, but Azeria could not hear what was said from where she was crouched behind a stack of lumber. She sent a trickle of power toward the two, allowing her desire to hear them to shape the power into the form she needed. Abruptly, their conversation became clear to her ears as if she were standing right there with them. Unfortunately, she still could not understand them since they were speaking Channerían.

Azeria cast her power upon her own mind and then sent it toward the woman. Once it had attached itself to the Maisey's mind, Azeria could hear every thought that flitted through the woman's mind. It was not a cast she would normally use. In fact, it was forbidden to use on a person without their permission, and it was not without risk. Linking with another's mind could have unintended consequences, so she would use the link sparingly. She filtered out the woman's errant thoughts and the fear that suffused her and focused on the conversation with the man at the window.

"I have a message for him," said Maisey.

"A message for who?" replied the man.

"For who? Who do you think?" Azeria watched as the woman leaned in and whispered, "The Raven."

The man laughed. "*You*? What message could *you* possibly have for *him*?"

"Shhh," hissed the woman. "Keep your voice down. This is important. He'll want to know about it."

The man sobered and leaned through the window to get closer to Maisey. "What message?"

"There's a woman looking for him."

"And?"

"And she wants to meet with him."

The man leaned back in surprise. "Why would she *want* to meet with him? That's suicide."

"I don't know, but she said she'll meet him by the old general's statue tomorrow night."

The man reached up to stroke his whiskered chin. "I don't know. It's strange, but I'm not sure this is newsworthy of *his* attention."

"Of course it is," snapped Maisey. "If anyone comes looking for him, he'll want to know about it."

"I doubt he'll meet with her."

"Maybe not. Maybe he'll just take off her head. But that's not for you or me to decide."

"I see your point," said the man. "Very well. I'll send the message, but there's no telling if he'll get it in time. He only checks in when he wants to."

"And we don't even know if he's still in Serret," said Maisey.

"He was as of last night. He made an appearance at one of the guildhouses. Apparently, he wasn't happy with the way things were going, so he made an example out of half a dozen men."

Even from where she was hidden, Azeria could see Maisey's face pale.

"Right then," said Maisey. "You have the message now. I wash my hands of this." She gave the man a firm nod then turned back the way she came.

Azeria let her go. She now had someone more important to follow—someone who knew how to contact the Raven. Only a few minutes later, the man shuttered the window and locked the door behind him as he left. Azeria followed the man back through the warehouse district, skirting a crowd gathered outside one of the buildings. They passed through two more districts, and Azeria was only forced to use her amulet once as she passed through the checkpoints. Luckily, she did not need any special documents to enter the adjacent districts, which confused her even more about the purpose of the checkpoints.

The shipyard worker she was following headed for a large circular building with a domed roof. The windows of the building were made of ornate stained glass, and there was gilding around the doorframe. Azeria followed the man into the large space beyond to find an open room with plentiful seating and a long counter separating the seating area from the device on the other side. Azeria recognized the device right away even though she had never seen one like it. It was a mage relay. She had seen the one designed by Rezkin on Cael, and it was similar but also different in many respects. For one, this relay was much larger than the one Rezkin built, and she did not think it was due to any extra functionality. As she peered past the counter to get a better look at it, she decided the one Rezkin built was simply more efficient at a smaller scale.

A pang of sorrow struck Azeria's center. She would not have admitted it while he was alive, but now that Rezkin was gone, she recognized how brilliant he had been. For someone raised as a human mundane, he had adapted to his power quickly. Of course, he had not come anywhere close to his true potential. If he had been, perhaps he would not have died, she thought. She regretted, now, opposing Entris's attempts to train Rezkin in the use of his power. At the time, she had thought only of the madness that would likely consume him should he begin using his power in earnest. She had not believed he could overcome the curse as he believed he would. In fact, she had encouraged Entris on several occasions to kill Rezkin and be done with it. Entris had seen through her, though. She had never truly wanted Rezkin dead. She had merely been scared by the connection they shared. Dreams of him had plagued her from even before they had met, and afterward, those dreams felt awkward and disconcerting. Now that he was dead, those dreams only reminded her of what she had lost—or what she had never truly had.

Azeria shook herself from her memories and musings as she returned her attention to the man she had followed. He was standing at the counter writing something on a small slip of paper. After he was finished, he waited his turn then handed the slip to the human mage who was operating the relay.

He said, "Bellingham."

The mage nodded and scrawled the name across the top of the paper before turning toward the relay. Once the message had been sent, the slip of paper was incinerated, and the man left the relay building. Azeria remained. A moment later, several of the runes of the relay lit up. The mage cast a few spells onto the device. Azeria watched the constructs carefully in case she needed to replicate them. Although the Eihelvanan did not use spells as the human mages did, they were still capable of doing so. The spell forms simply allowed human mages to control their power in a way that came naturally to the Eihelvanan. As such, Azeria did not know what the spells *did*, but she could recreate them.

The mage slipped a sheet of paper onto the flat pinnacle of the relay, and a new message began to appear there. When it was finished, the mage scrawled *Bellingham* on the edge of the paper then rolled it up, sealed it, and stuffed it into one of the many boxes that lined the wall behind the relay.

Azeria was confused at first. But after a few minutes of careful consideration, she thought she knew what had happened. The shipyard worker had sent a message to a Bellingham, and a minute later, the same message appeared on the relay *for* Bellingham. He had sent the message to the same relay so that it would be available for Bellingham when he came to collect it. It seemed a strange way to deliver a message, but humans were strange in many ways. One thing Azeria knew for certain was that Bellingham was the next man sought.

12

The sky was dark as Rezkin traversed the streets of Serret, despite the fact that sundown would not be for a few more hours. Seena scurried along beside him appearing very catlike to all but him. She had been cooped up in the satchel or hiding in the house he had commandeered, and she needed the exercise. He could not help the smile that spread across his own face as he watched her joyfully skip along the roadway dodging between passersby and stopping to sniff at every food stall they passed. One kindly old woman even gave her a nibble of fish, and Seena celebrated happily with a roll and a purr. The old woman laughed at Seena's antics and waved goodbye to her as they moved down the lane. The woman even had a coy wink for Rezkin, which he promptly returned causing her to blush and fan herself with her hand.

Rezkin, of course, did not appear as himself. He maintained the illusion of an old man with greying hair, a long white beard, and deep brown eyes. He walked briskly as he made his way toward the gate that led into the adjoining district. Once he and Seena had passed beyond the gate, it did not take long to reach his destination. The circular building with the domed roof stood by itself in the center of the square. He surveyed the surroundings before entering but found no spies watching.

The mage relay building was busy at this time of day, and people were lined up in a long queue waiting for their chance to send or receive a message. Just as Rezkin entered the line, he was suddenly struck with an alarming sight that made his heart nearly leap from his chest. There, standing against the wall not far from the counter, was a hooded woman. She was taller than most women, nearly as tall as he. She wore a soft grey tunic that went to mid-thigh and darker breeches as well as dark blue knee-high boots made of supple hide that laced up the front. The curved sword at her hip likewise marked her as unusual, and Rezkin would have noted her presence even if he had not immediately recognized her.

He was stunned. He could not move his eyes from her, and he completely lost track of his surroundings. When she turned her silver gaze on him, his will crumbled, and he nearly lost the illusion he was maintaining. In that moment, he was ready to give up his entire charade and go to her. When her gaze moved away from him and he could once again breathe, all his reasons for remaining dead in the eyes of the world crashed over him. Azeria and everyone else he knew were safer if Caydean thought he was dead. That and the freedom his death allotted him were enough to keep his feet from closing the distance between them.

Seena rubbed against his legs, shaking him from his thoughts, and he realized the line had moved ahead of him. As he moved up, he searched the grand space for anyone else he might recognize, hoping that Entris was not present. The Spirétua-lyé would be able to sense his use of power and see through his illusion. But Rezkin did not see Entris nor any of his other friends and associates. It seemed Azeria was there alone, which piqued his curiosity all the more.

What *was* she doing there? Was it pure coincidence that they happened to be in the same place at the same time, or was she looking for *him*? Perhaps she did not believe him truly dead after all. For some reason that thought pleased him. The more he thought about it, the more he realized he *wanted* her to know he was alive and well. But he could not yet reveal himself. If Azeria knew he was truly alive, she would feel obligated to tell Entris, and then Entris would insist on following him around again to watch for signs of madness. Rezkin still had many things to do that he would not be able to do with an entourage.

When Rezkin finally got to the front of the line, he spoke quietly, "*Are there any messages for Bellingham?*"

Azeria's gaze fell on him once again, and he suppressed a shiver. He had never reacted to anyone the way he reacted to Azeria. The fact that she could make him forget everything else with just her gaze made him want to retreat far from her, and yet the greater part of him desired her nearness. For a moment, he even wondered if she was using her power to muddle his thoughts, but he felt no vimara directed his way.

The relay operator handed Rezkin a message then called upon the next person in line. Ever cognizant of the steady gaze upon him, Rezkin stepped aside and quickly read the coded message. Azeria *was* looking for him. She just did not know it. For reasons he could not surmise, she was seeking the Raven, and she had even managed to find him. But, again, she did not know it.

Rezkin slipped the small missive into his pocket, then strode quickly toward the exit with Seena on his heels. It was not surprising when Azeria followed him from the building. Rezkin did not let on that he had noticed her, but when he turned a corner, he scooped Seena up and settled her in his satchel, then quickly changed his illusion to that of a much younger man wearing the livery of one of the noble houses. When Azeria rounded the corner, her gaze passed right over him. Despite her stoic demeanor, Rezkin noticed the moment she deflated having lost her quarry. Rezkin was again thankful that he had learned to cast illusions. Azeria was fast and cunning, and he did not think he could have evaded her otherwise.

With a pang of regret, Rezkin turned toward the docks. He had other things to take care of for now.

The following night, Rezkin slipped out of the window of his room so as not to disturb the home's other occupants. He wore a black tunic and pants beneath his newly acquired blackened armor. He left the black blade and Bladesunder in his quarters and chose instead to arm himself with the Sheyalin he had claimed from the felled Swordbearer. If he was to meet with Azeria, he would give her no cause to recognize him. He would use illusion to disguise himself to an extent, but he wanted all his power and focus available in case Azeria attacked. He could have ignored the summons altogether, but he found that he could not deny her. A part of him dearly wanted to speak with her, even if she did not know who he was.

Serret had no curfew, but Rezkin avoided the city patrols regardless. In fact, he tried to avoid as many people as possible. The fewer witnesses to his movements, the better. Rezkin slowed when he neared the statue of the long-deceased General Pickeny. Azeria stood in the moonlight beside the statue with a remarkable confidence that dared anyone to attempt to deter her. Rezkin searched the shadows around the intersection almost hoping to find more of his friends secluded there, but there were none.

When he was sure they were alone, Rezkin withdrew his crossbow. He notched the bolt he had prepared then took aim. He pulled the trigger, releasing the bolt at the same time he turned and dashed into the alley. He did not look back as he rushed through the streets. He had perhaps a minute or two for Azeria to read the note he had attached to the crossbow bolt before she would be after him. Luckily, he knew where he was going, whereas she would need to search for the location.

Rezkin made his way into the abandoned playhouse, checking his traps as he went. Then he ascended to the rafters to lie in wait. When the Eihelvanan lady finally appeared, she approached cautiously with her sword drawn. He could see the shimmer of a ward about her. He was glad to see her taking precautions. When she reached the stage, he called down to her using illusion to cast his face in shadow and to change his voice as he spoke. "You summoned me, my lady."

Azeria gave nothing of her thoughts away as she stared into the dark rafters. She said, "You are the Raven?"

The man in question tilted his head and tapped the hilt of his sword with impatience. The relief she felt for having finally found the elusive criminal overlord was palpable. She had not been sure about how he would receive her. She was taking a great chance in coming here. She did not like that he had taken control of the meeting place. She thought about attacking him with the force of her power but instead said, "I need to know why you stole his body."

With a grunt, he said, "There have been many bodies. You will have to be more specific." His voice was gruff and sent a shiver down her spine.

"Rezkin," she hissed as a sudden burst of anger surged through her. There was only one body of importance. How could he not know to whom she referred? "The Emperor of the Souelian. You stole his body from his tomb. Why?"

The Raven was silent for a moment. When he finally spoke, his voice grated against her nerves. "The emperor cannot die. He is yet needed."

She knew he was needed. Of course he was needed, but need did not negate death. She doubted the reasons *she* needed him and the reasons the Raven needed him were one and the same, though. "Needed for what? How does his death affect your criminal empire?"

"No, not that empire," said the Raven. "The Cimmerian Empire."

Azeria stiffened. "Why do you call it that?"

"That is its name, is it not?"

"No one calls it that but Rezkin. How do *you* know the name?"

"I know many things," he said cryptically.

"So you are perpetuating the myth that he lives in order to prevent the empire from falling?"

"One man's myth is another man's truth. Without a body, who is to say for certain whether he is dead or alive?"

Azeria grew suspicious. "I saw his body. I helped entomb him. I know he is dead."

"And yet I hear a question in your voice."

Azeria did not want to think too much about that question. Thinking about it gave her hope, and she knew that hope to be in vain. Choosing to ignore the comment, she said, "I want him back."

"Why?" He sounded genuinely curious, and Azeria was once again incensed.

"He deserves a proper burial."

"He had one," said the Raven. "I saw the tomb."

She felt her stoic visage crack for the first time. Her anguish overcame her. Her voice was barely above a whisper as she added, "You cannot keep him from me."

His voice softened, and he almost sounded sympathetic. "Rezkin will be returned to you in due time, Azeria."

Azeria did not move, but a cold lump formed in her stomach. "How do you know my name?"

"As I said, I know many things. You cannot hide from me. You need not cower beneath your hood."

Azeria was alarmed. How much did he know about her, and where had he gotten his information. Could it be that Rezkin told him? "Me, cower? You wear a hood as well. Why do you hide yourself?"

"I have many enemies."

About that Azeria had no doubt. She was not sure if she was among them. "You will return him? When?"

"When his present purpose is fulfilled."

"But he *is* dead, is he not?" Against her better judgment, hope filled her as she awaited his response.

He gave a deep bow then started to back away through the rafters. "I bid you adieu, my lady. But first, a warning. There is a spy in a position of influence in Cael—a woman."

"Who?"

He said nothing more, and Azeria acted on impulse. She shot a burst of wind into the rafters. The Raven was taken by surprise and fell from his lofty perch. He landed gracefully in a crouch facing her. "You will come with me as my prisoner," she said as she raised her sword.

The Raven drew his own sword as she advanced. She had no intention of killing the Raven, but she would not let him get away while she still had questions and Rezkin's body was still missing. She struck quickly so it was a surprise when he deflected her blade. Luck had been on his side. She knew no human could match her in speed. Her blade met steel on her next strike and again he was not deterred. She proceeded to issue a flurry of slashes and thrusts, each one causing him to retreat. Although he was backing away, and she could tell that he was pressed for speed, he was still meeting her strike for strike. He faltered, and she swept her sword at him from the right, drawing a line of blood from his arm as he dashed to the side toward the center stage. As she followed him, she wondered what enchantments he had about his person that would make him so unnaturally fast for a human. It was no matter. It was obvious he was being pressed to his limits to match her speed. He would tire long before she did, and then she would capture him and bring him to Cael. It was inevitable.

The Raven dodged and ducked and parried as her sword danced through the air. He suddenly dashed away from her, putting distance between them. He launched a throwing dagger, but not at her. It sailed past her. She heard a snap and then something dropped over her. As she struggled to free herself from the net, she heard a *thunk*, and then her feet were dropping out from under her. She tumbled down some steps and was suddenly enveloped in darkness beneath the stage. After a tense moment of yanking and twisting, she was finally free of the net. With her sword raised, she bounded back up the steps. Back on stage, she searched the shadows and recesses only to find that the Raven had disappeared.

Azeria's frustration was only surpassed by her sorrow. She had the Raven within her grasp, and yet he somehow had bested her. He could have taken the opportunity to kill her, but he had merely escaped. She had lost her only chance to retrieve Rezkin's body. She knew she would not get another. He had said he would return Rezkin's body, but the Raven was a criminal. There was no assurance that he was a man of his word. Devastation overtook her as the realization struck that she would never see Rezkin again. Finally, she saw her dreams of him for what they were—a blessing. She hoped they never ended.

Rezkin walked across the intersection quickly as he kept his senses honed for sounds of pursuit, but she did not follow him. Once he was around the corner, he switched his illusion to one of a rotund fellow who, having had too much to drink, swerved as he walked. When he was sure he was not being followed, Rezkin switched to another illusion and headed back to the house he was occupying.

He had escaped a confrontation with Azeria with only a minor cut, which had surprised him more than it had her. He had been pressing himself in his training since first sparring with her in Freth Adwyn, but he had not realized how much faster he had become. His satisfaction over his advancement could not overcome the pain he felt in his chest. He had been so close to her, and yet they were still separated by the agonizing distance of death.

She had not been able to hide her sorrow when she had begged for him to be returned to her. In that moment, he had nearly given up his pretense. The Eihelvanan were known for their stoic demeanors, and yet he had been told they felt emotions intensely. Although Azeria had shown him little favor in their time together, it had become clear that she did, in fact, have feelings for him. This was especially evident when they had kissed, a moment of weakness that Rezkin had hoped would be repeated. Now Rezkin endured a new feeling, one with which he had little experience.

Guilt.

When he had first considered his plan to remain dead to the world, he had not thought of the emotional impact that death would have on his friends. Now he could see Azeria's pain firsthand, and he perpetuated that pain knowing full well that it existed. He had been trained to do what needed to be done regardless of the emotions involved, but this felt wrong. Azeria did not deserve this pain he was inflicting upon her. Rezkin was filled with an unfamiliar desire. He did not want to merely exist for some preordained purpose. He had a desire to do something he had never done before. He wanted to fill Azeria with joy. That thought caused him profuse anxiety. He had no idea how to bring someone joy. He was not even sure what joy was. He only knew that he wanted to see it in Azeria, and he wanted to be the one to put it there.

13

Frisha emerged from her room feeling refreshed for the first time since they had arrived in Serret over a week ago. Until last night, her dreams had been plagued by images of Caydean's guards stalking her while she found it difficult to run and fight. Last night, though, her dreams had been blessedly peaceful. At least, she thought they were. She could not actually remember them.

She noted that Thresson's door was open and his room empty as she made her way down the hallway. It was not a large home, only three bedrooms upstairs and a sitting room, dining area, and kitchen downstairs. It was all they needed, though, and so much better than living on the road or in the Caydean's cave. She did not know how Urvuay had found such a comfortable home so quickly, and she worried at the cost. She and Thresson owed the man so much that she thought he could never be repaid. Therefore, it had not been difficult to convince her to allow him to travel with them to Cael. Even so, she maintained a little suspicion that the man was not quite what he seemed. She only hoped he was not a spy, but what were the chances that one of Caydean's spies would run into them on the road in the middle of nowhere?

When she entered the kitchen, she was greeted by a savory aroma that made her mouth water. Urvuay turned from the stove and graced her with a joyful smile. She immediately felt guilty for her suspicious thoughts. Urvuay had been nothing but kind to them. He settled a plate piled high with food in front of Thresson who was seated at the table then turned back to the stove. He filled another plate and set it on the table motioning for Frisha to take her seat. She smiled and thanked him as he turned back to grab a third plate, which he kept for himself once he was seated.

They all began eating, and after a few minutes, Urvuay said, "I go to the docks today to secure us passage to Cael."

Thresson looked up. "Oh, when do we leave?"

"We will have to see if there is a ship leaving for Cael soon."

"I hope so. How much do you think it will cost?" asked Frisha, worrying over the fact that she and Thresson had no money.

"I do not know the going rate right now," said Urvuay.

Frisha's gut churned with anxiety over how they might acquire the funds. She said, "Thank you, Urvuay. It's probably a good idea for us to come with you. We really appreciate all your help, but we can't expect you to do everything for us."

"Yes," said Thresson. "You have done more for us in these past weeks than anyone could hope for. I owe you a great debt."

Urvuay held up his hand. "No, I'll hear no more of that."

Thresson shook his head. "No, I cannot allow your kindness to go unrewarded."

Urvuay gripped Thresson's shoulder in a friendly gesture. "Then perhaps one day when you find your fortune, you will remember me, yes?" Then he laughed heartily as he dug into his food.

The docks were not far from the house, only one district over, so they only had to wait in line at one checkpoint. The guards waved them through with barely a glance, and Frisha was relieved she had not been required to speak the few lines of Channerían Thresson had taught her. As they passed a shipyard, Frisha turned her face toward the sky. Dark clouds threatened menacingly, and she worried that it might rain before they got to the ship. Their luck held out, though, and after inquiring with multiple officials, they found the ship that would take them to Cael. It was none other than *Stargazer*.

Frisha practically jumped with joy as she led the way onto the ship with Thresson and Urvuay following. She was a little disappointed when she realized she did not know the man who greeted them. She could not expect to know *everyone* in Cael as the island had been inundated with refugees and visitors hoping to secure trade agreements. Many of those refugees were skilled craftsmen, and Cael had begun to grow prosperous by importing raw goods and exporting luxury items such as jewelry, clothing, and art. Despite the turmoil on the Souelian, there remained a booming market for such items as the affluent desired goods generated in the capital of the new empire.

The one person Frisha did recognize was Captain Estadd. She hoped he remembered her in return. She straightened her ill-fitting clothes as she approached the captain. It turned out she had no reason to worry. As soon as the good captain saw her, his expression brightened.

"Lady Frisha, greetings. I did not expect to find you here," remarked Captain Estadd.

Frisha smiled. "Yes, Captain, I did not expect to *be* here." She waved to the two men behind her. "These are my friends. We are seeking passage to Cael."

Estadd returned her smile. "You have come to the right place. We set out for Cael on the morrow."

"Then you can accommodate us?"

"Of course, Lady Frisha."

"That is excellent, only we have no money …"

Estadd's brows rose. "No money? How did you end up in Serret with no money? No, never mind. It is none of my business. Of course, this will not be a problem. Lord Tieran would have my head if I were to leave you stranded in Serret. Your accommodations will be prepared immediately."

The tension left Frisha's shoulders, but it would take a while for her stomach to settle. "Thank you, Captain Estadd. I am so very glad to have found you."

Frisha and Thresson spent the night on the ship while Urvuay returned to the house they had been sharing to collect his belongings and settle matters with the landlord. She felt a little guilty leaving him to pay for the entire stay, but he had insisted. In the morning, Urvuay rejoined them aboard the *Stargazer*. Once they were underway, Captain Estadd greeted them on deck.

"Lady Frisha, it is my pleasure to escort you to Cael. I did not realize you were away from the island."

She smiled as the man gave her a courtly bow. "Thank you, Captain Estadd. No one knew I was away, I'm afraid." At his questioning stare, she added, "It's a long story."

"I see. I look forward to hearing it if you are willing to share. And who might be these friends who are escorting you on this journey?"

"Oh, allow me to introduce Prince Thresson of Ashai and Urvuay of Channería."

The captain gave Urvuay no more than a cursory glance, but his gaze bored into Thresson. "The missing prince? Truly?" Then he seemed to remember himself as he gave a deep bow. "Greetings and welcome aboard, Your Highness. I had no idea we would be carrying someone of your esteem on this voyage. I'm afraid we have made no preparations."

Thresson raised a hand. "All is well, Captain. Our journey thus far has been one of secrecy. It would not do for Caydean to discover my whereabouts."

"It is true, then? The mad king threatened his own brother?"

"Threatened? Yes, there was plenty of that. He has been holding me prisoner and the Lady Frisha as well."

Estadd's eyes rounded as he glanced between them. His surprise quickly turned to fury. "The emperor will hear of this—whoever that may be."

"What do you mean?" asked Frisha, her heart in her throat. "What of Rezkin?"

Estadd's eyes darkened. "You have not heard. Perhaps this news would best be shared over a drink. Please, come inside."

Frisha, Thresson, and Urvuay followed Estadd into the cabin. Estadd rounded his desk and pulled a decanter from a cupboard. After handing each of them a goblet, he turned with a heavy sigh. "Lady Frisha, I am certain you have heard the rumors. I am afraid Emperor Rezkin is dead. He was killed at the Battle of Garten Knoll about seven months ago."

Heat filled her veins as her stomach dropped. She said, "I don't believe it. We have heard equal rumors that he still lives."

Estadd nodded. "Yes, those are just rumors, I am sorry to say."

"It's not possible," she said stubbornly as tears filled her eyes. Her hands began to shake, and she set the goblet on Estadd's desk. She swayed on her feet, and it was not just from the motion of the ship. Thresson reached out with a steadying hand. She looked over to see anguish written across Thresson's face. Her heart broke for Thresson, who never got to meet his younger brother. She shook her head furiously. "No, he isn't dead."

Estadd said, "Lady Frisha—"

"No! He's too strong, too powerful, too *everything*. I simply cannot envision a world without Rezkin in it."

Estadd set his own goblet down after draining it. He looked at her with compassion. "There are those who believe that he lives. And with recent news, I cannot outright deny the possibility."

Hope surged inside her. She quickly uttered, "What news?"

"Well, it seems he is missing."

"What do you mean, he's missing?" said Thresson.

Estadd ran a hand over his well-kept beard. "He was interred in a tomb at Garten Knoll. Only a recent expedition to check on the state of the tomb revealed that his body has gone missing. The powers that be in Cael believe his body was stolen by the Raven. Others believe he walked out of his own accord after defying death."

Thresson narrowed his eyes at Estadd. "You are well informed for a ship's captain."

Estadd gave a curt nod. "I suppose I am, but then again, the emperor never treated me as just a ship's captain. Since the beginning, I have been more like a co-conspirator. Part of my responsibilities is to spread news of the empire as I travel between the kingdoms."

Thresson glanced at Urvuay. "Then it is our great luck that we ended up on this particular ship."

Urvuay spread his hands. "Luck had nothing to do with it. This was the only ship going to Cael."

"Then we are lucky it was in port when we needed it to be," replied Thresson. He turned to Frisha. "Are you well?"

Frisha shook her head as tears spilled over her lashes. "No, I'm not. I *need* to know that he is alive."

Thresson clasped her hand. "We will find out. I will make sure of it."

Tieran stopped abruptly as the air in front of him split open like an enormous, jagged tear in space. A moment later, Azeria stepped through, and the tear sealed itself shut. As he attempted to settle his galloping heart, Azeria strode forward until she was right in front of him. Without preamble, she said, "We have a problem."

"Oh? Was your mission successful?"

Azeria turned and gazed down each of the corridors before saying, "We need to go somewhere private."

"Very well, let us go to my office."

They were silent as they strode through the corridors toward his office, but Tieran's thoughts were loud. He had not expected Azeria's hunt to reveal anything. Her severe countenance and urgent words were enough to start his thoughts spinning. What could she possibly have figured out about Rezkin's death that would set her so on edge?

When they were secluded in his office, Azeria said, "There is a spy in Cael."

Tieran's brow rose. He said, "I am sure there are several spies in Cael. Do you care to be more specific?"

Azeria crossed her arms. "The Raven told me there is a spy in a position of influence here. It is a woman."

"You spoke to the Raven?"

"I did."

"What of Rezkin?"

"*Itsiyela*," Azeria said in exasperation. "The Raven will not return his body now. He said Rezkin still serves a purpose."

"And?" said Tieran, certain there was more.

"And he would not confirm that Rezkin is dead (*chisti*)."

Tieran threw himself into the chair behind his desk. "What does *chisti* mean?"

"It is a feeling."

"I know it is a feeling. Which one?"

"It is like … annoyed." Azeria sounded more frustrated with every word she spoke.

"Ah. It bothers you that the Raven would not confirm Rezkin's death? Why?"

"Because we *must* know."

Tieran released a heavy breath. "We already know. You were there. You helped entomb his body. You know he is dead."

Uncertainty flashed in her eyes, and Tieran realized Azeria no longer *knew* Rezkin was dead. She had begun to wonder about the veracity of the rumors. He realized, now, just how powerful those rumors were that even she—who had been there when he died—could begin to doubt his death.

"That is not the urgent matter," said Azeria. "This spy is. We must find her."

Tieran tapped his fingers on the desk in front of him. "That is going to be difficult. We do not even know where to begin."

"We begin with all the females in positions of influence. It must be someone kept in close confidence—someone especially adept at hiding her subterfuge."

Tieran pulled out a piece of paper from a drawer and picked up his enchanted pen. "We will make a list. I think we can exclude a few from the start—you, for example, and Frisha—"

"No, you must include Frisha on the list (*istak*)."

Tieran scoffed. "It is not possible that Frisha is the spy." Even as he said the words, he knew they did not ring true. Frisha had been different for the past seven months. He was no longer certain what she was capable of. Before Azeria could protest, he wrote Frisha's name at the top of the list. "Very well, are you happy?"

"Nothing about his makes me happy," muttered Azeria.

The golem waited around the corner until the mages passed. Then she followed them into the meeting hall. The expansive room had been fitted with a large seating area arranged in a semicircle around a raised dais. Mage Nanessy Threll stood upon the dais as she waited for everyone to be seated. The golem took a seat at the back, but still she was discovered.

"Oh, Lady Frisha, it is a surprise to see you here," said Mage Threll. "This is a meeting of the mages, and, well, you are not a mage."

The golem raised her chin and said imperiously, "I desire to know what goes on at these proceedings. I will stay."

Mage Threll was obviously uncomfortable. "Very well, you are welcome to stay, although I doubt anything said here will be of interest to you."

The golem said, "You have no idea what interests me, Mage Threll. Proceed."

Mage Threll did not look pleased as she commenced the meeting. In fact, she frequently glanced toward the golem as if she could not accept that Frisha might find the meeting to be of interest. The golem did not find it to be interesting. The golem had no interests of its own. In fact, it had no thoughts or feelings of any kind. It was bound to the will of its creator, though, and through an extension of her will, it was able to act autonomously as if it were a real person. And it found the meeting to be *very* informative, in particular, the part about the magical defenses of the kingdom of Cael and how they might extend those defenses to the ships in their growing armada.

The golem slipped out of the room once the meeting ended and started down the corridor in the direction of her room. Luckily, her ever-present shadow, Lus, had left her at the meeting room and had not yet returned. The golem wasn't sure what the relationship between Frisha and Lus was or why he followed her. That particular information had not been imparted to her during the imprinting process. In fact, much information had not transferred, and keeping up the ruse had been difficult in the beginning; but to her fortune, the emperor had died, and people excused *Frisha's* apparent absent-mindedness as due to the stress over his death.

The emperor's death had been sudden and unexpected. Of course, she had heard the rumors that he still lived, but she also knew that anyone who really knew him and had been there during the battle was certain that he was truly dead. That knowledge alone was enough to make the effort of creating her worthwhile.

Once back in her room, the golem retrieved the messenger device she had been given upon her creation. It was small, fitting in the palm of her hand, but still crude compared to the portable relay devices used by the people of Cael. It was all she had, though, so it would have to do. Unfortunately, for her message to get all the way to the contacts in Channería, she would have to send it from somewhere very high, which meant a long trek up to the pinnacle of the highest tower—and she had to complete her mission before Lus found her again.

The path up the tower was one long, winding corridor that seemed to tilt neither up nor down and had no stairs, but this did not bother the golem. She was incapable of the kind of thought that would make the mysterious citadel seem confusing. As she rounded a curve, she paused and glanced behind her. Had she heard footsteps? Was it the rustle of clothing? Something had drawn her attention, but she was not sure what it had been. She turned and continued up the corridor passing chamber after chamber. The golem had never explored these rooms. Most were unused so were of no importance. She only cared about information, and there was little to glean from empty rooms.

When she finally reached the top of the spire, the golem paused, glancing around. It was a wide, open space devoid of furnishings. The walls were dotted with windows that had no panes or shutters interspersed with shadowy alcoves containing doors that she had never opened. In the center of the tower hung an enormous ball of crystals that were presently devoid of light. The golem did not wonder about the purpose of the crystal ball. It was not relevant to her mission.

Shuffling over to one of the windows, the golem withdrew the messenger device from her pocket and set it on the windowsill. She turned the wheel at the top, aligning it with the one at the bottom, and it began to emit a low buzzing sound. When the buzzing ceased, she began speaking into the device, divulging all that she had heard in the mage meeting. When she was finished, she twisted the device so that the two wheels were no longer aligned and shoved it into her pocket. When she turned around, she stopped short. She was not alone.

"I did not want to believe it, but I cannot deny what I just witnessed."

"Tieran," she breathed. "How did you find me?"

"I have been following you all day," he said, his fury written across his face. "I knew something was wrong, but *this* …"

"I can explain," she stammered.

"Explain?" he shouted. "You are spying for Caydean! How could you, Frisha? After everything he has done. Were you always a spy, or did this only start after Rezkin died?"

She lifted her chin defiantly. "I am not a spy."

To her left, a door clicked shut, and Frisha turned to find Striker Kai striding toward her. On her right, Lus suddenly appeared. As they closed in on her, the golem began backing away. When her rear hit the windowsill, she stopped and looked over her shoulder to see the ground far, *far* below. The distance did not bother the golem, but she had been tasked with a mission she could not accomplish if she were splattered on the ground. She turned back to see that they were closer now.

Tieran waved a hand her way and said, "Capture her."

Kai moved to do his bidding, but Lus appeared torn. In fact, it almost looked as if he might fight Kai. Ultimately, though, he backed off and allowed her to be taken prisoner. Kai moved to march her back down the corridor, but Tieran stopped them. He grasped her jaw in a firm grip. "How could I ever have thought you were worthy of my love?"

The golem laughed. "What do I care for your trivial love?"

Tieran clenched his jaw and released her before stepping back. "Take her to the cells."

Over the prior several days, the wind and rain battered the ship from above while the sea tossed it around from below. Frisha had never been seasick before, but this was more than her poor stomach could take. She and many of the other passengers were ill for most, if not the entire, journey to Cael. Thresson and Urvuay, however, seemed well enough, and they both insisted on caring for her, which she appreciated even though there were times when she would rather have been alone.

When they finally entered the cliff-lined causeway that led to the island's protected harbor, Frisha's relief was almost palpable. After six months of captivity and another month of rough travel, she had finally returned home. And she *did* consider Cael to be her home now. This was where all her friends were, it was where she had found purpose, and it was where she felt safest. After all, she had been kidnapped only upon *leaving* Cael, a matter she was going to have to take up with Xa first chance she got.

When they disembarked, Frisha led the way through the massive warehouse beneath the mountain. She noted Thresson's awe at seeing the citadel for the first time. The enormous doors stood open, and light from the illuminated crystals on the ceiling shined brilliantly across the numerous carvings that adorned the pillars. Urvuay's reaction was much more subdued, and even though his gaze roved over everything, it was as if he was not seeing any of it.

They took the stairs into the upper part of the citadel, and even though what she really wanted was a bath and a change of clothes, Frisha headed straight for Tieran's office. Before she reached it, though, a couple of guards rounded the corner with swords drawn.

"Stop right there, Lady Frisha."

Frisha backed away in fright but stopped abruptly when a sharp point dug into her back. She looked behind her to find two more guards at her rear. Oddly, Lus—or *Xa*—was with them.

"What? What's going on?" she asked.

Several more guards came around the corner and with a nod from the lead guard moved to take Thresson's and Urvuay's weapons.

The door swung open, and Tieran stepped out. Upon seeing her, his expression fell, but Frisha rushed to him anyway. She threw her arms around him and kissed him soundly right there in front of everyone. He did not reciprocate. Instead, he grabbed her by the arms and snapped at the guards to seize her.

"What is happening here?" he said.

The lead guard said, "We caught her trying to escape. These two were aiding her."

Tieran's attention turned to the others, and he suddenly rocked back in surprise. His breath escaped on a word. "Thresson?"

"'Tis I, Cousin. Will you tell your guards to stop accosting us?"

Tieran's expression hardened. "What are you doing here with *her*? She is a traitor. Or have you been working with Caydean all along?"

Frisha rocked back on her heels and looked up at him with confusion. Anger surged up Frisha's throat as she remembered that the golem had been impersonating her the entire time she had been gone. Obviously, something terrible had happened. She needed to set the record straight immediately.

"Tieran, I've been gone for seven months. The woman you've been seeing was not me! She's a golem made to look like me. I've only just arrived on the ship, and I brought Thresson with me."

"You expect me to believe that?" snapped Tieran.

Frisha took both his hands in hers. Tieran snatched them away. She wondered what had happened between him and the golem in her absence to make him so cold toward her. "Please, listen to me. Seven months ago, Xa—I mean Lus—took me to Channería." She looked to Xa for confirmation, but he gave nothing away. She continued. "While we were there, he left me for a time in a safehouse. A mage came with a couple of henchmen, and they kidnapped me. Then the mage made a golem that looks and sounds exactly like me. When Lus came back for me, he took the golem with him, and I was abducted by the mage and her cronies. The woman you've known for the past seven months was not *me*. It was the golem."

Tieran's eyes were round as saucers as he looked at her with hopeful desperation, but then his expression shuttered. "Why bother with such lies? What game is this?"

Tears welled in Frisha's eyes. It was obvious things had not gone well for her while she had been gone. There was no telling how much damage she would need to undo. She shook her head. "Tieran, you have to believe me."

With vehemence, Tieran spat, "I do not have to believe anything *you* say." He looked to the guards. "Bring them." Then he began leading the way toward the cells.

Thresson said, "Please, Cousin. Believe her. We have only just arrived."

Tieran said, "We all thought you were dead. We thought Caydean had killed you. Where have you been?"

"You were pretty close in your assumptions," said Thresson. "Caydean has been holding me prisoner in a secret hideout in Sandea. It was only a matter of time before he killed me. We were lucky to escape."

"We?"

Thresson nodded toward Frisha. "She speaks truth, Cousin. She was imprisoned with me for six months. Together, we escaped, and it took us another month to get here." Now he motioned toward Urvuay. "And it was only thanks to this man here. He came to our aid a few weeks ago, saved our lives, and has been of great service since. This is Urvuay."

Tieran looked sidelong at Urvuay. "You must be a spy as well."

Urvuay walked with confidence and did not appear at all concerned that he was being taken prisoner. He did protest, however. "I am no such thing. I only seek a good life, preferably in Cael."

"Well, you will not have it. You will live the remainder of your days—as fleeting as they may be—in a cell beside these two."

Tears streamed down Frisha's face as she tried to think of a way to make Tieran understand. She said, "Please, Tieran, tell me what has happened."

He rounded on her causing everyone to abruptly stop. "It is Lord Nirius to you." He turned as quickly as he had stopped and continued down the corridor. When they reached the cells, all the doors were closed. Tieran stopped in front of one and ordered the guard to open it. When the door swung open, Tieran did not order them thrown into the cell. Instead, he stood staring into the space. Then he looked back at Frisha for a long moment before returning his attention to the cell. Finally, he stepped inside and came back out hauling a woman behind him. The woman looked exactly like *her*.

Frisha sighed in relief. The golem was still there, which meant Tieran would *have* to believe her. When the golem looked at her, it sneered, "What are *you* doing here?"

"I should be asking *you* that," growled Frisha.

With one hand firmly gripping the golem's arm, Tieran used his other to draw his sword. Then he ran the sword straight through the golem's chest. Everyone stared in shock.

The golem cackled as Tieran withdrew his sword. No blood poured from the wound, which sealed almost instantaneously. The golem sneered, "It has been rewarding being you—a *better* you."

"See?" shouted Frisha. "She's a golem. She isn't even a real person. Please, Tieran, I'm *me*. I'm Frisha."

Tieran flung the golem back into the cell and ordered it locked. Then he turned to them. He did not look at Frisha, though. As he spoke, he avoided looking at her directly. Instead, he focused his attention on Thresson. His voice was subdued when he said, "I am prepared to listen to you now, Cousin."

The guards marched them back through the corridors until they again reached Tieran's office. The three of them were escorted inside. When Kai arrived, shock tore through him. He fell to his knees before Thresson.

"My prince, I thought you dead. I dare not seek your forgiveness. I failed you."

Thresson laid a hand on Kai's shoulder. "Please, rise, Striker. You did not fail me."

“I did not protect you as I should have.”

“You followed your king’s orders as you were sworn to do. I do not blame you, Striker Kai. Now please get up. We have much to discuss.”

Kai rose, and Tieran dismissed the other guards. Xa remained behind, and for the first time, Frisha saw a crack in his stoic veneer. He looked shaken.

Tieran took a seat behind his desk, Kai leaned against the far wall, and Xa stood before the door. Thresson and Frisha sat on a settee while Urvuay took a seat in a high-backed chair. Tieran gave the man a calculating look before turning his attention back on Thresson. “I am listening.”

As Thresson relayed all that had happened to him, Frisha tried to get her tears under control. Tieran still would not look at her, and she worried that irreparable damage had been done. When Thresson got to the part about Urvuay coming to their rescue, Tieran turned to the man.

“I apologize for my brusque greeting earlier. You have returned my cousin to me. I am in your debt.”

“It was no problem. I was only in the right place at the right time.”

“Perhaps,” said Tieran, “but you must be rewarded for your service regardless.”

Urvuay scratched his head. “Well, there is one thing I might ask of you.”

“Name your price,” said Tieran.

“I’d like a place here. I could live here, work here. That would be enough for me. I am a master stone mason. I could be of use.”

“Done,” Tieran said without hesitation. “You will hold a place of honor. I assume you traveled light. You will be given all that you require. And I will find you a position worthy of your noble deeds.”

Tieran looked back to Thresson. “You must be tired from your travels. Come, we must find you a suitable living space. You will be housed in the citadel, of course. I believe there are some quarters available not far from mine. You will want a bath and a change of clothes. Have you eaten?”

Thresson nodded. “Fine, fine, Tieran, but I think you are forgetting something.”

“What is that?”

Thresson nodded toward her. “Frisha.”

With great effort, Tieran finally turned to her. “This traitor who spies for Caydean, who has flaunted herself before every man on the island, and who grates on my nerves to no end was not really you?”

Frisha winced. Of course, she could not have expected the golem to behave with civility in her stead, but she had hoped the spy would have been more subtle. "Yes," she said, "I have truly been imprisoned all this time. I missed you dearly."

Tieran dropped his gaze to the desk in front of him as if he could no longer stand to look at her. Frisha's tears threatened to start all over again, but she managed to hold them back. He said, "I knew something was wrong. You were so unlike yourself. I just could not see what it was. A golem. I never would have guessed."

"How could you? It's so farfetched. Even *I* had trouble believing it."

"I-I am sorry, Frisha, for your harsh treatment since you have returned."

She raised a hand to stave off the apology that hung on his lips. "I understand. I only hope things did not go *too* far." Her cheeks heated and her stomach soured at the thought.

Tieran shook his head. "She was forward, certainly, but so far as I know, your virtue—ah, *her* virtue—remains intact. I cannot say the same for your reputation, though."

Frisha's shoulders slumped. At least the worst of her fears had not come to pass. Still, the golem was a spy for Caydean, and there was no telling what information she had passed on.

Tieran's voice was but a whisper. "You were so different, so awful."

"I suppose I should be grateful that you at least noticed a difference," she said with a watery smile.

"Trust me, we *all* noticed," interjected Xa.

Tieran added, "But how could we have known it was not you? I have never heard of a golem that was so real, so independent."

Frisha wanted to be mad at them but could not. The golem *had* been convincing, and she doubted she would have been able to tell the difference had it been anyone *but* her. She looked at Tieran who seemed genuinely distraught. She said, "Are we okay?"

His expression softened, but again she saw doubt in his eyes. He replied, "I know now that she was not you, but so much has happened. It will take time for me to come to terms with it."

Frisha nodded. "Fair enough. I don't know what she put you through, but I imagine it was awful."

Tieran did not respond to that. Instead, he said, "Now we must do damage control. She was spying for Caydean for seven months. We must assume he knows everything. Coordinating the empire takes time and resources. It will not be easy to change our plans, but it must be done."

Urvuay pulled a folded paper from his pocket. "On that note, I have something that may interest you."

He handed the paper to Thresson, who passed it to Tieran. Tieran unfolded it, and after perusing the short missive, said, "Where did you get this?"

Urvuay shrugged. "I have contacts."

Tieran passed the note to Kai then looked to Thresson and Frisha. "Did you know about this?"

"Know about what?" said Thresson.

"According to this, Caydean is constructing a weapon that could destroy an entire city."

Frisha and Thresson stared at Urvuay. Frisha said, "Have you known about this all along?"

Urvuay shrugged. "I had more than one reason to come to Cael."

Tieran turned to Urvuay. "Who are you really?"

Urvuay appeared surprised by the direct question. "I am merely a stone mason from the north. But I do have contacts with the Fishers. I told them I was coming to Cael, and they entrusted me with this message. That is all."

"Then this came from the Fishers?" asked Tieran.

Urvuay nodded.

Tieran said, "How do the Fishers know about this?"

Urvuay stroked the stubble along his jaw. "My contact said it came from the Raven, but I know nothing about that."

"Do you know where this weapon is?" asked Thresson.

"My contact says it is in Kaibain. That is all I know," replied Urvuay.

"If this is true," said Tieran, "then we must either steal this weapon or destroy it *before* he has a chance to use it."

Tieran turned to Kai. "Have we heard from Mage Wesson? Is he still in Kaibain?"

"Last we heard, he was still there. That was a few days ago."

"Good. Get him a message that he is to wait there. We must put together a team to find this weapon, and we will need his skills."

14

WESSON STRAIGHTENED his tunic and ran a comb through his hair before leaving his humble quarters. The inn had seen better days, but Wesson was not concerned about anyone breaking into his room to steal his few belongings. He had warded the room to deter anyone from even *wanting* to enter. He wrapped a similar ward around himself, although this one would prevent people from looking too closely at him. Many people would not even notice his presence. It was a spell inspired by his time spent with Rezkin in which the warrior seemed capable of the same thing. The only drawback was that if another mage was close enough, they would detect his use of vimara and become suspicious. Rezkin had never had that problem since his power was not detectable by mages.

The streets of Kaibain were growing dark as he made his way through the throngs of last-minute shoppers and tavern visitors. When he neared the mage relay, he dropped his ward and clamped down on his power bleed so that no one would detect that he was a mage. Then he entered the building and waited. It was not long before the young woman handed him the message from Cael. He read the brief, coded message quickly before leaving the relay.

Once outside, he ducked down an alley and set the paper on fire. When it was nothing but ash, he exited the alley and headed toward the site of the temple construction. As he neared, the already-congested streets became nearly impassable. The newly converted devotees of Ygrethiel were filling the streets, and he knew it would only get worse the closer they got to the opening ceremony.

Wesson found a vantage from where he could watch the temple entrance unimpeded. He did not have to wait long. He had arrived just in time. The battle mage known as Avikeev came sauntering out of the temple with a pleased expression. Wesson wrapped his ward around himself and kept his distance as he followed Avikeev through the streets as he always did. This had been his daily routine for the past couple of weeks since he had arrived in Kaibain. The more he watched the battle mage, the more he knew something was not right about him. Avikeev was prone to moments of temperance interrupted by bursts of intense cruelty. Wesson had witnessed multiple instances of the man's sadism since he had been following him.

He followed the man to the same estate he had visited nearly daily, the old Marcum estate. Wesson had asked around about the place, and it turned out that Caydean had granted the estate to Avikeev after General Marcum had been declared an outlaw and disappeared with his wife. Of course, Wesson knew the general was gathering troops at the northern fortress where Rezkin had been trained, but either Caydean did not know it, or he did not see the general as a threat because no move had been made against him.

The estate was quiet as usual, and Wesson saw no one else enter or exit the home while he waited. Wesson's investigation had revealed that Avikeev was the new battle master, and Caydean had granted him the rank of general. Two more battle mages had also been designated generals. The female, named Ulessa, occasionally visited Avikeev's estate, but he had not seen the male, Trivian, since that first day he had followed Avikeev. Wesson did not know what they had done that day, but whatever it was, it had been big. Shockwaves of nocent power had suffused him even so far as across the street where he hid. It had happened a few more times since he had been watching the house, each time when Ulessa visited.

He desperately wanted to know what went on in the home, but he had no way of finding out. Every possible entrance was no doubt warded; and, while he could break the wards, he could not bend them to his will like Rezkin could. If he did break through, the generals would be alerted, and he might even trigger a trap. Still, the house was worth investigating since following Avikeev and Ulessa had not revealed anything more. He waited until Avikeev left the estate then scurried down the path to the main entrance. As he suspected, the door and windows were warded, so he slid around building searching for any weak points in the wards. When he reached the back of the house, he was forced to hide in the bushes to avoid notice by the servants who were going about their daily chores. A man stepped across the yard toward the stables, and a woman was hanging laundry on a line. Wesson wondered how it was that the servants could come and go through the wards, especially considering they had no power of their own. Then he considered how he might use that to his advantage.

The woman finished hanging her laundry, bent to retrieve her basket, and headed for the servants' entrance. Wesson watched carefully as she entered the home, passing through the ward. In his mind's eye he could see the intricate patterns of the ward and the power that suffused it, and with a heavy heart, he realized the power was not constructive in nature. That made sense since Avikeev was a natural battle mage and did not have access to constructive magic. His natural affinity for destructive, or nocent, power would override any constructive vimara he might possess. Only Wesson had been able to overcome the limitation through intensive training and dedication.

What was more interesting than the type of power used, however, was the way in which the ward had recognized the maid. It had been fast, but Wesson had seen that just as the ward probed at the woman, an answering power surged back from her. He was nearly certain that the seemingly mundane maid was possessed by a demon. The ward had been designed to recognize her demonic signature. Wesson realized that if he could mimic that signature, he might be able to trick the ward into believing he was the maid and allow him through. He needed to see the signature again to be sure, though. After all, he had only a split second to view it. He waited for her to return, and two hours later, she did. Wesson watched for her signature twice more as she came out to gather the laundry and take it back into the house.

Wesson had never attempted to mimic a demonic signature. Until now, he could not have thought of a reason he would want to. But as he crept toward the house, he formed in his mind the spell he thought might accomplish the task. It was a spell he designed while he waited for the maid and was untested. He considered waiting until dark to break into the home when everyone was asleep, but then Avikeev would have returned. He was not yet ready to confront the battle master general. The message he had received earlier in the day had indicated he was to remain in Kaibain in search of some sort of weapon. Apparently, a team would be coming to join him, and he wanted to have something concrete to report.

Wesson paused beside the doorway. His gaze roved the yard. Although he was warded to prevent people from noticing him, he was still cognizant of the danger. If the servants were demons, he could ill afford a confrontation that would alert the generals to his presence. Seeing no one, Wesson began concentrating on creating the spell that would mimic the demonic signature of the maid. Once he felt that he had it, he activated it and stepped through the ward.

The ward slid over him like oil with only the slightest resistance. So far as he knew, no alarms had been triggered, but he could not be certain. He entered the home through the servants' passage near the kitchen. A cook was busily preparing a meal as he tiptoed past the entrance. Then he was forced through the nearest doorway as someone rounded the corner into the hallway, and Wesson nearly tumbled down the stairs. Catching himself, Wesson decided to explore the cellar first. After all, if *he* were doing unscrupulous things, he would do it in the cellar. He picked his way past stacks of supplies then found that the cellar opened into an expansive space. It was poorly lit, but Wesson could just make out the bars of the cells. Past the rows of cells was a workspace that was presently empty.

A whimper from the side arrested his steps. Wesson stopped beside the cell and peered into the darkness. After a moment of searching, he finally found a darkened lump that might have been a person.

He spoke in a harsh whisper. "Hello? Who is there?"

The whimper came again, and the lump shivered.

Frustrated with his inability to see in the dark, Wesson cast a fireball over his outstretched hand. The large space was suddenly illuminated, and Wesson realized all the cells were occupied. There were six people in all, each cowering at the back of their cell. What caught his gaze next were the plentiful runes etched across the bars, the ceiling, and walls. The runes were intended to negate a mage's power and to prevent escape. Now that he was illuminated, he saw a few pairs of eyes blinking back at him. Curiosity won out, and one of the prisoners whispered, "Who are you?"

Wesson started to answer then realized his predicament. If he saved these people now, Avikeev would know someone had been there. If Avikeev knew someone was spying on him, it would become that much more difficult to find out what the man was up to. If he did *not* release these prisoners now, it would be better if they did not know anything about him in case they were interrogated. Plus, he would be leaving them to Avikeev's mercy, and he did not think the man had any.

Instead of answering the man's question, he repeated his own. "Who are *you*?"

The man looked at him suspiciously. "How do I know you're not one of them?"

"You don't," said Wesson. "But I give you my word, for what it's worth, that I am not."

The man glanced at the other figures who were huddled in their cells. Some still cowered, but others appeared cautiously curious. "I am Bargus. I—*we*—are all mages. The battle master brought us here for his experiments. I have already witnessed him kill four others since I've been here. Please, help us if you can."

Wesson eyed the bars with their unfamiliar runes. "Do you know where the key is kept?"

Bargus shook his head. "No. I'm not sure there is one. They use power to open the cells when they come for us."

"Really? With all these runes, they are still able to open the cells?"

"So it would seem. Are you a mage?" asked Bargus.

Again, Wesson did not answer. Instead, he moved toward the workspace to search for the key or any clues as to what the experiments were all about. He called back to Bargus. "Do you know anything about the experiments?"

Bargus said, "Only that the subject of those experiments always ends up dead. And that they're using nocent power, but that is obvious since they're battle mages."

Wesson examined the contents of the large worktable. A number of random items were strewn about. Some of the items looked costly while others were ordinary and of little value. A rack for securing a prisoner was situated to one side opposite a small writing desk. Wesson moved to the desk but found no notes or letters of interest save for one page full of arcane runes that seemed familiar even though Wesson knew he had never seen them before. Using a piece of blank paper and a stick of charcoal, he recreated the runes for himself before moving back to the cells. He placed another paper against the locking mechanism and used the charcoal to make a rubbing of the runes inscribed there. He folded the papers and tucked them into his tunic as he replaced the charcoal at the desk.

He said, "I am going to study these runes and find a way to release you. I will return as quickly as possible. Do not tell anyone I was here."

The man came forward and gripped the bars of the cell. His clothes were rumpled, and his face was scruffy, but his eyes still glinted with hope. "No, you must release us *now*! I have no desire to die here."

Wesson swallowed hard. "If I find a way to release you, they will know I was here."

"Not if it looks like we escaped on our own," said Bargus.

Wesson had not even left the cellar yet, and already the guilt for leaving them behind was eating at him. He turned his attention to the runes around the bars and across the walls and ceiling. Again, the runes seemed familiar. The longer Wesson stared at them, the closer he got to understanding them. Wesson felt his nocent power squirming at his core. It was responding to the runes he was studying. He drew up his power and fed a small stream into the runes probing for their meaning. And then it clicked. Wesson suddenly knew what the runes were for. He fed his nocent power into the locking mechanism of the first cell. There was a click, and then the cell door swung open.

"Thank you!" said Bargus as he came shuffling out. He headed for the stairs, but Wesson held him back with a firm hand.

"Wait," said Wesson. "You cannot go yet. You must wait here while I release the others. Then we will all escape together after I have set my plan in motion."

"What is your plan?"

"You need to die."

"*What?*"

"Not for real, of course. We are just going to make it *look* like you died during an escape attempt.

"How do you intend to pull that off?" asked Bargus.

"These runes here on the ceiling and walls hold enchantments that cause some serious incendiary effects if tampered with. It's possible that one or more of you were able to access a small bit of your power and attacked these enchantments."

"Not possible," said Bargus. "I tested myself against these enchantments for over a week and couldn't get a single spark of power."

"Nothing is fool proof," said Wesson. "Let us say you did access your power and you did throw it at these enchantments. You would cause an explosion that would wipe out everything in this cellar. It is a built-in failsafe. If you try to access these cells in any way other than the way I just did, you will set off the explosion—if you tried to escape, you would die."

"Is there no end to their cruelty?" muttered Bargus.

"I am afraid not," said Wesson as he opened the remaining cells. The prisoners all eyed the stairs, but none made a run for it. "All right, all of you huddle on the stairs but do not go up yet. I am going to set a spell to go off in ten minutes that will trigger the explosion. We are going to escape unseen before it goes off, but you must do exactly as I say. Understood?"

He cautiously ascended the stairs, listening for any indication that someone might be coming. Slipping through the doorway, he headed back toward the exit just as he heard the clomp of boots coming from the room at the end of the hallway. The owner of the boots did not turn his way, however, and disappeared around the corner. Wesson peered through the backdoor to see that the yard was clear. Then he motioned to Bargus who was waiting at the top of the cellar stairs. Bargus sent one of the prisoners down the hallway to stop when he reached Wesson. Quickly, Wesson created a sort of shroud of nocent power that he laid over the escapee. He hoped it worked to match the demon signature well enough to fool the ward on the backdoor. He crossed his fingers as he set the escapee through the doorway.

The ward slid over the escapee just as it had him when he had entered, and Wesson breathed out a sigh of relief. Then he motioned for the next prisoner. He repeated the same process with each one until all the escapees had made it across the yard. His heart raced as he quickly exited and dashed across the yard keeping his stealth spells in place so as not to be seen. Once he was back behind the cover of the foliage, he turned back to see Avikeev standing in the doorway surveying the yard. The man looked suspicious but not alarmed, so Wesson thought they had not been detected.

The explosion detonated at that moment, rocking the entire house. Avikeev darted back into the house, and Wesson and the escapees ran for their lives. When they were far enough into the city to go unnoticed, they paused for a breather in an abandoned workshop in a poor district. He instructed the mages to wait for him there while he acquired for them the supplies they would need until they could escape the city. Once Azeria arrived, he could send them back to Cael.

The sky was beginning to darken as Wesson hurried through the city toward the inn where he was staying. He took a roundabout route so as not to be followed. He was dashing down an alley when he suddenly stopped short. Three men blocked his path, each bearing a weapon. He started to back away when he heard the approach of two more from behind him.

"What do we have here?" said the largest one who held a wicked knife in front of him. "Hey, pretty boy, didn't your mama ever tell you not to go down dark alleys? The wolves will get you."

"You should be worried about why I'm not concerned with wolves," muttered Wesson. The knife-wielding thug lunged, slashing Wesson across the forearm just as he unleashed a spell that radiated, capturing all five ruffians and dropping them to the ground at once. As Wesson stepped over their unconscious bodies, he noted the mark of the Raven tattooed on each of them. He wondered what Rezkin would have done in that situation. He figured he probably would have killed all five without getting a drop of blood on him and then gone about his evening as if nothing had happened. Wesson felt momentarily guilty for leaving them alive to attack someone else, but he could not stomach the thought of killing them. He paused at the end of the alleyway. If he did leave them alive and they ended up killing someone else, then he would be responsible for that innocent person's death.

Wesson tugged anxiously at a lock of his hair as he considered his conundrum. He was utterly torn—and *angry* that this had landed on *his* shoulders. He knew what Rezkin would do. And he knew what he, himself, would have done a year ago. But who was he now?

Wesson returned to the unconscious men. Blood pounded in his ears and slid down his forearm as he bent over the largest one. He examined the man's rough, scarred face and imagined what kind of life he had lived. It was likely a sad, vicious one. Wesson reached out with his power and inscribed on the man's forehead a circle within a diamond with an *x* through it—the brand of a criminal. Then he removed the mark of the Raven tattooed on the man's collarbone. He repeated the process with the other four and left them to their fates. Henceforth, they could go nowhere without everyone knowing what they were. It was a desperate compromise but one he could live with.

When Wesson returned to the inn, he found his wards on his room to be intact, and the door was locked. He allowed himself into the dark room and closed and locked the door behind him. Then he lit the lamp on the table beside the door. His vision wavered as though he were seeing the room through water, and his head felt strange. It felt like it was no longer attached to his shoulders. He fell back against the door. Looking down at his bleeding arm, which had gone numb, he realized he had been poisoned. When he looked up, he saw that he was not alone. An enormous, looming figure stood at the center of the room. He wore armor and had an entire armory strapped to him, but it was his dominating presence that caused Wesson's heartrate to double.

Wesson stepped forward on shaky legs holding up the lamp to better illuminate the figure. He swallowed hard and said, "Rezkin?"

Just then, Wesson's ward wavered then shattered as the door blasted inward.

Wesson was knocked to the floor as the door collided with him. His head swam and his stomach lurched as he rolled over and shoved the door off him. He was woozy, but he could now see the men that were filing into the room and the marks upon their foreheads. They were the same men who had attacked him in the alley, but this time they wielded nocent power as they pummeled him with spells. Wesson managed to ward himself against their attacks, but he could not summon the mental acuity he needed to cast spells of his own.

It was a surprise when the first man fell, his head separated from his body. Wesson pushed himself to a sitting position just as a blast shook the room, shattering the window and causing Wesson to fall over again, his ears ringing. A light caught his attention, and he rolled his head to find the room on fire. The lamp had shattered, splattering oil across the floor and bedding. Wesson wrestled with his pyris power, desperately attempting to snuff the flames, but he could not gain control of it in his state.

He sluggishly turned his attention to the commotion by the door. One of the thugs—who Wesson now knew to be a battle mage—was slinging spells against the armored intruder who Wesson initially thought to be Rezkin. Obviously, it could not be Rezkin. Rezkin was dead. So who was this warrior who was holding his own against five battle mages? The battle mage's spell seemed to ricochet off the warrior, and the warrior brought his sword around to lop off both of the battle mage's arms. Then he ran him through. Something about the blade seemed familiar to Wesson, but as soon as the thought entered his mind, it flitted away.

Wesson tried to sit up again, but it was no use. His body had gone numb, and his muscles were like noodles. Nothing was responding the way it should have. As the warrior fought against the rest of the battle mages, Wesson laid back and gazed at the swirling ceiling. Pretty soon, his vision went black.

15

REZKIN KILLED the last battle mage with an efficient slash to the throat then turned back to Mage Wesson. He was unconscious on the floor with a sickly pallor, and the fire was quickly encroaching on him. It was now a race as to whether the poison or the fire would kill him first. Rezkin gathered the mage up and tossed him over his shoulder then grabbed Wesson's pack from beside the burning bed. He headed for the shattered window. He climbed through the opening into the alley and turned away from the burning building. Eventually, he hauled the unconscious mage onto a rooftop and laid him out.

Wesson's skin was cold and clammy, and he did not respond as Rezkin patted his face. Rezkin checked his pupils and sniffed the wound on his arm. He pulled a small vial from a pouch at his belt and tipped it into Wesson's mouth, rubbing his throat so that he would swallow. Rezkin was not certain about which poison had infected him, so he had used a broad-spectrum antidote that would account for the most common poisons.

Rezkin tucked Wesson's pack under his head and spread his own cloak over him. Then he waited, checking on his patient every so often. The sun was just cresting the horizon when Wesson finally stirred. He moaned and gripped his head then blinked blearily at Rezkin.

"What happened? Where am I? And who are you?" slurred the mage.

"Greetings, Mage Wesson," said Rezkin. "I am glad to see you are well."

Wesson jerked in an attempt to sit. "You! It *was* you. W-what are you doing here? You're dead!"

Rezkin spread his hands. "As you can see, I am very much alive."

"Are you? Perhaps you are an imposter. Or are you a wraith like at the citadel?"

Rezkin shook his head. So far, he thought this was going well, although he had thought that of all people, Mage Wesson might have conceived of the truth about his fate. He said, "I am no wraith. Only flesh and blood."

"By the Maker, what a relief," blurted Wesson as he finally managed to sit up. "You have no idea how much dread your death filled me with. I think I'll finally be able to breathe again. Where did you come from? How did you get here?"

Rezkin reached up to where Seena sat perched on his shoulder and stroked her long neck. "I have her to thank for that."

Wesson's eyes widened as he noticed Seena for the first time. "What is *that*?"

"This is Seena, my dragon."

"You have a dragon?!"

"She's still a baby, but she's growing quickly. She does not yet have her fire, but she can open portals to other locations within my memory."

"She reads your mind?" said Wesson in awe.

Rezkin nodded. "Yes, to a degree. I anticipate the bond will grow stronger as she gets older."

Wesson shook his head and poked at his singed pack. He said, "What happened? Where are we? And how are you *alive*?"

"Do you not remember? You were poisoned then attacked in your room. Who were those men?"

Wesson's brow furrowed. "I'm not sure. When I first encountered them, I thought they were just street thugs." He groaned as realization struck. "They were testing me. I must have been caught spying. They likely didn't know I was a mage. And now they will report back to their master."

Rezkin shook his head. "They will not be reporting to anyone. They are all dead and the inn burned down around them."

Wesson swallowed and clutched his pack to him. "Still, the deaths of five battle mages will alert the battle master. He will know I am here—or at least that *someone* is here. I don't know how much he knows." He looked back at Rezkin, pain etched across his face. "We all thought you were dead, most of us did, anyway. I saw your body. I helped lay you to rest. How did you survive?"

"I did not. The Sen Berringish retrieved me from death with intents on joining me with a demon. I killed him. There will be no more coming back from the dead."

Wesson lurched to his feet and threw his arms around Rezkin. Rezkin tensed, and Wesson quickly backed away. "This is great. You're back. You can come be emperor again, and everything will be as it was. Where have you been all this time? Why have you kept yourself a secret?"

"It is important for Caydean to believe I am dead. With me gone, he has little reason to target the others, and he will let down his guard."

Wesson appeared skeptical. "Okay, but why keep this from your friends? We care about you, Rezkin. You have no idea how much pain your death caused."

"I am sorry for that," Rezkin said truthfully. "It was never my intent to cause my friends pain. But I have a few reasons for keeping myself a secret from them. For one, there are spies in Cael. I cannot risk Caydean finding out I am alive. Two, I may now use my skills to do as is necessary for the advancement of this war. Without the burden of emperorship, I am free. Three, it liberates me from Entris's interference. If he knew I lived, he would insist on following me around to ensure I do not go mad."

"But are you mad?" blurted Wesson.

Rezkin sighed. "No, Wesson, I have not gone mad. I have reasons for everything I have done."

"I'm sure you do, but are they *good* reasons? Rezkin, the empire—*your* empire—is on a knife's edge. You don't realize how much damage your death is doing."

"My empire is stronger than you think. It will survive."

"No, Rezkin, it won't. The empire was built on *your* strength. Without that strength, it will crumble and Caydean will run rampant across the Souelian."

Rezkin was suddenly filled with uncertainty. Had he really overestimated the resilience of his empire in his absence? He had only ever seen himself as a figurehead in Ferélle and Gendishen and as a threat in Lon Lerésh. He had wanted those kingdoms for their armies but had no desire to rule over them. Was the emperor's reign really so tenuous?

Wesson must have seen his uncertainty because he said, "Rezkin, it's been seven months, and they won't even crown a new emperor because they won't admit you're dead. Everyone *needs* you to be alive." When Rezkin did not respond, Wesson said, "Why have you chosen to reveal yourself to me now?"

Rezkin shoved away his uncertainty. "It is to my benefit to have someone involved in Cael who knows of my existence."

"You need a spy."

Rezkin shook his head. "No, I have spies."

"You have people spying on your own kingdom?"

"Of course. Also, because you needed my assistance. You would be dead right now had I not intervened."

Wesson rubbed his throat as if the thought of losing his head had penetrated his mind. "I thank you for your timely assistance, then. I should have been faster, more aware, more—"

"Ruthless," said Rezkin.

"I wasn't going to say that."

"I know. But it is the truth. Had you been faster to kill, they would not have poisoned you or come after you later."

Wesson's face fell. "You saw all that?"

"I was following you."

"Why?"

"Because you were at Marcum's estate."

Wesson scowled. "It belongs to Battle Master General Avikeev now. What do you know of it?"

"Not as much as you. What did you find?"

Wesson ran a hand over his face. "He's keeping mages as prisoners and experimenting on them."

"What kind of experiments?"

"I don't know."

"You need to find out."

Wesson gave Rezkin a withering look. "That's what I was trying to do. Apparently, I got caught." He reached inside his tunic and pulled out some folded papers. "These were the only clues I could find."

Rezkin took the papers from Wesson and examined the runes. "What do they mean?"

"I don't know that either."

Handing the papers back, Rezkin said, "They look Adianaik but slightly different."

Wesson's eyes lit with realization. "That's why they seemed familiar."

"Entris or Azeria may know something about them."

"That's a good idea. About Azeria—she's been looking for you, or, rather, the Raven."

"I am aware," said Rezkin as a pang clenched his heart.

"If you tell no one else you are alive, you need to tell her. She took your death hard."

"Regretfully, I cannot. If Azeria knew I was alive, she would feel obligated to inform Entris, and I cannot have him following me around."

"Look, Rezkin, I've seen you two together. I know there is something going on between you. I don't claim to be an expert on women, but I do know they don't like to be deceived. You need to come forward before she finds out some other way."

Rezkin bowed slightly and said, "Thank you for your counsel, Mage Wesson. I will take that under advisement. For now, you must swear to keep my existence a secret from *everyone*."

Wesson shifted uncomfortably. "I don't feel comfortable swearing a mage oath to that effect."

"I will not ask it of you, but this is important. Swear it."

"Very well, I swear."

Before departing, Rezkin gave Wesson the location of a storehouse he could use as a safehouse. He turned to leave, but Wesson called out. "Rezkin."

"Yes?"

"I am glad you're alive."

Rezkin nodded then disappeared.

16

SEENA CLOSED the portal behind them, and Rezkin found himself standing in the forest that surrounded the northern fortress where he had trained since infancy. The conifers that dominated the landscape loomed ominously over the game trail. A cool breeze swept aside his hair, and Rezkin caught the scent of horses and men. His own horse shifted as Seena darted away, and he followed her path with his eyes. She stopped at the base of a large tree and began digging through the pine needles, no doubt in search of some small vermin she had detected. Redirecting his gaze, Rezkin peered through the trees to spy the fortress walls. The guards that manned the walls and towers remained vigilant as a hunting party exited the gates and entered the forest opposite from where Rezkin stood. The fortress looked different so filled with people. When he had been training there, it had been occupied by perhaps twenty people at any given time, and when he had left, it had been vacant save for the corpses he left in the yard.

Rezkin moved silently through the forest following the hunting party for a few minutes, getting a good look at its members. Then he returned to his horse and Seena. He stowed his swords with the horse and took up his bow. Then he asked Seena if she wanted to hunt with him. She gleefully scurried around his feet and then flitted up to his shoulder. Her wings were getting stronger since she had been using them more often. With Seena's help, Rezkin found and felled a young buck quickly. Then he secured his bow to his saddle, donned the illusion of one of the hunters, hefted the buck over his shoulders, and headed toward the fortress. He covered Seena with the illusion of a hound pup, given her size.

The gate guards barely looked at Rezkin as he passed beneath the portcullis, and they eyed the pup beside him only fleetingly. The bailey was awash with soldiers going about their duties or performing drills. Pages scurried amongst them, and other servants skirted the edges. Rezkin dropped the deer near the smoke shed then promptly changed his illusion to that of a soldier. At his urging, Seena scurried up his leg and into the messenger bag at his hip. She was nearly too large for the bag, but he smoothed the bulge with illusion and headed into the keep.

From the outside, the fortress was rough and functional, but the interior had been designed as an exact replica of the palace in Kaibain. Thanks to a lifetime of training there, Rezkin was familiar with every corner and crevice in the palace, and he had no trouble navigating the labyrinth of corridors as he sought General Marcum. He found the general in the suite that had served as his former masters' office and study. The rooms were filled with people engaged in deep conversations, and it was no trouble to sneak in unnoticed. Rezkin hovered around the perimeter as he listened to the bits of information while making his way toward where Marcum met with a couple of dour gentlemen. The conversation eventually shifted to something of interest to Rezkin.

"Yes, Atressian will be there," said the general.

A tall man with a short beard replied, "That will not sit well with Wellinven. The two are sworn enemies."

"It is true," said a shorter man with dull grey eyes. "I doubt even this trouble with Caydean can get them to set aside their animosity."

Marcum shifted his calculating gaze to the shorter man. "Wellinven knows what is at stake here. He will restrain himself from acting against Atressian. I cannot say Atressian will do the same."

"We will see soon enough," said the bearded man.

"Yes, we move out in three days' time. It will be a small contingent. I do not want to draw Caydean's attention," said Marcum.

The short man added, "So far as we know, he is unaware of this conference."

Marcum shook his head. "We should conduct ourselves as if Caydean knows all."

A page interrupted the exchange at that point, drawing Marcum's attention away from the two men. Rezkin had heard enough, though. He had arrived at the fortress in time to join the contingent destined for Wellinven. But first, he had to make sure he would be accepted. He quickly made his way out of the fortress and into the forest where his horse awaited him. He would camp in the forest and return to spy on the inhabitants of the fortress while he came up with a plan. It did not take him long to find his mark, and the plan fell into place from there.

On the third day, before the sun rose, Rezkin used a locked side entrance to access the bailey. It was not hard to identify the soldiers chosen for the mission as they were already awake and preparing to leave. He watched them surreptitiously for a while as he stalked his mark, a man named Gonery. Gonery was a lanky fellow with brown hair that curled over his ears and a mustache. He was quite unpopular with his comrades, and they tended to ignore him or, in some cases, taunt him. When Gonery headed for the latrine, Rezkin followed. He waited until the man had finished then shot him with a poisoned dart to the neck. He dragged Gonery behind a stack of crates and barrels. Gonery would not die. The poison was merely a strong sedative that would have the man out until the dinner bell at least. By then, the company would be long gone. Rezkin doubted Gonery would be taken seriously if he reported his incapacitation, or, more likely, Gonery would believe he had been the butt of some joke.

Rezkin joined Marcum's contingent disguised with illusion as the unpopular Gonery. Seena was not happy to be relegated to the messenger bag. She had ample energy and enjoyed running about hunting small creatures and attempting to fly. But Gonery did not have a companion animal besides his horse, so showing up with one now would draw notice, and he doubted Marcum would approve. So Seena stayed in the bag, shifting about anxiously as Rezkin held the illusion still. She spoke to Rezkin often using her mindspeak. She was learning new words and even forming short sentences, and Rezkin found their conversations intriguing as they rode.

They moved quickly toward Wellinven, with long days of riding, rising before the sun rose and making camp well after dusk. No roads existed between the northern fortress and Wellinven, so the company was forced to cut a path through the forest. For the most part, the other soldiers ignored Rezkin, and therefore he did not have to make excuses for not knowing their names or associations. Rezkin snuck away from the camp at night for two reasons: one, he was not certain he could maintain his illusion in his sleep; and two, to allow Seena time to play and hunt. On occasion, when she had cornered an animal, she would emit a screech and a small puff of smoke would stream from her maw. They continued with her flying lessons by moonlight. She could glide much farther now, but she still could not manage a takeoff or sustained flight. Rezkin was certain it would not be long, though, before she was soaring with the birds—and likely snacking on them.

After three weeks of travel east, they finally approached the Wellinven estate via a winding mountain road. It was a monstrous castle built upon a cliff overlooking the forested valley where the Tremadel River escaped the Zigharan Mountains. With seven towers ascending a slope, it was larger (and older) than the palace in Kaibain. Green and gold pennants flapped in the wind atop each of the towers, and similarly colored banners hung from their walls. The curtain wall surrounding the castle grounds arched away from the cliff and up the slope to encompass the entire structure, and such were the castle's defenses that those walls had never been breached.

Rezkin had never been to Wellinven. As he gazed upon its splendor, he appreciated its efficiency and defensibility. He rode at the back of the column under the guise of Gonery while Seena tossed and turned in the sack resting in front of his saddle. The guards in their green and gold tabards eyed them appreciatively as they rode beneath the portcullis. Rezkin's gaze was sharp as they passed the stone-faced homes and workshops that lined the roadway. He scanned every shadowed recess and alley in search of anything suspicious. Thanks to the information he had gained from the spies in Channería, he knew of at least one assassin, and likely more, waiting for their chance to strike out against the general and dukes. He did not discount the possibility that the assassin could even be a traitor in his midst.

Their procession slowed as they crossed a bridge that spanned the river falls and approached the gate of the inner curtain wall, but they continued through without issue. The courtyard beyond was lined with gardens and possessed a well attached to a decorative yet functional fountain. They came to a halt before the grand front entrance where awaited the duke and duchess as well as a number of retainers. Lord Nirius, Duke of Wellinven, was as tall as Marcum, broad-shouldered, and fit, and he bore a presence that demanded respect and promised swift punishment for any who defied him. Rezkin could readily see the physical resemblance between him and his son Tieran, yet their countenances were very different. Where Tieran eschewed responsibility and sought the pleasures in life, the duke was all severity and duty.

As the duke and duchess greeted Marcum, Rezkin searched the faces of the household staff who were present. On the surface, he saw no resentment or artifice that might indicate a traitor, but that was of little consolation. A skilled assassin would easily affect a placid demeanor up until the moment he or she sunk a blade into the target's back.

Marcum moved with the duke and duchess into the castle, and Rezkin and the rest of the soldiers were directed toward the stables. After seeing to their horses, they were assigned bunks in the barracks. When no one was looking, he slipped out and headed toward the keep, this time disguised as one of the Wellinven guards. He allowed Seena the freedom to run beside him disguised as Cat, and she was elated to stretch her wings and legs. Rezkin met no resistance as he entered the castle and passed through the ostentatious vestibule. The polished stone floors sparkled with flecks of mica in the sunlight that streamed in through the high windows. Along the walls stood pillars topped by various statues and behind them hung paintings of great and terrible battles. Rezkin gave all this a cursory glance as he headed deeper into the keep.

The grand hall could easily fit several hundred people. Its walls were smooth and draped in deep emerald fabric tied back in places by golden rope. At the head of the hall was a short dais upon which rested a large, ornately carved throne beside a smaller one of similar design. Neither were occupied at that moment, so Rezkin continued through to the sitting room beyond. He could hear voices emanating from within, so he silenced his steps as he cautiously approached the door.

Rezkin posed by the door as if standing guard while he listened to the conversations happening in the room. Wellinven's booming voice was delivering a scathing rebuke.

"It is precisely *because* of Caydean's recent graciousness that he cannot be trusted. He put to death half the noble houses, replacing them with his sycophants, and then had the nerve to brand us traitors. Now he issues edicts requiring conversion to this new religion of his, and still the people praise him for his generosity. His madness is spreading. If we wait much longer, our own forces are likely to start questioning us."

"Speak for yourself, Wellinven," said a second man. "My men are loyal and will remain so. I say we wait for an attack either by Channería in the east or the Jerean and Sandean forces to the northwest. That will give us the break we need to move our forces south."

A third man said, "Darning, you fool, we cannot entrust our fate to the actions of foreign parties. They may never gain the courage to attack, and what is to stop them if they do? We would have battle on two fronts."

Marcum said, "You both seem to be forgetting the fourth horse. The Emperor of the Souelian has amassed a sizeable force. We should coordinate our efforts with the empire. We could crush Caydean between us. And if this emperor's claim to the throne is legitimate then we would be better positioned to support a transition of power."

The third man, whom Rezkin presumed to be Duke Atressian, said, "*I* am the legitimate heir to the throne. The so-called emperor has no claim. He is a charlatan, and half the rumors claim him to be dead anyhow. His empire is on the brink of collapse. No, he will not be invading this kingdom to usurp the throne."

"Atressian, once again your claim to the throne is naught but fantasy. My son is the legitimate heir, and you know it," barked Wellinven.

"That's enough," growled Darning. "This matter can be settled *after* we oust Caydean from the throne."

"I think it is important that we settle this now," said Wellinven. "Once Caydean is overthrown, this kingdom will need a strong leader."

"And you think that is *Tieran*?" gasped Atressian in disbelief. "That boy of yours has never taken anything of import seriously in his entire life."

Wellinven said, "He is no longer a boy, Atressian. He is a grown man, and he understands duty."

"If you think I am going to support that twat on the throne—"

"This is getting us nowhere," interrupted Marcum. "We must be united against Caydean. And if this True King is alive and his claim is legitimate, then this entire discussion is irrelevant. We need more information. I have only just arrived. Let us adjourn and take this up again *after* dinner."

The others agreed, and Rezkin moved away from the doorway just as they began to exit. Now that all three dukes and the general had arrived, he had to be on high alert for the assassination attempt. Any one of them could be the first target. It was even possible that someone could try to take them all out at once. He was only one man. He could not possibly be watching all of them all the time. He pondered what he would do if *he* were the assassin.

Wellinven had the largest army with Atressian at a close second. Atressian and Wellinven were contentious already. It would not be difficult to pit them against each other, nor would it be surprising if one of them ended up dead by the other's hand. Then there was the question of the successor. If Wellinven fell, Rezkin had confidence that Tieran could take his place, but few others knew that. While Tieran had once been the irreverent fool Atressian thought him to be, he had changed in the many months since Rezkin had met him. Atressian's successor, Hespion, on the other hand, was cruel and ambitious in a way that would prevent any chance at cooperation.

Darning was the least significant of the three but would be easy to pick off while leaving the other two to fight amongst themselves. The general was the outlier. While he held no claim to the throne, his forces had grown to nearly match those of Wellinven. His influence was kingdom wide. He had the hearts of his men and the potential to draw more to his side. He also possessed the military experience to be a formidable threat against Caydean. Unlike the other three, Marcum was a mundane with no magical ability to protect himself. Rezkin thought that if he were to choose a target, it would be Marcum—but not everyone thought like him, and he could not afford to be wrong. The loss of any one of these men would be devastating.

Rezkin spent the rest of the day spying on the men. He changed his appearance often, sometimes appearing as a guard, other times as a servant. Seena scampered alongside him appearing as a cat, and when she grew tired, she crawled into his messenger bag. When the evening came, he watched the kitchen and serving staff carefully to ensure no one was poisoned. The tension was high around the dining table, and there was little conversation besides that in which the duchess engaged the men. Tieran's mother was a patient woman and having been raised at court beside her brother, King Bordran, she did not seem to be put off by the poorly concealed hostility around her table.

Before the men retired to their rooms that night, Rezkin checked for traps and poisons. In each of their rooms, he found a carefully hidden pin, likely laced with venom, so he knew the assassin or assassins were here. In Atressian's room, he also found a talisman hidden beneath the mattress, but he did not know what the magical item was intended to do. It could be something as simple as a relaxation spell to aid sleep, or it could be a magical trap. Rezkin found himself wishing Mage Wesson were present.

The following day, Rezkin disguised himself as one of Duke Wellinven's retainers, infiltrating the breakfast hall and ensuring that no poisons got past him. Seena slipped into the hall with him, and he instructed her to stay hidden beneath the serving tables. Apparently overcome with her excitement or hunger, Seena slipped out and scurried across the room. Upon seeing her, Wellinven barked, "Is that a cat in my dining hall?"

As Rezkin bent over to place Wellinven's plate in front of him, he said, "Pardon, Your Grace, but someone saw a rat. Shall I have the cat removed?"

"No, no," replied Wellinven. "Let the beast do its job. I'll have no rats in my home."

Rezkin was relieved. Seena was becoming harder to contain as her curiosity about her world grew. Her intelligence went far beyond that of an average beast, and he knew that she was becoming bored with her role.

Duke Darning was conspicuously absent that morning, which caused Rezkin some concern. Once all the food had been served, Rezkin gathered Seena and went in search of the missing duke. He took on the appearance of the duke's manservant and let himself into the suite. After a quick perusal, he realized Darning was not present and neither was his actual manservant. Rezkin was disappointed in himself for losing track of the duke, but he accepted that it was impossible for him to know where *everyone* was at any given time. Just as he began to search the castle, a commotion in the vestibule drew his attention. Several of Darning's guards came rushing in with Darning carried between them, his shirt bloodied and a branch sticking from his shoulder.

"Bring the healer!" shouted one of the guards.

Wellinven's butler hurried away, and the guards settled Darning on the floor. Rezkin hung back at the periphery as he observed the duke's pale, sweaty face. Darning was breathing, that much Rezkin could see, but his breaths were shallow and labored. Soon enough, Wellinven, Atressian, and Marcum all appeared along with a procession of guards and servants. When the healer arrived, she was forced to push her way through the crowd to get to the injured man. As the healer got to work, Wellinven barked, "What happened?"

One of Darning's guards said, "Your Grace, the duke went out for his usual morning ride. He got ahead of us, then something spooked his horse. He was thrown and landed on a broken branch. He was lucky, though."

"How so?" said Wellinven.

"The branch just missed his heart. He could easily have been killed."

Wellinven looked at the guard. "Are you sure this was an accident?"

"Yes, Your Grace. No one else was present."

Rezkin knew this was no accident. Someone had attempted to kill Darning, and he had not been there to stop it. He had not even known Darning had gone out for a ride. If he were going to keep all these men safe, he would need more information. He eyed the duke's manservant who stood back wringing his hands anxiously. The man had probably been in the duke's service for years and was unlikely to be the assassin. He could, however, provide Rezkin with the information he required. He just had to find a way to get it from him.

Wellinven's healer was a talented mage, and Darning was healed in a matter of minutes. She indicated that the duke would need to rest for a few hours, so he was led back to his rooms.

Rezkin followed Wellinven, Atressian, and Marcum back to the study. This time, they closed the door, so he was unable to hear what was said. With the potential targets sequestered in the study and likely out of danger at the present, Rezkin took the opportunity to study and question the servants. One of Wellinven's, two of Darning's, and one of Atressian's, he found out, were recently employed, within the past few months. Those he would watch closely. Of the guards, only two had joined their ranks in the past six months, one of them being Atressian's third cousin's son.

Getting information without raising suspicions was difficult, and Rezkin was pressed to try his hand at multiple illusions. Maintaining those illusions all day and night while also hiding Seena was taxing. Coupled with the fact that he was merely meditating and not sleeping meant that his energy stores were waning. As such, he needed to eat far more than the average human, and he spent a good amount of time near the kitchens. He was getting to know the kitchen staff well, and he had identified one particularly disgruntled young woman who could be a possible threat.

That evening, Duke Darning was recovered, and the three dukes and Marcum met in what Wellinven called his war room. It was a spacious chamber with shelves holding books and scrolls, seating around the perimeter, and a large oak table in the center. Spread on the table were maps of Ashai and its neighboring kingdoms. Mage stones glowed in the lamps that hung from the ceiling. Additional mage stones illuminated an imposing painting of the Wellinven castle standing strong upon its cliffside.

Rezkin, disguised as a servant, stood at attention by the sideboard, ready to do his master's bidding. Seena once again appeared as a cat and was thankfully sleeping nearby. Marcum and Darning stood in irritated silence as Wellinven and Atressian engaged in the well-worn argument over the ascension.

"Tieran will be king," said Wellinven.

"And just where is Tieran at the moment? I have it on good authority that he is presently a prisoner of the Souelian emperor."

"He is not a prisoner," growled Wellinven. "In fact, I have received word that he has been named crown prince of Cael and is next in line to be emperor."

Atressian's jowls jiggled as he jerked his head. "If that is true, which I doubt, then he cannot be king of Ashai. Ashai is not a part of this empire. And if he *is* next in line for the emperor's crown, why has he not been crowned. The emperor has been dead more than half a year."

"Bah, you put stock in unsubstantiated rumors. There is no proof the emperor is dead."

"No? Then where is he?" huffed Atressian.

Wellinven said, "Who knows why a man such as he remains hidden? The fact that his empire still stands despite his absence is a testament to his strength and leadership. I, for one, would like to meet this emperor."

Marcum cleared his throat and interrupted. "If he lives, then you may have the chance. As I said before, if we coordinate our attack from the north with the empire's from the south, we have a good chance at overthrowing Caydean."

"And what then?" snapped Atressian. "Does Ashai become a part of the empire? I'll not have it."

Darning said, "Perhaps it is better to become part of the empire than to allow Caydean's continued reign."

"Treason!" shouted Atressian.

Wellinven sighed, "Everything said here is treason. We are plotting against the king."

"But not the *rightful* king if this True King is to be believed, and if I am right about who he is, then I believe he has a legitimate claim. I have seen the proof of it myself," said Marcum. "If it is true, then Ashai is already part of the empire. You may not like to hear it, but it is the truth. Caydean has most of the army as well as mages and battle mages at his disposal. We can hold out against a siege, but if we do not coordinate an attack with the empire, we will fail."

Atressian growled his frustration. "There must be another way. Channería, Jerea, and Sandea are all positioned for invasion. Perhaps we could coordinate with one or more of them."

Wellinven barked out a mirthless laugh. "And what happens when we win? Do you think any of them will pack up and go back to their own kingdoms?"

As the conversation continued, Rezkin turned part of his attention to a servant who had just walked through the doorway. He had discovered through his research that this servant, a man named Pollick, had been with Wellinven for no more than a month. Pollick had short cropped red hair and a ruddy complexion that was more common in the south. He avoided Rezkin's curious gaze as he set a carafe on the sideboard beside Rezkin. The man's hands trembled as he turned and left the room.

Rezkin poured the wine into a pewter goblet and sniffed it. Sensing nothing out of the ordinary, he poured a bit into his mouth, rolling it around on his tongue. It was subtle, but there, beneath the essences of oak, cherry, and spice, was the telltale bite of crikisa venom. Rezkin spit the wine back into the cup and lifted the carafe just as Wellinven said, "Bring us some wine. All this arguing has left me parched."

Rezkin turned with the carafe and goblet in his hands and said, "Your Grace, I am afraid this wine has turned. I will fetch a fresh carafe."

"Very well," said Wellinven, "but be quick about it."

Rezkin exited the room, followed by Seena, and made his way outside where he dumped the poisoned wine on the lawn. Seena sniffed at it then released a very uncatlike screech as she backed away. Rezkin headed toward the wine cellar to procure more wine. As he strode through the corridors, he pondered the attempted poisoning. Pollick had been nervous, but was that due to guilt or because he was in the presence of the dukes? Had someone else poisoned the wine before Pollick brought it to the war room? Pollick did not have the countenance of a hardened assassin, but that did not mean he was not paid or blackmailed into poisoning the dukes. The man warranted additional investigation.

Upon returning to the war room with a fresh carafe of wine, Rezkin found that the dukes had begrudgingly agreed to make official contact with the empire. Rezkin decided to facilitate that contact by providing them with one of the portable mage relay devices. Since he did not have one, he would need to build it, and for that he needed supplies. When the men turned to discussing the particulars of their contact with the empire, Rezkin was dismissed, and the doors were closed.

Rezkin left the war room to go in search of the servant who had served the poisoned wine, assuming he was still in the castle. If *he* had served poison to four of the most powerful men in the kingdom, he would probably make a quick exit. The first place he checked was the stables. There he found Pollick doing a poor job of saddling a horse. He was obviously not an experienced rider. Rezkin came upon Pollick quickly, cornering him in the horse's stall. He did not bother with an illusion. For this, he could be himself. Holding Pollick at knifepoint, Rezkin said, "Where did you get the venom?"

Pollick shivered with fright as he chanced a glance at Rezkin's face. "W-what venom? I don't know what you're talking about."

Rezkin pressed the knife into Pollick's neck. "You poisoned the wine. Do not try to deny it. Where did you get the venom?"

Pollick started to shake his head, and Rezkin pressed harder drawing a rivulet of blood. Still shaking, the man said, "Please, they'll kill me if I talk."

Rezkin replied, "They're going to kill you anyway. People like these do not leave loose strings. What did they offer you?"

The man whimpered. "Money. They gave me money. I got half up front, and I'm to get the other half when I meet them by the river."

"Who are *they*?"

"I don't know, I swear. I didn't even see his face. He was just a voice under a cloak."

"When did you meet this man?"

"A-about a week ago. That's when he gave me the poison. I was to wait until the general arrived then put it in their wine. A-are they dead?"

Rezkin abruptly sheathed the knife up his sleeve then grabbed Pollick and shoved him out of the stall. "Walk," he ordered.

Pollick stumbled out of the stables, passing a surprised stableboy on the way. Rezkin directed Pollick to take him to the spot where he was to meet his patron. Pollick led Rezkin to the falls where the river cut through the city. Rather than crossing the bridge, he turned and walked up the cobbled road that ran along the cliff drop-off. The rows of homes and businesses gave way to store houses, and finally they reached the mountainside. Pollick stopped beside a small grotto near the waterfall. The recess was partially hidden by a gnarled tree growing from the mountain, and the entire area was in shadow. No one would see a thing unless they were actively searching for it.

Rezkin slid into the grotto, wrapping the shadows about him like a cloak. Pollick anxiously paced beside the tree giving frequent furtive glances in Rezkin's direction. He searched the shadows to no avail until he finally gave up looking. They waited about an hour before anyone approached the area. When a man eventually appeared, Rezkin immediately recognized the threat. Although the man was dressed as a peasant, he moved with the surety and grace of a trained fighter. His muscular build and the sword at his hip lent further evidence to Rezkin's appraisal.

The man approached quickly then stopped in the shadow of the mountain when he was a few feet from Pollick. He said, "You've done it?"

Pollick anxiously shifted from foot to foot. "Yes, it's done. I put it in their wine like you said."

"Well, you failed," growled the man as he drew his sword and stabbed it through Pollick's chest in one fluid movement. The man pushed a shocked

Pollick off his sword and over the cliff's edge. Pollick's body tumbled into the rocky falls below. The man turned and peered into the darkness of the grotto. After a moment, he hustled away.

Rezkin unfurled from his hiding place and followed the man, keeping his distance and shifting his illusion frequently so as not to alert the man to his presence. He had just switched his illusion from that of a male youth to a middle-aged woman when the man ducked into a tavern. Rezkin transitioned again to an older man with a silver beard and followed the man into the establishment. It was late afternoon and the tavern boasted only a few patrons. As Rezkin entered, he noted the swordsman taking a seat at a table in the back corner with another man of equal build wearing a green hood. Rezkin sat down at a table near enough that he could hear much of what they were saying but not so close as to be suspect. Seena curled up by his feet under the table. When the serving girl approached, he ordered ale then directed his attention to the men's discussion.

"Well, what happened?" said the hooded man.

"That lackwit said he put the venom in the wine, but he obviously lied. If he had, they would be dead now. I took care of him."

"We'll need another."

"I'm inclined to just take care of this myself."

"We've discussed this. If we take them one at a time, they will be on high alert after the first one. We need to do them all together. We'll try again with the poison."

"I could do it—go in dressed as a guard."

"Wellinven knows his guards too well," said the hooded man.

"Then a guard for one of the others. Atressian doesn't seem the type to get to know his people."

"It's too risky. We'll pay off another servant, and if that doesn't work then we'll move on to plan B."

"The explosives?'

The hooded man nodded. "I was assured the blast would be enough to take down an entire tower."

"Let's skip the poison and implement plan B now."

After a lengthy pause, the hooded may said, "Very well."

Both men abruptly stood and strode toward the exit. Rezkin dropped a thump on the table then followed the men out, changing his appearance once again as he exited. Seena scurried ahead, following the men a little closer but not so far from him that he could not maintain the illusion that she was a cat. The men did not acknowledge the cat in their midst. This time, Rezkin followed the men to a storehouse that was only a few streets away from the tavern. The only windows to the storehouse were high up near the roof, and it only had one entrance. If Rezkin used that entrance, he would easily be seen.

Rezkin lifted Seena onto his shoulder, instructing her to hold on tight. He winced as her little talons dug into his flesh. Then he moved to the narrow space between the storehouse and the adjacent building. He leapt, bounding off the wall to the opposite wall and then again in the other direction. He kept at it, leaping back and forth, as he ascended the buildings until finally he could reach the roof and pull himself over. Seena released his shoulder and skittered across the roof flapping her wings as if to take flight.

In a harsh whisper, Rezkin said, "Seena, no. Return to my side."

Seena lowered her wings slowly and looked at him, crestfallen. She dragged her tail along the roof as she slowly shuffled over to him. He knew she was eager to continue her flying lessons, but it was not the best time.

Rezkin padded across the flat roof toward the side with the high windows with Seena on his heels. There, he hung upside down from the roof to peer into windows smudged with dust. He found the two men inside standing over a crate discussing its contents. No one else was in the storehouse. Rezkin had a conundrum. He had no way of knowing if there were more assassins involved in this plot or if these two were it. If he took out these two now, it would alert any others that he was on to them. If he did not, he could lose them altogether.

Rezkin decided that killing these two now was worth the risk. He moved back to the side of the building he had scaled and descended in similar manner. He allowed Seena to glide down on her own, and when she reached the ground, she danced around happily. She abruptly ceased her celebration and followed him as he let himself into the storehouse through the only door. He had no armor and no sword on him since he had been disguised as a servant, but he had a plethora of knives secreted about his person. He palmed two throwing daggers as he entered the building.

As the door creaked open and Rezkin stepped into the dark interior, both men turned to look. Upon seeing him, they each drew a sword. They closed the distance. Rezkin threw his knives. The swordsman from earlier batted one away with his sword. The other dagger nicked the hooded man across the throat but failed to bring him down. Drawing two more knives, Rezkin dodged the first attacks by the two men.

They attacked in tandem with practiced ease. He ducked a strike and scored a cut across the first man's wrist. The man maintained his grip on his sword as Rezkin maneuvered to keep both men in front of him, one blocking the other. He dodged another attack and stepped into the man's guard, slashing his blade across the man's forearm. The man dropped the sword with a clatter. Rezkin stabbed his other knife into the man's kidney then pushed him into the second man. The hooded man shoved his comrade back and stepped around him. He came at Rezkin with quick, concise swings. It was not hard for Rezkin to figure out who—or *what*—these men were. Strikers.

Rezkin ducked, dodged, jumped, and rolled away from the hooded man's onslaught. The man remained between Rezkin and the dropped sword, while the first man lay on the ground groaning in pain and bleeding all over the floor. Rezkin rolled away from another strike. He came to his feet and stabbed the downed man in the neck. Leaving his knife there, he quickly palmed a throwing dagger. He turned and lobbed it at the hooded man. As the man dodged, Rezkin threw himself at the man's feet. The two tumbled to the ground. Rezkin slashed his knife across the man's inner thigh, severing the artery. Then he crawled upward grabbing hold of the man's sword arm in an iron grip. He stuck his knife at the man's throat with his other hand.

"What are your names?" asked Rezkin.

The man spit in Rezkin's face.

"How many more are there?" he asked as he pressed the knife deeper into the man's flesh.

"I'm not telling you anything. I'm dead anyway."

Rezkin knew it to be true. The man was bleeding out as they spoke.

"Who *are* you?" the man asked weakly.

Rezkin pondered that. Who was he now? He said, "They call me many things, but you may call me Death."

The man barked a pitiful laugh as his eyes became unfocused. He whispered, "You are too late." A moment later, he lost consciousness. Not long after that, he was dead.

Both men dead, Rezkin searched their bodies and collected his knives. Seena tiptoed around the pooling blood as she joined him. He could smell the smoke from her attempt to produce fire during the bout. Rezkin knew she wanted to join the fight. She always wanted to participate, but she was still too small, and her tiny teeth and talons would not do enough damage. She scurried up his clothing to perch on his shoulder as he peered into the crate.

An assortment of magical items was nestled in hay inside the crate. There were a few rods and pouches filled with rocks. Beneath those were clay jars containing a pungent powder. Rezkin did not know what any of the items were, and he had no way of knowing what enchantments they possessed, but he could guess that these were the explosives the strikers had been discussing. At least, some of them. The man's final words echoed in his mind. *You are too late.* Perhaps the explosives were already in place. Or perhaps there was another assassin.

He sealed the crate then hefted it onto a small cart he found in the corner. Disguised as the dead servant Pollick, whose body was unlikely to be found anytime soon, if ever, he began pushing the cart toward the castle keep. When he arrived, he informed the guards that the crate had been sent by an unknown party to the mages. He would let them figure out what was in it.

Once that was finished, Rezkin and Seena set off in the direction of the mages' ward. As he approached the corner to turn into the ward, he heard raised voices. Two men were arguing over an experiment gone wrong. Rezkin peered around the corner to see an older mage with a bald pate and glasses berating a younger mage with sandy blonde hair. The younger mage was not intimidated by the older mage, and Rezkin wondered what their relative power levels were. The younger mage stormed away turning down the corridor opposite Rezkin, and the older mage turned with a harrumph into a room.

With a bit of concentration, Rezkin transformed his illusion into a facsimile of the younger mage and headed down the corridor. He did not know the mage's name, but he had heard his voice enough to reproduce it using illusion. He just hoped no one stopped to chat with him. There was one other problem with impersonating a mage, though, and that was vimaral bleed. Most mages bled small amounts of power, especially when using that power, that could be detected by other mages. As Spirétua, Rezkin's vimaral bleed was not detectable by mages. Since he was disguised as a mage, it would be suspect if he did not have any. Rezkin strode down the corridor wondering if he could reproduce the effect.

From what he had learned from Entris and Wesson, power was a bit like the light spectrum. Vimara was split like light through a crystal into different bands of color. Human mages and most Eihelvanan had varying degrees of those colors, and the levels and combinations determined what kind of mage they were. A Spirétua, on the other hand, was blessed with the entire spectrum, the white light composed of all the colors.

Rezkin ducked into an empty workroom, pausing beside the doorway. He searched inside himself for his vimara. He could feel it pulsating at his core. He entered a light state of *eskyeyela* where he could visualize the vimara in its purest form. He could see the river of light flowing through him, could hear its melody ringing in his mind. As he did whenever he used his vimara, he drew a small stream from that river. Then he imagined separating that stream into the different colors of vimara. The stream split like a rainbow in his mind, and the melody changed becoming more animated. Rezkin released several of the colors pulling only on the blue for aquian or water, and violet for crystallis or earth. He did not know what the mage's affinities were, but a typical mage could not tell either. Only readers could see the colors. Rezkin took the blue and violet vimara and pushed them to the surface of his body and then outside it in a small amount. He could not tell for certain, but he was reasonably sure he was expressing vimaral bleed as would a mage.

That done, he withdrew from *eskyeyela* and turned his attention to the room. He still needed supplies for his portable mage relay, and he did not know where to find them. As he was searching, another mage walking by stuck her head into the room.

"Ferris? What are you doing in here?" she said.

Rezkin turned toward her with a look of chagrin. "I was just catching my breath. I had an argument."

The woman, a thirty-something brunette with a pleasant smile, looked at him sympathetically. "With Irdo. I know. I heard. I think *everybody* heard. I know you're both under stress with the coming war and all, but you shouldn't let him get to you. Just because he's older that doesn't mean he knows best."

Rezkin wanted the woman to leave, but now he was stuck having a heartfelt conversation with her on Ferris's behalf. "I know," he said, "but I don't think he does."

She smiled warmly. "Come on. We'll get some tea and talk it through."

"I would rather just stay here for a bit if you don't mind," he replied.

At this she seemed a little surprised, but she covered it well. "Okay, if that's what you want. You know where I am if you change your mind."

Rezkin nodded and thanked her. Then he took a chance and said, "Do you know where I might find some directional alloy?"

She furrowed her brow. "Why would you want that?"

"It's for a little side project," he replied.

"I suppose it's in the supply room if we have any," she said.

"I couldn't find it. Would you mind showing me?"

"Of course, I'll help you look."

Rezkin walked with the woman to a room three doors down. Seena scampered behind them chasing dust bunnies. The storage space was filled with shelves, crates, and barrels stuffed full to the brim with various magical and mundane supplies. The woman walked to a shelf and lifted a medium-sized trunk. She set it on a table in the center of the room and opened it to find a large chunk of directional alloy. Its silvery surface gleamed in the light of the mage stones on the ceiling.

"How much do you need?" she said eyeing the metallic lump.

"Not much, about the size of my thumb will do."

The woman pinched off the required amount and rolled into a ball before handing it to him. "Is that all?"

"No, I need a few more things, but I can find them. Thank you."

"All right, I will see you later."

"Oh, one more thing," he said as she was just about to exit. "How is my vimaral bleed?"

She looked at him curiously. "What do you mean?"

"I've been working on reining it in. Do you feel it?"

"Yes, I'm afraid you haven't been successful yet. It's coming through quite clearly."

Rezkin nodded and thanked her. Once the woman was gone, he began searching the storage room in earnest, stuffing items into a sack he procured from a stack in the corner. Rezkin was able to find everything he needed, although it would have been easier with some of the crystals from the citadel at Cael. Functionally, the only difference between the device he would create and those from the citadel was that only a mage would be able to operate this one. The construction of the relay would not be difficult. Linking it to the relay in Caellurum would be the challenge. Since he was not there to link it directly, he would have to do it based on memory alone. That was one of the advantages of being a *scrivener*, however. He had perfect memory and recall.

After acquiring all he needed to create the relay, Rezkin returned to the first workroom he had explored. He had seen many of the tools he would need in that workroom. He closed the door this time and worked quickly in case the real Ferris returned or someone else interrupted his work. He also needed to get back to the dukes and general before someone managed to assassinate one of them. Rezkin felt stretched thin. Having to protect four men at once while also affecting the war was strenuous, but he appreciated the challenge.

Since he had the materials and tools, he took the opportunity to make a second portable relay device, just in case something else came up where he might need one. When it came time to power the devices, Rezkin dropped his illusion and ceased the vimaral bleed. He would need all his concentration to link the devices to the mage relay in Caellurum. He instructed Seena to alert him if anyone entered, then dove into *eskyeyela.* He did not know how normal mages linked mage relays. He only knew how *he* had done it. He found the vimara infused in the mage materials of the relays and noted their pattern. Then he tugged on a number of streams of his own vimara and stripped away the pieces he needed. He bent, twisted, and curved the pieces to match the patterns of the mage materials then overlayed the two. Once the two patterns were linked together, he began manipulating them by memory into the intricate patterns that were specific to the mage relay in Cael. Once the patterns were locked into place, he withdrew his own vimara, leaving behind the linked signatures of the relay devices.

When he was finished, he cleaned up the workstation so there was no evidence of his being there. He tucked both relay devices into his pockets and reinstated his illusion of Mage Ferris. Then he headed for the door. When it swung open, he was faced with the very mage he was impersonating. Before Ferris could say anything, Rezkin switched the illusion to one of a servant. Ferris blinked at him looking thoroughly thrown.

"What's happening here?" said Ferris. "I saw …"

"Yes, master?" replied Rezkin with heavy deference.

"Well, I saw myself … but that's impossible."

"Excuse me, master? I don't understand."

Ferris wiped a hand down his face and shook his head. He muttered to himself, "I must be seeing things. Perhaps I do need more sleep." To Rezkin, he said, "What are you doing here? You know servants aren't supposed to be in these rooms."

Rezkin allowed fear to claim his face. "Pardon me, Master, but Mage Irdo asked me to come. Since he's not here, I was just leaving."

Ferris scowled. "Mage Irdo. Of course he would flout the rules. Go on. I will deal with Irdo if need be."

"Yes, Master. Thank you, Master." Rezkin ducked out of the room as if he could not leave fast enough. Seena followed, a rat clutched between her jaws as she pranced proudly behind him. Rezkin searched rooms as he traversed the corridor. This gave him the opportunity to familiarize himself with the castle in addition to finding what he was looking for. Finally, in the sixth room, he found a desk with a stack of paper and writing supplies. It was a small room, barely large enough to fit the desk, but that did not matter to Rezkin. He merely required the writing supplies. He sat down to compose a letter offering the portable mage relay to Lord Nirius, Duke of Wellinven. He explained its use and then left the letter unsigned. Then he placed the relay and the letter into a pouch he had procured from the storeroom. Finally, reapplying his illusion of Pollick, he delivered the pouch to the duke.

"What is this?" said Wellinven.

Rezkin held the serving tray so that the duke could reach the pouch. "A package, Your Grace. It just arrived."

The duke took the pouch, extracted its contents, and read the letter. As he did, his brows rose further and further toward the ceiling. He handed the letter to Marcum who read it with a similar reaction before handing it on to Darning.

"Do you think it is real?" said Marcum, indicating the device in Wellinven's hand.

Rezkin felt the sizzle of vimara as Wellinven probed the device. After a few minutes, Wellinven said, "I think it just might be. I have never heard of a portable mage relay. This is an ingenious design. I cannot imagine how it was done."

Marcum said, "If this works, it could give us a major advantage. Can you imagine the level of coordination we would have if we could give these to our officers?"

Darning said, "How do we know this is truly from Cael? This could be a trick of Caydean's—a trap."

"We will not know unless we try it," said Wellinven. "This would give me the opportunity to speak with my son. I say it is worth the risk."

Atressian tossed the letter onto the war room table. "Of course you would say that. This letter is unsigned. We do not even know that Tieran is on the other end. Even if you do speak with him, it could be an imposter. We might believe we are coordinating with the empire when really we are giving our strategy to the enemy."

"Then we will find a way to test him," said Wellinven. "I shall ask him questions to which only he would know the answers."

Wellinven abruptly looked at Rezkin. "Are you still here? Dismissed."

17

THE NEXT COUPLE of days were uneventful. Rezkin searched the castle for anything that might be an explosive device but had thus far found nothing. He continued to stalk and question household staff and guards while Seena single-handedly rid the place of vermin. During his time at the castle, he had taken upon himself another task—one that would see to the end of Caydean's reign.

The dukes had not been able to come to terms regarding anything—not about joining their forces, not about the ascension, not about working with or against the empire, and not even about contacting Cael. Rezkin knew that if left to their own devices, these days of endless meetings would lead nowhere. If Caydean was to be overthrown, the dukes and Marcum would need to make a unified front, and they would need to do it *with* the empire. Rezkin was to make sure that happened. Therefore, he needed more information.

With Seena's assistance, he stepped through a portal into a familiar forest speckled with sunlight streaming between the leaves and awash in the shadows cast by areas of thicker canopy. He was there for no more than a minute when he lurched to the side to avoid a flying dagger. Then a black clad figure dropped from a bough while another emerged from the underbrush. The man and the woman both wore masks to obscure all but their eyes, which took him in with threatening glares.

They attacked at once, the man with twin daggers and the woman with a shortsword. Rezkin did not draw his sword but instead stepped into the man's guard and blocked his attempted strikes. Rezkin kicked back at the woman while simultaneously grabbing the man's wrist and wrenching his arm around behind him causing him to drop one of his knives. He hauled the man around so that he was between him and the woman. He blocked another stab attempt, hooked his arm around the other man's arm and twisted his wrist until he dropped the second blade. Then he spun the man around and slammed him into a tree as he dodged another attack by the woman. She swiped at his legs, but he leapt out of the way before dashing around her in a burst of inhuman speed. He grabbed her around the neck in a choke hold and ordered her to drop the sword. She chose not to, so he rendered her unconscious. With both assassins out cold, he turned and padded softly over the detritus toward the Black Hall.

Shadows shifted in the trees, and a bird called out only to be echoed by another call from farther away. Rezkin knew they were communicating, and he was glad for it. These things went so much smoother when he did not have to fight everyone in his path to make his point. He could have portalled directly into the Black Hall, but he wanted to give them time to prepare for his arrival. When he reached the front entrance of the tower, a single assassin greeted him. It was Briesh, a master assassin and second to the grandmaster. Briesh appeared wary as he approached. He eyed Seena who was perched on Rezkin's shoulder disguised as a large raven.

"Raven," Briesh said. "It has been some time since we have seen you. Our slips did not recognize you."

"They were not meant to," replied Rezkin as he stopped in front of the slip.

Briesh nodded. "I can never remember your appearance. How do you do it?"

"That is a skill that cannot be taught."

"Indeed," said Briesh as if it were to be expected. "Why do you grace us with your presence?"

"I need information," said Rezkin.

Briesh cracked a grin. "Then you have come to the right place. We have gathered much since coming into your service. Please, come with me."

Rezkin followed Briesh into the hall. It was an enormous tower with rooms stationed around the perimeter and a multitude of training platforms ascending all the way to the roof. There, on the bottom level, were the most recent recruits, small men with only a handful of years to their short lives. Rezkin approved of their training starting so young, although he knew his friends would have felt differently. In *their* world, the innocent world of the *ro*, these were *children*, and they were meant to be protected and nurtured. But in the world of the *ruk*, those who knew the darkness that existed in the world, this early training would mean the difference between life and death for the future slips.

Briesh began climbing the platforms. The lower levels had stairs to accommodate the ascent, but as they rose, fewer accommodations were made. Eventually, they were leaping from platforms, ascending ropes, and climbing poles to get to the next level. About midway up the tower, Briesh led Rezkin into a series of rooms filled with tables, desks, and shelves. Upon these were stacks of papers, ledgers, books, and scrolls. Briesh turned and spread his arms wide.

"Here is all of your information," he said. "The librarians can help you find what you seek."

Rezkin eyed the two young men who stepped out from behind a stack of shelves. They were dressed like slips sans masks, but they each wore an apron with multiple pockets stuffed with scrolls. One of them had spectacles. They both wore expressions of uncertainty.

Eying the one with spectacles, Rezkin said, "It is unusual for slip to have such a visual deficiency."

The young man pushed the spectacles up the bridge of his nose and said, "I am Nimick, m'lord. My eyesight only went bad recently. It was why I was chosen to become a librarian." He lifted his chin defiantly. "But I am just as effective as I was before my eyesight changed."

Rezkin looked to Briesh. "Has he seen a healer?"

Briesh nodded once. "Yes. The healer was unable to correct his vision."

"Very well, so be it. I am looking for information on the dukes."

The second slip said, "Veshi, m'lord. Which dukes? The rightful dukes or Caydean's lot?"

"Darning, Atressian, and Wellinven. I need anything I can use against them."

The two nodded to each other, exchanged a few words, then moved toward different stacks of papers. As Nimick and Veshi went about gathering the information Rezkin requested, Briesh began informing Rezkin of the most significant happenings in the kingdom. Rezkin already knew much of what was discussed, but he found it interesting that the Black Hall had been able to garner so much. One area of pure speculation was Caydean's motivation for developing his own religion. On the surface, it appeared to be an attempt at unification of the kingdom under a single spiritual entity independent of the Temple of the Maker, which held much power in other parts of the Souelian. It appeared to be a progression toward order. Rezkin knew Caydean to be a demon, though, and demons were creatures of chaos. Did Caydean simply desire to be worshipped?

Was he hoping to sow discord between opposing religions? No one seemed to know the answer.

Briesh was explaining how Ashai's continued advance into Verril was affecting the neighboring kingdoms' sense of security when Nimick and Veshi approached, each bearing a short stack of papers.

Nimick cleared his throat and said, "Here is the information you ordered, Riel'gesh. If you would come this way, we have a place for you to study the documents."

Rezkin was led to a table lit by mage light bearing blank sheets of paper and an assortment of pens and inks. Before Nimick left, he said, "There is one more thing we thought you should know."

"Yes?"

"Someone issued a contract to kill the Leréshi queen."

Rezkin stroked his jaw thoughtfully. "Someone is always trying to kill the Leréshi queen."

Nimick bobbed his head. "Yes, but this time we could not confirm the source of the contract. We do not know who the client was."

This piqued Rezkin's interest. If the Black Hall could not figure out who the client was, then someone had gone to extreme measures to ensure that information stayed hidden. He said, "Did you take the contract?"

"No, Riel'gesh. You issued orders not to take contracts against the empire, and Lon Lerésh is part of the empire."

"Very good. Keep looking into the source of the contract. I want to know who issued it."

"Yes, Riel'gesh." Nimick bowed then left him to his reading.

For the next hour, he studied the documents, then he spent another hour making plans. Finally, he used the pens and paper to write letters and issue orders both for the Black Hall and for his numerous other retainers. After handing off some of his orders, Rezkin had Seena open a portal, and he stepped through. One matter was rather urgent, and Rezkin felt obliged to see to it himself. The passage was instantaneous, and Rezkin found himself standing in the market district of Kaibain. A man bearing a rickshaw swerved to avoid him, no doubt surprised and confused by Rezkin's sudden appearance.

It was evening by the time Rezkin made his way to the home of Miss Eliza Tomkins. The spacious apartment was on the second floor of a modest building in an area of the city that catered to the more affluent merchants, bankers, and city officials. Rezkin did not approach the apartment building directly for he knew someone would be watching. Instead, he waited for one of the tenants to leave the building, then used illusion to don the man's persona. He entered the apartment building disguised as the resident and took the stairs to the second floor. Then he knocked on the door of Miss Tomkin's apartment. The door opened to reveal a rough looking man in the uniform of an Ashaiian soldier. Rezkin punched the man in the face then kicked him backward into the apartment. He had to move fast. He did not know how many of the enemy inhabited the apartment.

Seena darted past Rezkin, and he slammed the door shut once they were inside. Before Rezkin could get to the next man, Seena wrapped herself around his thigh and sank her razor-sharp teeth into his flesh. The man shouted and reached down to wrench her off, but Seena was fast. She bit down on his hand eliciting another cry, and Rezkin launched a throwing dagger into the man's throat. Rezkin drew his sword and dispatched the man at his feet just as a woman screamed and a child began to wail. Rezkin turned to find a third uniformed man holding a small girl hostage at knifepoint. A woman yanked on his arm, but he shoved her away. While he was distracted, Rezkin launched two more throwing daggers. One skimmed past the man's head, clipping his ear, but the other found its mark. The man dropped dead with a dagger through the eye, and the child fell to the ground crying. The woman grabbed the child then turned toward Rezkin with terror in her eyes.

She said, "Did he send you? Please tell me he sent you to save us."

Rezkin stormed past the woman and child to search the other room before returning to look down at the woman who was huddled on the floor with her daughter. The woman looked to be in her late twenties. She wore a pale pink dress, and her hair was neatly arranged atop her head, but fatigue was evident in her eyes. She looked like she had not slept well for days.

Rezkin said, "Is the child well, Miss Tomkins?"

"Y-yes, she is unharmed."

"Good. We must move quickly. Pack your things. You may bring a single bag."

"We are leaving?"

"Yes, Caydean will send more men when these do not report in."

She nodded. "Yes, but what is *that*?" Her gaze went to Seena who preened atop the dead man she had attacked.

"Do not worry about her for now. You need to pack your belongings, or you will be going with only what you wear now."

"O-okay, but I do not have a bag. I have several trunks."

"I cannot carry a trunk for you. I need my hands free to fight. Wrap your belongings in the bedsheet. Do you possess the *talent*?"

"A little. Not enough to become a mage."

"Very well. Hopefully it will be enough to shorten the trip."

"What does that mean?"

"Never mind that. Go pack."

As Eliza packed a few meager belongings for herself and her daughter, Rezkin gathered the dead men and marked each with the symbol of the Raven. Eliza reemerged from her bedroom carrying a thick sack made of the bedsheet in one hand and gripping her daughter's hand in the other. Rezkin took the heavy sack from her, satisfied that he would have one hand free, then requested for Seena to open a portal to Cael. By the time they arrived, night had fallen. Rezkin secured Eliza and her daughter in an empty home in the city outside the citadel, then, with Seena's help, he returned to the Wellinven castle.

He was relieved to find that no one had been assassinated while he had been gone. The castle was quiet when he arrived in the dark of night. Darning and Wellinven were in the study arguing over whether they should attempt to coordinate with the Jerean and Sandean forces in the west or the Channeríans in the east, and Marcum was in his room poring over correspondence. Atressian was notably absent, and Rezkin found him seated by the hearth in the library reading a book.

Rezkin donned the disguise of a hooded figure, a warrior whose face was perpetually in shadow with a large raven upon his shoulder. Then he stealthily entered the room and seated himself in another chair by the fire without Atressian's notice. He waited patiently for Atressian to look up, but the man was engrossed in his reading material. Seena stretched and flapped her wings, and the rustle finally roused Atressian. The man startled and jumped to his feet dropping the tome on the floor. Rezkin remained where he was as he stroked Seena's long neck.

"Who are you, and what are you doing in here?" shouted Atressian and a mage ward appeared around him.

Rezkin inwardly cringed at the volume of the man's voice. He did not want others to come investigate. This conversation was better had in private.

Rezkin used illusion to deepen his voice. "Please, sit, Atressian. We have much to discuss."

Atressian drew himself up. "I will do no such thing. Who are you? How did you get in here without my noticing?"

Rezkin ignored the man's questions. "You have made several attempts to contract with the Black Hall to dispose of both Wellinven and Tieran Nirius, have you not?"

"I have done no such thing," huffed Atressian.

"Do not deny it. Yes, you made use of an assortment of assumed names and intermediaries, but I know it to be you."

Atressian's lips pursed stubbornly then his shoulders dropped. "You are he, then? You have come to fulfill the contract?"

With an edge to his voice, Rezkin commanded, "Sit."

Atressian slowly lowered himself back into his chair then looked at Rezkin expectantly.

Rezkin said, "If I had come to fulfill your contract you would never have seen me."

"What then?" asked Atressian. "Why are you here?"

"I have come to secure a counter agreement."

Atressian looked at him with suspicion. "What sort of counter agreement."

"I know of your mistress and her daughter—*your* daughter."

Atressian's face paled. "How could you? No one knows of them."

"I did not take you for a fool, Atressian. Of course people know of them. You are a duke. Your movements never go unnoticed. Caydean has been blackmailing you. He was keeping them under guard, threatening them, in order to secure your cooperation."

"What do you mean *was* keeping them? What has happened to Eliza and Zenia?"

"They are safe—for now."

"*You* have them?"

"I do, and if you want them to remain safe and unharmed, you will do as I command."

"Who *are* you?"

"I am known as the Raven."

Atressian clenched his fists in his lap. "I have heard of you. What is it you want from me?"

"You will set aside your petty grievances with Wellinven and work *with* him. You will agree to cooperate with the empire, and you will agree to contact Cael."

"Is that all?" Atressian said mockingly. "You ask me to sacrifice the kingdom."

"In addition, you will drop this nonsense of your claim to the Ashaiian throne."

"I will not! The crown belongs to *me*."

"Eliza's and Zenia's lives depend on it," said Rezkin.

"You think I will give up the throne for a mistress and bastard daughter?"

"I know you will, Atressian. You may carry no love for your wife or elder son, Fierdon, but I know you love Hespion, Eliza, and Zenia. You would not wish harm upon any of them."

Atressian tensed as Rezkin stood. He said, "You have your orders. See that you follow them. I will be watching closely." As Rezkin left the room, he immediately changed his illusion to that of a servant. Atressian appeared in the doorway a moment later peering down the corridor in either direction. Rezkin was pleased to have gotten away so easily and yet disappointed that there were no guards present. It was much more difficult to protect all the dukes if they did not attempt to protect themselves. They were not aware of the assassination attempts, however, so they had not been put on high alert. They no doubt felt they were safe within the Wellinven castle.

Seena scampered ahead of him as Rezkin made his way to the second tower where waited Duke Darning's quarters. He allowed himself into the suite and found the duke's manservant dozing noisily in the chair by the door. Rezkin withdrew a needle laced with a sedative from a small vial in his belt pouch and stuck it into the man's neck. The man never woke.

Rezkin crossed the sitting room to venture into the bed chamber. When Darning finally arrived nearly an hour later, Rezkin surprised him with his presence. The duke entered the suite and found his manservant peacefully napping, then he looked up to find the Raven staring at him from across the room. The duke's first reaction was an admirable one. He sent a ball of lightning streaking toward Rezkin. Rezkin did not dodge the attack, instead allowing the lightning to strike him. It sizzled around his body in glowing arcs before dissipating to no effect. Darning sent another ball of lightning at him with the same result. Then he turned toward the door either to run or call for guards. Rezkin snapped his power into action, casting a shield ward between the duke and the door, trapping him inside the suite.

The duke railed against the ward for a moment before turning back to Rezkin. He said, "Who are you? Are you here to kill me?"

Rezkin answered, "If I wanted you dead, you would already be dead."

"Well, what is it you want?"

"I have something for you, something I think will be of great interest to you."

"And you could not have given it to me through the regular channels?"

"I am afraid not, Duke Darning. I had to make sure you personally accept it."

The duke swallowed hard. "Very well. Hand it over and be gone."

Rezkin withdrew a scroll tube from where it was tucked into his belt and held it up. Darning looked at it, blinking a few times, before saying, "That is it? That is all you have for me?"

"I think you will find that it is enough," said Rezkin as he tossed the scroll tube toward the duke.

Darning fumbled the catch and had to stoop to pick the tube up from the floor. With shaky hands, he opened the tube and unrolled the contents, which were several pages of information. He glanced at Rezkin, then moved to the table in front of the settee to peruse the contents. As he read each page, his brows rose toward the ceiling higher and higher. Eventually, he looked up and said, "Is this true?"

Rezkin nodded in the affirmative even though most of it was *not* true—at least, nothing confirmed. The papers detailed a plot between the Jereans, Sandeans, and Channeríans to divvy up the kingdom of Ashai at the conclusion of a joint campaign. The proposed new borders went straight through Darning lands. Although the entire plot was fiction, Rezkin had used actual correspondence and intelligence to design it to appear authentic.

Darning said, "Who are you?"

Rezkin bowed with a flourish. "I am called the Raven."

Darning was silent for a moment before saying, "Why would a criminal overlord bring this to *me*?"

"Because you need to know the consequences of your proposed actions. The neighboring kingdoms cannot be trusted to ensure Ashai's autonomy. Your only hope lies with the empire."

Darning released a mirthless laugh. "And this *empire* will respect Ashai's autonomy?"

"The empire is already led by the rightful king of Ashai. Ashai's autonomy is not in question."

"Do you speak of the dead emperor or Tieran Nirius?"

"Does it matter?"

Darning rubbed a hand down his face. "No, I suppose it does not."

"You must lend your support to the proposal to coordinate with the empire and contact Cael."

Darning's suspicious gaze slid to Rezkin. "Why do *you* care?"

"For the same reason all Ashaiians should. It is in my best interest."

Rezkin left Duke Darning's suite satisfied that he had gotten through to the man. He had no need to visit Wellinven or Marcum since they were already of the mind to coordinate with the empire. He adjourned to the disused room in the sixth tower that he had claimed, and for the first time in several weeks, he slept soundly. That night, he was visited by another of his dreams.

He opened his eyes, and beside him lay a white-haired beauty with silver eyes. Those eyes turned wide as saucers upon seeing him, and her mouth formed a pert little 'o'. *Then tears filled her eyes and one rolled down her cheek.*

Her voice was husky as she said, "Why do you haunt me?"

Rezkin lifted a hand and wiped away her tear. He was suddenly overwhelmed with emotions he had never before experienced, at least not to this degree. He wanted nothing more than to wrap her in his arms and hold her close. He pulled her to him, and she came willingly. She crushed her lips to his, and he trailed his hand over the sheets, down her back to the curve of her buttocks. He pulled her in tightly as their tongues entwined. She pushed against him then rolled on top of him. Rezkin did not fight her despite the compromising position. For the first time since his youth, he did not feel threatened by a woman. He realized he trusted Azeria with his life.

Tendrils of guilt dug into his heart as his blood heated and his breath quickened. He trusted her, but she could not trust in him. Rezkin gripped her shoulders holding her back and breaking their kiss. He gazed into her confused eyes and made a decision. He said, "I need to tell you something."

"Cannot it wait," she murmured as she tried to kiss him again.

He held her back then sat up so that she was straddling his lap. The sheet fell, and he realized she wore nothing beneath it. With great effort, he drew his gaze away from her exposed breasts and said, "I need you to know something that must stay between you and me. You cannot tell Entris. Azeria, promise me."

Her brow furrowed in concern. "Tell me what?"

"Promise."

Her gaze was filled with questions as she stared at him. Finally, she said, "I promise."

For the first time in memory, Rezkin felt anxious. He released a breath and said, "I am alive."

. . .

Rezkin awoke with a start. Something had alerted him. He looked down to see Seena curled up sleeping peacefully at his side. She cracked one eye, looked at him, then rolled over onto her back exposing her belly. A moment later, she sniffed the air. Her eyes pooped open. She leapt to her feet and arched her back holding her wings aloft. Her attention was riveted on the door. Rezkin crept toward the door and eased it open. Peering into the darkness, he saw nothing but an empty stairwell. He listened for any sound of movement. After a moment, he thought he heard the slightest footfall—a mere scuff that would normally have gone unnoticed.

He padded down the stairs with a dagger in his hand and Seena at his heels. He had taught her to move as silently as he did, not an easy feat with a dragon. When they reached the next landing, Rezkin tried the door, but it was locked. He continued down the stairs as he listened closely. The dawn's first light peeked in through the arrow slits, but for the most part, he was enveloped in darkness. He reached the base of the tower without encountering anyone and began to wonder if the sound had been his imagination. Still, he would investigate. The sixth tower was attached to the curtain wall by means of a wooden bridge that could be dropped in the event of an attack. As it was, the tower could provide a means of entry into the castle if someone was skilled enough to scale the wall. That was why he had chosen that tower in the first place.

Rezkin searched the castle for over an hour before going to the kitchen to ensure no one poisoned the food. The general and dukes convened for breakfast in the dining hall, and Rezkin watched the servers carefully, ensuring that he knew them all. Then he returned to searching the castle for the intruder. It was then that he saw someone he did not recognize darting into the stairwell of the sixth tower.

Rezkin followed the stranger as he took the stairs two at a time. He could now hear the footsteps of his quarry, but he seemed to be getting no closer. With a burst of Eihelvanan speed he sped up the stairs, but the stranger still managed to stay ahead of him. When he reached the landing that led to the bridge he was breathing heavily. He caught sight of the stranger just as a black stream of energy struck him in the chest. Rezkin was thrown backward into the wall with a crunch. He nearly tumbled down the stairs before he caught himself. He struggled to sit up as his chest burned with a fiery pain that took his breath away. Seena perched on his chest hissing and spewing smoke toward the assailant.

Rezkin climbed to his feet and was halfway across the bridge when he spied the man about to descend over the crenelated wall.

The man stopped and looked back at Rezkin with a sinister grin. His eyes were black as night, and he exuded a dark aura all around him. He said, "You can chase me, or you can try to save *them*." Rezkin launched a throwing dagger at the man, but it fell to the ground uselessly when it encountered a ward. The demon said, "When the general and dukes gather, they will all die. You don't have much time to save them." Then the man jumped over the wall.

Rezkin hurried the rest of the way across the bridge and to the wall. He looked over the wall to see the demon running away far below. Rezkin had no means of following the man even if he did have the time. And time was a luxury he did not have. He was certain the demon had planted the explosives somewhere in the castle. His only clue as to where was that it would be near someplace where the men would gather.

Frustrated with having lost the assailant, Rezkin made his way back down the tower. Seena followed just as flustered as she flapped her wings with agitation. Rezkin did not know if she was truly bothered by the loss of their prey or if she were merely acting in response to his feelings.

The dukes and general had finished with their breakfast by the time Rezkin made it back to the dining hall. He knew that when they finished, they would gather in the war room to continue their negotiations. Hopefully, now those negotiations might lead somewhere thanks to his efforts of the past few days. In the meantime, however, Rezkin had to make sure they were not going to die. If the demon was to be believed, he had very little time to find the explosives and disable them—assuming he *could* disable them. Rezkin had never before handled magical devices that exploded, and he was not sure he had the necessary skills.

Rezkin went to the war room, which was presently unoccupied, and began his search. He had no idea what he was looking for, but he had made himself familiar with this room such that he would notice anything that did not belong. After a thorough search, he realized the explosives were not there. He was just leaving as Duke Darning entered the room. The other two dukes were arguing at the end of the corridor, and he had no idea where Marcum had gone. Rezkin had until they were all together to find the explosives. He hurried to the stairwell and looked up and down the stairs. Would the demon put the explosives above the war room or below it? Rezkin had only enough time to choose one, if that. Seena sniffed the air then darted down the stairs. Rezkin hoped she had caught the demon's scent and followed.

He hurried to the room that was directly below the war room. The men could gather at any minute, and he had no way of delaying them. The room was a large space used for storage of furniture and all kinds of treasure in every shape and size. There were rugs and draperies, books and candelabras and serving ware, chests and crates stacked everywhere with only a narrow path around them. Rezkin had no idea how he would find the explosive items amid the mess.

As Seena sniffed the air and scurried amongst the items, Rezkin turned inward. He sought the vimara at his core and pulled it forward. Then he sent a tendril outward searching for anything that might answer back. After a few minutes, he decided a single tendril was insufficient. He widened the flow then wrapped it around himself to radiate out in all directions. He was seeking anything bearing magic. The first item that answered was nothing more than a bespelled music box. The next was a silver ladle. He moved through the room setting it awash in his power. He and Seena eventually converged on one section that held an assortment of magical items. Several of them looked as if they *could* be an explosive device, but he did not know how to tell what their magic did.

He picked up an urn and rolled it over in his hands. It gave off a strong magical signature, but this magic felt different from the other items he had encountered. Something about it felt *off.* Rezkin probed the other items and found three more with the same magical signature. Rezkin gathered the four items in a bag and sprinted from the room. He did not know for certain if he had the explosive devices, but he had a feeling about these items. They were meant to be destructive, he knew it. He ran with a speed beyond human ability back up the stairs and out of the castle. He sped across the front lawn and down the street toward the inner wall. He slowed as he approached the wall so as not to draw attention. Once through the gate, he tossed the bag over the side of the bridge.

Seconds after it left his hands, the bag exploded. The concussive force blasted Rezkin off the other side of the bridge. He plummeted into the icy water only to be battered by rocks as he tumbled down the falls. He gasped as his head breached the surface before he was dragged back under. His ribs collided with a boulder and then his hip with another. It was all he could do with his hazy consciousness to protect his head with a small ward. He emerged from the water briefly as he plummeted through the air, then he slammed back down into the flow and his back collided with another rock.

When Rezkin finally stilled beside the shore, he was far below the castle.

The water lapped around him as he stared up at the morning sky. A bird soared high above him. It circled like a vulture looking for a meal. Then it began to descend. Something about it stirred a memory. This did not look like a bird. It had a long neck and an even longer, sinuous tail. And its wings were not feathered. Rezkin watched it descend until it landed somewhere to his right.

Rezkin did not turn to watch it further. He did not want to move. His whole body ached both with the pain of the blast and that of tumbling down the falls. He knew he was lucky the bag had not exploded while he was carrying it, but he did not feel lucky in that moment. Still, he was presently in violation of a number of *Rules* and if he were to adhere to *Rule 164—Do not depend on others*, then he would need to get moving on his own. Rezkin closed his eyes for a moment before he felt a weight press down on his chest. His eyes darted open, and he found a toothy snout in his face. Icy-blue eyes gazed down at him with concern, and a leathery tongue lashed out to rake his cheek. Rezkin slowly sat up, stifling a groan for his aching ribs. Seena leapt off and sat back on her heels as she watched him. Her wings drooped with worry, and she snorted a puff of smoke.

He took a painful breath and said, "I am well enough, all things considered."

"*You live*," she whispered in his mind.

"You worried I did not?" he asked.

"*I knew you did, but I worried you would not.*"

"I appreciate your concern, Seena. Thank you for finding me."

"*Of course. We are one.*"

Rezkin swallowed down his pain as he got to his feet. None of his limbs were broken, but he was sure to be black and blue by nightfall. He convinced Seena to open a portal into the castle to the room where he had stowed his belongings. There he changed into dry clothes and set his boots beside the fire he built in the hearth. With an illusion of the servant Pollick wrapped around him, he went in search of the dukes. As he stalked through the halls, he noticed the increased number of guards. Since the explosion, the castle had been put on high alert. He also noted a number of wards had been activated along the corridors and in doorways. At least these would help prevent the demon from returning.

He learned that the dukes and the general were once again in the war room, hopefully this time coming to a consensus. Rezkin obtained a tray of meats and cheeses from the kitchen, then reported to the war room to serve the men. When he arrived, Wellinven was using the portable mage relay to hold a discussion with Tieran in Cael. They seemed to have gotten past the initial surprise of contact and were well on their way to negotiating the terms of an alliance. Rezkin noted that although Wellinven seemed to be taking the hard line in the discussions, Tieran sounded knowledgeable and confident and was no less demanding. This seemed to take the dukes by surprise, and Rezkin could see the pride shining in Tieran's father's eyes.

Rezkin remained at Wellinven for the next day until the other dukes departed. There were no more assassination attempts during their stay, but he knew there was always a chance the dukes could fall prey to an ambush during their return journey. Rezkin traveled back to the northern fortress where he had trained with General Marcum, and once the general was safely ensconced in the fortress, he departed for Cael. He had other important matters to deal with.

18

WESSON STEPPED CAUTIOUSLY over the hummocky terrain as he made his way to the meeting point. The rain had stopped so he no longer needed the shield ward he had constructed to keep himself dry, but the tall grasses were still damp and so were his pant legs. He paused beside the tree line to cast a quick spell to dry his clothes. This far from the city it was unlikely any mages would be around to detect his use of vimara. At least, none that he had to worry about. He did not yet know if the party he was meeting had any mages in it. He knew only where and when to meet, and he was already late.

He cast his awareness into the forest searching for any signs of people. He was not particularly good at this spell, and results often varied. Still, it was better to try than be surprised. He sensed no one in the vicinity, and he deflated. Had he missed them? Had they left without him? Where would they go? Wesson shook off his disappointment and continued into the forest, hoping to find them farther in. He continued casting his awareness into his surroundings but only detected a few forest creatures, nothing large enough to be a person. When he reached a tributary, he stopped and settled on a boulder beside the river. He had only been sitting for a few breaths when a voice spoke from directly behind him.

"Mage Wesson."

Wesson nearly jumped out of his skin. Even though he had been casting, he had not detected the presence of another person. With chagrin, he noted to himself that he needed to practice that particular skill with more frequency.

Upon turning, his heart still racing, he said, "Y-yes, Striker Farson. I am here."

"Good. We have been waiting for you."

"I apologize for my tardiness. I was delayed in leaving the city thanks to the rain."

Farson nodded once, then said, "Come with me. I will take you to the others."

The sounds of Wesson crashing through the underbrush rendered Farson's silent passage all the more noticeable. Somehow, the striker was immune to thorny bushes and low-hanging vines. As Wesson's shirt tore on a branch, he wished he could be so graceful.

At one point, Farson looked back at him. "Must you break every branch in the forest? A toddler could track you."

"Sorry," said Wesson. "I am not much of a woodsman."

Luckily, they did not have far to go to reach the others. He found a neat camp of several tents arranged around a central fire pit that presently was not lit. Thanks to the rain, any wood they found to burn would produce too much smoke. Azeria greeted him as he approached. Connovan, who was seeing to the horses, gave him a nod. The former Rez did not speak often, and usually what he did say was not something you wanted to hear. He heard a yelp from within one of the tents. A moment later, Anda came tromping out looking a bit disheveled. Formerly one of Caydean's battle mages, Anda had finally opened her eyes to the truth once she had seen Cael and everything they were striving to create. Still, that did not mean Wesson trusted her, even if they had once been friends.

Wesson turned to Farson. "What is *she* doing here?"

"She is a battle mage. We thought she might be useful."

"But she has sworn a mage oath to serve Caydean."

"No," said Anda, holding up a finger. "I swore to serve *the king*, and you all have convinced me that Caydean is not the rightful king."

"How do we know she speaks truth?" asked Wesson.

Anda said, "Wesson, you know me. I have always tried to do what's right. And this feels right. You can trust me."

Wesson cringed at her words. That was exactly what a traitor would say. The problem was, Wesson *wanted* to believe her. Anda was not a particularly powerful battle mage, but they could use all the help they could get, and she *had* been his friend during a difficult time in his life.

Wesson sighed. "Very well. What are we doing?"

Farson answered. "You are going to tell us everything you have discovered since you have been here. Then we will formulate a plan."

Wesson nodded then proceeded to explain everything he knew about the battle mage generals, the experiments in Avikeev's cellar, the mage prisoners he had released, and then the news of the weapon Rezkin had told him about. He was a bit vague on where he had gotten that information since Rezkin had sworn him to secrecy. He also described the increased presence of the zealots of Caydean's new religion who were congesting the city. In fact, there were so many pilgrims arriving daily for the upcoming unveiling of the new temple that an encampment had been established outside the northern gates of Kaibain.

"The influx of pilgrims into the city means the guards are not checking everyone that enters. It is easy to come and go. There will be no problem getting you into the city," said Wesson.

"Did you find us a safe house?"

"Not exactly," said Wesson. "With so many pilgrims, it was impossible to find a room to rent much less an entire home. I did manage to secure a small storehouse near the market district, though." He neglected to mention that it was Rezkin who had directed him to the storehouse.

"Hmm, it will have to do," replied Farson. "What of this Avikeev? How much of a threat is he?"

"He is a demon. I am sure of it. If the power released during his experiments is any indication, he is pretty powerful, too," said Wesson.

Anda said, "Avikeev is the battle master since Rhone died." She glanced Wesson's way before continuing. "He is *very* powerful, and he's brilliant but merciless. There is a reason he was Rhone's second. I didn't see much of him at the Battle Mage Academy since he was usually in Kaibain, but when he was around, we all made ourselves scarce. I have a hard time believing in demons, but if anyone is one, then it would be him."

Wesson pulled the sketches of the runes from Avikeev's cellar from his tunic and handed them to Azeria. "I was wondering if you have seen anything like these before. I need to know what they mean."

Azeria examined the sketches and nodded. "Yes, I have seen this writing before. It is a form of Adianaik used by the Sen. I only know a few of these runes."

"That is great," said Wesson. "You have at least given me a place to start. Now that I know they are Sen, I can do some proper research."

"Your research will have to wait," said Farson. "Other matters take precedence."

"I am afraid this cannot wait," said Wesson. "This is pertinent to discovering what Avikeev is up to."

"Where must you go to do this research?" said Farson.

"There should be some books and scrolls on the Sen in the library in Kaibain. I am not sure if I will have access to them, though. Caydean has likely restricted access to them if he hasn't removed them altogether."

"Very well," said Farson. "Then our first order of business is to secure you access to the restricted section of the library."

"I would like Azeria to go with me. She knows what to look for." Wesson turned to her. "If that is all right with you, that is."

"Yes, I will join you," she said.

"Okay, then if you all want to follow me, I will lead you to the storehouse."

The group packed up their tents and covered the evidence of their presence. Then they followed Wesson into the city, blending with the pilgrims as they passed the gate guards. The storehouse was located near the market district. It was small but thankfully dry. The outer façade was made of timber and stucco. The interior was vacant save for a few dusty crates stacked to one side. It bore no windows, which would make it much more difficult for anyone to spy on them. The space would have been dark if not for the glowing mage lights stacked atop the crates. Those mage lights were powered by the mages Wesson had released from Avikeev's cells who were waiting for them. This made Striker Farson uneasy. Wesson made the introductions, then Farson pulled him aside.

"What are they doing here?" he said.

"They needed somewhere to go. They're in danger."

"But we do not know them. They could betray us," said Farson.

"They were going to be killed. I saved them. I don't think they'll betray us," Wesson replied.

"You do not know what oaths they have sworn. If they are sworn to serve Caydean, they will be compelled to betray us whether they want to or not."

"They were selected for the experiments because they refused to swear oaths to the king. But, I've been thinking about that. I think I may be able to come up with a way to break a mage oath if it was sworn under duress."

"Impossible," said Farson. "Mage oaths are unbreakable regardless of the conditions during their swearing."

"I can't believe that. It isn't fair—"

Farson barked a laugh. "Fair? Clear the muck out of your head. *Life* is not fair."

"Yes, of course, Striker. I understand." And Wesson did understand. Much of his life had been unfair.

He said, "What if Azeria takes them back to Cael?"

Mage Bargus cleared his throat as he approached. He said, "I could not help but overhear. If I may …"

"What is it?" barked Farson.

Bargus gave a slight bow. "I was held prisoner by Avikeev and the other generals for weeks. I witnessed many of my colleague's deaths while being held. Those were people I have lived and worked with, some for decades. I mourn them even now.

"I had given up hope of escape. I knew it was only a matter of time before I was selected for the experiment, and I knew I would not survive it. Mage Wesson saved me—all of us—from a terrible fate. I will forever be in his debt. And I hate Caydean and everything he stands for. I was at the Mage Academy when it was attacked. I know how treacherous and heartless he is, and I do not intend to stand idly by and watch him ruin this once great kingdom." He glanced back at the other mages before continuing. "I think I speak for all of us when I say I want to help. Please, allow us to be a part of your resistance. Let us put our powers to use."

Farson mulled that over for a minute before he finally said, "Mage Wesson is the emperor's mage. He is young, but he earned the emperor's trust and therefore has mine. Do you have a problem with answering to him?"

Bargus looked to Wesson and bowed more deeply this time. "It would be my honor to serve under the mage who saved my life."

Wesson said, "Thank you, Mage Bargus. You may join the new Mage Academy at Cael."

Bargus sounded surprised when he said, "There is a new mage academy?"

"Yes, we have a number of mages in Cael. We needed structure and a way to train new mages. It is a small academy right now, but we intend to rescue or recruit as many mages as we can find."

Bargus nodded. "There are a number of mages who, like us, refused to swear an oath to the king. Many of them are being held in the palace dungeons. I believe the only reason they have not been executed is because Caydean and Avikeev intend to use them for their experiments."

"Then we need to save them," said Wesson resolutely.

He, Farson, Connovan, and Anda spent the rest of the day making plans for that evening's activities while Azeria escorted the mages to Cael through the pathways. That night, Connovan, Azeria, and Anda joined Wesson in an attempt to infiltrate the library's restricted section. The library was as dark as the night when they arrived. It was a sprawling building, three stories high and made of stone with a terra cotta roof. Arched windows decorated the top two floors, and a series of columns lined the front where the steps ascended. Boxwoods occupied the spaces between columns, and decorative topiaries adorned the lawn on either side of the steps. There were no guards, but there was an active ward meant to bar entry to any who did not possess the magical key, a specific spell that only the librarians possessed.

They hid in the shadows of the columns at the top of the steps as they examined the ward for any defects. They failed to find any. The ward was as solid as the stone walls from which the library was built, and the large mahogany door remained undisturbed. Connovan suggested attempting to access the building by breaching the stained-glass windows via the roof, but Wesson wanted to avoid doing any actual damage to the premises if possible. Besides that, it was likely the ward extended to the entirety of the building.

Without thinking, Wesson muttered, "I wish I knew how Rezkin did it. He would simply walk through the ward and could take us with him."

Anda snorted as if she did not believe it.

He glanced at Azeria and could see the turmoil in her eyes at the mention of Rezkin. She seemed to brush it off, though, as she said, "The Spirétua are invulnerable to many spells and acts of magic because they possess the entire spectrum of vimara in equal parts. Only magic generated using the full spectrum or nocent power is guaranteed to work against them."

Wesson said, "So if we could use the entire spectrum, we would be able to walk through the ward as well?"

"Yes, but none of us possess such power," she replied.

Connovan said, "What if we were to combine our power to the same effect?"

"We would need to be able to cover the entire spectrum between us," said Azeria.

"And we would have to isolate each strand independently," added Wesson. "I don't know how to do that. I don't even know if it could be done."

"I can show you how," said Azeria. To Wesson, she said, "Yours will be most difficult because your nocent power may interfere, but Connovan should have no trouble. As a reflector, his power is already partitioned in such a way."

"But do we have the entire spectrum between us?" asked Wesson.

Azeria answered, "It is likely that between the three of us we cover the entire spectrum. Anda will remain out of the link because her nocent power renders her unable to control her constructive power. The difficult part is applying the power in equal parts as would a Spirétua."

"How can we do that?" asked Connovan. "Only a reader can see the ratio of power. How will we know how much to add?"

"We can link our power," said Azeria. "I can manage the link. You will each select your powers and feed them into me, and I will add the required amounts."

"You know how to do that?" said Wesson.

"Eihelvanan are not like human mages. You come into your power near adulthood. We are born with our power. Our parents and teachers use the link to guide our powers when we are young. I know how to form the link. I have never managed one, but I believe I can do it. A warning, though. Once the link is established, only the manager is able to wield the power. You will no longer have the ability to cast so long as the link is in place."

Wesson was alarmed. He possessed a vast amount of destructive power, and he did not like the idea of someone else wielding it. He said, "How long does the link last?"

"Until I, as the manager, release it. Technically, I could maintain the link indefinitely. This is why it is dangerous to form a link with someone. Is breaching this ward worth the risk for you?"

Connovan said, "I say we try to go in through the window."

Wesson scowled at Connovan. "The ward likely extends to the windows as well."

Connovan shrugged. "It is worth a shot."

Wesson wrestled with the idea of putting his power in the hands of someone else. He liked Azeria, but he barely knew her. He did not think she would take advantage of the link, but he did not like the idea of being vulnerable. He would not be able to use his own power so long as she maintained the link, and if she never released it, he would be relegated to the life of a mundane. He also had to consider that while Azeria had developed a working relationship with him, she did not trust him or even particularly *like* him due to his allegedly being a demon. She could take this opportunity to end the threat. He took solace in the fact that she had actually warned them of the danger of forming the link when she could have kept that part to herself.

His stomach flipped as he said the words he was sure to regret. "I'll do it."

Azeria nodded then they both looked at Connovan. Connovan gave nothing of his feelings away, but Wesson knew the former Rez was weighing the risks just as he had. If Wesson had learned anything from Rezkin, it was that allowing himself to be vulnerable like this was definitely against the rules. With a final glance between them, Connovan released a breath. "Very well, I will participate." After that, Anda agreed with little hesitation.

Azeria guided them through the linking process, a wholly unpleasant experience as far as Wesson was concerned. As soon as his power left his control, he began to panic. He could feel the power at his fingertips, yet he could not wield it. His heart raced, and his palms began to sweat as he tried to get ahold of himself. After a few minutes, Azeria looked at him and said, "I need you to feed the threads of power to me one at a time."

Wesson anxiously tugged at a lock of his hair as he worked to quell his nerves. Then he dove into himself and began pulling the power forward, feeding it into Azeria as she had requested. He did not know what Azeria did, but her face was a mask of concentration as she took control of the power. She had Connovan do the same, and after a few minutes, she said she was ready to try to breach the ward. They all agreed, then Wesson felt a drag on his power. His nocent power tried to grab hold of his constructive power, and Wesson had to wrestle it down. Azeria stepped toward the ward, then raised her hand and pressed against it. It stood as solid as ever. Wesson felt Azeria pull harder on his power, and his panic returned. The feel of someone else wielding his power struck Wesson deep at his core. Connovan was tense and seemed to be struggling as well.

Azeria pressed her hand against the ward. "I am attempting to find the right balance," she said. After what felt like forever, her hand suddenly fell through the ward. She turned and took them each by the arm, and together they walked through the ward. Connovan did not wait before hurrying forward to pick the lock on the door. The door swung open, and they all shuffled through to the dark interior of the library. Azeria did not release their power right away. She held onto the link in case they needed it again to enter the restricted section, and Wesson's stomach churned with anxiety over the loss.

They made their way quickly through the stacks to the stairway at the rear of the library. Then they ascended three flights until they came to a locked door. Connovan made quick work of the lock, but when the door opened, they were met with another ward, this one stronger and with offensive capabilities that would not only deter entry but could potentially cause harm to any trespassers.

Azeria once again pulled on Wesson's power to attempt to access the ward, but this time the ward fought back. Azeria yelped and withdrew her hand when the ward sent a warning shock through her body. She shook her hand then tried again. After several long minutes, she finally broke through the ward and was able to pull them through with her.

The restricted section of the library was an entire level of tomes, scrolls, pamphlets, maps, and even clay tablets. Some were written on paper, others on parchment or vellum, and some carved in stone. The latter were mounted on short pedestals, and there were a number of glass cases displaying ancient or notable works. A few tables and chairs occupied space between the shelves. Unlit mage stones hung from the ceiling and plush carpets lined the walkways. Wesson would have been happy to spend weeks perusing the writings in this space, but they were pressed for time. Since they did not know how this section was organized, it would be difficult to find what they were looking for.

Several hours passed before they found the first tome containing information about the Sen. After that, it was easy to find more as the materials seemed to be organized by subject. Although Wesson learned a number of interesting tidbits about the mysterious necromancers of the old world, there was very little about their language. That is, until he found the narrow volume bound in leather that he currently held. It seemed to be a journal written by an unnamed Sen. What was curious about it was that someone had gone through the journal and translated the writing into Ashaiian. Assuming the translation was correct, this journal would be invaluable to his study of the ancient language.

Wesson tucked the journal into his tunic then continued searching for additional writings on or by the Sen. Azeria found a book that detailed a number of Sen rituals, which they also pocketed. Connovan and Anda did not find anything of import regarding the Sen, but they did collect a few other works of interest. They made their way out of the library in much the same way they had entered. Wesson's muscles were tense, and his skin crawled as he struggled against the bond that tied his power to Azeria. He could feel his power within him, could even grab hold of it, but no matter how hard he tried, he could not cast a spell. Thankfully, once they were on the street, Azeria released the link connecting their powers, and Wesson felt like he could breathe again. He had not realized how much stress the link had been inflicting upon him until it was finally gone.

After returning to the storehouse, Wesson elected to get some sleep. He spent the following afternoon translating the runes he had copied from Avikeev's workshop. He had not yet completed the translation, but what he found was disturbing.

"It seems he is trying to find a way to place a person's soul inside an object while keeping them alive," he announced at an impromptu meeting that night.

"Why would he want to do that?" said Connovan.

"He would be able to control them," answered Azeria. "It would be like the Shielreyah of the citadel in Cael except that they would continue to have the bodies and powers of this world."

"That's why he was using mages," muttered Wesson. "He wants to control their power."

"We need not worry about this," said Azeria. "It is impossible. With the soul drawn out of the body, the body dies. It is a frivolous experiment."

Wesson said, "That is not exactly true." He tensed when they all looked at him. He was not sure how much he should say. He did not know what they knew of Yserria's predicament, but it seemed important to mention now. "Rezkin did it. It was an accident, but it happened. Yserria's soul was partially pulled from her body into one of the crystals from the citadel. We were concerned that if she carried the crystal herself, her soul might be completely drawn into the crystal, so Rezkin gave the crystal to Malcius to carry for her. He ordered Malcius to stay near Yserria since it could cause further harm for her to be too far separated from the crystal."

Connovan said, "That is why he follows her wherever she goes. I thought he was merely smitten."

Wesson said, "We should be grateful that Avikeev has failed thus far, but for every experiment he conducts, someone dies."

Farson said, "The question is why does he think this can be done in the first place? Is it just coincidence that he would try, or does he know it has already been done and he is trying to recreate it?"

Connovan added, "If it is the latter then that means his spies have fed him sensitive information that only a few in Cael know. There is no telling what else he knows."

"We should assume that what Avikeev knows Caydean knows as well," said Farson.

Anda interjected, "So is this the weapon Caydean is creating or something else?"

"That is a good question," replied Farson. "We may be looking at two different plots here."

"What I want to know is why has he continued to fail?" said Wesson.

Azeria replied, "Most likely for two reasons. The first is that he is probably trying to pull the entire soul out of the body, which will end in death every time. As for the second reason, you said you found a number of mundane items in his workshop. If he is attempting to use those to hold the soul, I doubt it will work. In order to create shielreyah, it is necessary to use a vessel capable of housing the soul. The crystals at the citadel in Caellurum are one such vessel. They have unique properties that allow for it."

Wesson said, "So Avikeev needs the crystals to make it work? Let us hope he hasn't figured that out."

Azeria said, "I will return to Cael and warn them to check for anyone attempting to smuggle the crystals out."

Farson said, "In the meantime, we will continue looking into this weapon of Caydean's." To Wesson, he said, "It would help if you told us where you got your information about the weapon."

Wesson's muscles tensed as he considered how to answer. He could not tell them that it was Rezkin who had given him the information. He had hoped no one would ask, but he was not that lucky. He guiltily glanced at Azeria remembering her distress over Rezkin's death. He wanted to tell her that Rezkin was the source. He wanted to tell them all. Choosing a likely scenario that the striker would not be able to verify, he said, "Avikeev mentioned it." He felt no relief for the lie, but at least he had kept Rezkin's secret as he had sworn to do.

19

AZERIA WALKED the pathway alone with her sword drawn and a shield ward surrounding her. One could not be too careful in the pathways and walking them alone was never safe. Doing so in her state of mind was particularly dangerous. Ever since her dream two nights ago, she had been shaken.

"*I am alive.*"

That was what he had said. But was it truly him or a figment of her overburdened mind? She had never been clear on exactly what the dreams were. She had thought them merely dreams, but it seemed Rezkin had them as well. Were they somehow sharing one dream? If so, did that mean he spoke truth? Was he really alive? She tried to stifle the hope that rose in her chest, but it would not be snuffed.

Walking the paths alone gave her mind the freedom it needed to explore all the possibilities. If Rezkin really was alive, what did that mean for them? They had had a spark, but what did it mean? Where was it going? Could she see herself bonding with him beyond the bond they already seemed to share? Could she fall in love with him? Did she already love him? That thought sent her mind awhirl.

She had never meant to fall for the human Spirétua who was doomed to madness. And when that happened, what would she do? Would she allow Entris to kill him as was his responsibility? Perhaps Rezkin was already mad. Why else would he perpetuate the falsehood of his own death when he should be ruling an empire? Should she tell Entris her suspicions that Rezkin might be alive? Entris would insist on seeking him out. She had made a promise to Rezkin that she would not tell Entris, but could she be held to a promise made in a dream? What if she was wrong? What if all of it truly was just a dream and Rezkin was actually dead? She would be alerting Entris for no reason.

She was so engrossed in the turmoil in her mind that she missed the signs that she was no longer alone. She was suddenly jerked off her feet. A tentacle had wrapped around her ankle and wrenched her toward a gaping maw. Azeria slashed with her sword, slicing through the tentacle with ease. Somehow the creature had gotten through her ward, though. As another tentacle lashed at her, Azeria jumped out of the way. Her forward momentum took her into the path of another tentacle that wrapped around her waist. As it began to squeeze, she hacked away at the thicker appendage. Another tentacle surged forward and wrapped around her sword arm halting any more attempts to free herself. A dozen more tentacles wrapped her in an ever-constricting cocoon. She struggled for breath as she gathered her energy forcing it into a tight ball at her core. Then she released the pressure. It exploded out of her in a shower of tentacle bits and gore.

The creature screeched and flopped around on its few remaining tentacles as it spewed blood from its injured stumps. Azeria grabbed her sword from the ground and ran at the creature. She slipped in the pooling blood but caught herself before she fell. She closed in on the creature then shoved her sword through its one large eye. Its choked cry ended on a gurgle. The creature was dead, but Azeria was a gory mess as she set back down the pathway to Cael.

When she arrived, she headed for her room to retrieve fresh clothes then went straight to the baths. Once clean, she went in search of Striker Kai. She found him speaking with the man named Urvuay, the Channerían who had arrived with Prince Thresson and Frisha. Something about the man always sent a chill up her spine. It was something in the way he looked at her, and she was not sure she trusted him. Then again, she did not particularly trust any of the humans.

"Striker Kai, I must speak with you privately," she said as she stopped in front of the two.

Kai nodded toward Urvuay who walked a good distance away so that he was out of ear shot. Kai then looked at her. "General Azeria, what may I do for you?"

Azeria explained about Avikeev's mission to create soulless minions out of mages and his need for the crystals of the citadel. Kai assured her he would increase efforts to search anyone leaving the island. As they spoke, Azeria kept an eye on Urvuay. It was not obvious by any action on his part, but she got the feeling he was somehow listening in on them—which was impossible given the distance and the fact that he was not a mage.

When she was finished speaking with Kai, she sought out Entris. She felt compelled to discuss Rezkin with him, and she was not sure how to go about it. When she found him, he was training in the practice yard. She watched him for several minutes before speaking. His long hair was pulled back high on his head, and he was stripped bare to his waist. His sculpted muscles flexed and contracted with his every movement. He was a perfect male specimen to admire, yet she had never coveted him. Even now, she longed to see Rezkin in his place, and that made what she had to say all the more difficult.

"Entris," she said, "I must discuss something with you."

He paused in his motions, then turned toward her. Her gaze did not track his movements as he stalked toward her but was instead riveted on the memory of another male walking toward her in much the same way. When he stood in front of her, she pushed the thought from her mind.

"*What is it, Azeria?*"

"*I must speak with you about Rezkin,*" she said.

"*What of him? Have you found his body? (Curious)*"

"*No. I need to know what you thought of his state of mind before his death. (Interested)*"

His expression remained placid, yet she could see the surprise in his eyes. "*What is this about, Azeria?*"

"*Please, just tell me. Was he going mad?*"

"*He was always a difficult one to interpret,*" said Entris. "*He did not behave like a typical human, so it was difficult to tell whether it was madness or cunning. (Thoughtful) I do not believe he was mad, though. (Earnest)*"

Azeria was only partly relieved. She said, "*What if the rumors are true and he lives? (Curious)*"

Entris shook his head. "*You know that is not true, Azeria. We helped entomb him. He is dead. (Earnest)*"

The reminder hurt like an arrow to the chest, but Azeria pushed on. "*But what if we are wrong, and he secretly lives? Would you say his mind remains intact? (Curious)*"

Entris released a breath and dropped his gaze to the ground as he thought. Eventually, he looked up and said, "*He would have abandoned his own empire during a time of war, abandoned his friends and family, abandoned* you, *to go hide away in solitude. These do not seem like the actions of a sane mind.*"

Azeria's heart froze. "*So you do believe him to be mad?*"

"*I believe him to be dead,*" said Entris. "*But if, by some miracle, he does live, then it is my responsibility to find him and end the threat if need be.*"

Azeria knew that, as Spirétua-lye, it was Entris's responsibility to kill a mad human Spirétua, but to hear him say it so succinctly regarding Rezkin was alarming. She felt a sudden protectiveness toward Rezkin, and she reconsidered sharing her dream with Entris. Still, what he said was true. If Rezkin really were alive, why would he remain hidden? She did not think him a coward. He had faced every foe they had encountered with strength and courage. What could he possibly gain by pretending to be dead? What was worth the heartache he had caused his friends, he had caused *her*? And why would he tell her now? Why did he trust her not to tell Entris what she knew—or, rather, what she *hoped* to be true? Did he really think she could keep something like this from Entris?

Her emotions were a roiling mess as she considered her options. If he were mad, he would need to be dealt with, and Entris would be the one to do it. If he remained sane, she would be putting his life at risk for no reason by telling Entris. She was not even sure her dream was real. All of her internal conflict could be without merit. That was the point she grabbed onto. She did not know that Rezkin was alive, so she had nothing to tell Entris. Until she had proof, she would say nothing.

Maintaining his disguise, Rezkin watched as Azeria stalked away through the citadel. He considered following her but figured she was likely going to find Entris. The Spirétua-lye would see through his illusion with ease, so Rezkin was avoiding him. Rezkin had found out some disturbing information while in Cael, and it was time to investigate. He took Seena into an unoccupied courtyard and instructed her to open a portal. The rift materialized in front of him, and he stepped through. It took him about an hour through the pathways to reach his destination. Gendishen was unusually warm for that time of year, and the hard-packed dirt of the road was dry and cracked. The crops outside Drovsk were withered and brown, more evidence that the recent drought was wreaking havoc on the kingdom.

Rezkin disguised Seena as a small dog then headed toward the fort located just past the northern boundary of the city. The fort at Drovsk was the center of the Gendishen Army. It was a sprawling complex of training grounds, the command center, the military academy, armories, stables, smiths, fletchers, barracks, and other support structures. But none of that interested Rezkin. To him, the only important detail was that this was the last place Tam was seen before he disappeared. Nearly eight months ago, after Tam's escape from the slave quarry and subsequent trip to Pruar, Rezkin had sent Tam to Gendishen to lead the army. According to his intel, Tam had arrived in Drovsk as scheduled but had been reluctant to take the lead. After news of Rezkin's death had reached them, Tam had disappeared—again. Rezkin did not know if Tam had become overwhelmed and voluntarily left his position or if something nefarious had occurred. Unfortunately, Rezkin was just finding out about this, and the trail had surely gone cold.

Rezkin donned an illusion of a plain-faced man in his thirties. He was well-dressed for a commoner in a pair of dark grey slacks, a burgundy vest over a white shirt and a dark grey overcoat. After a moment's thought, he removed the overcoat from the illusion as it was entirely too hot outside for the garment. After searching briefly for the office of the administrator, Rezkin found a woman in the position. While this would have been expected in Lon Lerésh, it was unusual for a woman to hold such a position in Gendishen. She was older, probably in her sixties, she had grey hair and warm brown eyes. She smiled pleasantly upon seeing him.

"*I'm Girdy, the administrator here. How may I help you?*" she said in Gendishen as he entered the office.

Rezkin offered her his forged papers and spoke in Ashaiian. "I am Investigator Coulson of Cael. I am here about the disappearance of General Blackwater."

Her eyebrows reached for the ceiling. "Oh? It's been some time since he's been gone. I'm surprised anyone is still looking into it. The last investigator said he hadn't found a clue."

"I am reopening the case," said Rezkin. "I will need any notes and reports from the previous investigator."

"Of course, Inspector Coulson. I will have my assistant pull those for you immediately. She nodded to a young man sitting at a small desk in the corner of the room. The young man hopped up from his seat and hurried out the door. Girdy eyed Seena who appeared as a small dog to her and looked at him questioningly.

"She is in training," said Rezkin without further explanation.

Girdy still appeared confused but pointed to a chair. "Please, have a seat, Inspector Coulson. I will be happy to answer any questions you might have."

Rezkin sat down in the proffered chair. He was surprised by Girdy for more than one reason. Besides her being a woman in what was typically a man's position, she was open, friendly, and helpful—not typical traits of the Gendishen. He said, "When and where was the general last seen?"

"Now that is interesting," she said. "A couple of the men reported seeing him enter his chambers shortly after dinner that night. No one saw him leave after that. He was just gone, and most of his belongings remained behind."

Rezkin nodded as if he had known the details all along and said, "I will need to see his chambers."

"Of course, but they have been reassigned. Goulen Julik may take exception to you snooping around in his quarters."

Rezkin gave her a cold, icy stare. "Mistress Girdy, I have been given the authority to investigate this matter by any means necessary. Goulen Julik will have to accept that."

She gave him a wobbly smile. "Of course, Inspector. I will see that you have access to the suite. General Blackwater's belongings are in storage if you need to see them as well."

With a nod, Rezkin said, "Thank you, Mistress Girdy."

At that moment, the assistant reappeared with a notebook stuffed with loose papers. He handed the notebook to Rezkin with a small bow. Mistress Girdy gave the young man the additional instructions regarding access to Tam's rooms, and he hurried out of the room again. Rezkin took a few minutes to study the papers stuffed into the notebook as well as peruse a number of entries scrawled in a handwriting that was somewhat difficult to decipher.

Rezkin said, "I see here that Fyer Lansing and Fyer Sorel were the last to see General Blackwater. I will need to speak with them."

Girdy retrieved a large, leatherbound tome and dropped it on her desk with a *thump*. She licked her fingers, then flipped through a number of pages. After a couple of minutes, she said, "Fyer Sorel is no longer here. He was transferred two months ago. Fyer Lansing is still here, though. I will have him sent for." Girdy stepped around her desk and left the room for several minutes. When she returned, she held a key. She said, "I can take you to Goulen Julik's quarters now."

Rezkin followed the woman out of the building and around the corner. They entered a larger stone building that had an open veranda and a statue of a long-dead goulen, the Gendishen equivalent of a general. By the time they reached the top of the stairs to the second level, Girdy was breathing heavily and favoring her right leg. At Rezkin's inquiry, she said, "It's my knees. They aren't what they used to be."

She led Rezkin to an ornately carved door and handed him the key. "This will get you through the door."

"Thank you," answered Rezkin as he slipped the key into the lock. The door swung open, and he stepped across the threshold with Seena on his heels. Being in Gendishen, he knew not to expect a ward, but he prepared himself for the encounter anyway. The suite consisted of a bedroom, a study, and a sitting room. Each was furnished in dark wood, and the seating areas were adorned in green and beige fabric. Paintings and tapestries graced the walls, some portraits and others battle scenes. At the back of the study was a bar complete with glassware and bottles filled with colorful liquids.

Rezkin searched the rooms, ignoring the personal items belonging to Goulen Julik. He was searching behind the tapestry in the bedroom when he found his first clue. The wall there was deformed, as if the stones had been melted into a single slab. Upon sniffing it, Seena began to snarl at the wall. Rezkin examined the area first with this eyes and hands, then with his vimara. He sent a thread of power into the stone seeking any sign that magic had caused the anomaly. After so many months, it was unlikely he would find anything, but he searched anyway. He was rewarded for his efforts. The stone held the slightest signature of power, but it was unlike any mage Rezkin had sensed. In fact, it was unlike *anything* magical he had known. Except that was not quite right. Something about it felt familiar. This power did not feel like a human mage or even Eihelvanan. Nor did it feel demonic. It felt like the fae.

Rezkin left the goulen's quarters with more questions than he had entering. Did the fae have something to do with Tam's disappearance? Why would they want him? Did he make a deal with them? He knew Tam had interacted with the fae Goragana at the quarry in Verril, but he did not think Tam had agreed to anything. If he had, then Rezkin was not sure he could help Tam. His past interactions with Bilior had shown him that his power was next to useless against the fae.

Girdy led Rezkin back to the administration building where she left him in a small office with instructions to wait for Fyer Lansing. Rezkin waited around fifteen minutes during which time he pondered his own deal with the fae. They had agreed to provide his people with a safe haven, while he had agreed to provide them with an army. He had since realized that it was not a human army the fae expected him to bring, but an army of the Eihelvanan. There had been no discussion about the size of the army, though, and he wondered how many they would require to consider the deal fulfilled. It seemed a moot point, though, considering he did not have an army of the Eihelvanan. He had two, and they presently considered him to be dead. He had never said he would bring the Eihelvanan, though, so he hoped a human army would suffice.

Fyer Lansing eventually appeared in the doorway, and Rezkin set about questioning the man. When asked where he had last seen Tam, Lansing said, "I spoke to him shortly after dinner outside his quarters. He went into his quarters and that was it."

"What did you speak about?" asked Rezkin.

"He was asking about the northern forest," replied Lansing.

"What about it?"

Lansing shrugged. "I don't really know what he wanted to know. I told him it was unsettled forest rarely visited. Those who stray into the woods often don't return. Some say it's cursed. I say it's the drauglics."

"Did General Blackwater give you any indication that he meant to go there?"

With a shake of his head, Lansing said, "No, he didn't mention it; but now that you ask, I remember that he did ask me if I knew where he could get a compass."

"What did you tell him?"

"That I didn't know where he could get one. I've never seen one, myself, but I've heard of them. They're made by the afflicted—I mean, by the mages. Of course, we wouldn't have anything like that here."

"Of course," said Rezkin before dismissing the soldier.

Next, he was taken to the storehouse where Tam's belongings were being kept. All of Tam's things fit into two trunks. Rezkin was glad to see that Tam's sword was not among the items. That meant there was a chance that wherever Tam ended up, he was armed. What he did find in the trunks, besides the clothing and usual personal affects, was a small, smooth milky-white stone. While the stone was pretty, it would have otherwise been unremarkable if not for the faint trace of power that suffused it. The power felt the same as the power that had deformed the wall in the bed chamber. He held the stone out for Seena to sniff. Her wings snapped out as the spines along her back stood up, and she released a very dragon-like roar. She seemed to surprise herself with the latter and fell over, shattering the effect. Rezkin chuckled then pocketed the stone.

Rezkin had Seena open a portal to Kaibain. He had investigated all that was to be seen at the fort, and now he needed an expert. He had given Seena instructions to open the portal into an alley near the market district that he recalled. What he had not expected when he stepped from the portal was the multitude of people camped in the alley. There were a few surprised faces when he appeared seemingly out of thin air, but most of the people were preoccupied with listening to a man at the end of the alley. He stood upon a crate and was shouting about the glory of Ygrethiel and how only through Ygrethiel could they be saved from damnation.

Rezkin stepped around the people in his path and made his way through the throng of pilgrims toward the storehouse he had instructed Wesson to use. He watched the storehouse for some time before Mage Wesson emerged alone. Rezkin scurried across rooftops and down alleyways as he followed the mage. Once Wesson was a suitable distance away from the storehouse, Rezkin stepped into his path. Wesson came up short as he almost ran into Rezkin.

Wesson said, "Pardon me, sir, I didn't see you there." When Wesson made to step around him, Rezkin stopped him with a hand to his shoulder. This time, Wesson really *looked* at Rezkin. Genuine surprise showed on his face when he recognized him.

"Rez—"

Rezkin pulled Wesson into the alley. Once they were both out of sight of prying eyes, Rezkin said, "Where are you going?"

Wesson straightened his tunic and with a huff said, "It is good to see you too." He lowered his voice and said, "I was going to spy on Avikeev. What are *you* doing?"

"I was looking for *you*," replied Rezkin. He pulled Tam's milky white stone from his pocket and held it out for Wesson. "I need to know what this is."

Wesson took the stone and turned it over in his hands examining it with his senses of sight and touch as well as magic. After a few minutes, he said, "It bears unique power unlike any I have sensed. That being said, I believe it is a beacon stone."

"What is that?" asked Rezkin.

"It is used to locate someone or something. It has a matching stone, called a twin, that is placed with the person, object, or place you wish to find. When vimara is fed into this stone, it will lead you to its twin."

"How does it work?"

Wesson handed the stone back to Rezkin. "Once it is powered, you will feel a pull in the direction of the twin. You just follow the pull, and you will find the stone. This stone will begin to glow when it is in proximity to the other one." He looked at Rezkin curiously. "What are you looking for?"

"Not *what*. Who. I am searching for Tam."

Wesson's face fell. "Yes, I heard of his disappearance. An investigation was opened, but nothing came of it. Where did you get the beacon stone?"

"It was with his belongings in Drovsk," explained Rezkin.

"Oh?" said Wesson. "I'm surprised the investigator missed it."

"It is Gendishen," said Rezkin. "They would have assigned a mundane to the case. To him, this probably just looked like a pretty stone. He would not have known to look for magical significance."

"No, I suppose not. We should have sent our own investigator, but it's still too dangerous for the *talented* in Gendishen. The people hate us, and the purifiers still hunt us."

"The people do not hate you," Rezkin replied. "They fear you."

"It's the same thing so far as our lives are concerned," said Wesson.

"Perhaps, but fear can be overcome through experience and education. One day, you may go to Gendishen and change the fate of the *talented* there. For now, we have other priorities. What have you found out about Avikeev's experiments?"

Wesson explained to Rezkin what he had discovered—that Avikeev was attempting to remove the soul from a mage and store it in a vessel while keeping the mage alive to do his bidding.

Rezkin said, "If he knows of Yserria, then she is in trouble. He will want to use her life stone to control her. And he will want to see how it was done so that he may reproduce the effect."

"Can he do it?" said Wesson.

"I am not certain. It is possible that with the crystals from the citadel he may be capable of it. It is pertinent he does not get his hands on the crystals or Yserria and her life stone."

Wesson said, "I can warn her using the mage relay."

Rezkin nodded. "You do that, but she is not aware of the life stone nor the fact that Malcius carries it. You warned me against telling her in case the knowledge causes her soul to slip further into the stone."

"That's right. I did say that. I am not certain that would happen though."

"Just warn her that someone powerful may be after her but do not tell her why. I am not certain it will be enough. If Avikeev is as smart as you say he is, then he has already sent someone after her—someone with enough power to overcome her considerable skills."

"What do you propose?"

"I will go to her after I seek out Tam."

"What if she's attacked in the meantime?" said Wesson.

"She and Malcius will need to be on high alert. Hopefully with this beacon stone, it will not take long to locate Tam."

"Assuming he's still alive," muttered Wesson.

Rezkin did not respond to that last statement. The possibility that Tam truly was dead weighed heavily on his mind. Had he sent Tam to his death when he sent him to Gendishen? Was he to blame? Rezkin pushed the thought aside. Blame was irrelevant. He needed to focus on what he did know. He squeezed the beacon stone in his hand. At least now he had something to go on. He had thought that, after the last time Tam had been taken by slavers, he would have made a more difficult target, but if the fae were involved, he could not blame Tam for his failure to protect himself. The fae were powerful and cunning. If the stories were to be believed, then when the fae wanted something, they usually got it.

Rezkin fed a small amount of power into the beacon stone, and immediately he felt a tug toward the east. He bid Wesson adieu then instructed Seena to open a portal back to Gendishen. The portal opened to the windswept plain near Drovsk. The day was gloomy, and the tall, dead grasses swayed like a turbulent sea. Shadowy copses stood out like droplets of black paint on a muted landscape. Rezkin entered Drovsk briefly to obtain supplies and a horse then headed back out onto the blustery plain heading north.

20

YSERRIA STEPPED off the ferry then turned to ensure her horse had no trouble following. Malcius was beside her doing the same for his own mount. She glanced over and saw that he was deep in thought, and she wondered what troubled him. She knew he was anxious about returning to Lon Lerésh. The last time they had been there, they had gone from starving castaways to battlefield warriors, and she had been forced to claim him lest he be claimed by some other matria. He was still angry about the mark he had received when he inadvertently accepted that claim by recognizing it outside Lon Lerésh. She was not happy about it either. Although she and Malcius knew the claim to be a ruse, so far as the rest of the world was concerned, they were now married. At least in Lon Lerésh he was only her consort, which was somewhat better than husband. Still, nothing had come of the accidental union but resentment. She did not know why he insisted on traveling with her everywhere she went.

Upon exiting the ferry, they were greeted by an entourage of her own echelon. Since she was now leader of *two* echelons, she had a full contingent of retainers ready to do her bidding. That included Japa, the servant she had acquired after winning the battle to claim the Third and Fourth Echelons. Japa had been a good servant. He was quiet but always ready with a smile and a gentle deportment. He was formally educated and specialized in farming, but he had a bit of the *talent* in him, which came in handy. Japa was presently bringing up the rear while leading his own horse and the pack horse from the ferry. Yserria turned away from Malcius and Japa to face her welcoming party.

"Greetings, Echelon," said the woman in front. It was Wolshina, Japa's mother.

Yserria said, "Greetings, Wolshina. It is good to see you well."

Wolshina's gaze cut to Japa then back again. "We are pleased to have you with us once again, Echelon. We do not wish to overwhelm you, but there are many things to go over since your long absence."

Yserria withheld the sigh that threatened to escape her. "Of course, I will address all your concerns once we have reached the villa."

Wolshina motioned toward the others who were gathered to greet her. There were three other women and eight men, presumably their consorts. The men were all armed with swords, knives, and short bows, while the women each wore an embellished dagger at the hip. There were also three wagons, one laden with supplies and the other two possessing a tentlike structure. Wolshina led Yserria toward a tented wagon and said, "We would be pleased for you to ride here for our journey."

Yserria said, "Thank you, but I would prefer to ride out here where I can see the enemy coming."

Wolshina's eyes widened. "Do you expect trouble, Echelon?"

"I always expect trouble," replied Yserria.

"That is because she *is* trouble," muttered Malcius barely loud enough for Yserria to hear. Wolshina seemed not to notice as she went about introducing Yserria to the others. Yserria recognized some of them and did her best to remember all their names and how they were related.

While the women rode in the tented wagons, Yserria remained mounted with the men. Malcius stayed ever-present at her side, although he said little. Malcius had been broody ever since leaving Coledon's court in Ferélle, and Yserria longed to send him back to Cael. She would not admit it to herself, but part of her was glad Malcius was with her. She had grown used to his presence. She never lacked for companionship, and that gave her comfort. Even his grousing no longer irritated her the way it once had. He seemed to be coming to terms with it as well. He complained less, and somehow the silences had become less awkward.

It took two days to reach the villa of the Fourth Echelon. It was nestled within the walls of the city of Previs. The city was clean and bright, the buildings freshly painted, and balconies and patios were well-maintained and decorated with flowers. Beyond the walls were sprawling vineyards and quaint farmhouses. The rolling hills across the verdant countryside were peaceful and inviting, a far cry from what she had experienced the last time she had been in this country. Their caravan pulled to a halt as a shepherd drove his flock across the road. Yserria smiled at the bleating sheep with their fluffy white coats. She was glad she was outside the wagon to see the stunning sites around her.

Upon entering the city, the serenity was abandoned as were many of the homes and shops. People rushed down the street toward the city's center to calls for all to attend. Something had alarmed the populace, but Yserria did not think the city was under attack. She had seen no evidence of invaders upon approach. She looked over to her entourage. Two of the men were conferring, then one rode ahead in the direction of the crowd.

The other, a man named Gillis, said, "Echelon, Nexius will find out what is happening."

By the time they saw Nexius again, the caravan had reached the city center where the crowd was gathered around the mage relay station. The people seemed to be eagerly awaiting some news, but it was not forthcoming. Nexius rode back to meet them and stopped in front of Yserria. He said, "Echelon, the people have gathered because a message from the palace at Kielen has come through the mage relay for you. They eagerly await the news."

Yserria looked at the man in surprise. "All these people are here to find out what a message says?"

Nexius shrugged. "Very little of interest happens in this city, and we are far removed from Kielen. When a message from the palace arrives, everyone wants to hear the news."

"What was the message?" said Yserria, glancing over the crowd once more.

Nexius held out a message written on a slip of relay paper. It read:

To the venerable Fourth Echelon,

On this day an attempt on the life of our merciful queen has been carried out by an unknown assailant. You are summoned to the court of Kielen by her majesty the queen. Present yourself within one month's time.

. . .

Yserria read the missive twice searching for meaning in its words. It seemed the queen was *not* dead, but someone had tried to make her so. Nearly all Leréshi queens ended their reign by assassination, but until now Erisial had been untouchable thanks to her marriage to Rezkin. If Erisial died, the throne would go to Rezkin, a man, and no one in Lon Lerésh wanted that to happen. Although it was the official stance of the crown that Rezkin still lived, some people were counting on him being dead, in which case the throne would go to the most powerful woman to seek it.

Yserria did not know why Erisial wanted to see *her*. She had nothing to do with the attempt on Erisial's life. But Yserria was also backed by Rezkin's power, so perhaps Erisial saw them as kindred spirits—or at least two people with the same motivation to keep Rezkin alive.

She handed the missive to Japa who stowed it away then turned to the crowd. She rode through the throng and turned her mount to face them once she was at the front. She raised her hands, and the crowd slowly hushed. She said, "*An attempt has been made on the queen's life, but Queen Erisial lives. You may all go home.*"

People began muttering amongst themselves and a few shouted questions to her. Several of her guards came forward calling for the crowd to disperse. Once the people had gone, Yserria and her entourage continued toward the villa. The villa consisted of several buildings all finished with stucco and roofed with red clay tiles. The main house was a two-story affair surrounded by tall columns with arches between them. Many of the windows contained colorful stained glass depicting animals or flowers, and mage-lit sconces illuminated the shadows. Azeria had never visited the villa, but she immediately adored it. It was too bad she would have to leave almost immediately for the capital city of Kielen to answer the queen's summons.

Trivian peered through the spy glass until he could no longer see the flame-haired woman when she entered the villa. As one of Caydean's demon-bound battle mage generals, he had the power to just waltz into the compound and take her, but he wanted this to remain quiet. It would be easier to get her back to Ashai if he was not having to fend off her protectors at every turn. No, it would be better to steal her away in secret.

There was also the matter of the crystal that bound her soul, the one his source had called her life stone. He did not know where the crystal was located, and he could not return to Ashai without it. He assumed she carried it with her since the life stone was too precious to entrust to anyone else, but he could not be certain about where she kept it. There were a few gemstones in her scabbard, and she wore a torque possessing several larger stones, but he did not know if any of them were the life stone he sought. He would wait and watch her until he had identified the crystal. Then he would take them both back to Ashai for their experiments.

Avikeev was nearly certain that one could be controlled through their life stone, and Trivian was eager to find out. He enjoyed controlling people, manipulating them into doing things they normally would never do. He especially relished betrayal. The shock and horror suffered by the victim was almost as decadent as the guilt and self-loathing experienced by the perpetrator. As an empath, he thrived on the feelings and experiences of others. The more devastating the better. Trivian would delight in Yserria's palpable misery.

Trivian eyed Yserria's companions as they each entered the villa. There was a man who stayed at her side. He did not wear a ribbon in his hair as did the Leréshi, but based on the tattoo-like markings on his face, he was Yserria's consort. Then there was a bigger man, a Leréshi with a blue ribbon braded into his hair indicating he belonged to a matrianera's household but was not of relation to her or claimed as consort. In other words, he was a servant. After him came several women. The men stayed with the caravan and began unloading the wagons.

He put away his spyglass, then dislodging himself from his hiding place on the rocky hillside beyond the city buildings, he began making his way toward the villa. He smiled to himself. How many could he convince to turn on her? Could he get Yserria to turn on *them*? He was going to have fun tearing these people apart from the shadows.

Yserria settled into her quarters at the villa with a sigh. It was a beautiful room decorated with tasteful paintings of the countryside, a number of seating areas covered in embroidered pillows, and a large bed draped in grey silk with dark blue accents. The wardrobe had a variety of dresses in varying degrees of modesty. Most of them Yserria would never wear, but there were a few she admired.

She had not been in her room for long when her lady's maid entered bearing a tray of fruits and cheeses and a pitcher of wine. She said, "Thank you, Hestress. You are very much appreciated."

Hestress smiled and touched her wrists to her forehead. Then she said, "There are a number of officials waiting to see you, my lady. Shall I tell them to come back another day?"

"No, no, we will not be here that long. We need to leave for Kielen as soon as possible. Have the officials brought to my study one at a time. I will see them individually to make sure all their needs are addressed."

"Yes, my lady. Shall I have your consort join you?"

"Malcius? Um, yes, that would be helpful. Thank you."

Yserria helped herself to a bit of the repast. Then she changed out of her travel clothes and into a mauve silk gown that fell in waves over the curves of her body. It was more appropriate garb in which to meet the officials as they would be dressed similarly. Yserria left her sword in her wardrobe and exited her quarters. Gillis and Nexius were waiting for her in the corridor. She gave them a questioning look, and Gillis said, "We are here to escort you to your study, Echelon."

"Oh? Thank you, Gillis. It isn't far, though. I remember where it is. Why don't you and Nexius go rest after the long ride?"

Nexius smiled and said, "Thank you, my lady, but we would rather see to your safety, especially seeing as how you are not carrying your sword. As leader of two echelons, you have twice the number of vultures vying for your position."

Yserria suppressed a shiver. She did not like having a target on her back. At least when she had been out of the country, she had been less accessible. Now that she had returned, those so-called vultures would be circling. She said, "Thank you for your concern. I do appreciate your service."

"You are most welcome, my lady," replied Gillis.

Yserria walked down the corridor and then another flanked by the two guardsmen. She had inherited both as members of her household upon defeating the previous echelon. At the time, she had questioned their loyalty, but since then they had proven to be honorable and dedicated. Gillis had even confided in her that he had hated working for the previous echelon and had been glad for the change.

Yserria waited as Nexius opened the door to the study then proceeded into the room. It was spacious with plenty of room for a number of bookcases, although they were sadly lacking in books. The meager collection they had pertained to Leréshi laws and customs. Apparently, the previous echelon had not been a big reader. It was no matter. Yserria did not have time to read. If she ever were to spend a good amount of time at the villa, she would want to fill those bookcases.

When she entered the study, the minister of common affairs was awaiting her. She greeted her by name and invited her to sit and enjoy a glass of wine. Malcius entered a moment later and joined them. Hestress had returned to pour the wine, and the head scribe named Polimas sat in one of the chairs with a lap desk. As they discussed the workings of the echelon, Polimas kept copious notes. Every once in a while, he would beg them to pause while he caught up. Malcius made helpful comments about issues Yserria had not considered. Having been raised as a commoner, she had not been prepared for the rulership of two echelons. His insights and advice had been invaluable.

The process continued as official after official sat across from Yserria, and by the time she was through meeting with them, her voice had nearly abandoned her. When the meetings ended, Yserria returned to her quarters to dress for dinner. This time, she wore a dark blue skirt and blouse that wrapped around her and tied at the back, exposing quite a bit more flesh than Yserria was used to. Yserria did not see the point in changing clothes for dinner, but it was the Leréshi way, and since she was the leader of her echelons, she was expected to be a model of Leréshi custom.

A knock sounded at the door, and Hestress answered. She turned to Yserria, and said, "My lady, your consort is here to escort you to dinner."

"Thank you, Hestress. You may let him in."

Yserria turned to find Malcius standing in the doorway. He was dressed in traditional Leréshi fashion in a white wraparound tunic belted at the waist and tight, black trousers tucked into knee-high boots. It struck her that Malcius naturally fit the role of noble no matter which country he was in—far better than she did.

They entered the dining hall together, arm in arm, and the attendants sat them beside one another. Yserria no longer felt awkward being so close to Malcius. Over the many months that he had been following her around, she had grown accustomed to his presence. It felt natural to eat beside him, and she wondered what that meant.

The first course was a chilled soup that Yserria did not care for. She sent it back to the kitchen with instructions to give it to someone who would enjoy it.

They had just finished the second course of lentil salad when Hestress came rushing over.

"My lady, Raki has become terribly ill!"

Yserria's felt a yank at her heart. "The kitchen boy?"

"Yes, my lady. We believe it was poison."

Yserria became alarmed. "Poison? How? Who would want to poison a kitchen boy?"

Tears trickled down Hestress's cheeks. "It was the soup, my lady. The soup that was meant for you. Raki ate it then quickly fell ill."

Yserria dropped her fork with a clatter. "Someone tried to poison *me*?"

"We believe so, my lady."

Her stomach dropped. Someone had tried to kill her, and poor Raki could be dying in her place. "Have you called for a healer?"

"Yes, we did so right away."

"Good," said Yserria. "See that he is kept comfortable." As Hestress hurried away, she turned her attention to her tense guardsman. "Gillis, you will lead an investigation into the poisoning."

"Yes, my lady," replied Gillis before he, too, headed in the direction of the kitchen.

Yserria looked down at her half-eaten dinner, and her stomach churned. She no longer had an appetite. She looked to Malcius who appeared nearly as shaken as she. "It was poison, Malcius. If I'm being honest, it terrifies me. I cannot fight poison."

Malcius pushed his own plate away. "We should have a mage check your food from now on."

Yserria wiped her sweaty palms on her napkin. "Would a mage be able to detect poison?"

"Not always but sometimes. If the mage is particularly skilled and is familiar with the poison, he or she might be able to identify it."

"We have a number of mages here, but I don't know if any of them are familiar with poisons. And if they were, wouldn't that make them a suspect?"

Malcius drummed his fingers on the table thoughtfully. "I suppose so, but what else can we do? You have to eat."

Yserria swallowed the lump that had formed in her throat. She could not help but assess her current physical state. Was she already poisoned? Was the churning in her stomach a sign of impending death or just nerves? Was her sweating due to some toxin in her food, or was it from fear? Yserria had the sudden urge to see the healer, but she would wait until the woman was finished with Raki. Yserria dearly hoped the young man did not die. Already the guilt was consuming her. She felt responsible for Raki. She felt responsible for all her people. They were hers to lead and hers to protect. She wondered if this was the way Rezkin had felt about his empire. Was this the reason he sacrificed himself that day on the battlefield?

Raki died that night. Even though she had barely known the boy, she mourned his loss as much as anyone. Two days later, they celebrated Raki's life with a feast, but Yserria could not bring herself to enjoy the festivities. The food tasted like death on her tongue. Every bite she ate was potentially the bite that would end her. Yserria had faced many an enemy with strength and courage, but nothing could quell her fears over poison.

On the third day, they were prepared to leave for Kielen to comply with the queen's summons. Yserria was dressed for battle in her tunic and breeches and armor. Her sword slapped against her thigh as she walked, and she was grateful for its companionship. Malcius would accompany her, of course, as would Hestress and Polimas. Gillis and Nexius led the guardsmen of which there were twenty-four. In addition, they would be accompanied by three mages, Zelida, Lilith, and Eshi, the first being a healer and the latter two being battle mages. In addition, several of the mages' consorts would be traveling with them. It was a relatively small entourage, but they would be traveling through several echelons, and Yserria did not want to be mistaken for an invading force. Plus, time was of the essence.

They traveled as quickly as the wagons would allow. There was little trouble along the route until they crossed the border into the Second Echelon. The sky was overcast, and the mood on the windswept plains was nearly as dreary as the weather. They stuck to the few remaining forested hills for cover's sake, but on by the second day in the echelon, the hills were no more. Yserria sat atop her mount in the cover of a small copse on the last hill as she gazed across the plain before her, and Battle Mage Lilith was beside her. They watched as a patrol of the Second Echelon traveled in orderly formation across the expanse.

Yserria said, "Do you think we can avoid them?"

Lilith was quiet for a moment before she spoke. "It is unlikely."

"Perhaps if we wait here for a time, they will pass, and we can follow behind them."

"I doubt it. Look, they are moving slowly, and they keep sending out scouts. We will be seen as soon as we descend the hill."

"Then we should make contact," said Yserria. "If we take the initiative, they will be more likely to accept our passage across their lands. Besides, we have the summons from the queen. They should not interfere in queen's business."

"That is assuming they give us a chance to show them the summons," said Lilith. "These Seconds are more likely to attack first and not bother asking questions."

Lilith was a petite woman in her forties with a thin frame, long, black hair, and large grey eyes that saw everything. The woman was friendly enough but a bit jaded, and she often saw treachery in the most ordinary of circumstances.

Malcius rode up to Yserria's other side. "Shall we parlay?"

"I think we must," said Yserria.

"A small contingent then?"

"No, we will ride down together," replied Yserria. "We must appear strong and make it clear that we will fight if pressed."

Malcius said, "Are you sure that is the best course of action? With a smaller contingent, we will appear less threatening."

Yserria shook her head. "These are Leréshi soldiers. They respect strength and boldness. A small contingent will be weak and is likely to be killed on sight. At best, it would provide them with hostages."

Lilith said, "You do not understand Leréshi ways. You should not question your echelon in front of witnesses. As her consort, you should always show her support in public."

Malcius began, "I did not mean to—"

"It's fine," interrupted Yserria. "I appreciate Malcius's insight and invite him to offer his opinion. I invite *all* of you to share your counsel."

Lilith looked at Yserria appraisingly. "Very well, Echelon. In that case, I suggest we approach the patrol sooner rather than later. We do not want to chance them spying us before we are ready."

"Then we will go now," said Yserria. "We will leave the wagons here with the servants and a small guard."

"What should we do if they attack?" asked Lilith.

"Defend ourselves but try not to kill anyone. We are more likely to gain peaceful passage through their lands if we do not have blood on our hands."

They descended the hill in battle formation with the battle mages at the fore flanking the standard bearer. Swords were drawn, shields were raised, and arrows were knocked, but they approached the patrol at a steady trot so as not to cause undue alarm by closing the distance too quickly. Their efforts went unrewarded. As soon as they were within firing distance, the opposing mages began their assault. Shield wards flashed all around them as blasts shook the ground. Large clods of dirt were blasted into the air. They were forced to slow as the field became riddled with pits in which a horse might break a leg.

A hail of arrows came next. Many were deflected by the shield wards, but some were able to break through to spear horses and guards. Lilith returned fire with a blast of energy that broke through their shield wards and slammed into the enemy like a wall. Their horses faltered and many of the patrolmen were tossed to the ground. The two lines crashed into each other in a clatter of hooves and steel.

"Defense!" shouted Yserria. Then something stabbed her in the back. Yserria doubled over as she tried to catch her breath. She coughed and blood sprayed across her horse's mane. She had been stabbed, and it had come from *behind* her. She steadied herself and looked around. In all the chaos, she could not tell who had assaulted her, but she knew it had to have been one of her own.

Yserria wiped her mouth on her sleeve and looked for the nearest mage. She found Eshi only a few paces away. The blonde battle mage was using a blade of light to cut through the opposing mage's shield ward. Yserria pushed her way through to the mage and said, "Eshi, can you project my voice?"

Eshi looked at her startled. "Yes, Echelon. Would you like me to do it *now*?"

"Yes, now," said Yserria. Then she turned to face the patrol commander who was in a mounted sword battle with Nexius. She called out in Leréshi, "*We are here on a summons from the queen. We are not your enemy. We merely seek passage through these lands*."

The commander looked her way and nearly missed a strike that would have laid open his throat. Luckily, Nexius pulled back at the last second to avoid killing the commander, but he did manage to unhorse the man. Yserria leapt from her horse and closed in on the downed commander. He was on his feet by the time she got there. He raised his sword and swung at her head. Yserria dodged and brought her own blade around. Pain ripped through her back. The commander pivoted and parried. The blades clashed. She did her bast to ignore the pain as she danced around him. The man was skilled with a sword, but he was no Swordmaster. Her blade struck. The ring of the steel reverberated up her arm. She twisted bringing her sword up and around. The commander lost his grip. His sword sailed away, and Yserria stepped into him. She hooked her leg around his and slammed into his chest, knocking him off balance. The man fell to his knees. Yserria stood over him, her blade to his neck.

She said, "*Call them back. We are here in peace. I don't want to have to kill you.*"

The commander raised his fist and shouted, "*Halt! Patrol, pull back!*"

It took a few minutes for the message to get through to everyone and for them to separate themselves. Yserria stepped back, allowing the commander to stand.

He glanced toward his sword that lay several paces out of reach. Then he lifted his chin haughtily. "*What's this about a summons from the queen?*"

Yserria sucked in a painful breath, "*I have a summons from Queen Erisial to attend her in Kielen.*"

"*And who are you to have a summons from the queen?*" said the commander with more than a hint of disdain.

"*I am Yserria Rey, ruler of the Third and Fourth Echelons. You must not interfere with official business of the crown.*"

He looked back to his patrol unit that was comprised mostly of men with a few women. He said, "*How many have we lost?*"

One of the patrolmen said, "*None, sir. Mostly minor injuries. A few will require the work of a healer.*"

The commander nodded. To Yserria he said, "*You are lucky no one died, or we would not still be speaking.*"

Lilith laughed. "*You no longer possess a sword with which to issue threats. And you will speak to the echelon with the respect due her position. It was not luck that no one died. We were ordered to restrain ourselves.*"

"*Hmph, is that so?*" replied the commander. "*I would see this summons from the queen.*"

Drawing the missive from the scroll tube secured to her belt, Yserria handed over the summons. The commander scowled as he read it then handed it back. "*We will escort you to the castle where Echelon Lisbet will decide what to do with you. She will surely invite you to stay overnight.*"

Yserria did not want to stay overnight. She had no desire to surround herself with a multitude of strangers from an opposing echelon, even though the more immediate threat was someone within her own party. Tucking the scroll back into the tube, Yserria said, "*I'm afraid that is unacceptable. We will continue on our way directly to the palace at Kielen with no further interference. If you test us, it will be seen as an act of war against the Third* and *Fourth Echelons, and it will be reported to the queen that you attempted to detain us while on official business from the crown.*"

The commander's jaw clenched, and he glanced over Yserria's forces, his gaze pausing on the battle mages. Yserria's soldiers were outnumbered two to one, but the battle mages were worth two or three patrols on their own. He finally returned his dark gaze to Yserria. "*You are injured.*"

Yserria coughed into her sleeve, and it came away bloody. She said, "*We have a healer. I will be fine.*"

He glanced toward Lilith, who gave him a scathing look. Then he returned his dark gaze to Yserria. "*Echelon, it would be our honor to escort you to the eastern border.*"

Yserria thanked the commander, then a wave of dizziness assailed her. She gripped a nearby stirrup tightly so as not to fall over then called for everyone to return to the wagons. As they headed across the plain, Malcius rode up beside her.

"You are bleeding, Yserria."

"I know," she said, sucking in a breath. "I was stabbed in the back." She lowered her voice, "By one of *ours*."

Malcius's eyes widened. "The assassin is *here*?"

Yserria shrugged and pain sliced across her back. "*An* assassin is here. Who knows how many there are."

The stab wound was painful, but she was confident Healer Zelida could repair any damage done. She did not fear battle as she feared poison even though it was just as deadly. Yserria hoped they caught the perpetrators and that she never had to face poison again.

Two weeks later, they arrived in Kielen. The multitude of flowers and colorful drapes and pennants gave the city a cheerful disposition, but Yserria knew the city had a darker side. With the number of nobles and officials in the city, assassination attempts were nearly a daily occurrence.

Nexius rode ahead to alert the palace to their coming. When they reached the palace, they were greeted with all the fanfare due the arrival of an echelon. Gawking courtiers were lined up on the steps, servants scurried everywhere to tend to the baggage and horses, and a troupe of minstrels played from the lawn. Yserria and Malcius were led to a grand suite containing four bedrooms and a sitting room. The two larger bedrooms were richly appointed in colorful silks and hardwood. The two smaller bedrooms were reserved for the lady's maid and manservant but were still lavishly decorated. The sitting room held a seating area near the blazing hearth that possessed two settees and four chairs. A smaller space held a long table and chairs for dining. The suite was larger than her entire childhood home.

Hestress unpacked Yserria's trunks, filling the wardrobe with more gowns than Yserria intended to wear. Then she drew out a green blouse and skirt that was made mostly of a gauzy fabric with small strips of silk to cover the important bits. Yserria balked at the idea that she was expected to wear the garment, but being in Kielen, such adornment was expected. Hestress went with Yserria to the baths, where Yserria selected a private stall. After she was clean and dressed in the revealing gown, she returned to her suite. When she arrived, Malcius was there, also freshly washed. His back was turned when she entered, but he called over his shoulder, "A message arrived while you were gone."

Malcius turned around, and his eyes widened. He stared at her for an uncomfortable moment. Yserria shifted anxiously trying to pull the silk to cover more of her. Malcius shook himself and said, "You are summoned to the queen's chambers. Some guards will be here soon to escort you."

Yserria shivered. She felt naked, exposed, and not because of her revealing dress. The thought of walking the halls of the palace without her sword left her tense. It would not be appropriate or even permitted for her to wear her sword to the queen's chambers, however. A few minutes later, a knock sounded at the door. Hestress opened it to reveal a pair of palace guards. One of them bade Yserria to join them, and she went with little hesitation. She was eager to find out what Erisial wanted with her, and she was glad not to have been made to wait.

Erisial's chambers were much like her own except that at one end there was a row of long windows and a glass door that led to a broad balcony. The windows faced north, so the afternoon sunlight did not shine directly into the room but bathed the space in a warm glow. Yserria was told to wait, so she stood in the sitting room, her hand continually straying to her side where her hilt would naturally lay.

The bedchamber door opened. It was not Erisial who emerged but Serunius, Erisial's one and only consort. Serunius was the most powerful battle mage in Lon Lerésh, and it was largely because of him that Erisial had managed to hold on to the throne for more than a decade. He cut an imposing figure with his dark features and black mage garb, and Yserria worked hard to quell her fear. Like poison, Yserria could not fight against the *talent*. It was beyond her and therefore made her vulnerable. She did not like feeling vulnerable.

Serunius stopped a scant two feet from her, his towering figure pressing in on her personal space. He held his arms behind his back as he stared at her with hard eyes. A muscle ticked in his jaw, and Yserria swallowed the bile that rose from her tumultuous stomach. His gazes descended to take in all of her, then he turned and left. Obviously, he had decided she did not pose a threat to Erisial. Yserria would have been offended if not for the fact that Erisial, herself, was a mage.

When Yserria looked back to the bedchamber, Erisial was standing in the doorway. Her creamy silk dress wrapped around her chest and hips and little else. Her golden hair was piled atop her head in an intricate do of curls and braids, and jewels glistened at her ears and throat. Erisial smiled pleasantly as she came into the sitting room, but Yserria was not fooled. This woman was a viper, and she would not hesitate to cut down any threat.

"*Please, sit,*" said the woman, indicating the settee in front of her. Yserria did as the queen bade, and Erisial sat in one of the high-backed chairs across from her. "*I must say, you look quite lovely in that dress. My Serunius thought so as well.*"

Yserria's heart set out at a gallop. Did Erisial think she was after her consort? Yserria had recognized Serunius's interest during her last visit, but she did not return the sentiment. She opened her mouth to make that clear, but Erisial continued.

"*Yes, I know he fancies you, but nothing will ever come of it. A pretty bobble may catch his eye, but he is ever dedicated to* me."

Yserria uttered, "*I don't—*"

Erisial raised a hand to cut her off, and the tiny jewels at her wrist twinkled in the light. "*You are no doubt wondering why I brought you here.*"

Yserria snapped her mouth shut. Erisial apparently had no interest in her rebuttal.

Erisial continued. "*As you know, the official stance of the crown is that my husband, Rezkin, still lives. His very existence is an unspoken threat to the foundation of this queendom. I took a great risk in taking him as my husband. I angered many, but no one will move against me so long as he lives. More and more, though, people are rejecting the notion. My advisories claim him to be dead, which leaves me vulnerable. Since your rulership of the Third and Fourth Echelons also hinges on him being alive, you, too, have become vulnerable.*

"*I do not know your sentiments toward me, and I do not care. You and I have a shared purpose. We must see that Rezkin is made immortal in the eyes of the nobles.*"

"*How do you intend to do that?*" asked Yserria.

"*You will claim to have contact with him. You will claim to have seen him with your own eyes and to regularly correspond with him.*"

Yserria's brow rose. "*No one will believe me.*"

"*Those who wish to believe will. Others will be convinced by the documents.*"

"*What documents?*"

"*Serunius and a loyal master forger will create correspondence from Rezkin to both you and myself.*"

"*And what will this correspondence say?*"

Erisial waved a hand through the air. "*Oh, the usual. Plans for the troops and such. There will be a few more personal communications to me—all in line with what one might expect of a husband to his wife.*"

Yserria shook her head. "*Rezkin would never send anything like that. Anyone who knows him will know you're lying.*"

Erisial smiled. "*You see? This is why I needed you here. I've barely had any time with the man. You know him. Your input will be invaluable.*"

"*That's all you want me to do? Pretend that Rezkin lives?*"

Erisial's pleasant demeanor turned hard. "*No, there is one thing more. If Rezkin lives, then you are too powerful. You will renounce your claim to the Third Echelon. I will replace you there with one of my supporters.*"

Yserria straightened her back as her muscles tensed. "*I won both echelons fairly in challenge. They are mine until someone takes them from me.*"

This time Erisial's grin was positively villainous. "*That can be arranged. You and I both know Rezkin is not coming to champion you should you be challenged. If you do not acquiesce, both echelons will be taken from you, and you will be buried alive.*"

Yserria clenched her fists, wishing once again that she had the familiar weight of her sword at her hip. "*If you kill me, your plan to immortalize Rezkin will fail.*"

Erisial dipped her head. "*It will be more difficult, but not impossible without you. That is why I would prefer you live. But I will not suffer a single woman ruling two echelons so long as I am queen.*" She rose from her chair, and her tone lightened as she made her way back toward her room. She paused in the doorway. "*Now go, make your preparations. I will see that all is arranged for a peaceful transition of power.*" Then Erisial was gone.

Yserria wanted to argue, but the queen had dismissed her as if her opinion had no bearing on the issue. She had wondered for many months how Erisial would finally respond to her acquiring two echelons. She had thought maybe with a garrote. Perhaps it would have been if not for the fact that Erisial needed her to pull off her plan regarding Rezkin. Yserria did not feel right lying about having seen Rezkin. Yes, it would make things easier, safer, but she knew Rezkin to be dead. His body had been entombed. Services had been held. People had mourned. It was time for the empire to move on. It was time for a new emperor to be crowned. If she perpetuated the myth that he lived, the empire would grow weak without leadership.

21

REZKIN ENTERED the woods as the sun was setting. His beacon stone continued to pull him deeper into the northern forest, but he was weary and in need of rest. He had ridden hard to get to the forest in only a few weeks, meditating in *eskyeyela* while in the saddle rather than sleeping, and stopping only for short breaks to feed and rest his horse. Rezkin dismounted and began making camp in the final rays of light offered by the setting sun. He set his saddle beside his pack and began brushing down his horse. He smelled them before he saw or heard them. The putrid stench of decay offended his nose and set him on alert.

He drew the black blade as the first of the drauglics came loping into the small clearing wearing stolen armor and carrying a stone-topped club. Before that one reached him, five more appeared from the woods, some wearing torn and filthy clothing and armor and all bearing weapons. The first to reach him came from his right wielding a sword with little skill. Rezkin lashed out with the black blade, disarming the drauglic and running him through. He wrenched his blade free just as another attacked from his other side. His horse was no battle charger. It shrieked then bolted back the direction they had come.

As Rezkin hacked down the first six drauglics, the clearing filled with more. They were attacking in droves. They were crude and unskilled, but what they lacked in fighting prowess, they made up for in numbers. The black blade crackled with green lightning as Rezkin felled one creature after another, and still they came. Battle energy surged through him as he engaged the enemy. At his side, Seena would no longer hold back. She eagerly jumped into the fray, biting and gouging their attackers with tiny razor-sharp teeth and claws. Concerned for her safety, Rezkin called for her to fall back, but she pretended not to hear him.

Rezkin searched the dark forest as he hacked away at the seemingly endless stream of drauglics. He waded into the densest crowd of the creatures looking for the ukwa. If he could find and kill the leader, the rest of the drauglics would likely retreat. Four of the scaly creatures suddenly attacked him at once. A pulse of vimara escaped him unbidden. The wave of power knocked back the drauglics that were surrounding him. Those closest to him lost their footing as they were thrust into those behind them. Many dropped their weapons, and confusion abounded. He was confused, too. He did not know what had just happened, but he was more than willing for it to happen again.

The drauglics soon recovered and began to merge on him once again. Rezkin swung the black blade in a flurry of elven speed. Seena released a painfilled roar, and his heart skipped a beat. Rezkin turned to look for her just as another pulse blasted from his body. The drauglics were tossed away, and Rezkin could finally see the small lump that was Seena. Her scales were covered in blood and one wing hung limply at her side. Her long neck snaked upward, and she growled, exhaling thick, black smoke but still no flames.

With Rezkin's attention on Seena, the drauglics were able to close on him from behind. He turned just in time to avoid a club to the back of the head. He shoved his sword into the midsection of the nearest drauglic then kicked the next creature away. He backed away, moving closer to Seena. He wanted to protect her, but he also needed to fight the creatures and find the ukwa. After hacking down three more drauglic attackers, Rezkin swept Seena into his arm. He tried to be gentle with the hurried movement, but she screeched nonetheless. With Seena tucked under his left arm and the black blade in his other hand, Rezkin waded back into the mass of drauglics. Fighting was made more difficult by the burden, but the alternative was to leave her undefended.

One drauglic reaching for Seena raked his claws down Rezkin's arm. With a mighty swing, Rezkin lopped off its head. Then he heard it. One of the creatures called out to the others in a darkly grating primitive language. Rezkin followed the sound with his eyes and ears. One drauglic was larger than the others. It wore a polished breastplate and carried a longsword pocked with rust. It seemed to be issuing orders to those nearest it, and Rezkin was nearly certain this was the ukwa. As Rezkin moved toward the ukwa, the attacking drauglics packed in tighter making it nearly impossible to make progress. Rezkin thought that if he could somehow recreate the blast of power, he might be able to clear a path to the ukwa. He had no idea how to do that, though, and in the midst of a battle was hardly the time to experiment.

Rezkin ducked beneath a low-hanging branch just as an axe sank into it. He dodged a second attack by the axe wielder then smashed it in the face with his pommel. As the drauglics drew closer, completely surrounding him, he felt an energy building up inside him. This was different from the battle energy he usually felt when he fought. It formed a ball at his core and began to bleed out toward the edges. His black blade began to glow green. Rezkin directed the energy toward his sword, and it surged out in a streak of green lightning, striking all the drauglics in its path. A blast of sound rocked him a moment later. Rezkin made a run for it. Closing the distance quickly, he launched himself at the ukwa.

Unlike the other drauglics, the ukwa was not unskilled with the sword, but still he was no match for Rezkin. The black blade sliced through the ukwa's neck with ease. The ukwa's head toppled to the ground, followed by his body. The other drauglics roared something unintelligible, then they began to scatter. Within minutes, the clearing was empty save for Rezkin and Seena and dozens of dead drauglics.

Rezkin gazed down the path he had used to get there and wondered how far his horse had run. He doubted he could find the mount again, especially in the dark. He briefly considered having Seena open another portal back to Drovsk so he could procure another horse but decided against it. The forest was only getting denser, and it would be easier to go on foot. Besides, Seena was injured and needed her energy.

Grabbing his pack, Rezkin hiked with Seena deeper into the forest away from the bloody carnage. It was fully dark by then, and the moonlight could not reach past the dense canopy, so Rezkin depended on the light of a mage stone to find his way. Once he felt he was far enough from the battle site, he lit a fire and began seeing to Seena's wounds. She was not as injured as he had first thought. It turned out most of the blood was not hers. Her hard scales protected her from most injuries, but her wing was another story. It was broken in two places. Rezkin attempted to splint the wing, but the way it was broken made it difficult. He was concerned that if it healed improperly, she might never fly.

Rezkin considered his options. He could splint it as well as he could and hope for the best or open a portal back to civilization and find a healer. He was not sure he could find a healer who was willing and able to heal a dragon. The first option was unacceptable, and the second was unlikely. That left him with the third and most distasteful option. He could try to heal Seena himself. Entris had insisted he had the power to heal, if not the willingness. Well, Rezkin had a willingness now. He wanted Seena well again, and it looked like he was her only chance.

Seena lay on the ground groaning every time her wing shifted. She looked up at him with imploring icy-blue eyes and said, "*It hurts. Help me.*"

Rezkin sat down with his legs crossed, his hands resting on his knees. Entris had said he needed to empathize with his patient. Rezkin could not imagine what having wings was like, but he was no stranger to broken bones. He thought of the pain he had endured each time he had broken something and his desire for that pain to be taken away. He said to her, "I will try to help you, but I do not know what it feels like to have wings. I am not sure I know how."

Suddenly, Rezkin's mind was inundated with sensations. He felt the satisfying stretch as the appendages lengthened and the release as they folded back again. The air felt solid beneath them as they glided through its currents. He felt the tension in his back and chest as the wings flapped to hold her aloft. Seena still had not successfully flown, but she could glide, and now, through their mind bond, he was feeling all the sensations that her wings endured as she did so. Not only could he feel what it was like to have wings, he could feel what it was like for *Seena* to have wings. And he could feel her pain, pain unlike any she had experienced in her short lifetime.

In that moment, Rezkin felt more than anything else a desire for her pain to be gone. He wanted to heal her, to make her body work again the way it was supposed to. He wanted to take away all that distressed her and give her back her joy. Rezkin gently took Seena's wing in his hands as he focused on his desire to heal. Then he found the ball of power at his core, the same power that had created lightning during the battle with the drauglics. That had been a release of raw power, though. Rezkin knew he could not release that into Seena. She would likely be burnt to a crisp. No, he needed to form the power into something else, something healing. But he did not know how.

The sound of rain reached his ears, but Rezkin felt no drops. Seena released a small roar that was mighty for her size. He opened his eyes and found himself staring into two yellow-orange orbs. The word escaped him before its meaning struck. "Bilior."

The katerghen danced backward. He hung his head to the side and blinked at Rezkin. "The spawn of Nihko be broken. The shattered one seeks to heal."

"Bilior, how did you find me?" said Rezkin as he got to his feet.

"Through the pathways I go. The way you did show. At the drahg'ahn gates, the shattered one waits." Bilior's twiggy limbs hung askew as he danced.

"Why do you call me the shattered one?"

Bilior raised a finger and traced Rezkin's shape through the air. "Your aura be broken. In pieces it lay. Shattered and sharp, a price you did pay."

"What did I pay for?"

The feathery leaves around the katerghen's head flitted in the breeze and sounded like rain. Seena hissed at the katerghen. Bilior hissed back. Then he said, "Many lives lived, many deaths died. The marks on your skin, the cracks in your aura. The *we* see."

"You knew I was alive?"

"To know and to follow."

Rezkin squatted down to stroke Seena's long neck trying to settle her. He was ever aware that she was still broken and in pain, and she seemed to have an aversion to the fae. To Bilior, he said, "Why are you following me?"

Bilior froze in place then slowly crept closer until he was just out of arm's reach. He looked at Rezkin pointedly. "An army was promised. An army for the we."

Rezkin nearly groaned aloud. He did not have time to deal with the fae. He needed to heal Seena, find Tam, help Yserria, and end Caydean. He swallowed down his frustration, separating from his emotions. "I have an army—several, actually. You will have them too."

The feathery leaves rustled again. "The old ones we need. The ahn'an will bleed."

"The old ones? You mean the Eihelvanan?"

Bilior simply stared at Rezkin expectantly. Rezkin said, "That was not part of our deal. You said an army. I am bringing an army—a *human* army."

"'T'will not be enough. All life they will snuff. Spirétua we need, to fight the daem'ahn horde."

"So far as our deal is concerned, I have fulfilled my part of the bargain. I have an army. It will have to be enough."

A concussive force suddenly blew Rezkin from his feet, and he sailed into a tree. He struck with a *whomp* and then stuck there as if a great force was pressing against his chest. He struggled against it but made no progress. Like the many times before when he had faced the fae, he was no match for Bilior's power. The power at his core suddenly began building up once again. Rezkin held on to it, allowing it to fill him beyond what was comfortable. Then he set his gaze on the katerghen. He released the power in a singular, focused direction. The wave struck the katerghen blasting him from his feet and tossing him into another tree. The twiggy creature crumpled to the ground, and Rezkin was abruptly released.

He hurried forward with his sword drawn. For the first time, Rezkin had a chance to stand against the fae creature. Bilior bounded to his feet and created a stave out of his own limbs. The two weapons met in a dazzling display of green lightning. They danced around, meeting each other strike for strike. Rezkin filled his blade with power and swung at the greedy fae creature. At the same time, Bilior's stave became thicker with a slight greenish glow. When the two met, Bilior's stave shattered, and Rezkin's sword was wrenched from his hands.

Roots and twigs suddenly shot out from Bilior's body. They wrapped around Rezkin, yanking his arms to his sides and securing them there. Bilior leaned forward so that his yellow-orange eyes were mere inches from Rezkin's face. He said, "The shattered one grows strong. His power be great but not great enough. The we prevail."

Seena roared again, and Rezkin looked down at her. He could feel her misery through their bond. He said, "I need to heal her. Release me and be gone."

Bilior hissed at Seena then turned back to Rezkin. "The price must be paid. A general claimed. An army be made." Then the twigs and roots retreated, releasing Rezkin. Bilior backed away but did not leave.

Rezkin watched him cautiously as he moved toward Seena, claiming his sword on the way. He said, "I must heal her. Please leave me to concentrate."

Bilior collapsed into a pile of twigs not far from Seena. It seemed he would not go, and Rezkin could not *make* him leave, so Rezkin split his focus to remain aware of Bilior yet set his mind to the task of healing. It was difficult to concentrate with the powerful katerghen so close. Rezkin knew Bilior was not his friend. He could not depend on the fae creature's good will. The katerghen could decide at any moment that Rezkin was in breach of contract and attack him again. But Seena needed him, so he turned his mind inward to the power at his core. After several moments of fumbling around, he heard a voice directly beside his ear.

"The power that is you be the power that is her. To heal is to be one."

A shiver went down Rezkin's spine, and all his muscles tensed. He did as the voice said, though, and tried to match the pattern of his power to Seena's. He could not see her aura, but he could feel the power within it. After many attempts, he was finally able to match the patterns, and he released a satisfied sigh. He did not know what to do after that, though. He thought back to when Wesson had first taught Reaylin to heal. Wesson had directed her to form her desire in her mind then push the power toward the wound. Then Wesson had used his knowledge of anatomy to guide that power in healing his donkey. Rezkin did not know the anatomy of a dragon, but he could imagine how the wing was meant to function.

Rezkin formed in his mind his desire to heal then pushed his power into Seena's body. Then he directed that power to set the broken bones and heal the damaged muscles and ligaments. Before he had even withdrawn his power, Seena began to flap her wing wildly. She crooned with pleasure then scurried up his arm to perch on his shoulder. When he stood, she leapt off and glided down to the ground. Rezkin watched her with a grin as she flopped around gleefully.

Bilior's craggy voice said, "We go now. The army you bring?"

Rezkin turned back to the katerghen. "No, now I will rest, and then I go to find my friend."

Bilior was not happy, but he did not press the issue and finally departed. Seena had slept most of the day in the satchel, so she was to stand guard and alert Rezkin if anything threatened them. Rezkin lay on the hard ground that night, his sleep broken by discomfort from all the tree roots and pebbles that dug into his backside. He slept in his armor with his sword at his side. He had attempted to place a dome ward around them for the night, but he kept losing control of it each time he fell asleep. When he woke in the morning, he was exhausted. Seena's screeching awoke him. He opened his eyes to the sight of Bilior leaning over him. The katerghen had returned.

After covering over his campfire, Rezkin gathered his pack and pulled out the beacon stone. It was leading him farther into the forest. Seena was enjoying the trek. She scurried up trees and leapt from branch to branch, sometimes gliding to the ground before repeating it over again. Bilior trailed Rezkin, sometimes maintaining his tree-like visage and other times taking on the form of an animal. Rezkin did not like being followed by the fae creature, but there was nothing he could do about it. At least Bilior was following him in the open where he could see him.

Rezkin traveled through the forest for the better part of three weeks. The land became steep and rocky as they entered the foothills of the Eastern Mountains, and the foliage began to change. The thick, squat trees of the plain gave way to towering conifers. The shadows shifted between the trees as the sun rose into the clear sky. It was a few hours past midday when Rezkin came upon a fissure in the rockface. The beacon stone drew him into the cave that apparently extended far into the hills. Rezkin used the light of a mage stone to find his way through the tunnels and caverns. The air was cool and damp inside the caves, and every scuff and footfall echoed through the chambers. The caves eventually opened into a clearing surrounded by more trees and then steep, rocky slopes. At the center of the clearing was a structure unlike any Rezkin had ever seen. It appeared to be made from living trees that had been twisted together to form a sort of cabin.

Seena released a smokey roar. She arched her spine and spread her wings as her neck and tail lashed back and forth. Rezkin drew the black blade and held it at the ready. He did not know what alarmed Seena, but he knew something was not right. He had the sense they were not alone. He could feel someone watching him, although he saw no one. Rezkin began to move through the clearing as though he were seeking prey. He walked stealthily in a circuitous route toward the cabin in the center. A *crack* resounded around the space, then rocks upon the slope began to slide. Rezkin searched the area for a hidden source but saw nothing.

The hairs on the back of his neck began to stand on end, and he spun. Behind him was a tree like any other tree, but it was one he did not remember being there before. He searched for Bilior and found him watching from a dozen feet away. Rezkin peered at the tree a moment longer then continued toward the cabin. When he was about twenty feet away, he tripped. He managed to catch himself before he fell flat on his face, but he was perplexed. He looked down to see a root sticking up from the ground—one he had not seen. It was as if the thing had risen up and grabbed his foot. And then it did.

The ground began to shake as roots shot through the soil and snagged his legs. A tree suddenly appeared behind him, its branches bending down to wrap around his arms. He lost his grip on the black blade as the branches wrenched him around. Then stones from the cliffside began pelting him. Rezkin jerked his head out of the path of a flying stone, and he found Bilior was now only a few feet away. The katerghen simply watched as Rezkin was entangled in roots and branches and assaulted by rocks. He shouted, "Bilior!"

He heard another small roar and looked down to see Seena attacking the roots that were wrapped around his legs. Her sharp teeth and talons dug into the fleshy roots to little effect. New roots shot out of the ground to wrap several times around the little dragon. Smoke billowed from her mouth as she roared again. A blade suddenly cut through the branches holding Rezkin's left arm. Rezkin turned to look, but he could not see the wielder through the thick branches. The blade came down again, this time from the other side, freeing his right arm.

"Release him!" hollered a voice that Rezkin knew all too well. "I said release him, now! He is not the enemy."

The rocks stopped pelting him, and the roots around Rezkin's legs went slack. He untangled himself before snatching up his sword from the ground. Then Rezkin began hacking at the roots restraining Seena until she was free. Seena continued to attack the roots even though they were no longer animated.

Rezkin turned to his savior. "Tam, it is good to see you."

Tam sheathed his Sheyalin and threw himself at Rezkin, wrapping him in a tight hug. He said, "I'm so glad to see you, Rez. I heard you were dead."

Rezkin said, "I was, but I did not prefer it."

Tam leaned back with surprise. "Rez, was that joke? I didn't know you were capable."

Rezkin sheathed his own sword. "The Sen Berringish brought me back from the dead. I killed him for it. It will not happen again."

With wide eyes, Tam said, "Why would you kill him for saving you?"

"He tried to put a demon in me."

"Oh, I guess that was a good reason."

Rezkin waved around at the limbs and roots then the offending tree. "What is going on here?"

Tam appeared embarrassed. He said, "Sorry about that. They got a little excited. You are the first of the ahn'tep races they have encountered, besides me, of course."

"Then they *are* ahn'an?"

"Yes," said Tam. "Come. I will explain over tea."

Rezkin followed Tam into the living cabin. It was a small, one-room affair with an equally living table and chair to one side. Tam offered Rezkin the chair and announced, "I need another chair." Roots began growing rapidly out of the ground. Then stalks began to form on them, and these grew into a twisted frame of a chair. Tam went to the stone hearth and retrieved a clay pot that had been heating over the fire. Then he produced two wooden cups and filled them with steaming hot tea from the pot. When Tam sat down, he breathed out heavily.

"You got my beacon stone?" said Tam.

"I did. Where did you get such a thing?"

"From *them*," he said, motioning with his head toward the fae creatures outside. "Where to start?" muttered Tam. "I guess it started back at the quarry. Maybe a little before that. It was all because of that hole in my mind. The one *you* had put there."

Rezkin felt a pang of guilt slice through him. Tam had almost died because of him. "I am sorry about that, Tam. I never should have—"

Tam held up a hand. "No, no. If you had not, I would likely be dead right now. You see, that hole in my mind opened an entirely new world to me. I began to hear and see things, to *know* things that I didn't before. It's like the world is constantly chattering, sometimes even speaking to *me*, and I could understand it. I thought I was going mad. But it turns out it was all real.

"Back in the quarry, a creature came to me—one of the fae. I think I told you about it. It was a rock monster. At least, that's what I thought at the time. Now I know it to be ahn'an. Its name was Goragana, and it is one of the Ancients. It spoke to me, and I could understand. It saved my life because of the deal you made with the Ancients."

"Anyway, I thought I was done with the fae after that, but it turns out they weren't done with me. I came to Gendishen like you asked, but things weren't going well for me. I didn't have the confidence to take charge of the army like you wanted. I realize that now. Anyway, one night, Goragana came to me—came right out of my bed chamber wall. Goragana said that I was part of the army you had promised them and that it was time for me to take my place. I thought it meant as general of the Gendishen Army, but it turns out that's not what they wanted. Because of my ability to understand them, they had selected me to be *their* general. They stole me away through the pathways and brought me here where they made me the general of the fae army. I've been training with them here ever since. They won't let me go. They want me to be the liaison between them and the rest of your army."

Rezkin felt a burst of red-hot anger burn through him. The ahn'an had conscripted Tam without his consent into a position he was not meant to fill. Had he unknowingly given the fae the right to take his people for their own use in the coming war? He had promised them an army. He had not specified that it would be made of people of his own choosing *or* that he would be the one to lead that army. Now they had Tam. Who knew for how long or in what capacity?

Rezkin found himself apologizing a second time. "I am sorry, Tam. I never meant for this to happen to you. I did not fully consider my deal with the fae, and now you are at their mercy."

Tam's eyes widened. "Are you saying you can't get me out of this?"

Rezkin shook his head. "No, I believe they feel that they are satisfying the terms of our agreement. They have claimed you as part of the army I promised them."

"So I'm stuck here? For how long? What will they have me do? Rez, I can't do this. I'm going insane here among them. They keep trying to make deals with me."

"You must be very careful of anything you say to them, Tam. Do not agree to anything, even something simple. When I made the deal with them, I felt I had no other choice. They will try to put you in the position to feel the same way."

Tam hung his head. After a moment, he looked up and said, "I guess it's not all bad. I mean, I always wanted adventure. He tapped the table then stood. Pacing the floor, he rubbed his hands together as he thought. Then he turned to Rezkin. "Yes, this will be good. No, it'll be great! I'm the *leader* of the fae army. How much more adventurous could it get?"

"I am truly sorry, Tam. This was never my intention. I will try to come up with a way to get you out of it."

"Don't' be sorry, Rez. This is exciting, isn't it?" He looked down to where Seena was attacking part of the living table leg. "Now, are we going to discuss the dragon?"

22

After a week, Rezkin left Tam with a gnawing guilt he could not ignore. It was *his* fault Tam was stuck with the fae, and he had no idea how he would get Tam out of it. The pathway to Caellurum was a long one, not due to the distance but because of the burden he carried in his heart. First, he needed to make sure Yserria was safe, and he had to thwart whatever plans Caydean had for Lon Lerésh, then he needed to find a way to free Tam, even if Tam did not presently want to be freed. He stopped in Caellurum to get the latest news. He needed to know where to find Yserria. According to the latest report, she had been summoned to the queen's court in the Leréshi capital city of Kielen and had traveled there during the time Rezkin had been searching the forest for Tam.

He had Seena open the portal directly into a storeroom he had once visited in the queen's palace. He disguised himself as a Leréshi servant intending to go in search of Yserria. Since animals were not common in the palace, Seena had to travel in the sack at Rezkin's hip. She did not like being cooped up in the sack and protested by shifting around as much as possible. At least she was quiet. He could cover up her movements with illusion, but it was much harder to hide the noises.

Upon stepping out of the storeroom, Rezkin was nearly run over by a team of guards. The guards paid no attention to him as they ran past. A commotion at the other end of the corridor caught Rezkin's attention. A maid was crying, and several other servants stood around looking pensive. The guards rushed into the queen's chambers at the end of the corridor. Then Rezkin heard a shout.

"The queen is dead!"

Rezkin's blood ran cold at the proclamation. If it was true, and Erisial was dead, that meant he was now the ruler of Lon Lerésh. At least, he would be if people did not think him dead. Another queen would soon take Erisial's place, and there was no guarantee she would be sympathetic to his cause or that she would adhere to the agreements made between him and Erisial. If Rezkin was to maintain control of Lon Lerésh's military, he would need a supporter on the throne.

Footsteps thundered toward him from the opposite end of the corridor. Erisial's consort Serunius dashed toward the queen's chambers. Rezkin waited to see the battle mage's reaction to whatever had happened in Erisial's quarters. The servants hurriedly vacated the corridor as Serunius arrived. A moment later, there was an explosion, and the doors to the chamber flew off their hinges to slam against the wall on the opposite side of the corridor. That was all the confirmation Rezkin needed. Erisial *was* dead, and now he had a choice to make. He could either come forward and seize the throne for himself, or he had to ensure the right person took the throne.

News of the queen's death spread like wildfire throughout the palace. Already servants began scurrying through the corridors covering portraits and statues in black fabric as the guards searched the entire palace for the assassin. With all the commotion, it was not difficult for Rezkin to move about undeterred. He questioned a few of the servants and learned that Yserria *was* at the palace and had gone to the practice yard that morning. Malcius had gone with her. Rezkin was pleased the two were maintaining their *Skills*, and he longed to practice with them. He realized that he missed training with his friends.

Rezkin hurried toward the practice yard so that he would not miss them. When he arrived, he found that news of Erisial's death had already reached the grounds. The guards normally training there were quickly vacating the yard. Yserria and Malcius were heading into the small building near the practice yard used for storing supplies and for resting and recuperating, and they both looked distraught. Rezkin waited until no one remained in the practice yard, then headed for the building. When he entered, his attention perused the storage area where practice weapons and padding were stacked and piled and then turned toward the seating area. He found Yserria and Malcius alone. He spoke in Leréshi.

"*Pardon me, Matrianera Yserria. May I have a word with you privately?*"

Yserria glanced at Malcius, but of course Malcius had not understood him. Rezkin could tell that Yserria was suspicious of the unusual request, but she nodded graciously.

Rezkin said, "*Might we speak alone?*"

Yserria responded, "*What you have to say to me, you can say in front of him. He won't understand you anyway.*"

Rezkin stared at Malcius for a long moment rethinking his chosen course of action. Finally, he nodded and allowed his illusion to drop away. Yserria and Malcius both jumped as he changed before their eyes. Malcius found his voice first.

"Rez! You're alive! But … *how*?"

Rezkin looked at Yserria, who stared at him speechless. He turned back to Malcius. "A Sen retrieved me from death. I live again."

Malcius suddenly closed the distance and threw his arms around Rezkin. "Oh, thank the Maker, we are saved." Then he reared back, and his face screwed up in anger. "It's been *nine months*! And you're just now coming forward. How could you do that to us? How could you let us believe you were dead all this time?"

"I realize you are upset—"

"Upset?! Upset does not begin to cover it!"

"But I had my reasons, and I still do. I am only showing myself to you now because circumstances demand it."

Yserria released a squeak and pointed at his satchel. "It's moving!"

Now that his illusion was gone, they could see where Seena was shifting around irritably.

"*I want out!*" Seena shouted into his mind.

"*Not now,*" he replied with his thoughts. Receiving her thoughts had been easy, but responding through thought had been more challenging, and she did not always hear what he was saying. This time she heard but was not cowed. She popped her head out of the satchel then sprang onto a nearby table. Malcius jumped away, knocking over a chair, and Yserria drew her sword. Seena stretched her wings and neck and tail to their full extents then shook herself like a wet dog.

"Is that a dragon!?" shouted Malcius.

Rezkin reached for Seena, but she scurried away from his grasping hands. "Yes," he said, "this is Seena. She is my companion." He reached for her again and just missed catching her. "She is usually better behaved, but she has been cooped up in the satchel for too long."

Yserria hesitantly sheathed her sword. "You've been keeping a *dragon* in your satchel?"

"Well, I cannot very well walk around the palace with her frolicking in the hallways, and she cannot be left alone. She is only a baby and does not yet have adequate defensive capabilities."

Malcius said, "Just when I think I know you, Rez, you rise from the dead and capture a dragon. No one will believe this."

"You can tell no one about me," said Rezkin. "You must maintain the secret for a while longer."

"You want *us* to pretend you are dead?" asked Malcius. "You want me to lie to our friends? To what end, Rezkin?"

Yserria finally spoke. "Erisial is dead. We just heard. That means you are now the ruler of Lon Lerésh. You must come forward and claim the throne."

"I cannot do that. I must remain hidden a while longer."

"But you will lose Lon Lerésh," said Yserria. "It will no longer be a part of the empire."

"That is why I have come to you now. I must ensure that a loyalist wears the crown."

"How do you intend to do that?" asked Malcius.

Rezkin looked to Yserria. "I need *you* to claim the throne, Yserria."

Yserria's eyes widened. "*What*? You want *me* to become queen?"

"Yes."

"How do you expect me to do that?"

"I think you will find you have more support than you know. You are already the leader of *two* echelons. You have more clout than most at court."

"But without you backing me, I am less of a threat. I'm surprised I haven't already been assassinated."

"That is why I need you to claim a new consort."

Yserria cut her hand through the air. "Absolutely not." She glanced at Malcius from the corner of her eye and said, "As far as I'm concerned, I have one too many."

Malcius scowled at Yserria but did not argue the point.

Rezkin said, "There is something else you need to know. Someone is coming for you, someone against whom your blade will have little effect. It will be a battle mage, and likely a demon. You need the protection of a mage and not just any mage. You need a battle mage. You must claim Serunius."

"But I don't *want* Serunius!"

"This is not right," interjected Malcius. "You cannot force her to take a consort."

Rezkin returned his gaze to Yserria. "What you do—or do *not* do—with him is your business, but you need his protection. He is the most powerful battle mage in Lon Lerésh."

"What makes you think he will accept my claim?"

"He loved Erisial. He will be in mourning, but he is experienced at court. He will see the wisdom and necessity of your claim. He is attracted to you. He would rather have your claim than that of another, and he will not remain unclaimed for long. You may have several challengers for him. If you secure Serunius as your consort, your claim to the throne may go unchallenged. Serunius is the key."

Yserria's jaw tensed. "You are forgetting that I don't *want* the throne. And I don't want Serunius. Why should I do any of this?"

"You must do it for the empire and the fight against Caydean."

"*Your* empire. None of this would be necessary if you just came forward."

"As I have said, I cannot at this time. Only a few people know I am alive, and it needs to stay that way for now. You cannot discuss it with anyone, even amongst yourselves. Caydean must not find out. Besides, even if I came forward, the queendom would be thrown into turmoil. It would be civil war. The queendom *needs* a queen. Will you do it?"

"It seems I have no choice."

"You always have a choice, Yserria. If you decide against this, I will find another way—one that likely will include much more bloodshed."

Yserria took a deep breath and released it slowly. She looked at Malcius, who appeared anxious and almost fearful. Then she turned back to Rezkin. "I will do it, but I know nothing about running a queendom."

"Serunius was with Erisial during her entire reign. He will help you. The echelons are largely independent and will run themselves. It is up to you to keep them under your thumb. You do not have to do this all on your own, Yserria. I will remain here working in the shadows until you secure Serunius and the throne."

Rezkin turned to go, but Yserria called out to him. "Wait. This battle mage you said is coming for me. Why? Why me?"

"That I cannot tell you without risking your life."

"My life is already at risk. Tell me."

Rezkin turned back to her. "Very well, but even knowing this could put you in more danger. Are you sure you want to know?"

"If it is so important, I think I should," replied Yserria.

Rezkin nodded solemnly. "Back on Cael, when you were being held for that demon ritual, something happened to you. Your soul was being drawn into the bonfire to allow for the demon to enter you. I stopped the ritual by trapping the fire inside some crystals. Unfortunately, part of your soul was drawn into one of the crystals as well. We believed that had you known, the process would have continued until your entire soul was trapped."

"You're saying my *soul* is trapped in a crystal?"

"Only part of it. If it was your entire soul, you would be dead."

"So where is this crystal? I should have it. It's *my* soul."

"Again, we believe that it would be detrimental for you to carry your own crystal. It could draw the remainder of your soul inside and kill you. But it could be equally dangerous for you to be too far parted from that piece of your soul. Therefore, someone else needed to carry the crystal, your *life stone*, for you and remain close to you. Someone I trusted."

Rezkin could see the thoughts whirling through Yserria's mind through her pale eyes. Then her gaze slid to Malcius. "*You*? *You're* carrying this life stone?"

Malcius dug under the neck of his tunic and produced the pendant holding a brilliant red crystal.

Yserria punched Rezkin in the arm. "You gave my soul to *Malcius*? Of all people! He hates me."

"Malcius is loyal and honorable," said Rezkin. "He has only ever treated the stone with the reverence it deserves. He has been at your side for more than a year, has hazarded all your trials, even endured Lon Lerésh, for the sole purpose of bearing your soul, to keep you alive and well. And he has never attempted to foist the burden onto someone else."

Yserria was taken aback. She stared at Malcius as if seeing him for the first time. She whispered, "I didn't know. I'm sorry, Malcius. I didn't know."

Malcius tucked the stone back under his tunic. "You were not *supposed* to know."

Yserria's thoughts tumbled around in her mind as Rezkin walked away. She had no idea the burden Malcius had borne all this time. What he had done for her was beyond her imaginings. He had taken voyages, endured battles, been claimed, and permanently marked as wed—all for *her*. Not once had he given any hint that he carried the stone, nor had he expected her gratitude or recompense. She was left in wonder over why he had done it. Sure, Rezkin had asked him to, but as Rezkin had said earlier, there was always a choice. Malcius could have insisted someone else take the burden, but instead he had taken it upon himself.

Malcius hated her. He still blamed her for his brother Palis's death. He had made it clear that he could not stand to be around her, yet he had followed her wherever she went. Yserria had barely questioned it. It had grown to feel natural to have Malcius, in all his moodiness, at her side. Given this revelation, she now saw all that time spent together, usually quarrelling, in a new light. Practically everything he had done for more than a year at been for *her*.

"What?" snapped Malcius.

Yserria jumped. She realized she had been staring at him. She said, "It's just —I don't know what to say."

Malcius released a frustrated breath. "You do not need to say anything. We should be getting back to the palace. I may not be Leréshi, but I know something of court politics. The vultures will be swarming over Erisial's dead body. You need to make an appearance and begin testing the waters for support for the throne. That is, if you really intend to go through with this."

Yserria swallowed the lump in her throat. "I do."

"You are really going to claim Serunius?" he said. She noticed how he clenched his jaw and fisted his hands.

"It seems I must if I am to take the throne," she answered as she exited the building and began walking the path back to the palace.

"Then you had best do it now before someone else does," said Malcius as he kept pace beside her.

Yserria's eyes widened. "Erisial's body isn't even cold yet, and you want me to claim her lover?"

"*I* do not want you to, but I did not get a say in this insane scheme. Rezkin is right. You are going to be challenged for him. You need to make it known that he is yours and you will not take no for an answer."

"If he accepts my claim, I doubt anyone will challenge me. It would mean he can act as my champion, and no one will want to go up against the most powerful battle mage in Lon Lerésh."

"True. That does not seem like a fair fight."

"How do you think Erisial held on to him for so long? Serunius is powerful enough that he will not be claimed unless he wants to be. Only Rezkin might stand a chance against him—and maybe Wesson. That is one reason why Erisial married Rezkin. She could not afford for him to act as someone else's champion against Serunius." She paused for a moment, then said, "I am concerned that Serunius will not accept my claim."

Malcius barked a short laugh, but his tone was dark as he spoke. "Serunius wants you. I have seen it in the way he looks at you. He will accept your claim."

They were stopped and questioned by no less than three sets of guards as they entered the palace and made their way toward the throne room. Already the corridors were draped in black fabric, and the mage lights in the wall sconces had been changed from a warm, fiery yellow to a cool blue.

As they began walking the path toward the palace, Yserria said, "Why are you doing this? Why are you helping me?"

Malcius huffed. "It is my job."

She shook her head. "No, your job was to carry the stone. That's it. No one ever said you had to help me, yet you've done so everywhere we've gone."

Malcius muttered, "I have nothing better to do."

Yserria did not believe him for a moment. She knew he had some ulterior motive for helping her, but she could not fathom what it was. She pushed thoughts of Malcius aside as she entered the throne room. A few courtiers who had been in residence at the palace had already arrived, but she knew more would begin arriving over the coming weeks. The Sixth Echelon, Matrianera Nayala of House Tekahl, rushed over to greet her as soon as she stepped through the doorway. She took Yserria by the arm and spoke in hushed tones as they slowly crossed the throne room. Malcius kept pace at her other side.

"The palace is in an uproar," said Nayala in Ashaiian. "It has been over ten years since a new queen took the throne, and there are no certainties about who it will be."

Yserria said, "Who are the contenders?"

"First Echelon Alania Dormisk will certainly issue a claim. She has made no secret of her plans to one day rule Lon Lerésh. I doubt she has the support to succeed, though. She has been very unpopular both at court and with her people over the past year. She imports more than she exports and as such has a budget deficit, which she makes up in higher taxes and customs.

"A second contender will likely be Ninth Echelon Thia Helanis. She is most popular among certain social circles, and she runs her echelon well. Her people are generally content, and her borders have been stable since she took the position.

"In my opinion, the most likely to succeed is Twelfth Echelon Grizelda Tynan. Her champion is undefeated in battle. He has served as general of the army for the past five years and wields his *talent* with the expertise of a master mage. Grizelda is also very popular at court for her shrewd business dealings and generosity. She is a patron of the arts as well as the primary contributor to the efforts to house and feed the poor. If rumors are true, however, she is something of a deviant. People often go missing in her echelon, and some say she is sacrificing them on the altar of her heathen god."

Yserria looked at Nayala sharply. "Do you believe the rumors?"

Nayala shrugged. "I have no evidence to support them, but the tales are too rampant to be ignored. She has never been seen at the Temple of the Maker."

Yserria pulled her arm from Nayala as they stopped amongst the growing crowd only a few paces from the throne. Yserria noticed how Malcius kept his hand on his hilt as he surveyed the crowd with sharp eyes. She could not blame him for being anxious. She was anxious, too. Where there was one assassination, there could be more. Yserria looked back to Nayala.

"You have no designs on the throne?"

Nayala's gaze swept over the crowd, and she nodded toward her consort Banen, who quickly began making his way toward them. She swept her many braids over her shoulder and said, "No, I like my head right where it is. Only those with a death wish vie for the throne."

A chill went through Yserria, and her fingers grazed her own hilt. Banen joined them and wrapped his arms around Nyala in a warm, protective embrace. Yserria briefly wondered what it would feel like to be held like that. Palis had ever been the gentleman and had not so much as touched her in the short time she had known him, and there had been no other men for her. She contemplated that as she thought about what she was about to do. She was about to claim a second man she did not desire as her consort, this time for political reasons so that she could claim a throne she equally did not want. Rezkin was her emperor, though, and what he asked of her was for the greater good. She felt obliged to answer his call.

Yserria turned back to Nayala. "What happens now?"

Nayala tapped Banen's arm, and he retreated to stand behind her. She said, "Now begins the true efforts to sway the court toward the contenders. We will likely be here for hours as people mingle and attempt to convince each other that their preferred contender should rule. This will occur every day for the next several weeks until there is a clear winner. You must be on guard. Assassinations are common during this time. Someone is likely to challenge you for one or both of your echelons." Nayala glanced over Malcius, then added, "You would do well to claim another consort to act as your champion. You cannot fight all your battles alone."

"I intend to," said Yserria as Serunius entered the throne room. He wore his ceremonial battle mage attire of a black tunic and pants embellished with gold embroidery. His dark hair was cut short and styled, and his face was clean shaven. His eyes, though, were slightly red and puffy. Yserria's gut churned, and she felt even worse for what she was about to do. This strong, powerful man had cried over his beloved only a short time ago, and she was about to try to steal him away.

Yserria saw that other people were beginning to notice Serunius's presence, and she knew she had to move quickly if she were to stake her claim first. She pushed past the few courtiers standing between her and the dais then mounted the steps quickly. No one paid her any attention, and she knew her voice would not be heard over the din. A shrill whistle sounded from right beside her, and she realized Malcius had followed her onto the dais. A silence descended over the room, and every head turned her way. She looked over at Serunius. He met her gaze with a hard stare that gave nothing away.

Turning back to the crowd, Yserria called out in the strongest voice she could muster. "I, Yserria Ray of House Palis, Third and Fourth Echelon, claim Serunius Pendrant as consort." There seemed to be a collective inhale as all eyes turned toward Serunius, but his gaze was riveted on *her*. His cold, dark eyes penetrated her soul, and that voice of empathy inside her cried out for his pain. Yserria swallowed hard, and her hands began to tremble as she awaited his rejection. If he did, she would have to fight the champion of anyone else intent on claiming him until she had defeated all other contenders. And if he accepted someone else's claim, she would likely have to fight *him* in order to claim him against his will.

Her discomfort stretched as silence prevailed. Serunius clenched his fists at his sides but otherwise did not move. His thoughts were loud enough to fill the silence as resentment ignited in his eyes. Finally, he dropped his gaze and said in a voice that could barely be heard, "I accept."

Yserria tore her gaze away from the grieving man and spoke over the fresh muttering of the crowd. "I, Yserria Ray of House Palis, Third and Fourth Echelon, lay claim to the throne of Lon Lerésh."

The previously muted crowd erupted in a discordant chorus. Malcius loosened his sword in its scabbard as he stepped closer to Yserria. He muttered, "I think we should get out of here."

"We cannot," she returned in an equally low voice. "We must stay to convince them to support my claim."

"It is not safe," he hissed. "You are the first to lay claim, and they will not want to fight Serunius in an open challenge. They will assassinate you."

The next moment, they were surrounded by nobles pelting her with questions. Yserria fielded the questions as best she could, hedging on the more difficult subjects, and allowing Malcius to answer for her on several occasions. She was not prepared for the onslaught, and she knew she was doing a poor job of representing herself. After an hour of non-answers and political double speak, Serunius came to her rescue. He pushed his way into the group and held up a hand as he raised his voice.

"*That is all the questions for now. I require a private conference with my matrianera, if she would oblige.*"

"*Yes, of course,*" said Yserria, drawing away from the group quickly. Malcius followed her and Serunius out of the throne room and down a short corridor, but when they reached the doorway to the sitting room, Serunius barred the way from Malcius with an outstretched arm.

He looked at Malcius and said, "My words are for Yserria alone. You will wait out here."

Malcius scowled at Serunius and turned to Yserria. "Are you okay with this?"

Yserria was *not* okay with it. She did not want to be alone with Serunius and especially not now while he was grieving his beloved. She did not say any of that, though. Serunius had accepted her claim at the most inopportune time, and Yserria felt that she owed him an explanation. She nodded. "Yes, I will speak with him."

Malcius looked to Serunius, "Do not touch her or—"

"Or what?" interrupted Serunius. "If I wanted to harm her, there is little *you* could do about it." He released a pulse of power that reverberated through Yserria's chest. "She may have claimed you before me, but do not make the mistake of thinking *you* are First Consort."

He did not wait for a response as he turned and entered the sitting room and closed the door. Yserria backed farther into the room, gripping her hilt even knowing that her sword would be virtually useless against the battle mage. Serunius stalked toward her like a large cat hunting its prey. She hit the back of the sofa, and she could go no further. He stopped with no more than half a foot between them. Looming over her, he said, "*Never before have you shown the slightest interest in me, then today, mere hours since the death of my matrianera, you are the first to lay claim to me. For months, you could not be bothered to set foot in your echelons, yet in the very next breath, you claim the throne. What game are you playing?*"

"*This is not a game,*" said Yserria. "*The stakes are too high.*"

His dark eyes were calculating as he stared down at her. Finally, he spoke in a soft voice. "*My heart has been torn from my breast this day. I have no love to give you.*"

Yserria nearly shivered at the cold, emptiness of those last words. "*I do not require your love, Serunius, only your service.*"

"*Then I am but a pawn in your wicked game. I have accepted your claim. Now you owe me the truth. Why do you want the throne?*"

Yserria straightened her back and lifted her chin. "*For the empire.*"

"*Ah, the empire with no emperor.*"

"*It is the official stance of Lon Lerésh that the emperor still lives.*"

The corners of his lips lifted in a sardonic grin. "*That is something Erisial said to keep the vipers from taking her throne. With her gone, Lon Lerésh will become independent once again.*"

"*Not if I become queen,*" said Yserria.

He lifted a finger to make a point. "*You cannot become queen if the emperor lives, for* he *is the rightful ruler.*"

Yserria crossed her arms. "*I will hold the position until he returns to claim it.*"

"*And you want* my *help in doing that.*"

"*Would you prefer I allow someone else to claim you? I will ask nothing of you beyond serving as my champion and protector. What will another matrianera desire?*"

He shook his head. "*It matters not what they desire. I cannot be forced to do anything I do not wish to do. If I am to serve you, then I need certain assurances.*"

Yserria had known Serunius would not make this easy, but she was anxious to hear his demands. "*What would you have?*"

The pain in his voice raked across her nerves. "*I must be given time to mourn Erisial.*"

"*You may mourn Erisial for as long as you need, forever if you must.*"

He looked at her for a long time, as if searching for signs of deceit. His eyes hardened. "*I am first consort. No others will be above me—ever.*"

Yserria nodded slowly. Malcius would not like it, but like Serunius, Malcius was her consort in name only. Therefore, his feelings on the matter were moot. She said, "*So shall it be. Is there anything else?*"

"*Yes, I will be free to do as I please. Anything beyond my duties as champion and protector is my business and mine alone.*"

Yserria shook her head. "*That I cannot do. If I am to be queen, then I will rule this queendom as I deem necessary for its prosperity and that of the empire. I need you to act in accordance with my design. And, as a member of my household and first consort to the queen, what you do reflects on me. I am responsible for the things you do. I cannot look away.*"

"*I am accustomed to certain freedoms—*"

"*I do not believe for a moment that Erisial gave you full autonomy.*"

"*Perhaps not,*" he admitted. "*But she trusted me to act in her interests and for the good of the queendom.*"

"*I, too, may come to trust you some day, but that kind of trust takes time to build. Besides, I do not know that your interests and mine are aligned. Do you support Rezkin and the empire?*"

Serunius tilted his head thoughtfully. "*I do not care for him, but I do respect him. He is a powerful man, and he has come into that power through battle prowess, intelligence, and cunning. Do I trust him to rule Lon Lerésh? No. Do I trust him to support* your *rule? I do. That is assuming he lives.*"

"*He does,*" she said, "*and I think it will not be long before that truth is known.*"

His eyes hardened. "*If anyone else takes the throne and then he comes forward to claim his rightful place as king, there will be civil war. I would rather not have Lon Lerésh torn apart.*"

"*Then you will support my claim to the throne?*"

"*I will on one condition. You do not marry Rezkin. I will not share another matrianera with him.*"

"*That will not be an issue. I have no intention of marrying him, nor would he marry me.*"

"*We are in agreement, then. We shall go forth and claim the throne together.*"

For the following days and weeks, Yserria, Malcius, Serunius, and Nayala campaigned for support among the courtiers. Alania Dormisk and Thia Helanis both arrived within two weeks, and each made her own claim to the throne. Unlike other challenges, claims for the throne were decided via popular vote amongst the nobility, and the men and women of the noble households were granted equal votes. Yserria's pro-empire stance made it more difficult to garner support among the noble ladies; however, she experienced growing popularity among the men who saw the empire as a means for greater personal independence.

The three contenders for the throne and their retinues were gathered in the throne room campaigning amongst the nobles when Grizelda Tynan arrived. She swept into the room like a tempest, grabbing everyone's attention as she flaunted herself before the nobles. With her chin raised and her silk gown trailing the floor behind her, she strutted across the room to ascend the dais. When she turned toward the crowd, she grinned smugly and said, "I, Grizelda Tynan, ruler of the Twelfth Echelon, claim the throne of Lon Lerésh." She met Yserria's gaze. "Any who stand against me will perish."

Yserria leaned over and whispered to Nyala. "What is she talking about?"

Nayala shrugged one shoulder. "I do not know, but I doubt she will leave us wondering for long."

They did not have to wait long. Grizelda waited for the curious mutterings to die down. Then she said, "I invoke the right of trial."

The nobles burst into a chaotic chorus. A shiver went through Yserria. She did not know what the right of trial was, but she was certain it was nothing good. Beside her, Nayala hissed.

"What is it?" asked Yserria.

"She has invoked the right of trial. That has not been done in more than a hundred years. This does not bode well for any of you."

"What does it mean?"

"It means you and your champion and possibly members of your household must endure three trials if you choose to remain a contender for the throne."

"So if I win the trial, then I become queen?"

"No. The trials do not determine who will be queen. They are designed to showcase your talents and experience so that the nobles will be more inclined to vote for you."

"That doesn't sound so bad."

"Do not be fooled. The trials are not easy. And you need not win every trial. Your primary goal is to survive."

Yserria's eyes widened. "The trials are deadly?"

"Oh, there *will* be death. It is guaranteed."

Yserria gripped the hilt of her sword for the comfort it brought her. "What are these trials?"

Nayala lifted her chin toward a group of women speaking heatedly in the corner. "That is for the Queen's Council to decide. They will design and administer the trials. In some of the trials, the nobles will cast their votes of approval. In others, the council will decide the winner. As both a foreigner and a mundane, you will be at a disadvantage."

Yserria *was* at a disadvantage as she was the only mundane among the contenders. Alania, Thia, and Grizelda were each accomplished mages, traditionally trained with rule in mind. With Serunius as her champion, though, she had a chance at overcoming the deficiency.

After Grizelda's harrowing announcement, the council members adjourned to discuss the trials, and Yserria and Nayala met Malcius and Serunius back at Yserria's suite. They sat sharing tea in the sitting room as Nayala further explained that the trials were designed to test the contestants' political, economic, and martial aptitude. Two hours later, a page brought the news that the first of the trials was announced. It would be a public debate. Each contender would be given one day to consider the topics and form their opinions. Then each had to present their stance before the court and defend it against any who would oppose it. The catch was that there were deadly consequences for failure.

"Not everyone will survive the first trial," said Nayala in Ashaiian for Malcius's sake. "Each contender and her champion will be placed in a cage covered in runes to prevent them from using their *talent*. The cage is then hung over a massive fire pit. With each poor answer, the cage is lowered farther into the pit."

"That's horrible," gasped Yserria. "Why would anyone want the throne if the stakes are so high?"

"Will you withdraw your claim?" asked Nayala.

"I cannot," replied Yserria as she inwardly cursed Rezkin.

"Then you will have to endure the debate," said Nayala. "You will receive the debate topics tomorrow morning. You will have one day to consider them. The trial will begin the following day." She paused in thought, then said, "Ienia Vesqu will no doubt champion Thia. They are close friends. Ienia is the foremost debater in Kielen."

"I am ill-suited to a debate," said Yserria. "I have never participated in one." She looked to Serunius. He merely stared back at her. Then she turned to Malcius. He anxiously ran a hand through his hair.

He said, "I have participated in numerous debates and came out the victor in most of them. I can teach you."

"There isn't time for that," said Yserria. "You will have to act as my champion."

Malcius's eyes widened. "But I cannot! This is Lon Lerésh. I know nothing of debate here. I know very little about their politics. I do not even speak the language."

Yserria said, "But you must, Malcius. I know no one else to ask."

"Fire, Yserria. We will die by *fire*."

"You do not have to win the debate," said Nayala. "You just have to impress enough people with your answers that the cage is not lowered too far. There will be five questions. You will be given four of them in advance so that you may prepare your answers. The fifth question remains a secret until the end."

Malcius sat heavily in a chair and dropped his head into his hands. After a moment, he looked up. "What about the language barrier? Surely this debate will be held in Leréshi."

"I have a solution for that, "said Serunius, breaking his long silence. "There is an amulet used in negotiations with diplomats that will enable you to speak and understand any language so long as you are wearing it. I will ensure the runes on the cage do not interfere with the amulet."

"An amulet?" said Malcius. "It would have been helpful to have that all this time."

Serunius said, "There is only one in existence, and it is property of the crown. It is only to be used for official business. I think the selection of the next queen of Lon Lerésh qualifies."

Malcius groaned. "You all have answers for everything except how we are going to survive the fifth question."

"Hopefully, we will not be lowered so far after the first four questions for the fifth to matter that much," replied Yserria.

Malcius looked at her meaningfully, "You are gambling with our lives, and you are depending on *hope*?"

23

REZKIN WAITED for Nayala and Serunius to leave Yserria's suite before letting himself in. Yserria and Malcius both drew their swords as he shut the door. He pushed back his hood, and they visibly relaxed. Sheathing their swords, they advanced on him.

"What is the meaning of this, Rezkin? Did you know this was going to happen?" said Malcius accusingly.

"Know what was going to happen?" replied Rezkin.

"The trials. The cage and the fire and whatever else they have planned."

"The right of trial has not been used in over a hundred years. I did not know Grizelda would invoke it now, nor did I know which trials they would choose," he said as he walked past them. He warded the room against anyone attempting to listen, magical or otherwise. They watched him curiously as he set about searching for traps, poisons, and listening devices.

"Just what are you looking for?" huffed Malcius.

"Things that should not be here."

Yserria walked over to him and planted herself in his path. "What are we going to do about the first trial?"

"Do? We are going to prepare you for a debate."

Yserria crossed her arms. "*I* am not debating. Malcius is."

Rezkin nodded. "Good choice. Malcius is an excellent speaker."

"I am a decent speaker in Ashai, not in Lon Lerésh," said Malcius.

"On the contrary, the Leréshi may find your style to be different and refreshing."

"And if they do not?" queried Malcius.

"Then your answers to the questions will see you through," replied Rezkin as he finished searching the room.

Yserria said, "How do you know our answers will suffice?"

"Because I am going to help you," said Rezkin. "And because I already have the questions." He said this last as he pulled a folded paper from his tunic and held it forth in offering.

Malcius snatched it out of his hand and unfolded it. Then he grunted and held it out for Yserria. "It is written in Leréshi. Even so, I can count. There are only four questions on the page. What of the mysterious fifth question?"

Rezkin tried to look apologetic. "Unfortunately, I cannot help you with that one. It will be decided the moment before the trial begins."

"Great," said Malcius. "Then we just have to come up with some answers the Leréshi will like for the other four questions."

"It is not that simple," said Rezkin. "The cages will contain a spell that will force you to speak only truth. You will not be able to hide your true sentiments."

Malcius threw up his hands. "Of course they will. Why would they not? It makes perfect sense. We are doomed."

"Not doomed, Malcius. We only have to word your answers in such a way that the Leréshi will *think* you are in agreement with them. Shall we get started?"

They worked diligently through the remainder of the day then gathered again the next day. Malcius did his best to memorize the answers as they progressed, but given such little time, it was difficult. Seena remained hidden in Rezkin's satchel the entire time he was working with them but not without complaint. Her interruptions of his thoughts came frequently, and he found that his concentration was not ideal. Finally, Rezkin allowed her out of the satchel. She scurried onto the table and promptly spilled a bottle of ink.

"A baby," said Malcius, shaking his head. "That means she will get bigger."

"Much bigger," replied Rezkin as he attempted to keep Seena from tracking ink all over the table. "Although how much bigger is hard to say. I believe her growth was hindered during the time she spent in her egg without vimara to feed her. It was only after I began wearing her egg around my neck and inadvertently sharing my vimara with her that she matured enough to hatch."

Malcius crept forward to get a better look. "That stone you wore was an *egg*?"

"Yes, although I did not know it at the time. I felt better when wearing it because it was syphoning off my vimara thereby holding the madness at bay."

"And now?"

"Now I am linked with her, bonded. It is not unlike the bond I share with Tiseyi, the omessa she-wolf."

"You are bonded to them both?" said Yserria.

"Yes," said Rezkin. He believed he was also bonded to Azeria in some way, but he did not say that. He was still uncertain of the nature of that bond, and he did not care to divulge that secret, even to them.

"What do these bonds *do*?" asked Malcius.

"Each one is different," said Rezkin. "Perhaps most importantly, though, they are preventing the madness from claiming my mind."

"I do not know about that, Rezkin," said Malcius. "I cannot help but think that what we are doing here is madness itself. If you just came forward, there would be no need for Yserria to claim the throne."

"If I came forward, Lon Lerésh would be thrown into civil war. We cannot afford to be fighting a war within while war rages on the Souelian. Lon Lerésh needs a queen whether I live or not. I intend to make sure that queen is Yserria."

"And if we are sacrificed in the process?" asked Malcius.

"Have faith, Malcius," replied Rezkin.

Malcius scoffed. "I have never known you to depend on faith in the Maker."

Rezkin shook his head. "No, I was saying to have faith in *yourself*. I believe you have the *Skills* to accomplish this. You are only lacking the confidence."

"You're not the one staring down a fiery death."

Rezkin motioned to the copious notes scrawled across the pages on the table in front of him. "All you need is here, Malcius. You will do well."

A knock sounded at the door, and Rezkin called for Seena to get back in the bag. Luckily, she complied, and he was quickly striding across the room to flatten his back against the wall next to the door. Yserria glanced at him as she went to open the door, and her eyes widened as they darted around the space. He knew she could no longer see him since he had pulled the illusion of the wall around himself and Seena. Someone knocked again, and Yserria turned back to the door with a shiver. She opened it to find Serunius standing there.

"Are you prepared?" he said without further greeting.

Yserria turned to look at Malcius. He wiped his palms on his tunic and said, "I believe so. I have only to memorize a few more things."

Serunius held out an amulet with a large, fiery opal set into a gold disk decorated with runes. Yserria took the amulet as Serunius said, "Good. You are nearly out of time. Wear the amulet during the debate, and you will be able to understand and speak Leréshi. The amulet must be returned after the debate.

"Of course," said Yserria as she held the amulet up for her perusal. "You are sure this will work inside the cage?"

Serunius nodded curtly. "Yes, it has already been tested. I will return in the morning to escort you to the debate arena." He met Yserria's gaze. "Are you certain you want *him* to be your champion. There is little time, but we may still find a worthy debater to take his place."

Yserria shook her head. "No, Malcius can do this."

Rezkin slipped through the doorway behind Serunius, quickly taking on the illusion of a palace guard. Then he headed toward the arena. He was traversing the palace corridors, when he spotted Thia and Alania heading toward a door to a courtyard. They looked around suspiciously then exited. When Rezkin got to the door, he peered through the window beside it and saw that Grizelda awaited them in the courtyard. Curious, he hurried down the corridor to the next courtyard. Once outside, he scaled the wall that separated the two courtyards and peered over the top. The three women were preoccupied, and none were looking his way, so he wrapped his invisibility illusion around himself and dropped down into the courtyard. He hid behind some foliage close enough that he could hear their conversation.

"She does not belong here. She has no right to the throne," said Grizelda with vehemence.

"The Queen's Council recognizes her Leréshi heritage," replied Alania.

Grizelda scoffed. "When I am queen, my first order of business will be to replace the council."

"You mean *if* you become queen," said Thia. "But that will not help us now. She is already recognized as a contender."

Grizelda said, "That is why we must work together to ensure she does not survive the trials."

"Work together?" said Thia with a chuckle. "Since when do you work *with* anyone? Everything you do is for your own advancement."

"Of course it is," snapped Grizelda. "But there are great rewards to be had for supporting me as queen. You would do well to cease this charade and recognize my claim."

"You are no more likely to be queen than either of us," said Thia. "I believe you have fewer supporters than you think."

Alania huffed, "That is enough. We each want to be queen, but only one of us can prevail. At least if it is one of us, it will be a Leréshi. I agree that something has to be done about Yserria."

Rezkin peered through the branches to spy on the three women.

Grizelda raised a fist. "She will not make it through the trials, are we agreed?"

"Agreed," said Thia and Alania in unison, each of them raising a fist in return.

Thia and Alania exited the courtyard, and a man stepped out from the shadows on the opposite side from Rezkin. He recognized the man as Grizelda's first consort. Grizelda turned to him. "What did you think, Martis?"

Martis grinned. "I think it is a clever plan. They will be so focused on Yserria that they will not see you coming for them. As far as Yserria goes, all the plans are in order. I have done as you asked and contracted with multiple assassins to end her before the trials are through. You need no longer worry about her."

Grizelda closed the distance between them and planted a passionate kiss on Martis's lips. Then they turned and left the courtyard together. Rezkin wished they had said more about the assassins to give him some direction, but wishing was frivolous. He would need to find these assassins before they followed through on their contract.

"No, Malcius can do this," said Yserria. She said the words with a confidence she did not quite feel. Malcius may have been an excellent debater in Ashai, but they were in Lon Lerésh, and his disdain for the Leréshi ways was sure to be reflected in his answers should he stray from the speeches they had written.

Serunius nodded then left them to finish preparing. Malcius did not even take the time to complain. He immediately threw himself into the work of memorizing his lines. Yserria was disappointed that Rezkin was no longer there. He had disappeared right before their eyes. Somehow, the warrior emperor had grown *more* mysterious the longer she knew him. His power was unlike anything she had known, and now he had a dragon as well. His speak of bonds and madness had concerned her. Although his reasoning for maintaining the illusion of his death made sense, she could not shake the feeling that Rezkin was not thinking clearly. Why would he give up the power of being emperor in favor of skulking in the shadows?

The next morning, Serunius showed up at her door. His ceremonial battle mage garb highlighted the severity of the situation, and Yserria's nerves were frayed. Malcius looked no better. His face was pale, and his eyes were a bit too wide. Malcius muttered under his breath the entire way to the arena, no doubt going over his speeches. When they entered the arena, he suddenly clamped his mouth shut and said nothing more.

The arena was shaped like an amphitheater with seating carved into the hillside. At the center of the amphitheater was a massive flaming pit that sent waves of heat across the entire arena. The first several rows were empty, but hundreds of nobles dressed in Leréshi finery occupied the seats farther back. Over the fire pit was a grand structure of metal and stone, and from this structure hung four gilded cages just large enough to fit two people. Serunius led Yserria and Malcius up a winding staircase and across a platform before stopping in front of an open cage. Alania and her champion followed behind them, and Thia and Grizelda approached from the opposite direction. Thia looked upon her with disdain, but Grizelda merely looked smug.

Serunius motioned to the cage. "You must enter now."

Yserria peered over the platform to the fiery abyss below. The heat billowed from within in waves, and already she was beginning to perspire. She said, "There's no smoke."

Serunius's expression did not change as he said, "It is mage fire. It produces no smoke but burns hotter than normal fire." He motioned again to the cage.

Yserria said, "All right, all right, I'm going." The cage swayed as she stepped into it, and she gripped the warm bars to steady herself. Malcius entered after her, and the door was shut and locked behind him.

"Remind me again why I am doing this," said Malcius.

Yserria gripped his shoulder and met his gaze. "Because you are loyal to the empire. You are loyal to *him*."

For a moment, it looked as if Malcius would argue, but then Thia called out from her cage, "Your sword cannot save you this time, and neither can Serunius. Without your precious emperor, you are nothing."

"He is *your* emperor, too, and he yet lives," shouted Yserria. "Your soul will quake as you kneel before him again."

Thia laughed then, and her champion, Ienia, joined her. Yserria looked past Thia to see Grizelda standing in her cage alone. She would be representing herself in this test. Grizelda looked back at her and grinned as she offered a little wave. She did not appear concerned at all. Yserria wondered what advantage the woman had to make her so confident.

Turning, Yserria saw Alania in deep discussion with her champion, an older man with dark skin and a thick, grey beard. Alania looked anxious until she caught Yserria staring at her. Then she sneered and offered her a crude gesture. Yserria's cage jerked, and her heart sped up as it began to descend. All the cages stopped about halfway between the structure and the fiery pit. The air was stifling hot. Yserria fanned herself with her hand to no avail.

She looked Malcius in the eyes and said, "You can do this, Malcius. I have faith in you. My life is in your hands."

"Is that supposed to make me feel *better*?" muttered Malcius as he turned to look over the crowd. He was sweating, and it was not just from the heat. These were the people he had to either sway to his way of thinking or convince that he thought the same as them. It was going to be a difficult task since he abhorred the Leréshi way, and he doubted he would be able to convince them that his way was better. He wondered if the part about the cage forcing him to tell the truth was true or if Serunius was just trying to scare him. He opened his mouth to utter a lie, and the words stuck on his tongue. No matter how hard he tried, he could not say the words. He swallowed them down and hoped that Rezkin was right and the way they had worded the responses would see him clear.

The crowd applauded as the contenders and their champions were announced. Malcius noted with angst that the reaction was rather muted for him and Yserria. He hoped it was not a sign of things to come. He wiped the sweat from his brow and turned to Yserria. As he looked at her pensive expression, he could not help the resentment that welled up within him—not for her, but for Rezkin. He was angry with Rezkin for putting them in this situation. What Rezkin had said about Lon Lerésh needing a queen had made sense. Logically, he knew it was true. But in his heart, he still felt the sting of Palis's death, a senseless death that he was certain Rezkin could have prevented if only he had tried. Ever since meeting Rezkin, his life had been one terrifying and deadly experience after another. Rezkin was his friend, and he respected him, but there was a part of Malcius that hated him, a sentiment currently being reinforced by these deadly trials.

Malcius was so wrapped up in his thoughts and feelings that he barely heard the first question. Alania's champion answered in a deep, resounding voice that rolled across Malcius's frazzled nerves like silk. Unfortunately for them, although delivered beautifully, the crowd did not like the answer. Malcius watched the crowd as every person present voted. It was quick and efficient. Each person held two tokens, one blue and the other white. If they pressed the rune on the blue token, their vote was counted as approval. If they pressed the white, it was considered disapproving. In this case, more white tokens were pressed than blue, and Alania's cage was lowered closer to the fire.

When the question was posed to Malcius, he froze. It was not just his life that was at risk but Yserria's as well. She was depending on him to make a good show. He gripped the life stone tucked into his tunic. The familiar weight brought him comfort and reminded him that he was a dedicated protector.

"Malcius, you're supposed to answer," hissed Yserria as she nudged his arm.

Malcius took a deep breath of warm air and then began speaking. His words were stilted at first. He was not used to speaking in Leréshi. Although he was speaking the language properly, his mouth was making unfamiliar motions that tangled his tongue. His annunciation became smoother the longer he spoke, and by the end of his answer, he felt a slight confidence that he had not completely bungled it. The vote came back quickly for blue. Malcius released a pent breath as their cage was raised.

Yserria patted him on the shoulder. "Good job. Only four more to go."

Next, Thia's cage was raised. She smirked at them and said, "You got lucky this time. It was an easy question. I think you will not be so successful on the rest considering you are a man and a noble foreigner who is accustomed to living under a patriarchy."

Malcius kept his mouth shut as he practiced his response to the next question in his mind. Thia was right, though. The next three questions were centered around the balance of power between the males and females of their society and the positions each was permitted to hold. Malcius could not come out and say that he abhorred the matriarchy and felt that men should have equal standing to the women. He could not say that their system of claiming consorts, often against the man's will, was detestable. He had to somehow speak around the truth to answer the questions posed to him and do so well enough to impress the crowd.

Grizelda's cage was lowered after the first question. The look of shock that came over her face was priceless. They moved on to round two. The next question was regarding a specific case in which a piece of land was claimed by two different matrianeras. The land was won in challenge by one matrianera, but in a second challenge, the predominantly male workers of that land were won by the other matrianera. The landholder petitioned her echelon that the workers should be considered part of the land and that the second challenge should not have occurred. Malcius thought the whole notion of winning people like property was repugnant, but he was even less inclined to agree that people were part of the land.

He tried to stick to his script and speak around the subject so that his true feelings on the matter were not exposed, but thanks to the truth spell, his disdain for the topic showed through. The crowd was unmoved by his response, and their cage was subsequently lowered. He failed on the next two topics as well, and their cage was lowered twice more. He could no longer touch the bars of the cage as they had become so hot they would scorch the flesh from his bones. The heat and lack of oxygen stole the air from his lungs, and his clothes were soaked through and stuck to his body by sweat. Malcius turned to Yserria who looked no better than he felt.

"I am sorry, Yserria. I have failed us."

She panted, "There is one more question. We can still pull through."

Malcius sucked in a lungful of hot air. "We do not even know what the last question will be. I do not have an answer for it. If we are dropped any farther, we will be in the fire."

"Rezkin will not let us burn. He will find a way to help us," said Yserria.

Anger as fierce as the fire below them surged through Malcius. "Like he helped Palis? You put too much faith in him, Yserria. He cares more for his empire than he does for his friends."

"That's not so! He's always saying rule number one is to protect and honor your friends."

"But are we his friends? Are we really? For *nine months* he has allowed us to believe him dead. Who does that to their friends?"

Yserria did not have time to answer as the final debate topic was announced. Upon hearing it, dread flooded Malcius's mind. The question was whether Lon Lerésh should remain part of the Souelian Empire or declare independence. Malcius knew what his answer would be, and he equally knew it would not be a popular answer among the Leréshi.

The first to answer the question was Alania's champion, and to Malcius's surprise, he answered in favor of remaining with the empire. He argued that it provided for a more financially stable future for Lon Lerésh and for a better relationship with Gendishen. Malcius agreed with everything the man said. The nobles remained unconvinced. Alania and her champion wailed as their cage was lowered into the fire. The flames billowed up around them, and the scent of charred flesh and burnt hair permeated the air. All action ceased in the debate until the screams died, along with the people who issued them.

Malcius quaked inside. He doubted his answer would be better than the one just given. His throat was dry as he swallowed, and he looked to Yserria. For the first time since he had met her, she truly appeared frightened. Her wild gaze darted over the crowd, and he knew she searched for Rezkin. Her savior was nowhere to be seen.

Malcius looked up at the cages containing Thia and Grizelda. They were in no danger of burning regardless of how the final answer went for them. His gaze fell to the gathered nobles. They no doubt already knew which argument he would make, and they were already preparing to send him and Yserria into the flames. He had to change their minds. He had to convince them that what was right for the empire was right for Lon Lerésh. He thought back to the speeches Rezkin had given regarding the strength and fortitude of the empire in the face of adversity. Lon Lerésh had not yet experienced that adversity—at least as far as Caydean was concerned.

He looked down as Yserria placed her hand in his. Looking back up at her, he saw a tentative smile play at her face. She said, "You can do this, Malcius. I trust in you." She released his hand, and he turned once more to the crowd. The hot, dry air scorched his lungs as he took a deep breath. Then he began to speak.

He spoke first of the greatness of Lon Lerésh. This was difficult for him, but although he did not appreciate the matriarchy, he could not deny the nation's wealth and success. Then he spoke of the threat of Caydean. This he spoke from the heart. He gave, in great detail, the horrors and injustices inflicted during the King's Tournament. He spoke of his brother's death and the pain it brought to him and those who knew him. Then he spoke of the Souelian Empire, of its indomitable ruler and his gracious rule over the kingdoms he had claimed.

He said, "But the empire is not built on one man, alive or dead. It is an empire of many. It is an empire of survivors. The men and women, the magical and mundane, the warriors, builders, servants, and farmers are all treated with dignity and fairness. They in turn spread that dignity and fairness to all they touch.

"You heard moments ago of the financial and social advantages of remaining with the empire. That was not enough to sway you. But think on this. Lon Lerésh has long been outcast—a queendom within a sea of kingdoms. Its advancement stymied by bigotry, derision, and suspicion. Within the empire, Lon Lerésh is an equal, revered for its unique culture and accomplishments. Long has Lon Lerésh endured conflict with Gendishen to the north and Ferélle to the west. As part of the empire, those nations will be your brothers, living in peace, sharing their wealth, and ready to lend aid at a moment's notice.

"With Yserria Rey as queen, you will experience the world as not one lonely nation but as many nations speaking with one voice and flourishing under the single banner of the Souelian Empire. Emperor Rezkin is not just a man, not just a leader. He is a force. He is *the* force of good and right, of justice and nobility in its purest sense. He does not fight for wealth or power but for the safety and honor of those under his banner. He does not believe that the people belong to the emperor, but that the emperor belongs to the people. Remain with the empire, and he will be *your* weapon against the darkness that assails us. He will belong to you, *your* champion against all that threatens you."

Malcius surprised himself as he said those words. He realized he truly did believe that Rezkin would protect them, that he would fight for them until his last breath. Tears welled in his eyes and dried on his cheeks as his resentment slipped away. He realized then that Rezkin had not failed Palis. The person to blame for Palis's death was Caydean. Rezkin had only ever sought to honor his friends, and sometimes doing so meant he had to let them fight their own battles, just as Malcius was fighting a battle now. And suddenly, he had no doubt that Rezkin was out there somewhere ready to step in and save them should he fail.

Calm for the first time since arriving in Kielen, Malcius finished his speech in the strongest voice possible. Yserria grabbed his hand once again, and he turned to look into her pale, glistening eyes. Her hair was stuck to her face, and sweat dripped off her chin, and yet he could not help but notice how beautiful she was in that moment—in *every* moment. As he gazed at her, his ears were attuned to the crowd. There was no applause, no mutters of dissent or agreement. All was silent except for the crackle of the flames beneath them. The cage jerked, and Malcius's heart leapt into his throat. In that moment, the moment before his death, he felt the sudden need to confess. He opened his mouth to reveal his dark secret, but before he could draw in a scorching lungful of air, the cage began to move *up*. Malcius was so relieved, he thought he might become sick.

Yserria jerked her hand away then threw her arms around him. Malcius tightened the embrace, reveling in the sensation before she pulled away.

"You did it, Malcius! I know you would."

Malcius gulped down cooler air then released his breath. His lungs and throat felt raw as he spoke. "To be honest, I did not believe I could. I appreciate your faith in me."

Yserria fidgeted with her dress, and Malcius's attention was drawn to the way the silk was plastered to her magnificent form. He pulled his eyes up to meet her gaze as she said, "I wouldn't have chosen you as champion if I didn't believe in you."

He released a husky laugh. "I thought I was your only resort."

"Nonsense," she said. "I could have found a debater or orator to do the job. I wanted *you* to do it because you believe in the empire, and as angry with him as you are, you believe in Rezkin."

"I believe in *you*," said Malcius.

Yserria wiped sweat from her face and flicked it away. "You believe *I* can be queen."

"I do," he said, and he meant it.

So wrapped up in their survival were they that neither heard Thia's and Grizelda's answers. Their cages were both lowered, though, so they knew their sentiments were not popular with the nobles. A short time later, the remaining cages were raised back up to the platform, and they were released. Serunius met them at the bottom of the stairs.

"You succeeded where I thought you would not," he said with an unflinching expression.

Yserria narrowed her eyes. "You doubted us?"

Serunius tipped his head toward Malcius. "I doubted *him*. Especially where the last question was concerned. Somehow you convinced the nobles that remaining with the empire was in their best interest—for now. Popular opinion changes on a whim."

Yserria said, "We are done with that trial. We need not concern ourselves with popular opinion for now. When will the next trial begin?"

"The trial to test your economic prowess will begin tomorrow. It will not be as easy as the debate, and you will not enjoy the consequences of failure."

"What are they?" said Malcius.

"That is yet to be determined," replied Serunius as he stepped aside to allow them to pass.

Malcius walked Yserria back to the suite. He collected a change of clothes as she did the same. Then he walked with her and her maid to the baths, past the guards stationed at the entrance. The bathing chamber was a large room with high ceilings and stone floors. The baths themselves were recessed into the floor, and each possessed a ledge for sitting. Soaps, salts, and bottles of oil were lined up neatly along one side of each bath, and several racks with towels were situated about the room. Most of the baths were enjoyed by men and women together, but there were a few private baths separated by scarlet curtains. Yserria claimed the first private bath, so Malcius continued to the second. A few minutes later, he heard Yserria say, "Thank you, Hestress. You may go. I would like some privacy."

Malcius stacked his clean clothes on a table beside his bath then peeled off the sweat-drenched clothes he was wearing. Then he stepped down into the warm water that felt a little too hot after his fiery ordeal. He soaped and oiled his body and hair then rinsed away the evidence of the trial. Once he was clean, he sat back on the submerged ledge and relaxed as the warm water soothed away the tension in his muscles. He closed his eyes and thought back on the trial. They had come so close to dying a horrible death. He could still hear Alania's and her champion's screams as they burned. If he thought about it too hard, he could smell the seared flesh. A shiver racked his body, and he opened his eyes.

It took him a moment to register what was out of place. Then he realized it was the shoes he could see beneath the curtain. They were men's shoes in Yserria's bathing chamber. He acted without thinking. He propelled himself from the bath and tackled the intruder, yanking down the curtain between them. His momentum carried them into the bath beyond, and Malcius heard a woman's scream just before he plunged under water. The intruder, now trapped beneath the water and wrapped in the curtain struggled against him. Malcius found his footing and stood, yanking the intruder up with him. He gripped the man around the arms and torso as the man desperately tried to get away. Malcius shouted for the guards as he struggled to maintain his hold on the intruder. A moment later, the guards arrived, swords drawn and calling for him to release the man.

Malcius breathed heavily as he stepped back. As the intruder worked to untangle himself from the curtain, Malcius turned to check on Yserria. She stood outside the bath wrapped in a towel, holding her sword aloft. Water dripped from her red hair to run in rivulets down her bare arms and legs. Malcius had never seen so much of the woman, and he was enraptured.

Yserria snapped, "Malcius!"

He wrenched his gaze up to her face. "Are you well?"

Her face was scarlet, and she avoided looking at him.

"What is wrong?" he asked with concern.

Yserria waved her sword at him but still would not look at him. "You're naked!"

Malcius looked down at himself. With all the commotion, he had overlooked his lack of modesty. He was grateful that he was at least somewhat hidden by the churning water. Ignoring his state of undress, he said, "But are *you* okay?"

Yserria risked a glance but immediately looked away. She shifted her towel tighter around herself and said, "I'm fine. I was half asleep when you barreled into my bath."

Their attention was drawn back to the intruder as he finally yanked the curtain off his head revealing blonde hair and a square, clean-cut jaw. Malcius did not recognize the man, but he noted the blue and red ribbons entwined with the braid at his temple. This indicated he was claimed by a matria but that he was of no relation to his matrianera. Malcius wondered which one had put him up to this.

"What's going on here?" asked one of the guards in heavily accented Ashaiian.

Malcius pointed to the intruder. "This man intruded on my matrianera's private bath."

"So you attacked him?" asked the other guard. "Why did you not just ask him to leave?"

Malcius was searching for an answer when something caught his eye. There, beneath the water, a glint. He dove into the bath and came back up holding a large knife. "He intended to kill her," Malcius said as he wiped the water from his face.

"That's not mine," said the man in question, not even glancing at the knife.

"Well, it is certainly not mine," said Malcius drawing attention to his naked body.

"Nor is it mine," said Yserria. "This was an attempted assassination. You should arrest him."

The two guards shared a look. "For what?" said the first guard. "Wandering into the wrong bathing chamber?"

The second guard waved his hand around the scene. "There is no evidence of a crime here."

"What do you call *this*?" said Malcius, holding up the knife.

"That could have been left here by anyone," said the second guard. "You have no proof it belongs to this man."

Yserria started, "This was an assassination attempt—"

The first guard interrupted her. "If you can't handle the heat, you should go back to Ashai, foreigner."

Yserria straightened. "I am *not* a foreigner. I am Leréshi."

"In birth only," said the first guard. "Then you come here to claim the throne for your Ashaiian emperor."

The second guard added, "It's a wonder you have not yet been assassinated."

Yserria looked as angry as Malcius felt. She said, "If you will do nothing about this, then I shall challenge his matrianera. What is your name, and to whom do you belong?"

The intruder grinned. "Good luck with that. My name is Lindon, and my matrianera is Grizelda. She and her champions will defeat you at any challenge she chooses."

"Come," said the first guard to the intruder. He eyed Yserria's sword and added, "We will see you safely out of here."

Malcius's anger nearly bubbled over as he watched the intruder trudge from the bath. Yserria never flinched as she held her sword between them. When the guards and the intruder were gone, Malcius looked to Yserria.

"Will you challenge her?"

Yserria's shoulders sagged. "It is unlikely. If I challenge *her*, she gets to choose the challenge, and no doubt she will choose something in which we cannot prevail." She sheathed her sword and propped it back against the table where she kept it. Then she looked back at him. "Well?"

He stared back at her. "Well, what?"

"Get out of my bath."

24

Yserria paced the corridor anxiously as they awaited news of the next trial. She had no champion for the economics trial. Malcius was good with numbers, and he had a basic education in the subject, but he was no economist. Neither was Serunius, although he was somewhat more suited to the subject due to his experience at Erisial's side. Serunius was still in mourning, though, and Yserria was not sure his head would be in the game. In short, she would need all the help she could get to prevail in this trial. And that was one of the reasons for the system of champions the Leréshi employed. It was a test to see how well one chose others to perform tasks for which they were better suited, how well they could delegate, and how much support they would have.

While they awaited Serunius's news, Nayala appeared, accompanied by a strikingly similar, albeit a bit younger, woman. Nayala said, "Yserria, I would like you to meet my sister Bridania. She is Mistress of Trade in my echelon. She has agreed to serve as your champion if you will have her."

Yserria's knees nearly buckled in relief. "Bridania, I am so pleased to meet you, and I am elated to accept you as champion. But are you sure you want to do this? The consequence for failure in the last trial was death, and you don't even know me. Why would you risk this?"

Bridania smiled and tossed her braids over her shoulder. "I have several reasons, one of which is that I do not wish to see Thia or Grizelda made queen. There has long been contention between our echelons. But, also, I have seen the good of becoming one with the empire. We have developed excellent trade deals with Ferélle since becoming part of the empire, and we are even in talks with Gendishen, something I never thought to happen in my lifetime. Not to mention we do a decent trade with Cael for their wine, which I might add is above reproach. I do love a good wine."

"That is all very good to hear," said Yserria, "but we don't even know what the trial will be yet."

Bridania nodded down the corridor to where Serunius was heading toward them. "I think we will not have long to wait."

His expression was dour as he approached. He stopped before them and looked from Yserria to Malcius then to Nayala and Bridania. If he was surprised by Bridania's presence, he did not show it. He returned his attention to Yserria and said, "The trial is to be trade based. Each contender will be given the opportunity to meet with the trade delegates from Ferélle, Channería, and Gendishen. The quality and quantity of those trade deals will determine your status in the trial."

So far, the trial did not seem too terrible to Yserria, so she knew there had to be more to it. The Leréshi coveted the dramatic like water in the desert. She said, "What's the catch?"

"The catch is that you must balance those deals by imposing taxes to maintain a sustainable economy. For every tax you implement, you will be given a certain number of points. At the end of each round, you, your champion, and four members of your household will be provided with a selection of wines to toast the occasion. The number of points you have acquired will determine how many of those drinks will be poisoned."

"Poisoned?" cried Malcius. "Must every trial be deadly?"

Serunius turned his attention to Malcius. "The idea behind the trials is to test the contender's fortitude in the face of death." His gaze became distant as he continued. "A Leréshi queen must face the possibility of death every moment of every day. Not everyone who wants to be queen can withstand the pressure."

Malcius said, "I suppose there is a kind of sense in that, but why do members of her household have to be involved?"

"Because in the real world, there are severe consequences for poor governance. If taxes are too high, people will suffer. They may revolt, ending in much bloodshed, or they could starve to death. There must be deadly consequences in the trials just as there are in real life."

Yserria said, "I have very few household members here, only those who escorted me from my echelon. How am I supposed to choose who will face death with me?"

"If you wish to be queen, you must make this kind of decision often. I will make it somewhat easier on you though. I volunteer to be one of the participants."

"Why would you do that?" asked Yserria.

Serunius looked away. "I have my reasons."

For the past two days, Serunius's melancholy air had been growing, and Yserria wondered if his reasons involved a desire to join his late lover in death. It was difficult to watch such a powerful man with a towering presence reduced to a state of woe. She had no idea what kept him going.

Yserria turned to Bridania. "Do you still wish to serve as my champion?"

Bridania lifted her chin and boldly said, "Yes, Echelon, if you would have me."

"Then I guess I just need three more members of my household."

Malcius released an exasperated breath. "Fine. I will do it."

Yserria shook her head. "I wasn't asking—"

"I know," he said with a wave of his hand. "But I cannot have *him* besting me." He motioned toward Serunius.

"It was not a challenge," said Serunius.

"Bloody Hells, it was, and you know it," replied Malcius.

Yserria stared at Malcius for a long moment. On the one hand, she appreciated his support and offer of service; but, on the other, she did not want to see him dead. She could not imagine telling *anyone* in her household that they had to participate in the absurd trial. Once again, she wondered if it would not be better to allow someone else to take the throne. Both Thia and Grizelda were against remaining with the empire, though, so she could not bow out. She had to see this through for the empire, for Rezkin, and for Lon Lerésh.

Yserria called for a meeting of her household. Hestress and Polimas attended, as well as Nexius and a few others including a servant named Indini and two guards named Brent and Larramont. She explained about the trial and the potential consequences of gaining points then said, "I need two of you to participate." She paused as she tried to decide who she would order to face potential death.

Nexius spoke before she had made a decision. "I volunteer to be a participant."

Yserria looked up at the man surprised. "Why would you do that?"

"I can see that the thought of ordering us to do this weighs heavily on you. The very fact that you have brought us here and explained what you need shows that you are considerate of our needs. You have been a good and fair ruler of the echelon. I believe you will make an excellent queen."

Hestress stepped forward. "I volunteer as well. I have seen your virtues first-hand, and I believe you will bring honor to the Leréshi people."

"I will volunteer as well," said Polimas as he set down his pen and stood from the table. "It makes no sense for Nexius to participate. You need him for protection, especially in Kielen. But you can always find another scribe, and I have no family to leave behind should I perish."

Yserria looked from one face to the next as every member of her household who was present volunteered to participate in the deadly trial. Tears slipped from her eyes as she made her decision.

It was only an hour later that Yserria and Bridania met with the trade delegate from Channería. He was a haughty man with a sour disposition, and he was obviously annoyed by the turn of events. The man knew he had them over a barrel, so he was unwilling to budge even the slightest. Yserria's silk was in far less demand than the lumber that so many kingdoms were using to build their ships for the war. Bridania still managed to acquire a deal that was only slightly in Channería's favor. Per the rules of the trial, taxes would need to be raised to make up for the deficit. Yserria received one point, which meant one drink out of the ten they were provided would be poisoned.

After the deal was made, Yserria, Bridania, Malcius, Serunius, Hestress, and Polimas, met in a hall designated the poisoning room. It was a modest sized hall with three tables arranged in a triangle. The three contenders for the throne and their respective retinues each gathered around one of the tables upon which sat ten glasses. Each glass held a thumb's width of wine, and the number of poisoned glasses would be equal to the number of points gained. In Yserria's case, one of them would be poisoned. Spectators stood around the perimeter of the room chatting and casting bets as though they were watching a game of sport. Guards ringed the table behind the contenders, ready to step in should someone refuse to drink. The other two tables were a short distance away, and at those stood Thia and Grizelda with their respective households.

Yserria eyed the ten glasses before them. It was impossible to tell which glass held the poison. She raked her gaze over the faces of her household, and her pulse quickened. There was a good chance that one of these people would die. Her arms began to shake, and she nearly cried out that she had changed her mind—that she did not *want* the throne. A firm hand on her shoulder steadied her. She met the man's gaze and realized he was a stranger, one of the guards she had never met. Something about the way he looked at her said otherwise, though.

The official stepped into their circle and said, "You must now choose."

Everyone looked to Yserria. She reached with a shaking hand toward a glass and collected it from the table. Each of the others followed suit with varying degrees of trepidation.

Serunius said to her, "You are afraid."

"Of course I'm afraid," she replied tersely.

He raised one brow. "You would fight any foe in battle, yet you tremble over a glass of wine."

"I can fight in a battle. I have a good chance of winning. I cannot fight poison."

Before Serunius could respond, the official said, "You will drink now."

Yserria raised the glass to her lips, but she could not force herself to tip it up. The official frowned at her then tipped the glass up for her. Yserria swallowed down the contents, but they threatened to come right back up. The others drank down their own wine as they followed her lead.

A commotion caught their attention from across the room. One of Grizelda's household had set her glass back on the table and was backing away while shaking her head.

"No, I cannot do it," she said.

Then she turned to run. A second later, a foot of steel was protruding from her back. The woman slid to the ground. Yserria ran over to her.

"What have you done?" she shouted at the guard who had run the woman through.

The official stepped over, avoiding the blood that was pooling on the floor. She said, "Per the rules of the trial, anyone who does not drink will be killed."

Yserria looked back to Grizelda and noticed a stunning lack of concern. Not a single tear graced her cheeks. It was no wonder that someone of her household had run. The woman was cold as ice. A moment later, Yserria heard a thud. She turned to find Polimas collapsed, frothing at the mouth and his eyes wide. He jerked and spasmed as his limbs contorted in disturbing ways. Yserria hurried to his side. She said, "Polimas, no! I am so sorry Polimas. I'm so sorry."

Polimas's gaze focused on her, and he sputtered, "For my queen."

Yserria gripped his hand as tears streamed down her cheeks.

A cry sounded from across the room and then another closer. Yserria looked over to see that two more of Grizelda's household had collapsed and one of Thia's. Thia was distraught, obviously having been closer to her household member than Grizelda was. Yserria felt a mountain of guilt crash over her. One of her household members was dying after volunteering to participate for *her*. At that moment, Yserria could not remember why it was so important that she become queen.

Serunius's eyes were devoid of emotion as he said, "The path to the throne is brutal."

Malcius pulled Yserria away from Polimas's side. "This was not your fault," he whispered to her.

"Yes, it was, Malcius. I ordered him to be here."

"No, he volunteered because he believed in you. If there is any fault here, then it is this accursed queendom. These trials are designed to be cruel and uncompromising."

Yserria met Malcius's concerned gaze. "I don't know how to do this, Malcius. There are still two more rounds, and already we have lost one person."

Malcius cupped her cheek in his palm. "We will have to make sure there are no more points accrued. We will do this together."

Yserria knelt beside Polimas again but hesitated to touch him lest she inflict upon him even more pain. His neck muscles were strained, and his face was turning purple. A moment later, Polimas's movements stilled, and his bloodshot eyes stared sightlessly at the ceiling. The poison had not worked quickly or kindly while it stripped Polimas of his life. Yserria was struck through with a real and visceral fear unlike any she had previously experienced. Any one of them could meet the same fate as Polimas. She could be dead by the end of the next round. She looked over at Malcius, and an even greater fear cut through her. It occurred to her that she would rather be dead than watch him suffer this fate. She resolved to find a way to prevent him from participating in the final two rounds.

Later that night, Yserria paced the floor of her bedchamber. As she moved back and forth across the azure carpet, she racked her brain for some excuse to exclude Malcius. As his matrianera, she had the right to simply order him to remain out of it, but she had never before given him an order, and she did not feel right about doing so now. Still, if it could save his life, she would do it.

She wrenched open her door and strode across the sitting room to Malcius's bedroom. Her nerves danced beneath her flesh as she raised her arm and knocked on the door. When it swung open, she found Malcius only half dressed. His chest was bare, exposing an expanse of muscles far more prominent than she had expected of him prior to seeing him in her bath. Her cheeks heated as she lifted her gaze and found him watching her.

"Do you need something?" he queried.

Remembering why she was there, Yserria lifted her chin and said imperiously, "You will not participate in the rest of the trial."

His face fell as if she had just stabbed him with her sword. "You do not want my help?"

Yserria's resolve faltered at his look of pain. "It's not that, only I do not want you to volunteer as part of my household."

His voice heated as he said, "Have I displeased you in some way? Did I embarrass you? I drank the wine same as you."

"No," she said, shaking her head adamantly. "You have not displeased me."

"Then I shall volunteer same as before."

"No! As your matrianera, I forbid it. I am ordering you to stay out of the trial."

"*Ordering* me? No matter what these Leréshi think, I am not beholden to you. You have no right to order me to do anything. I thought we had an understanding." He waved his hand between them. "*This*, between us, is just for show, nothing more."

A pain struck Yserria in the chest, and she was not sure why. She balled her fists. "Look, Malcius, we are in Lon Lerésh, and in Lon Lerésh, I *am* your matrianera, and you do as I say."

"If this is what you want, then you may *ask* me, and I will decide. Give me one good reason why I should stay out of it."

"Because I don't want you to die! Okay? I can't stand the thought of you dying, so I *need* you to stay out of it." Yserria could not stop the tears that slipped from her eyes.

A look of understanding overcame him, and Malcius said, "I understand. But, Yserria, I will not let you do this alone. If you are facing death, then I shall face it with you."

"But why? You hate me."

His gaze was unwavering as he stared at her for a long moment. Then, as if he had come to some conclusion, he said, "I have treated you unfairly in the past. I regret my actions and my harsh words. I understand if you cannot forgive me, but you must let me explain.

"Back in Skutton, at the registration for the tournament, I saw you first. From that first moment, I was bewitched. Everything about you called to me. But my heart and my duty were at war. You were a commoner, and as the first son and heir, I knew you were beyond my reach. And then Palis saw you, and he said all the things I was thinking. When he staked his claim, I was furious. Jealousy suffused every piece of my soul, and not just because he wanted you; but because he was willing to do what I was not. He would have given up everything for you, but I could not turn my back on my duty to my family. The fact that he would have you and I would not—I hated him for it. Then he died, and I was devastated. I had spent my last days with my brother hating him. It was too much for me to handle, and I ended up blaming you for it. I blamed you for my guilt because even after he died, my feelings for you did not change.

"I know it was not your fault that Palis died. It was never your fault. And you were not responsible for my feelings of jealousy, guilt, and self-loathing. I do not hate you, Yserria. I never hated you. I love you, and I have loved you since the first time I saw you. That is why I *must* be a part of this. That is why I will face death for you every time."

Thoughts and feelings flooded Yserria's mind and heart so quickly that she was having difficulty parsing them out. Words escaped her, but she knew he was awaiting a response. She blurted, "You *love* me?"

Malcius reached out and took her shaking hands. "I do, with every fiber of my being."

"That's why you've been following me around? That's why you agreed to carry my life stone?"

Her heart rate picked up as he rubbed the back of her hand with his thumb. "It is."

Shaking her head, she said, "I don't know what to say, Malcius."

"You do not have to say anything. I was prepared to suffer my love in silence. I will take as much or as little as you will give me."

"But you were so upset about the bond between us."

"I was upset about the *way* in which it happened. It was forced upon us, and I knew it was not what you wanted. I would never be disappointed to be bound to you."

Yserria yanked her hands away. She threw her arms around him, and her lips crashed into his. He was shocked into stillness for a moment before he seized her in his arms and opened to her. Her heavy breathing matched his when she finally pulled away. She said, "I think I love you too, Malcius."

"You think? I shall endure my longing until you are certain; but know then that I shall claim you properly, and you will be mine and I shall be yours for always."

His words raked over her heart tilling away her doubt and sowing the seeds of desire. She flushed when she realized her hands had found his bare chest, and she pulled them away. He grabbed one and pulled it to rest over his heart. He said, "This beats for you. You may touch me anytime."

If she thought her face could not have gotten any redder, she was wrong. She was saved from having to respond by a deep voice from behind her. "Pardon me," said the man. She spun at the sound, but she did not have her sword. Her heart galloped as Malcius stepped around her to face the intruder.

She was flooded with relief and not a small amount of embarrassment when she realized the intruder was Rezkin. "We were just … um …"

"I know," said Rezkin. "I did not wish to interrupt."

Yserria wanted to hide having been caught groping a man who was not her husband. Well, technically he *was* her husband as far as the rest of the world was concerned. Instead of hiding, though, Yserria straightened and stepped around Malcius to face Rezkin.

"How did you get in here? The door was locked. I made sure of it."

Rezkin said, "That simple lock was no hindrance. The ward I have placed around the door, however, will be."

"You can create wards, now?" asked Malcius incredulously.

"I can, and I have. You may sleep the better for it."

"What are you doing here?" said Yserria. "And where were you earlier? Two of my people died today."

"I apologize that I was unable to assist you during the trial. I was making arrangements. I have prepared and *negotiated* a deal with the Ferélli trade delegate." He held out a piece of paper inscribed with the terms of a lucrative deal that would certainly see them through the next round of the trial.

Malcius, who was reading over Yserria's shoulder, said, "How exactly did you negotiate this deal?"

"It is probably better that you do not know," said Rezkin. "The delegate has already agreed to the terms. You need only present them to him during the trial."

Yserria's tight muscles relaxed as relief suffused her. With Rezkin's help, she had hope that no more of her people would die.

The following day, she and Bridania presented the deal to the Ferélli trade delegate. The delegate frowned as he reviewed the terms, and it suddenly struck Yserria that the man could still choose not to honor the deal he had made with

Rezkin. Her heart rate picked up and she began to perspire as she awaited his response. He pointed to the page and opened his mouth as if to argue a point. Then his gaze caught on something behind her, and his mouth snapped shut. He laid the contract on the table, picked up his pen and signed the paper without a word. Yserria turned to look behind her but saw nothing suspicious, only spectators.

Afterward, out in the corridor, Bridania gushed at her, "When you brought me that contract, I thought you were crazy. I thought there was no way he would accept such terms. Tell me, how did you do it? Was it a bribe? Did you threaten him? What is your secret?"

Yserria shook her head. "Honestly, *I* did none of those things, and I wasn't sure he would accept. I'm so relieved."

"You and me, both. I am certain we shall have no poison in our glasses today."

"Thank the Maker," said Yserria, but in her mind, she was thanking Rezkin.

Rezkin did not reappear that night with another deal. In fact, he did not show the next day before the trial either. Yserria paced the corridor outside the negotiation room. Malcius stood to one side giving her space.

"Where is he?" she hissed.

"Be calm, Yserria. He will come," said Malcius. His body language belied his words, though. He was tightly wound, and she could see the concern written across his face.

A door opened down the corridor. Yserria stopped and stared at it in anticipation. When Bridania stepped into the hallway, Yserria's shoulders drooped. It was not him. By the time Bridania reached them, the door to the negotiation room had been opened. Yserria, Malcius, and Bridania entered the room to find that many spectators, including Serunius, had already arrived via another entrance. The spectators lined the perimeter of the room, surrounding a table in the center. A man in his thirties sat at the table opposite two empty chairs. His fingers were steepled in front of him as he waited patiently for the proceedings.

Yserria and Bridania took their seats opposite the delegate after offering him a formal greeting. The delegate smiled pleasantly. "I look forward to seeing what deal you ladies have brought to me."

Yserria felt somewhat reassured by the man's affable demeanor, but her nerves were still frayed. She said, "I think you will see that this deal is favorable for both our peoples." She nodded to Bridania who produced a list of the terms and handed it over to the man. The delegate perused the list nodding his head every so often. Finally, he placed the page on the table with a smile. He spoke the Ashaiian trade dialect with a thick Gendishen accent.

"This is well considered, but I think we will need to make some adjustments."

Yserria swallowed hard, but Bridania asked, "What kind of adjustments?"

"Well, you see here you have asked for too much wool and woolen fabric in exchange for these silks."

"I disagree," said Bridania. "We could get nearly twice as much from Verril."

"Ah, but Verril is not at this table," he said, his grin turning wolfish. "No, I believe you need to make a deal with *me*, and I say you ask too much. I will give you half as much."

"But silk is far more valuable than woolens," protested Bridania.

"Not so!" said the man with a chuckle. "We are in a time of war. Woolens are in high demand. Uniforms, tents, cloaks, blankets, stockings, saddle blankets, you name it. Armies require supplies, and silk is of little use."

Bridania scowled. "We cannot trade the silk for so little. What of the salt? Surely your army requires salt."

"Yes, of course," said the delegate, "but we have already made a profitable deal for salt with the Twelfth Echelon. We need no more salt."

"The olive oil, then, and the cheese," said Bridania.

"You cannot offer enough olive oil and cheese to warrant a trade in woolens *and* iron. We could work with the granite, but I'm afraid that with the call to arms, we haven't the labor to get it to you."

Yserria's concern mounted as Bridania and the delegate haggled back and forth. Nothing Bridania proposed was acceptable to the delegate, and everything he proposed was preposterous. Thanks to the nature of the trial, he knew they were desperate to make a deal, and he was taking full advantage. Yserria's mind wandered to dark places. She glanced down at the time piece displayed on the table, and her heart leapt. They had only ten more minutes to make a deal. If she failed to do so, she would automatically be awarded six points. With only ten cups of wine and six people drinking, it would be guaranteed that at least two people would die and likely more.

"We have a deal then?" said Bridania, breaking Yserria away from the edge of panic.

"We do," said the delegate with a broad grin that did not bode well for Yserria.

Yserria did not know what the deal was. The turmoil in her mind had interrupted her focus. She looked to Bridania for some hint of how they fared, but the woman's expression gave away nothing. The scribe who had been recording the terms set forth in the negotiations came forward and laid a contract on the table before her. She glanced over the contract. They were trading olive oil, cheese, jewels, silk, and enough vimarium to fill a small storehouse. She had no idea why someone would want so much of the rare but practically useless metal. Yserria looked at Bridania again. The woman frowned but nodded. Yserria's hand shook as she lifted the pen to the page and scrawled her name across it. The spectators began chattering amongst themselves, and she did not think their mutterings were positive.

The trial official approached the table, and raising her voice, said, "Three points to House Palis."

Yserria's heart seized. Three points. Three cups of poison. She searched for Malcius in the crowd and found him staring back at her. He nodded once, but her nerves were not quelled. Hot anger surged through her veins. Where was Rezkin?

25

REZKIN WIPED the blood from his blade and sheathed his sword. The would-be assassin had put up a good fight, at least on par with a striker. He had not been the only assassin that night. After Rezkin had taken out the other two, the man had eluded him for most of the night and several hours that morning. Unfortunately, it prevented Rezkin from working out a deal with the Gendishen delegate or appearing before the trial. Now that they were heading into the final stage of the trial, Rezkin had to hurry. He had no idea how the negotiations had gone, but going into them, he had been concerned about the Gendishen representative. He was a shrewd and devious man, and Rezkin did not doubt that he had gotten the upper hand. Now it was time to do damage control.

The jaunt through the city back to the palace was made easy by his illusion of a city guardsman. Once at the palace, he replaced that illusion with one of a palace guard. Once in the trial room, he took on the appearance of a nobleman and blended with the crowd. Yserria, Malcius, Serunius, Yserria's champion Bridania, and two more of Yserria's household were gathered around the central table, while Grizelda and Thia's entourages were at adjacent tables. Ten goblets of wine sat on each table. One of the officials approached Yserria's table. She said, "Three points to House Palis. Drink."

Serunius selected a glass and knocked it back quickly. The others were slow to follow. Rezkin noted that Malcius and Yserria drank theirs together, followed by Bridania and the other two household members—Yserria's maid, Hestress, and another servant named Brent. Nothing happened for several minutes. Then, suddenly, Brent collapsed. A moment later, Malcius doubled over and fell to the floor. Yserria screamed and knelt, clutching at him. Disguised as a guard, Rezkin rushed to his side. Yserria looked up, not recognizing him through his illusion. She cried, "No, stay away from him!"

Rezkin grabbed her shoulders and pulled her closer. He allowed his illusion to slip away for her eyes only, permitting her to see his true self. Yserria blinked at him in confusion but did not protest as he took her hand. He pressed a small vial against her palm, then backed away into the crowd. He watched as Yserria stared down at the vial. He saw her resolve as she tipped Malcius's head back and poured the glowing contents down his throat. Slowly, Malcius's spasms stilled, and his breathing became regular. Tears streamed down Yserria's face. She said, "Please, Malcius, be okay. I'm certain. Do you hear me? I'm certain."

Sobs from a short distance away stole their attention. Hestress leaned over Brent's quaking form as she wailed her sorrow. Across the room, there was a shout. Thia had collapsed and was spasming on the floor. But Yserria was not looking at Thia. He followed Yserria's gaze, and his eyes landed upon Grizelda. She appeared much too smug as she stared at Thia convulsing on the ground. Rezkin had no doubt that Grizelda had something to do with Thia's poisoning, and he thought Yserria knew it too.

An official rounded the table and looked down at Malcius. He barked, "What is happening here?"

"Nothing," said Yserria. "He's fine."

The official scowled down at Malcius who was now conscious and blinking his eyes. "He was poisoned?"

"No," replied Serunius. With a smirk, he said, "He fainted."

Rezkin backed away through the crowd. Now that the second trial was over, the attempts on Yserria's life would increase. He still had not identified the battle mage from Ashai sent by Avikeev. Rezkin was fairly sure he knew who it was, but he could not be certain. He had kept a close eye on Caydean's battle mage generals; and, according to his sources, one of them, Trivian, had gone missing from Kaibain not too long ago. If Avikeev was so keen on discovering how to control a person by extracting the soul, then it would make sense that he would not entrust the task of collecting Yserria to just anyone. Rezkin had no proof, but he felt it likely that Avikeev, Trivian, and Ulessa were possessed by demons. Unlike people, Caydean could control demons through the power of the summoning, and Caydean would not entrust such positions of power to anyone that he could not control.

Rezkin strode through the palace in the guise of a guard. No one stopped him at the check points, and he made it to Grizelda's chambers unhindered. No guards were posted at the door, so he let himself in.

"*Are you back so soon, Matrianera?*" said a young Leréshi woman Rezkin recognized as Grizelda's maid. She stopped short as she came into the sitting room. "*Oh, who are you? I wasn't expecting anyone.*"

Rezkin put his blowtube to his lips and ejected a dart into the woman's neck. She squeaked and pulled out the dart, looking at it in confusion before her eyes rolled back in her head, and she slumped to the floor. Rezkin had made it across the room by the time she fell, and he caught her before she could strike her head. He gathered her into his arms and took her into the small room that served as her quarters, laying her on the bed. He examined her closely as he formed an illusionary likeness of her. He was not thrilled with the idea of imitating the woman. He was not well-practiced in feminine behaviors, and a Leréshi woman, in particular, would be difficult if not impossible for him to pull off for any length of time. He had watched this woman, though, and he thought he could affect her mannerisms briefly.

Rezkin did not have to wait long for Grizelda and her entourage to return. When the woman swept into the sitting room, Rezkin was there waiting.

"*Are you back so soon, Matrianera?*" he said with the maid's voice.

"*Yes, Liza, it was horrible,*" said Grizelda as she threw herself on the settee quite dramatically. "*Thia is dead. She succumbed to the poison. We lost Terril, Manik, and Erinia. I am sorry, Liza, I know you were close with Erinia.*"

Rezkin attempted a pained expression and allowed a quaver to his voice. "*She is dead?*"

"*Yes, my love,*" said a young man who hurried over to Rezkin. The man reached for Rezkin, wrapping him in his arms and bringing his lips down onto Rezkin's. It took all of Rezkin's strength to stop himself from putting a blade between the man's ribs. The man leaned back and said, "*Are you well, my dear?*"

"*Yes, it is just a shock,*" said Rezkin in the maid's voice.

"*It is all that Ashaiian woman's fault,*" said Grizelda.

Rezkin took a chance and said, "*But didn't* you *have Thia's drink poisoned?*"

Grizelda huffed, "*Yes, but if that Ashaiian woman had not laid claim to the throne, Thia and Alania would not have had the courage to stand against me. Now they are both dead, and I should be queen.*"

"*Ashaiian? I thought she was Leréshi by blood.*"

"*By blood, perhaps, but she was raised in Ashai and has Ashaiian values. I will not allow her to rule over Lon Lerésh. We need a true Leréshi queen.*"

"*We need you,*" said Rezkin putting some more distance between himself and the clingy young lover.

"*Precisely.*" Grizelda balled her hand in a fist before turning back to her first consort. "*Martis, what news of the assassins? Why is Yserria still alive? She should be dead by now.*"

"*I have heard nothing, my dear, not since they were contracted.*"

"*This is what happens when you hire men to do a woman's job. We should have contracted with the Adana'Ro.*"

Martis said, "*You know the Adana'Ro have aligned themselves with the empire. They would not take a contract against its champion and likely would have killed you for the attempt.*"

Grizelda sighed. "*Then we will have to end her during the final trial.*"

"*What of your deal with the foreigner?*" asked Martis.

"*I have accepted. I do not know how effective he will be, but he assures me I will be queen. Are you prepared to stand against Serunius?*"

Martis moved around the settee to kneel at Grizelda's side. He took her hand in his and met her gaze. "*I would stand against the Maker for you, my matrianera.*"

Grizelda's expression softened. "*But can you prevail?*"

"*I have been training for years for this. Serunius may have once been the most powerful and skilled battle mage in Lon Lerésh, but I believe this no longer. I can best him. I am sure.*"

"*Good because I am depending on you to contend with him while I deal with Yserria.*"

"*And what of the woman?*" asked Martis.

Grizelda laughed. "*She is what? A mere Swordmaster? She has no power. She cannot stand against the* talent. *Even Liza with her paltry power could defeat her.*"

They both looked to Rezkin, and he attempted to look demure. Apparently, he failed. They both frowned, and Grizelda said, "*Liza, I have never seen such a ghastly look on your face. Are you feeling well?*"

"*No,*" said Rezkin, crossing the room. He attempted to sway his hips in a seductive Leréshi style. "*I am feeling out of sorts. Erinia's death and all.*"

"Yes, yes, I am sorry. I did not think. Please, go lie down before you fall over. You cannot even walk straight."

Disappointed that he had failed in his femininity, Rezkin retreated to Liza's room and went straight to the window. It was warded, of course, but Rezkin bent the ward around himself and slipped through with little effort. The small courtyard was cast in shadow, which allowed Rezkin to move through it without concern. The courtyard opened onto the lawn that was illuminated in green and gold by the sun's last rays. Rezkin worked his way around to the front of the palace and exited the grounds through the main gate.

The city beyond was awash in celebratory décor, the lanterns were already lit, and the streets were crowded with festival goers and vendors catering to every class. News of the day's events was on everyone's lips, and every person had an opinion about who would be the next queen of Lon Lerésh. Surprisingly, a good number of people believed the next queen's life would be cut short when the emperor returned to claim his throne. It was a scenario Rezkin found himself contemplating should Yserria fail to take the crown. Rezkin did not relish killing an innocent to reclaim the throne, but neither Thia nor Grizelda were innocent. Both had conspired to assassinate Yserria and probably each other as well. In fact, Rezkin was nearly certain that Thia was to blame for Alania's fiery death. Thia was dead, though, so he had only Grizelda to contend with.

The streets became quieter the farther he got from the palace, and by the time he reached the residences on the adjacent hillside the encroaching darkness had chased away any passersby. Rezkin wore no disguise as he approached the sprawling manse near the top of the hill. This location had taken him some time to find. The branches of towering oaks framed the pathway, and Rezkin was happy to allow Seena the chance to flit between them. As he mounted the steps to approach the front door, Seena glided down to perch on his shoulder. Rezkin cast an illusion to make her appear as a large, black raven, a vision that seemed all the more ominous by the smoke that billowed from her nostrils.

Rezkin gripped the thin chain that hung down from the porch ceiling and yanked on it several times. A moment later, the front door swung open to reveal a young man dressed in livery. The man did not ask his name, nor did he question Rezkin's motives for coming there. He merely stood aside, and Rezkin proceeded into the foyer. The foyer opened into a rotunda with polished marble floors and a dark mahogany banister tracing the curve of the spiraling staircase to the right. Large potted plants were interspersed with marble statues of men and women dancing in the nude.

The young man who had greeted him disappeared through a doorway, and Rezkin waited, knowing he was being observed. He could feel the greedy gazes thirsting for blood upon him, but he had yet to find the source. Eventually, a woman wearing a dress that barely brushed her upper thighs descended the stairs. Her dark auburn hair fell in waves down her back, and her large, brown eyes were cunning and alight with intrigue. Nothing about her was so telling as the large daggers strapped to her thighs. She unsheathed one of these daggers as she approached him, spinning it about in her hand with practiced ease.

"*A visitor, how interesting. I doubt you have come to this house by happenstance.*" She closed the distance between them and rested the tip of the dagger at the base of Rezkin's throat. With her other hand, she stroked his cheek. "*A handsome visitor and unclaimed, I see. Perhaps I should claim you for myself.*" She narrowed her eyes. "*You look familiar, yet I cannot place you. Most unusual.*" Her voice hardened. "*Who are you?*"

Seena said into his mind, "*Shall I bite her?*"

"*No,*" he thought. Rezkin caught the woman in his icy gaze. "*You know me because you serve me.*" He saw a shiver run through her.

She drew her dagger back a fraction and said, "*I know not what you mean. We serve none other than the Riel'gesh.*" Retreating a step, she said, "*Ophelia, attend me.*"

The wall to Rezkin's left opened on silent hinges, and a woman slipped out, shutting the opening behind her. This one wore soft black pants and tunic and had a length of black fabric covering the lower half of her face. Large, grey eyes stared at Rezkin as she made her way to the other woman's side.

"*Ophelia, you have seen the Riel'gesh. Do you know this man?*"

Ophelia's voice quivered as she said, "*Yes, Secrelé. He is the Riel'gesh.*" Then she dropped to her knees and bowed her head to the ground before him.

The secrelé immediately dropped her dagger and joined her subordinate on the floor. "*Forgive me, Riel'gesh, for I have drawn a weapon against you. I did not know you. I live to serve you, as do all of the Adana'Ro.*"

Rezkin bent and plucked the dagger from the ground. He said, "*Rise.*"

The secrelé quickly gained her feet then met his gaze unflinchingly. "*I recognize you now. I saw you once from afar. I accept whatever punishment you deem fit. My life is yours.*"

Rezkin held the dagger out to her, handle first. She tentatively took the dagger as if he might flip it around and thrust it into her at any second. He said,

"*I am a stranger in your home. I expect such treatment from the Adana'Ro. The viper does not apologize for striking its prey.*"

The secrelé released a breath. "*You are dismissed, Ophelia.*"

Ophelia rose from the floor and disappeared back through the opening in the wall. The opening was seamless, undetectable to the naked eye. Rezkin made a mental note of where it was located then turned back to the secrelé. She said, "*We have awaited your visit.*"

"*You knew I was alive?*"

"*You are the Riel'gesh. You cannot die. You have come to claim your throne, then?*"

"*No, I am here to ensure that my contender succeeds and that she survives.*"

"*Your contender is Yserria Rey, yes?*"

Rezkin nodded.

"*We are a small contingent here in Lon Lerésh. Do you wish for us to kill her opponent, or do you wish for us to ensure her survival? We cannot do both.*"

"*Neither,*" said Rezkin. "*I need you to find someone.*"

Her eyebrows rose. She said, "*Who?*"

"*A battle mage from Ashai has been sent to kidnap or kill Yserria. I do not know his identity for certain, but I believe it to be one of Caydean's generals, a battle mage named Trivian.*" Rezkin withdrew a page from the scroll tube secured at his waist, unrolled it, and handed it to the woman. "*This is his likeness. I doubt he will use a disguise. He is not a striker. You are not to engage him unless Yserria or her companion, Malcius, are in imminent danger. I will deal with Trivian myself.*"

"*Yes, Riel'gesh, it will be as you command. There is something else, though.*"

"*What is that?*"

"*Someone attempted to hire us to assassinate the queen. We rejected the contract, of course, but it seems they found another way.*"

"*Do you know who it was?*"

"*The contract was brought to us by a man who we traced back to Grizelda Tynan. During the course of our research, however, we discovered that Grizelda was only the middleman. We have only just discovered that the contract originated in Ashai. We contacted the Black Hall and found that a similar contract had been offered to them. They were finally able to trace the source of their contract all the way back to the king.*"

Rezkin was not surprised, but he was concerned. He thought back to Caydean's plans for Lon Lerésh. He had not gotten there in time to save Erisial, but he did not think her assassination was the whole of Caydean's plan. Caydean needed something from Lon Lerésh. But what was it? Rezkin had no idea, but he aimed to find out,

Yserria looked across the arena as the thrill of the upcoming battle coursed through her. She had been in an arena before, but this time was different. She was not fighting for fame or a heavy purse this time. She was confident that with Serunius's help, she could win spectacularly, and should that happen, she could secure the throne of the entire queendom. With Thia and Alania dead, she had only Grizelda and her champion, the battle mage named Martis, to deal with. Grizelda was reported to be a talented mage in her own right, but as far as anyone know, she had no martial skill. If Serunius kept them both occupied, Yserria could move in and strike them down. At least, that was the plan.

Her gaze traced the structures that had been erected throughout the arena. Some were made to look like buildings, others hills and trees. There were plenty of places to hide. She could easily sneak up on her opponents so long as they were distracted. Yserria wondered if Rezkin would make an appearance. Perhaps he was hiding in one of the structures, ready to take out the enemy when they neared. She saw no movement or figures from her vantage, but that meant little. Rezkin could disappear when he wanted.

"*Are you ready?*" asked Serunius as he approached from her left.

Yserria loosened her grip on her sword. "*Yes, so long as you do your part, I'll do mine.*"

"*Martis thinks he is a match for me, but I have seen him train. He is good, but not as good as me. And Grizelda will hardly put up a challenge. She is not a trained battle mage. We should easily prevail.*"

Yserria looked at him sharply. "*Winning is not enough. It needs to be epic if I am to gain enough favor with the nobles to take the throne.*"

Serunius winked at her and grinned. "*Then we shall make a grand show of it.*"

The official appeared down the corridor and moved toward them with a shuffling gate. The elderly woman wore a sour expression. She stopped in front of them and said, "*There is some kind of unrest in the city. We were delayed, but we have received instructions to go ahead with the trial. The sooner a queen is chosen, the sooner the people will settle.*"

"*I understand,*" said Yserria.

"*Good, then you may enter the arena now. The trial has begun.*"

Yserria did not pause. She gripped her sword and darted into the arena, heading for a large structure that looked like a three-story tavern. Its façade was made of stone, so it appeared sturdier than the structures around it. Serunius walked up the central pathway completely exposed. Yserria could not see the ward he erected around himself, but she knew it was there. He had assured her that none of Grizelda or Martis's attacks would get through the shield ward.

The tavern was empty inside. Only the building's structure existed. Yserria ducked beneath a window and then peered out. She had not seen Grizelda or her champion as she rushed through the arena. An explosion to the left rocked the building on its foundation. Yserria jumped and turned her gaze toward its source. From her vantage, she could see Serunius, but she could not see whoever it was he was fighting. She hurried to the back entrance of the building and turned to the right, dashing across another open space and behind a small hill across which grew a smattering of trees. Yserria darted from tree to tree as she ascended the hill. Once at the top, she peered past the trunks toward the other end of the arena.

"Careful," said a voice from behind her. "Your back is exposed."

Yserria spun to find herself face to face with Rezkin. Her breath left her in a whoosh. "You are here. How do you plan to help with the trial?"

"I cannot," he said, and her heart plummeted. "There has been an attack in the city. From what I heard, monsters are running rampant through the streets killing indiscriminately."

"*Monsters?* Drauglics?"

"No, not drauglics. I believe them to be demons brought here by General Trivian to capture *you*. I must contend with them, so I cannot stay. I have no doubt you and Serunius will be victorious here."

"Should we come with you? If there are multiple demons, you surely cannot stand against them alone."

"No, you focus on this trial. I will deal with the demons. I have other resources should I need them."

Yserria nodded once, then Rezkin disappeared completely right before her eyes.

Rezkin left the arena under cover of illusion. He had found that if he reflected his environment and bent the illusion around himself, he could effectively disappear. Due to its mental demands, he could only hold the illusion for a few minutes, so its use was limited. Rezkin hurried toward the market district, which was where the monster attack was supposedly taking place. If he was right, and the monsters really were demons, it would take a lot more than the city guard to stop them. The fact that the demons had attacked in the city, when it was well-known that Yserria would be at the arena, was not surprising. According to Entris, so long as the demon maintained human form, it was more easily controlled by the host. Once the demon shed the human form, the demon took over and was nearly uncontrollable. They tended to wreak havoc wherever they were.

Rezkin heard evidence of the attack long before he saw it. Loud crashes and explosions punctuated the screams of the dying. When he finally rounded the corner onto the main thoroughfare, he saw the monsters for himself. There were five of them, each eight or nine feet tall. Some were thick and bulky dark brown creatures with black hair in patches across their bodies. Others were long-limbed, sinuous beings with pasty white skin speckled with luminescent scales. One of the monsters was a rusty hue and had spikes covering its back, arms and legs. All five of the demons were crashing through market stalls, smashing holes in buildings, and slaughtering anyone who got in their path. Black snakes of power lashed out from their bodies to snag those attempting to flee, and blood ran freely in the street.

Rezkin instructed Seena to remain where it was safe, and she half-heartedly agreed. He drew the black blade from the sheath at his back and stalked down the street toward the chaos. One of the white demons ripped a man in half right in front of him, and Rezkin dodged the torso as it was discarded like refuse. The monster's black gaze snagged on him, and black snakes of power surged toward him. Rezkin deflected them with a shield ward, but he could feel the dark power chipping away at the ward. He swung the black blade at the creature's neck, but the demon raised an arm. Rezkin's sword glanced off the iridescent scales with a spark. Green lightning flashed through the dark blade. He dodged a swipe of claws. He swung at the monster's midsection. Again, the blade failed to cut through the scales.

The demon leapt toward him, and Rezkin raised his blade just in time to impale the monster as it tackled him to the ground. Green lightning erupted from the blade, crackling as it wrapped around the demon searing its scales and flesh.

Never before had the blade produced such an effect. The creature screeched and propelled itself away. Rezkin nearly lost his grip on the sword as it was wrenched from the creature's body. Black blood slid down the blade to coat his hands in the slippery substance. Rezkin wiped his hands on his pants as he regained his feet and prepared to strike the creature again. It was more cautious this time. It lashed at him with its long tail while simultaneously swiping at him with its claws. Rezkin blocked the claws with his sword while leaping over the tail. The creature reared back and released a furious roar.

The other demons abruptly stopped mid-rampage and turned toward him. Then they began merging on him, surrounding him. As the openings between them began to close, Rezkin thought quickly. He could retreat, try to separate them, and pick them off one at a time. But while he was fighting one demon, the others would be wreaking havoc on the city, killing countless people. On the other hand, he could engage all five at once, keeping them busy until the city guard and mage force arrived. Rezkin opted for the latter, and in those precious few seconds that he had been deciding, his chance for retreat closed.

The black tendrils of power suddenly broke through Rezkin's ward and wrapped around his torso. They compressed his chest so that he could not catch a breath. At the same time, the white creature in front of him stumbled forward and scored him with its claws. The claws failed to penetrate Rezkin's armor, but he still could not breathe. With his left hand, Rezkin drew a dagger from his sleeve and launched it at the monster. It struck the creature in the eye. The demon reeled backward as it yanked the dagger from its skull taking the eyeball with it.

The black tendrils loosened somewhat, and Rezkin sucked in a deep breath. One of the hairy demons suddenly crashed into him. The impact shot him across the street. He smashed into a stone wall and crumpled to the ground. He groaned as he regained his feet. His ribs ached, and his shoulder pained him. Rezkin rolled his shoulder around, grabbed his sword from where it had fallen beside him, and met the next demon head on. A hairy monster, perhaps the same one, came at him like a charging bull. Rezkin crouched as if preparing for the impact then dodged at the last second. The demon crashed into the stone wall, breaking through it and bringing the entire wall down onto it.

As the hairy monster struggled to free itself, Rezkin faced off against the second hairy demon. It reached for him, while at the same time one of the white demons lashed him with its tail. Rezkin could not dodge both attacks, and in avoiding the white demon's tail, he placed himself within reach of the hairy demon. It wrapped its thick, muscular arms around him, trapping his arms by his sides, and squeezed until he thought his bones would break. It opened its giant snout revealing two rows of sharp, yellow teeth. Just as it made to close its mouth around his head, Rezkin released a pulse of raw power into the creature's chest. They were blasted apart, and Rezkin landed in the pile of stone beneath the broken wall.

The first creature he had fought, still bleeding black blood over its shiny white scales, advanced on him again. Rezkin raised his sword as he released a pulse of power into the black tendrils of demonic power that reached for him. They skittered away, and he leapt forward. He thrust his sword through the demon's chest. Green lightning snaked over the demon's body. Rezkin withdrew the blade and quickly thrust it into the chest again. This time the green lightning ignited the demon's flesh. The demon crashed to the ground with an agonized groan. It writhed and screamed as green flame enveloped it.

Rezkin breathed heavily, but he did not have time to watch the creature die. The fight had taken much out of him already, and there were still four more demons to dispatch. At this rate, it would take him all day to kill the monsters. Rezkin was about to run into the fray when he saw a woman appear at the end of the nearest alley. He recognized her as the Adana'Ro Ophelia. Her eyes were wide as she took in the scene, but she turned and waved toward him anyway. Rezkin ran to meet her, stopping only to avoid a flying wagon. She bowed when he stopped before her.

"Riel'gesh, I am glad to have found you. We have news of Battle Mage Trivian. We have found him."

"Where is he?" Rezkin said as he kept his focus on the demons rampaging in the square.

"He was just seen entering the arena."

It suddenly occurred to him the real reason for the attack. This had been a diversion. Trivian would go after Yserria himself.

Ophelia drew her sword. "I shall assist you in defeating these monsters."

"Demons. They are demons, and there is little you can do against them. Your efforts are better spent helping these people. Get them out of here."

She nodded and sheathed her sword. "As you wish, Riel'gesh. It will be as you command."

Rezkin was torn. He needed to get back to the arena to save Yserria, but if he left now, these demons would ravage the city. His spinning thoughts were punctuated by the screams of the dying. There was no one to protect these people save for him. Rezkin resolved to dispatch these demons first and hope that Serunius and Yserria could hold out against Trivian until he could get there.

26

YSERRIA ROUNDED a rocky outcropping in the hillside and stopped in her tracks. She had finally managed to flank Grizelda's champion, Martis, but she had no idea where Grizelda had gone. Martis was engaged in an exchange of incendiary spells with Serunius. Yserria knew this might be her only opportunity to sneak up on him, and she was not about to waste it. She waited for an explosion to cover the sound of her movements then rushed forward. Just as she was closing within striking distance, a searing heat tore across her back. She was knocked forward into the gravel, and her sword skittered away from her. She cried out from the pain as she got to her knees and crawled toward it. Just as her fingers closed around the hilt, another blast flattened her to the ground.

Yserria rolled onto her side to see her assailant. Grizelda was still some distance away, but she was closing in quickly. Yserria was thankful the woman had not been closer, or those two attacks would certainly have killed her. She quickly got to her feet. She tried to ignore the horrendous pain in her back, but tears sprang to her eyes. Yserria knew she could not face Grizelda alone in a head on battle. She needed Serunius to distract the woman, but Serunius was presently engaged with Martis. Yserria made a calculated decision. She turned away from Grizelda and ran the rest of the way toward Martis. Then, while he was distracted, she shoved her sword through his back.

A scream tore through her as an explosion catapulted her from her feet. She managed to hang on to her sword this time, but nearly impaled herself when she landed. Serunius rushed to her side, helping her to her feet. He did not waste energy on words as he lobbed a sizzling globe of power toward Grizelda. He looked ragged as he sucked in a deep breath. He had been battling both Grizelda *and* Martis for some time as Yserria tried to find an opening for attack. She wondered how near depletion he was and hoped he still had enough in him to keep Grizelda at bay.

His gaze slid to her. "*Are you well enough to continue with the plan?*"

Yserria ignored the tears streaming down her face. "*I don't have a choice.*" He nodded to her once, and she said, "*Cover me.*"

She took off running toward Grizelda. The woman attempted several attacks, even tearing up the earth between them to strike at her with chunks of rocky dirt. Serunius deflected all the attacks and even managed to launch a few of his own. His attacks, though, were weakening, Yserria could tell. None of them were making it through Grizelda's shield ward. With a burst of power, Grizelda wrenched the earth open, creating a forty-foot-deep pit at the base of a rocky tower. Yserria skidded to a stop, nearly toppling over the edge. She peered down into the pit as she pinwheeled her arms. At the bottom of the pit was a roiling pool of lava. The heat and fumes smacked Yserria in the face as she regained her balance.

Yserria turned and skirted the pit. She was only about ten feet away from Grizelda when she noticed a motion from behind the woman. A man stepped out from one of the buildings. He wore the traditional black garb of a battle mage, only his pristine uniform bore an arcane insignia on the breast that Yserria did not recognize. His eyes suddenly bled into nothing but black pits as he grinned maliciously. A thick, black tendril of power surged from his palm to strike Grizelda in the back. Grizelda shrieked as she fell to the ground. Black veins crawled through her skin, and she struggled to breathe. The man came to stand over Grizelda. He smiled down at her.

Grizelda was choked as she said, "Trivian, we had a deal. You said you would kill them, and I would be queen."

The man, Trivian, shrugged. "I lied. Now that I have her, I no longer need you." Then he kicked her in the head, breaking her neck. He looked up at Yserria, still smiling as though he had not just murdered a woman. Yserria turned to run, nearly colliding with Serunius who had closed the distance. Yserria glanced back as black tendrils of power smacked against Serunius's shield ward. The ward illuminated where it was struck, and she could see that it wavered under the force of the man's attack.

Trivian chuckled. He said, "Come back, my little pet. I will not kill you now. I will claim you, then my brethren and I will raze this city to the ground."

Serunius grabbed Yserria by the arm. His gaze was fathomless. "We must stay and fight. He will kill everyone in Kielen if he lives."

Yserria's nerves quaked as she looked back at the demon. This was surely the battle mage general, Trivian, who Rezkin said had been sent to collect her. What chance did she have of defeating such a powerful creature? Without Serunius, she would be killed or taken within seconds. She did not get the chance to contemplate it further. Trivian sent a searing blast of black power directly at Serunius. The dark power shattered Serunius's shield ward and crashed into him. Serunius landed in a crumpled heap a good fifty feet away.

Yserria did not wait. She immediately turned and ran. Trivian laughed and said, "Run, pet. Once I catch you, you will wish you had died with him."

Yserria made for the arena exit. Coming toward her was a unit of palace guards and three battle mages. A powerful explosion tore through the ground in her path, and the guards and mages scattered. She pivoted and ran for the cover of the rocky outcrop to her right. The battle mages began sending volleys of power attacks at Trivian. He turned toward them, and Yserria took the momentary distraction to circle around behind the demon. While the battle mages kept Trivian busy, the guards reformed and advanced. Trivian cast demonic spell after demonic spell, but the battle mages together were managing to hold him back. The swords and spears of the palace guards were nearly within striking range when Trivian suddenly reared back and roared. As he did so, his skin ripped open.

A monster emerged from within his human sack of skin. The demonic monster was inky black and had a long neck and tail like a dragon. It had no wings, though, and the entire length of its back was lined with sharp spines. Its feet and hands were tipped in sharp talons, and its snout was filled with razor-sharp teeth.

Yserria abandoned her plan to attack from behind as the monstrous demon began sending more powerful spells at the battle mages. Their shield wards were blasted apart. The demon raged as it began tearing through them with its teeth and claws. The swords and spears of the palace guard seemed ineffectual against the monster's thick hide. Seeing her people—and they *were* her people—being torn to pieces reignited her determination.

Yserria again set herself to attack the demon from behind. She ran forward, dodged a swing of its tail and brought her sword down on the demon's back. Her blade glanced off the impenetrable hide. The demon was too preoccupied with the mages to acknowledge her, so Yserria proceeded to attack it again and again. She searched for its vulnerable spots and found none. A stab to its side barely sunk in more than a couple of inches.

The demon suddenly pivoted to face her, and Yserria realized the mages were dead, as were the palace guards. Yserria needed time to think of a way to defeat the demon. She turned and ran. She glanced back as the demon cast a bolt of power her way. She dodged, and the bolt sailed by her to crash into the rocks ahead. The next volley struck her in her already injured back, and she shrieked in pain as she tumbled head over heels. Gravel dug into her flesh, tearing through it like paper. She had no time to take note of her many scrapes and lacerations as she grabbed her sword and ducked behind the outcrop. Heavy footfalls crunched across the gravel toward her, and Yserria darted in the only direction she could go. Up. Up the hill she went, knowing full well that she was running into a trap. Once at the top, she would have nowhere to go save through *him*.

Her lungs burned as she reached the top of the hill, the highest point in the arena. She desperately searched for an escape, but short of jumping from the cliff, she could find none. She spun around as the footsteps grew louder behind her. She raised her heavy sword, both palms on the hilt, and waited as the demon approached. He stopped a few feet from her and began to change. A cloud of dark power encased the demon. When it cleared, the man Trivian stood before her. He smiled that menacing smile.

"You are mine, little pet. Drop your sword, and I will capture you with no further harm—for now."

Yserria shifted her feet as she faced him, sword raised. She swallowed hard and tried to settle her writhing nerves. She did not want to be captured by the demon, but neither was she ready to die. She glanced behind her, over the edge of the cliff as she backed away as far as she could go. She was stalling for time as she thought quickly. If he captured her, he would have what he wanted. He would use her to find a way to control people through the life stone. Then he would continue his killing rampage throughout Kielen. Many Leréshi would die.

Her thoughts suddenly shifted to Malcius. He was in trouble, too, since he possessed her life stone. Surely the general would go after him next. She was not ready to die. She had to find a way to help Malcius, a way to help the Leréshi people. At least if she were captured, she would have a chance at escape. With trepidation, she loosened her grip on her sword and dropped it to her feet.

"Good, little pet. Now kneel."

Yserria adjusted her stance for attack and said, "These are *my* people, and I will not abide you harming them."

Trivian laughed. "You have no choice. I will take you either way. I had hoped to take you without further damage, but I only need you alive. Kneel and I will spare you more pain."

Yserria remembered her goals as she swallowed her pride and knelt at the demon's feet. He pulled a length of cord from his pocket and moved to her side.

"Place your hands behind your back."

Yserria did as he asked. He leaned down to tie her hands. Yserria said a quick prayer to the Maker then sprung upward. She grabbed hold of the demon and threw her entire weight at him. The demon flailed as they both tumbled off the cliff toward the lava pit below. Yserria's last thought as she fell was anguish that she would not see Malcius one last time. She would never get to say goodbye.

She saw the demon plummet into the lava ahead of her, and then she jerked to a stop as her arm was wrenched behind her. Her body swung down to smack into the side of the pit, and the wind was knocked from her. Yserria blinked upward. A strong hand gripped her arm. She followed the arm upward to find Malcius gazing down at her, on his face a tortured grimace of pain. He reached down with his other arm, and she swung her free hand up to grab on to him. He pulled her up and over the side of the pit then released her. He rolled his shoulder around as though it pained him. He must have injured it when he caught her.

Yserria said, "What are you doing here?"

"What, did you think I would allow you to fight a demon by yourself? I came to help, and it was a good thing I did."

"You caught me," she said, her voice relaying her shock.

Malcius pulled her in for a searing kiss. Yserria's heart now raced from more than the fall. When he released her, he said, "I will always catch you."

Yserria kissed him again. Then she leaned over the edge of the pit and searched the lava below. There was no sign of movement from the demon. It did not emerge as she had feared. Relief flooded her as she realized the demon was no more. She had nearly died, and her hands shook with the realization. She had Malcius to thank for her life.

A few minutes later, an assortment of guards, mages, and healers surrounded them. Serunius was carted away, and some of the healers fussed over Yserria's many injuries. As she was being poked and prodded, Yserria's gaze lingered on the crowd of spectators. No one had attempted to interfere when Trivian appeared in the arena, most likely believing it to be part of the trial. They may not have known he was a demon, but they had surely heard his threats against the queendom via the sound amplifying spells focused on the arena.

A commotion at the arena entrance drew her attention. A parade of colorfully dressed men and women marched toward her. About halfway down the column was a group of men bearing a litter upon which sat a golden throne similar to but smaller than the one in the throne room. The column arched into a circle around her, and then Yserria was surrounded. The healers backed away as several of the colorfully dressed women approached. They carried with them a length of creamy silk fabric, which they draped around Yserria, securing it across her bosom at the shoulder. The men settled the litter on the ground as the women backed away. Then everyone in the arena dropped to their knees before her, placing their palms on their foreheads and bowing down to the ground.

Yserria's heart raced faster than it had when she had been fighting the demon. Her gaze darted around the arena taking everyone in. There were trial officials, mages, counselors, and palace guards in addition to a plethora of servants; and they were all bowing to *her*. It took her mind a moment to catch up. All the other contenders were dead. She was the only one vying for the throne who was left to claim it.

Where there should have been relief, she suddenly felt the grip of dread. *No!* her thoughts raced in alarm. *I cannot be queen. I am not meant to rule a nation. I can't do this.* Everything was closing in around her. Her vision became black at the edges, and she swayed on her feet. A man approached, but she could not see him clearly. As he neared, Yserria's knees buckled. He caught her before she hit the ground.

"Breathe, Yserria," he said into her ear.

She recognized the voice. It was Malcius. He had come to save her from the demon, and now he would save her from the horrible mistake she had made. She grabbed onto his arm and turned into him, hugging him tightly. He gripped her just as tightly and whispered, "I nearly lost you."

Yserria released a shuddering breath. "I'm okay, Malcius. I'm alive."

He stroked her hair, "I am not a religious man, but today I thank the Maker."

Yserria looked up into the stands to see that many of the spectators remained, and they were cheering. "This is real, isn't it?"

"Yes, Yserria. You are queen of Lon Lerésh. You *earned* the right to wear the crown. It is yours."

"But I cannot do it," she mumbled into his neck.

"You doubt yourself? You are the strongest woman I have ever met. You are intelligent and skilled and completely dedicated to the queendom's success within the empire. You are a worthy queen."

Yserria pulled away and looked up at him. "Do you really believe that?"

"I do," he said as he met her searching gaze. In his eyes she saw certainty and ... *love*.

Yserria steadied herself on her feet and returned her attention to the kneeling crowd. She *had* worked hard to earn her place on the throne. She had prevailed against all the other contenders. *And* she had defeated a powerful demon. Rezkin had confidence in her. Malcius had confidence in her. She felt an upwelling of strength and resolve. It was the kind of feeling she had during a duel. She knew she could prevail.

She turned to Malcius and nodded. He smiled and took her hand. He led her toward the litter and leant her support as she climbed atop it and sat in the throne. Then she lifted her chin and said loudly, "*Rise.*"

The single word echoed throughout the arena, and everyone rose to their feet. The crowd parted, and a woman Yserria recognized came forward. It was Lidia Oppena, head of the Queen's Council. Lidia genuflected appropriately.

"*My queen, if I may. You have defeated not only the other contenders for the throne but a great enemy of the people as well. You felled, in single combat and without the aid of the talent, a powerful battle mage—a monster—bent on destroying this city. You could have submitted to him, but instead you chose to sacrifice yourself to save the people. All of Lon Lerésh is in your debt. Your strength, courage, cunning, and perseverance are proven on this day and throughout the trials. Although you no longer need the vote of the nobles, it should be known that you have won their hearts and fealty. We recognize your claim to the throne, Yserria Rey, Queen of Lon Lerésh.*"

She felt the burden of leadership settle onto her shoulders, but she was undaunted. She had started the trials to accommodate Rezkin's initiative, but she had ended them with a resolve to protect the people. Before they carried her away, Yserria looked down upon Lidia and asked, "*The attacks in the city—what of them? Are the people still in danger?*"

"*A great warrior fights the monsters that plague our city. Much damage has been done, and many lives have been lost.*"

"*And this warrior? What of him? Who is he?*"

"*No one seems to know.*"

"*What of our forces?*"

"*Half the city guard is stationed outside the palace in case the monsters make it this far. The other half as been called in to deal with the creatures themselves.*"

Yserria said, "*Send the entirety of the city guard and the mage force to fight the demons.*"

"*But, Your Majesty, the palace will be unprotected!*"

"*Palaces can be rebuilt. Protect the people first,*" said Yserria.

Lidia's brows rose in surprise, but then she smiled. "*Yes, my queen, I will see to it right away.*"

Yserria stood and made to climb down from the litter. Malcius blocked her way.

"What are you doing?" he asked even though his expression said he already knew.

"I'm going to fight the demons."

"No, you're not. We went through hell to put you on the throne for the sake of the queendom *and* the empire. It will all be for naught if you get yourself killed now."

"Rezkin needs me, Malcius."

"Rezkin *needs* you to be queen. He can handle the demons."

Yserria's nerves were compelling her to go fight beside her emperor. "But what if you're wrong? What if he gets killed for good this time?"

Malcius shook his head. "Do you not understand, yet? Rezkin cannot die."

27

A VIVID PURPLE flame shot out of the white demon. Rezkin strengthened his shield ward but dodged anyway. The flame splashed against his ward, eating away at it. The ward abruptly failed, and Rezkin was momentarily unprotected from magical attack. Black tendrils of power whipped out of the white demon to wrap around him again. Out of desperation, Rezkin slashed at the tendrils with his blade. When the sword made contact with the demonic power, it ignited in scorching green flame, and the tendrils burned away. Rezkin did not have time to consider the newfound power of the black blade. He erected a new shield ward and turned toward the nearest threat.

The rusty red demon two dozen feet away turned and ejected a number of its spikes, shooting them straight at Rezkin. He swept the black blade through the air, catching most of the spikes and knocking them aside. One got past him, penetrating his armor and stabbing into his pectoral muscle. Rezkin yanked at the spike, but it would not come free. He had to abandon his efforts to face the two hairy demons who were coming at him from either side. The white demon suddenly leapt forward, spinning and lashing at him with its tail. Rezkin dropped his sword and caught the end of the tail. He used the creature's own momentum and a bit of vimara to propel the white demon into one of the hairy demons.

He kicked his sword up into his hands and thrust it forward into the chest of the charging hairy demon on the other side. Green lightning enveloped the demon. The demon reared back, then grabbed the hilt of the sword and wrenched the blade from its chest. Then it threw the black blade across the street into a pile of rubble. Rezkin jumped and rolled out of the way of an attack from behind. The white demon and the other hairy demon had recovered and were now attacking in unison.

Rezkin's heart turned to ice at what he saw next. Seena was running toward the battle, her brilliant blue scales glinting in the sunlight. He shouted within his mind for her to go back, to retreat, but she paid him no heed.

Rezkin retrieved his miniature crossbow from where it hung at his belt and aimed at the white demon's head. Just as he released the bolt, the hairy demon behind him raked him with its claws. The strike failed to penetrate his armor, but it sent his crossbow bolt awry. Rezkin skirted the hairy demon and ran after his sword. Seena met him halfway and scurried up his body to perch on his shoulder. She arched her wings and back and straightened her tail in preparation for battle. It was then that a new sound reached his ears. It was the sound of thundering footsteps and clanking armor. It was the shout of a commander and the responding call from his troops. Rezkin bent to grab his sword and came up spinning. From every street and alley in the vicinity came the troops of the kingdom. At the fore were dozens of mages, many of them battle mages.

He was both relieved and alarmed. He could finally get a brief respite, but more people would die. The troops charged the four demons in the square as the mages began sending volleys of flame, lightning, and ice in their direction. The nearest demon swept the troops aside as though they were dolls made of paper. It ignored their swords and spears as it shredded their flesh from their bones. Rezkin looked to the other demons who appeared to be doing the same to all who engaged them. The mage attacks fell uselessly against shield wards made of demonic power. A few of the attacks landed, but the demons were undeterred. They began targeting the mages next.

As the mages died, the troops were far less protected thanks to the collapse of their shield wards. Within minutes, the troops were decimated, and those left alive ran away. Rezkin watched their retreat with relief. Part of him hoped they would regroup and return with a better plan of attack. The other part hoped they stayed far from the battle and the death that awaited them.

Rezkin took a deep breath then ran toward the nearest demon. He grabbed on to its hairy back and yanked it backward off its feet. It crashed to the ground, and he stabbed it through the chest. As he did so, he fed some of his vimara into the black blade. Green lightning snaked over the demon. He pushed more power into the blade. The demon abruptly ignited in fiery green flames. It shrieked and writhed as the flames spread across its flesh. Black tendrils of power erupted from the demon to slam against Rezkin's shield ward. Within seconds the demon was reduced to a charred husk amongst a pile of ash.

He was suddenly yanked off his feet. The black tendrils had broken through his ward. They now held him suspended upside down a dozen feet from the ground, and his black blade was still stuck in the remains of the hairy demon below him. Seena clung to his chest as she screeched at the demon, dark puffs of smoke streaming from her mouth and nostrils. The remaining three demons merged on him. Rezkin launched throwing daggers at each of them. The daggers hit their targets but did nothing to deter the demons. He needed to release himself from the clutches of the demonic power. He closed his eyes and sought *eskyeyela*, not an easy feat with three demons bearing down on him. He sought his power. Once he heard its melody and witnessed its bright luminescence, he captured it. He drew it into a ball at his core. Opening his eyes, he released it.

A brilliant sphere of pure white light surged toward the center demon. It smashed into it and exploded in a cloud of sizzling lightning that zapped all three demons. They all three dropped to the ground as they jerked and spasmed under the assault. Rezkin grasped another thread of his vimara and fed it into the black tendrils holding him aloft. The tendrils released him, and Rezkin crashed to the ground rolling head over heels to absorb the impact. He ended on his feet and immediately retrieved the black blade. When he turned to face the demons, they were already bearing down on him. They were noticeably slower and weaker than they had been previously, but they were still a formidable foe.

A streak of light abruptly split the air between him and the demons, and Rezkin realized he was staring into a portal. Seena clambered up his body once again and shouted into his mind, "*Go!*"

Rezkin did not know where the pathway would take him, but he jumped into it nonetheless. He did not get one step before he was exiting the pathways. He realized he had reappeared behind the demons.

Inspired by his successes, Rezkin opened the gates between his power and the black blade. The blade glowed with green lightning as he ran toward the first demon. The hairy monster spun and raked its claws through the air, just missing Rezkin's face. Rezkin brought the blade up and down again. It sizzled with power as it sliced through the monster's appendage. The demon wailed as black blood spewed from its stump. Lightning crackled through the creature as Rezkin sliced through the beast's abdomen, spilling its entrails across the ground. The demon fell forward, and Rezkin brought the glowing blade down upon its neck. The head tumbled from its body to land at the feet of the white demon.

Rezkin did not wait a single heartbeat before he was slashing at the white demon. It whipped at him with its tail, so he severed the lengthy appendage from its body. Black tendrils of power threatened to capture him once again. Rezkin allowed his power to leak from him, wrapping him and Seena in a cocoon of white light. The black tendrils recoiled from the light, abandoning their mission. The red demon rolled into a giant spikey ball and tumbled toward him. He dodged, but it followed him as he raced around the square. Meanwhile, the white demon began spewing purple flames at him, catching buildings alight and turning the square into a flaming bonfire.

Turning, Rezkin ran straight at the white demon. Its violet flame surged toward him, but he did not leap aside. At the last minute, a portal opened before him, and he leapt through. He came out to the right of the white demon just as the flames splashed into the rolling red demon. The demon became a giant red and purple fireball as it rolled right over the white demon. Rezkin followed in its wake. He ran the black blade down into the chest of the white demon as he released his power. Green flame mixed with purple flame, and the creature was consumed. Rezkin chopped off its head for good measure. Then he turned toward the remaining demon—the red spiked demon.

The fiend uncoiled and turned toward Rezkin. It issued a terrifying howl then began a slow and calculated advance. Rezkin felt a surge in battle energy as he faced down the demon. The beast pulled two of its spikes from its arm and held them in front of it as it began muttering in a strange language that sounded like little more than a growl. A black vapor appeared around the spikes, then it coalesced on them to create an inky coating. The fiend bared its teeth then reached back and launched the spikes at Rezkin. The spikes flew at him faster than he could dodge. One of them missed altogether nearly clipping Seena, but the second impaled his arm through his armor.

Numbness spread through Rezkin's arm until everything from his fingers to his neck felt dead. He tried to make a fist, but his hand would not cooperate. Then he noticed the black veins that stood out against his alabaster skin. He became alarmed when he realized the numbness was spreading. If he did nothing, soon he would be unable to move. He sheathed his blade and yanked the black spike out of his arm. Red blood mixed with black ink poured from the wound. He backed away from the advancing demon. Seena provided him with a pathway that took him out of the demon's path. Then he sought *eskyeyela*. This time when he found it, the melody was distorted, and black veins were converging on his glowing river of vimara. Rezkin pulled on his vimara, but it was slow to respond. The glowing aura that surrounded him began to wane, and he was gradually losing sensation in his chest. The demon screeched, and he knew he had to end the threat now, before he was rendered incapable.

The demon turned toward him, and he took off in the opposite direction. As he ran, he drew the black blade once more. Black tendrils of demonic power reached for him. He batted them away with his sword, and each time he did so, the blade glowed green. It occurred to him that the black blade had a power of its own. He wondered if he could somehow use that power for his own sake. He continued to circle the square, avoiding the red demon as it chased after him.

Splitting his focus, Rezkin sent his mind into the blade just as he had with the crystals on Cael. Diving into the strange mage material from which it was made, he became surrounded by green lightning that crackled all around him. He reached out with his mind and connected with that power. It surged through him unimpeded. His anxiety spiked. He had failed to block the power from consuming him, and now he would endure a fiery death.

Rezkin tried to erect blockades against it. The green power broke through his pitiful barriers as it reached for his core. There, it crashed against the insidious demonic power that suffused him. Green lightning erupted over Rezkin's body. He desperately fought it lest it char him to a crisp. His alarm only subsided once he realized he was unharmed. The black veins of power that poisoned him ignited and burned away, and sensation began to return. The green lightning did not dissipate. It continued to arc over and through his flesh destroying the demonic power every time it reached for him.

Rezkin stopped running. With the black blade in his right hand, he drew Bladesunder with his left. Then he turned back to the demon. He met it in a clash of blades and claws. Seena launched herself at the demon's face, clawing at its eyes. With the black blade in one hand and his Sheyalin in the other, Rezkin released the full force of his fury on the spiked demon. The monster raised its arm to block a strike, and Rezkin sheared away the spikes. With his other sword, he scored the creature's side. Black tendrils of power lashed at him, and the green lightning that protected him crackled. Rezkin tapped into the flow of power between the black blade and his river of vimara. He sent power surging into the blade as he struck at the demon. Green flame and lightning crashed over the demon causing it to rear back in a spasm. Rezkin stabbed Bladesunder into the demon's side. The demon grabbed on to the blade and yanked it from Rezkin's grasp.

Rezkin took the black blade in both hands and spun, swinging in a mighty arc. The blade dropped down on the demon's shoulder and continued through its body to the opposite hip, cleaving it in two. The two halves of the creature's body fell away. Still, it battered at him with the insidious dark power. Rezkin again brought his sword down on the creature, this time severing its head from its body.

Rezkin fell to his knees over the corpse breathing heavily. Seena joined him on the ground. The battle with the five demons had taken much out of him, both physically and magically. He felt his energy waning, and his stomach rumbled with hunger. Now that the battle energy was wearing off, he began to feel all his aches and pains. He reached up to the spike that still impaled his shoulder and yanked on it until it finally came free. He was bleeding heavily both from the wound to his shoulder and to his arm as well as numerous other lacerations. His ribs hurt, and every breath was agony.

He looked up when he sensed motion ahead of him. He saw a woman in battle armor bearing a sword sitting atop a white horse. Behind her were more mounted soldiers. And Malcius. Rezkin turned his gaze back to the flame-haired woman and realized it was Yserria. He rose to his feet and collected Bladesunder. Yserria called out for the troops to stay where they were, and she and Malcius rode forward. Rezkin backed away. He was exhausted and severely injured. He could not allow himself to remain so vulnerable. It was time to retreat.

28

REZKIN SHEATHED HIS SWORDS, but he realized he had not yet released the power that suffused him. Green arcs of lightning danced along his skin, and a white glow surrounded him. Splitting his focus again, he maintained watch on the troops as he also sought *eskyeyela.* Once there, he withdrew his connection to the black blade and ceased drawing upon his vimara. When he looked down upon himself, he noted that he once again appeared as an ordinary man.

He called to Seena to open a portal, then held in his mind his destination. A moment later, he was standing in a small kitchen he had visited one other time when he had been injured. Seena was disguised as a cat at his feet. A man who had just entered the kitchen jumped in alarm at Rezkin's sudden appearance. Rezkin drew his Sheyalin and laid it on the table in front of him. The man's eyes grew wide as he stared at the blue-swirled blade. He looked back to Rezkin and said, "Who are you? How did you get in here?"

Rezkin said, "That is not important, Healer Yerwey Dulse. I require healing."

Yerwey glanced back at the sword and said, "Of course. I have learned not to ask questions in circumstances like these. Please, have a seat."

Rezkin sat still as stone as Yerwey healed him. The man's shaking hands lent evidence to his anxiety, but he did an admirable job regardless. As he worked, Rezkin eyed the sigil on the man's tunic. When Yerwey was finished, Rezkin stood. He said, "You are sworn to Caydean?"

Yerwey shook his head adamantly. "Yes, of course. I swore my oath, you can check the record."

Rezkin said, "How do you feel about that?"

Yerwey's eyes widened, and Rezkin could see the fear within them. The man said, "I am loyal to the king."

"You swore the oath under duress," said Rezkin.

"Yes," Yerwey drawled as he clasped his hands to keep them from shaking, "but a mage oath is an oath that cannot be broken. You can report back that I will uphold it."

Rezkin replaced the Sheyalin in its sheath, then called to Seena to follow him as he headed for the door. Once he had left the apartment, he had her open another portal back to Kielen. This time, the portal released him directly into the queen's chambers in the palace. He sat in a high-backed chair and entered *eskyeyela* as he waited. As servants came and went, he used illusion to vanish so that they would not see him. He felt somewhat refreshed when Yserria and Malcius finally entered hours later.

Yserria dismissed her maid as soon as she entered. As soon as the door shut, Malcius had her pressed against it, kissing her soundly. Rezkin cleared his throat to get their attention. They both jumped, then scowled at him once they recognized him. They both moved farther into the sitting room and stood before him. Yserria scrutinized him for a long moment. Then she said, "You look terrible."

"But you are alive," Malcius quickly added.

Rezkin remembered the scene from mere hours before. The square was destroyed, but it was the blood and bodies he was seeing. He said, "Many others did not survive."

Yserria nodded solemnly. "Yes, but you saved the city. You were injured. Let us bring you a healer."

Rezkin waved her off. "My injuries have already been seen to."

Yserria looked skeptical as she took in his bloody clothes and armor. She said, "How did you defeat five demons on your own?"

"Those demons were strong but not undefeatable. Trivian was not with them. He is still the greater threat."

"No, longer," said Malcius. "Yserria defeated him when he came for her at the arena."

Rezkin's eyebrows rose. "Is that so?"

Yserria lifted her chin. "He threatened the people. I could not let that stand."

Rezkin gave her a genuine smile. "Said like a true queen. Tell me about it."

Yserria and Malcius sat down on the settee before they began telling the tale together. Yserria did most of the talking while Malcius filled in bits and pieces from his perspective. Yserria was sure to mention how Malcius had saved her, and he caught the adoring look she sent Malcius's way. Then Yserria's attention turned back to Rezkin. "I am queen now. Will you come forward and let the people know you live? Will you let them know that you have saved them this day?"

"No, I must remain dead a little longer. You all are safer if Caydean thinks I am dead, and I still have much to do."

"What will you do now?" asked Malcius.

"I have many tasks ahead of me. I need to find out what Caydean wanted here besides Erisial's death."

"There's more?" said Yserria.

"Yes, I believe killing Erisial was a means to an end. He needed something here, and I want you to find out what it was."

Yserria nodded. "I will investigate."

Malcius shook his head, "No, you are queen now. You do not do the investigating. You assign someone else to do it."

"Oh, right. It's going to take me some time to get used to that."

Malcius cast his gaze toward Rezkin. "Yes, that is something our emperor should learn as well."

Yserria looked back to Rezkin. "I will assign a team to investigate."

"Good," said Rezkin, "I also plan to return to Ashai. I have unified the dukes and General Marcum against Caydean. They know Caydean's good will there is a ruse. He is planning something treacherous, and I aim to find out what it is. Mage Wesson is leading an investigation into Caydean's plans as we speak. I intend to follow it closely.

"And then there is the matter of the fae. They have taken Tam as their general. I intend to see that he is not conscripted for life."

"Tam is alive?" said Malcius with surprise. "I had heard he was missing and presumed dead."

"He is well," said Rezkin.

Malcius leaned forward. "Rez, you do not have to do it all on your own. You have an entire empire to help you."

"There are some things that I must do myself."

Malcius nodded sadly. "I understand that but have faith in us. We are capable. We can help."

"I know that, and I will not hesitate to call upon you when you can be of use."

Malcius made a fist and pounded his knee to punctuate his words. "Not just when we can be of use. You need us for more than just the tasks you assign to us."

Rezkin furrowed his brow. "What more is there?" But even as he asked the question, he knew the answer. The loss of his friends had cut deeper than he would have expected. Sitting there with them, talking as they were, he felt more at peace than he had in months.

"Comradery," said Malcius, "moral support, friendship, trust. These are the things that are important, Rez. These are what we are fighting for. You need us whether you realize it or not. Do not lock us out."

A pang of regret struck Rezkin. He had spent the better part of the year pretending to be dead, and he had missed these interactions. Now he was wondering if it was worth it. "You are right, Malcius. I will take your words under advisement. Thank you for your loyalty."

Malcius said, "You have always had my loyalty. Even when I hated you, you had my loyalty."

"You hate me no longer?" asked Rezkin with an unfamiliar stirring of hope deep in his chest.

Malcius shook his head. "I realized that I was wrong to blame you for Palis's death. You have always put the safety of your friends above all else. Even now, you sacrifice your happiness, your empire, to see that we are safer from Caydean. Forgive me for doubting you."

Rezkin stood. "All is forgiven, Malcius. You are a true friend."

He called to Seena who was once again disguised as a cat. She scurried up his side to perch on his shoulder. Using his mindspeak, he requested she open a portal. She released a very uncatlike screech, and the air split before him. Rezkin bid his friends farewell then stepped through the portal.

29

Rezkin stepped out of the other side of the portal into a humble dwelling built of stone carved long ago by an ancient race. He stood in what would eventually become a sitting room once it was furnished but that, as yet, held merely a woven rug and a single wooden chair. To his right stood a kitchen, equally bereft save for a single pot, a ceramic dish, and a pewter mug.

He shucked his weapons, armor, and bloody clothes then climbed into the basin in the adjoining room. He ran his fingers over the runes on the wall beside the basin, and water began to flow from a spout at his feet. He first washed his hair then used a wash rag and soap to remove the sweat, dirt, and blood from the day's battle. Once he was finished cleaning himself, he stroked a second rune, and the dirty water from the basin drained away through a hole in the bottom. He grabbed the only drying cloth on the rack and dried himself as he stepped into the next room. This one held a bed and a wardrobe and nothing else.

He opened the wardrobe to select fresh clothes. He donned a fine black tunic and black breeches. He shrugged on his blackened armor, then pulled on his boots and belted the Sheyalin blade he had acquired from the dead Swordmaster to his hip. Finally, he braided his hair and tied it back with a black ribbon before pulling a black hood over his head. He had no mirror, but he connected with Seena's mind and saw how he looked through her eyes. Dragons did not see things in the same way humans did, so it was a little disorienting. He was familiar enough with this disguise that he did not really need to see it to know how he looked.

Rezkin applied an illusion of his own design to himself then left his abode. Seena stayed in his satchel as he began making his way through the ancient city streets. The city of Caellurum was very different than it had been when he had first seen it. Then, it had been an empty, barren place visited only by the wraiths that inhabited it. This part, at least, was now bustling with people. The mages had even gotten plants to grow in plots spaced around the city. After half an hour of searching, he finally approached Kai.

The striker said, "Greetings, Urvuay. What has you visiting the citadel?"

Rezkin replied, "I am looking for General Azeria. Have you seen her?"

"Yes, I do believe she is practicing in one of the outer courtyards on the western side. I would caution you against interrupting her, though. She has been especially brusque of late."

"Thank you, Striker Kai. Perhaps I will approach her another time. Good day."

Rezkin finally found his quarry practicing her *talent* in a disused courtyard at the base of the citadel. The space was naught but cobblestones and dirt as the mages had not yet populated it with the plant life they were encouraging to grow on this side of the corveua. Two long tables had been set up along the wall at one end of the courtyard, atop which were multiple clay vessels of varying size and shape. Azeria stood at the other end of the courtyard, the wind swirling around her in a turbulent eddy. She raised her hand and slashed it downward. At the other end, a clay pot shattered, leaving the pots around it unblemished. She slashed her other hand downward, and another pot broke. Then, with an anguished scream, she danced in a flurry of movement, and the pots across from her broke in quick succession.

When all the pots were broken, the wind died, and Azeria fell to her knees. Her head hung forward, her face hidden by her hair, but her shoulders shook. Rezkin knew she wept, and he knew why. Never had he seen such emotion from her. He could not have imagined her so despondent, in such pain.

Rezkin dropped the illusion and left only his face shrouded in darkness as he walked toward her, intentionally scuffing his feet so as not to startle her. Azeria's head snapped up, and she quickly wiped her face as she got to her feet. When she turned to fully face him, her visage was as cold and stoic as ever. All the emotions she had just been expressing were now hidden behind her silver eyes.

Her shrouded torment tugged at something inside him, an answering anguish of his own.

"Raven," she said as he closed the distance to stand before her. His battle energy spiked as his nerves quaked. He felt as if he were heading into a fight he could not win, and his instinct was to retreat. Now that he was face to face with her, he could not bring himself to speak. He was considering abandoning the mission when she spoke again.

"What are you doing here? How did you gain access to the island?" She slid her sword free of its scabbard.

With great effort, he suppressed his anxiety and cleared his throat. "General Azeria, I have come to make good on my promise."

She tilted her head curiously. "You have brought Rezkin back to me?"

"In a manner of speaking."

The way she stared at him once again left him at a loss for words. His stomach churned and his nerves danced. Not long ago, he had faced down *five* demons without hesitation, yet this one woman rendered him speechless.

He cleared his throat again to dislodge the lump that had formed there. He steeled his nerves and said, "You need to know that Rezkin lives."

Shock stole across her face before she could cover it. She took an aggressive step toward him. The next instance, Rezkin was sprawled on the ground beneath her, her sword nearly at his throat. He had drawn the Sheyalin and blocked her just in time, although he did not think she intended to kill him. Her face was mere inches from his own as she scowled down at him. "Where is he?"

Rezkin was nearly certain he could get away from her should he try. In that moment, however, with her pressed against him, he wanted nothing more than to be so close to her. He met her gaze as he dropped the illusion that hid his face. She blinked at him several times. Then her lips came crashing down onto his. She did not release his mouth as she tossed away her sword and grabbed his face. Rezkin pushed the Sheyalin away then threaded one hand through her hair and wrapped the other around her body, pulling her closer. He closed his eyes as their tongues tangled, trusting that she would not try to kill him. They both dove in with abandon, tasting each other's very souls.

After several long minutes, Azeria suddenly lurched away. She stood over him with her hands on her hips and a scowl on her face. Then she began pacing, never glancing away from him for more than a second, as if he might disappear.

Rezkin lay propped up on his elbows, unmoving so as not to spook her. She paused, poised as if to berate him, then resumed her pacing. She finally stopped, dropped to her knees in front of him and deflated. Her face was a mask once again.

"It was you in Serret? *You* are the Raven?"

"I am."

She inhaled deeply as if the news upset her. She was surely thinking of the time he spent with her as the Raven without revealing himself. She said, "You were dead. I saw you with my own eyes, touched your cold body. (*despondent*)"

"Yes," Rezkin said slowly as he sat up. "I was dead. Sen Berringish brought me back."

"That was *nine* months ago! Why have you hidden yourself from us—from *me*?"

Rezkin reached out to take her hand, but she pulled it away. "Because I wanted Caydean to think I was dead. With me dead, he is less focused on the empire and more concerned with his own nefarious plans. Also, I knew that if I told *you*, you would be obliged to tell Entris. I cannot have him following me around all the time."

"That will no longer be a concern."

Surprised, Rezkin said, "Why?"

"Because he believes that if you live, you are most likely mad, and he will kill you. He is Spirétua-lye. You cannot defeat him. (*earnest*)"

"You can convince him that I am not mad."

Azeria shook her head. "I cannot. He knows I am compromised. (*frustrated*)"

"Compromised how?" asked Rezkin.

She met his stare. "Because of my feelings for you. (*exasperated*)"

Usually, Rezkin felt a person's feelings toward him were immaterial, but Azeria was different. He wanted to ask what those feelings were, but he was not sure he was ready to know. Not until he understood his own feelings better. He *needed* to understand them better because he had come to realize that he could not separate himself from them. He carried Azeria with him at all times. She was never far from his thoughts.

There was one thing he wanted from her that he felt he did not deserve. He asked anyway. "Can you forgive me?"

She blinked a few times as she thought. Then she said, "There is nothing to forgive. I understand why you did it. Regardless of what Entris thinks, I see the wisdom in your actions."

Rezkin released a breath he did not realize he had been holding. For a woman so rich in emotions, she was remarkably reasonable. He said, "Good, because I'm afraid I must leave again."

"I know. You cannot stay here, or Entris will kill you. He may not give you time to explain yourself."

Rezkin pushed down his alarm over having created an enemy out of Entris. He said, "Not just that. I have much to do still."

Azeria's expression was resolute. "Then we will do it together."

"Together?"

"I am coming with you." He started to argue, but she stopped him. "This is nonnegotiable. I have spent enough time separated from you in mourning. I will not be parted from you now. Besides, you can use my skills. I intend to ensure you survive. Together we are stronger. We will face your enemies together."

"And if the enemy that comes for me is Entris? What will you do?"

Her face was stony, but he could see the conflict in her eyes. Still, she did not hesitate when she said, "I will do all in my power to protect you, even from him."

"And if I do go mad?"

"Then I shall end you myself, or die trying." She paused, then said, "I have many questions."

Rezkin nodded knowingly. "I will answer all of them."

She looked at him skeptically. "You will keep nothing from me?"

Rezkin thought about all the secrets he held. The many identities, the mass killings, the subterfuge. If he disclosed all of them, she might begin to think him mad. But looking at her now, with the cool autumn breeze tousling her long, white locks and her silver eyes glinting in the afternoon light, he knew that he wanted her to know him—to know *all* of him. And if the truth drove her away, then he would cast aside all his other plans and follow her. Because he wanted her.

He did not think Azeria was the kind of woman to be wooed in the traditional fashion. The lessons he had learned from his trainers, from the books he had read, and from the plays he had watched would not go far with her. He thought she valued honesty and reason above all else.

Rezkin could not ignore the voice in his mind saying *trust no one, be one and alone, reveal nothing, do not depend on others, always be on guard.* Would Azeria turn on him? If he did trust her, would she ultimately be his demise? She was asking him to go against a lifetime of training—his only way of living.

He considered lying to her. He could tell her what she wanted to hear to keep her on his side. But as he met her earnest gaze, he knew he could not do that to her. If he turned her down now, would she side with Entris? What would he do to stop her from divulging that he was alive? Could he kill her? The thought sent nausea rolling through him. He knew he could not. No, if Azeria turned on him, he would let her. He would deal with the consequences. The fact that he would let a potential enemy live, to walk free, made him realize he was already lost.

In his most momentous grasp of courage yet, he said, "You shall know all that I am, all that I have ever been, and all that I become."

End of Book Six

Rezkin will return in *King's Dark Tidings,* Book Seven

CHARACTERS

Caydean - King of Ashai
Thresson - Second son of King Bordran of Ashai
Frisha - young woman from Ashai; one of Rezkin's companions
CidHarga - Ancient Ahn'an slayed by Ygrethiel
Gorokin - Father of Daem'Ahn
Ygrethiel - Crown Prince of H'khajnak
Avikeev - natural battle mage; Caydean's volunteer
Trivian - mage; one of Caydean's volunteers
Ulessa - mage; one of Caydean's volunteers
Wesson Seth - battle mage; Rezkin's companion
Zankai (Kai) – Tresdian striker; Rezkin's companion
Celise - Leréshi who claimed Wesson
Rezkin - secretly trained warrior
Seena - Rezkin's dragon companion
Finwy - Minder of the Temple
Farson - striker from northern fortress
Jimson - Ashaiian captain; Rezkin's companion
Reaylin de Voss - healer-warrior; Rezkin's companion
Nanessy Threll - elemental mage; Rezkin's companion
Tiseyi - omessa bonded to Rezkin; she-wolf
Azeria - Eihelvanan general
Entris - Eihelvanan Spirétua-lye
Anda - battle mage Wesson befriended at Battle Mage Academy
Brin Meyner - investigator for Caydean
Bobbi - inn keeper in Umbrell
Drake Banting - Rezkin's alter ego
Rodry - merchant in tavern in Umbrell
Pivar - merchant in tavern in Umbrell
Ikrus - Diamond Claw guildmember in Kaibain
Terishi - Lead coliseum architect and earth mage
Bergmon - General at Fort Krellis
Jeiro - Swordbearer who serves Caydean

Darning - Duke
Wellinven - Duke
Atressian - Duke
Peebs - bandit
Urvuay - stranger on the road
Gavain Claud - merchant in Channería
Bendin - Avikeev's butler
Lord Genever - lord in Ferélle
Lord Palsby - Lord accused of treason in Ferélle
Fedro - Lord Palsby's son
Erisial - Queen of Lon Lerésh
Bargus - prisoner of Avikeev
Gonery - soldier at northern fortress
Pollick - Wellinven's servant
Ferris - Wellinven's young mage
Irdo - Wellinven's older mage
Briesh - master assassin of the Black Hall
Nimick - slip with Black Hall who wears spectacles
Veshi - librarian with the Black Hall
Eliza Tomkins - Atressian's mistress
Gillis - A guard and member of Yserria's household
Nexius - A guard and member of Yserria's household
Raki - kitchen boy of Fourth Echelon
Tamarin (Tam) Blackwater - Rezkin's best friend
Girdy - Gendishen Army's administrator
Inspector Coulson - Rezkin's disguise
Goulen Julik - Gendishen Army general
Goragana - fae Ancient of earth
Serunius Pendrant - Consort to Queen Erisial, battle mage
Nayala Tekahl - Sixth Echelon; matrianera of House Tekahl
Alania Dormisk - First Echelon
Thia Helanis - Ninth Echelon
Grizelda Tynan - Twelfth Echelon
Ienia Vesqu - Foremost debater in Kielen; debates for Thia
Lindon - intruder in the baths
Bridania - Nayala's sister; Mistress of Trade in the Sixth Echelon
Hestressa - female member of Yserria's household

Polimasa - male member of Yserria's household
Liza - Grizelda's maid
Terril - member of Grizelda's household
Manik - member of Grizelda's household
Erinia - member of Grizelda's household
Martis - Grizelda's first consort
Lidia Oppena - Head of the Queen's Council of Lon Lerésh
Zelida - mage of the Fourth Echelon
Lilith - battle mage of the Fourth Echelon
Eshi - battle mage of the Third Echelon
Lisbet - Second Echelon

DEFINITIONS

ahn'an - beings with the power of Mikayal and Reyna
ahn'tep - beings with the power of all three gods (e.g. humans)
daem'ahn - demon; beings with the power of Nihko and Reyna
Spirétua - magic wielder with access to entire spectrum of vimara
Spirétua-lye - leader of the Spirétua
vimara - magical power; "life water"
Myer - Gendishen Army officer
Adianaik - ancient language often used in spells
Fyer - Gendishen Army soldier
Goulen - Gendishen Army general
Vimarium - metal that serves as a conduit for vimara; found in Lon Lerésh

Fersheya
ahdohuana - determined
itsiyela - exasperated
spretu - serious
istak - certain
yelouis - sadness
chisti - annoyed

Channerían
brach nih - greetings

OTHER BOOKS BY THE AUTHOR

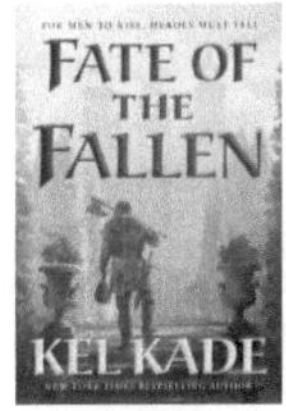

Not all stories have happy endings.

Everyone loves Mathias. Naturally, when he discovers it's his destiny to save the world, he dives in headfirst, pulling his best friend, Aaslo, along for the ride.

However, saving the world isn't as easy, or exciting, as it sounds in the stories. The going gets rough, and folks start to believe their best chance for survival is to surrender to the forces of evil, which isn't how the prophecy goes. At all. As the list of allies grows thin and the friends find themselves staring death in the face, they must decide how to become the heroes they were destined to be or, failing that, how to survive.

ABOUT THE AUTHOR

New York Times Best Selling Author Kel Kade is a full-time writer and parent living in a quiet semi-rural town on the outskirts of the Dallas metroplex in Texas. She cohabitates with three crazy dogs, three lazy cats, and one boring fish. Prior to becoming an author, Kel worked as an environmental consultant and later entered a doctoral program to complete research in big data studies of volcanic rock geochemistry and marine research in the Izu-Bonin-Mariana and Central America volcanic arcs.

Growing up, Kel lived a military lifestyle of traveling and living in new places. Experiences with distinctive cultures and geography instilled in Kel a sense of wanderlust and opened her young mind to the knowledge that the Earth is expansive and wild. She has a deep interest in science, ancient history, cultural anthropology, art, music, languages, and spirituality, which is evidenced by the diversity and richness of the places and cultures depicted in her writing. Her hobbies include creating universes spanning space and time, developing criminal empires, plotting the downfall of tyrannous rulers, and diving into fantastical mysteries.

NOTE FROM THE AUTHOR

I hope you enjoyed reading this sixth book in the *King's Dark Tidings* series. Please consider leaving a review or comments so that I may continue to improve and expand upon this ongoing series. Also, sign up for my newsletter for updates or find me on my website (www.kelkade.com), X (@Kel_Kade), Facebook (@read_KelKade), or Instagram (Kel_Kade). Rezkin will return in *King's Dark Tidings* Book Seven.

Also, check out my *Shroud of Prophecy* series published by Tor Books. It begins with *Fate of the Fallen* and includes everything from simple foresters to endearing thieves, mysterious reapers, powerful yet flawed gods, dragons, the walking dead, and more!

www.ingramcontent.com/pod-product-compliance
Lightning Source LLC
Chambersburg PA
CBHW030422310726
48979CB00009B/1568/J
9781952687082